A DETECTIVE (     'VEL

# CROOKED
# WAS HIS CANE

NEW YORK TIMES #1 BESTSELLER **TONY LEE** WRITING AS

# JACK GATLAND

---

Published by Hooded Man Media.
Cover photo by Paul Thomas Gooney

First Edition: June 2024

# PRAISE FOR JACK GATLAND

'Fast-paced and action packed, Jack Gatland's thrillers always deliver a punch.'

'This is one of those books that will keep you up past your bedtime, as each chapter lures you into reading just one more.'

'This book was excellent! A great plot which kept you guessing until the end.'

'Couldn't put it down, fast paced with twists and turns.'

'The story was captivating, good plot, twists you never saw and really likeable characters. Can't wait for the next one!'

'Totally addictive. Thoroughly recommend.'

'Moves at a fast pace and carries you along with it.'

'Just couldn't put this book down, from the first page to the last one it kept you wondering what would happen next.'

Before LETTER FROM THE DEAD...
There was

# LIQUIDATE THE PROFITS

Learn the story of what *really* happened to DI Declan Walsh, while at Mile End!

An EXCLUSIVE PREQUEL, completely free to anyone who joins the Declan Walsh Reader's Club!

Join at bit.ly/jackgatlandVIP

## Also by Jack Gatland

ROGUE SIGNAL

*For Mum, who inspired me to write.*

*For Tracy, who inspires me to write.*

# CONTENTS

# PROLOGUE

Stuart Laws didn't see the car that killed him.

It wasn't that he was careless, or hadn't paid attention while crossing the road; in fact, when Stuart Laws was struck by the London black cab, he was walking along the pavement in the pouring rain, the vehicle veering off from the road to take him out.

It could have been an accident, a sudden slip of the wheel or a foot hitting the accelerator instead of the clutch, but the witnesses who saw Stuart struck by the car would never know, as the driver carried on in what seemed to be a hit and run. The same witnesses would claim, in the days and weeks to come, they couldn't be sure whether the driver even *realised* they'd hit Stuart, because the cab had simply carried on down the street – even if it looked scarily like Stuart, while walking from his house to his own parked car, had been deliberately targeted.

Stuart wasn't hated. He had no enemies that anyone could think of. And over the following days, when asked by the police about this, many of his friends and neighbours would say that Stuart was a nobody, the kind of person that stood in the background of a room and never really got involved in conversations – but when you looked around, you'd see him standing, there all along.

It was a strange personality for Stuart, a cab driver, to have. Often, black cab drivers were gregarious, talkative men and women, happy to chat to whoever was in their cab, but with Stuart, he was happy just to sit and simply drive. It was one of the reasons why, a few years earlier, he had quit being a London cab driver after almost fifteen years of being in the job, and had moved into a higher level of chauffeur work, driving a black Mercedes-Benz limo for high-paying passengers, often foreign visitors who didn't speak English, anyway.

Stuart had liked that. He had spoken about this several times to friends, pointing out that if his passengers didn't understand what he was saying, it meant he didn't have to talk, and he was completely fine with this business arrangement.

Of course, after the accident – if it indeed was an accident – people had wondered whether Stuart had been struck down by somebody connected to this other line of work. Maybe he had angered someone; there was even talk of him angering the local yakuza after chauffeuring some Japanese visitors in his car, although that was later decided as just random scuttlebutt, and mildly racist conspiracy theories by people who should know better. He'd been nervous, twitchy even for a few weeks before the accident, which didn't help the rumours. But the fact of the matter was that Stuart Laws had been struck by a car in the middle of a morning rush hour, one that had veered during a terrible rainstorm, killing Stuart almost instantly before driving on.

Nobody had gained the number.

Nobody had seen the driver.

All that was known was that it was a London black cab, just like the one Stuart Laws used to drive.

Rather ironic, really.

———

ALFIE REYNOLDS HATED HIS JOB.

He knew many people detested their jobs, but he truly loathed his with a vengeance. He disliked the job, the hours, the people he worked with, his boss, and the arrogant, utter prick that owned the company. If it weren't for the fact he made money from it, and that he knew he'd be leaving eventually, he would probably have told them to go stuff themselves and punched his boss in the face.

Alfie worked for a company that specialised in telemarketing. This was a posh way of saying that they sold unwanted items to people; mainly goods that people didn't want. His job often involved calling random strangers from a list given to him by some other marketing company, which had probably obtained the list from yet *another* marketing company, informing them that because of some random computer algorithm, their name had been selected off a massive list, and they'd won the opportunity to have a carpet, or another item (usually a sofa or a curtain) of their choice, steam cleaned free of charge.

*Hooray, what a joy,* and at a time when people didn't think they got much for nothing. To be told this often gave a little jolt of joy to the person who received the phone call.

Well, he hoped so, anyway.

Of course, it was a lie. They hadn't been selected by a machine, except for the fact that the machine that generated the names had spat out a thousand different numbers. Some of the larger companies even did away with the telemarketers, and robo-dialled the numbers, either playing recorded messages, or instantly connecting to a waiting agent in an Indian call centre the moment the phone was answered. Some even stopped after two rings, and therefore made the person dial back, thus saving the phone bill for the company, but Alfie didn't like those because the caller was always suspicious as to what the call had been for and was therefore defensive when calling.

*Better to just keep to the tried and tested rules.*

Of the numbers he dialled, one in ten would answer. Of the people who answered, one, maybe two (depending on how persuasive he felt on the day) in ten again would likely agree to have their carpet or sofa steam cleaned, not realising that the chances were the company that did it would arrive, steam clean a square foot, and then do their best to sell the item that did the steam cleaning, explaining that this was the greatest, most wonderful device in the world and for less than *eight hundred quid,* they could have it all to themselves. And when the competition winner said no, they thought they were getting something for nothing, they were persistently pushed until they eventually agreed to take it on a rather expensive hire purchase agreement.

The lists targeted people who were in their sixties and upwards, people who liked the idea of having an item steam cleaned, and keeping their house pretty, but wouldn't confront a younger, burlier man when they turned around and said, "now buy the item".

Alfie had heard horror stories of the sales agents, too. Often only commission-based, there was one story that had even made the papers, where a sales agent stayed the night in his own sleeping bag on the couch of the hapless "winner", just so he could go with them to the bank the following morning, and they could get the money out.

It was horrid. Alfie hated the job.

However, Alfie was also *very good* at the job.

Alfie wanted more than anything to leave the job, even if it had been given to him by someone his uncle knew.

Because of this and the hours, Alfie finished work at nine in the evening every day, travelling home to his small, box-sized room in a shared flat in Bermondsey, grabbing a few hours' sleep, and then, usually around four or five in the morning he would get up, get on his bike, and cycle around London. Not that he wanted to stay fit or healthy. It wasn't that he had places to go. In fact, a lot of his journeys were quite random because Alfie Reynolds had a plan.

He was learning the *Knowledge*.

This was the comprehensive examination, around since 1865, that all of London's black cab drivers had to pass to obtain their licence; a task of memorising every street and significant landmark within a six-mile radius of Charing Cross, over twenty thousand streets and places of interest that helped them navigate around London. Sure, there were sat-navs and other devices out there that could help you do such things, but London taxi drivers, they had the Knowledge. Which meant they could find the quickest way from A to B through the centre of town without a problem. And it wasn't easy, either. Aspiring drivers would often study for an average of three or four years, navigating the city on motor scooters or electric bikes to learn the fastest routes. The test itself was divided into stages, starting with a written exam, and followed by a series of one-on-one oral examinations, where candidates would have to verbally navigate between any two points in London without referring to a map, visualising the routes in their head, using "runs" – basically preplanned routes through London.

They'd need to know the relevant hotels, museums, government buildings, embassies, railway stations, theatres, clubs, and historical sites they'd pass, as well as the one-way systems and restricted turns. It couldn't be learnt by book or rote, you actually had to travel the roads.

Even when you passed, Alfie had been told you still spent another six months learning the timing of the city, knowing which routes, although longer, may be quicker during rush hours.

It was a lot. But Alfie knew this was a way to work for himself for a change; to create his own opportunities.

Alfie had started the course convinced that this was nonsense. Sat-navs were surely better, especially the ones that could tell you where roads were closed or diverted. But surprisingly, the Knowledge was very good at providing information, and the cab network of black cab drivers was just as good as some of the other devices for telling you where you could or couldn't now drive, as well as the "blue book" of cab runs – which wasn't really a book, and definitely wasn't blue, but was filled with over three hundred "runs" Alfie had to learn.

He had first ridden along with his Uncle Marshall, who had been a cab driver for just over twenty years now. Although Marshall had been the one to get him the job he currently had, he'd also been the one to suggest Alfie did this, and watching Marshall ease his way through the crowded streets of London while watching Waze on his own phone, monitoring to see which one worked faster, Alfie had learned quickly that there wasn't much of a difference.

So, every morning before rush hour started, Alfie Reynolds would get on his electric bike and ride the routes of London, given tests based on the "blue book" by his uncle, learning the waypoints and the points of interest that cab drivers would use to navigate their way around London. He returned to his Bermondsey apartment before nine, and then headed to one of the various London Knowledge Schools out there, a small but functional one in Old Street. Here, his uncle learned his Knowledge too – for a couple of hours each day in a classroom environment, of his own volition, where he talked and worked through runs with other students before returning home, watching TV, and then back to the call centre in the mid-afternoon for his day job.

During those morning runs, he found it was cathartic. He didn't listen to music, he didn't have an audiobook in his ears, as many people commuting in and out did. He listened to London. As he rode, he examined the streets, looked for the symbols on the walls, the graffiti markings that would help him, the police plaques; anything that his uncle had pointed out the previous day, or that his teacher at the school had suggested he check into. And by process of elimination, he would find his way around.

Today, however, was different.

The previous day, after his uncle – who was also one of the part-time tutors at the college, which helped a ton with the monthly fees – had spoken about them, the other students had been discussing London trap streets. These were fictional addresses that were placed on maps back in the day when copyright meant something. Mapmakers would add roads or rename streets purely to prove, when additional maps were created by other people, that if their street was on it, then they'd obviously been copied. They were also known as "Map Traps" and had even once held an entire fictitious "paper town" on a New York map. The London A to Z still used by a lot of cabbies was believed to hold over a hundred of these, although Marshall claimed this was bollocks and only held a couple, but part of the training Alfie received was to know where the trap streets were; not to drive to them, but to use them as waypoints, like all the others.

Today, Alfie was hunting his first trap street, as he finished one run he'd been learning. He'd heard about the more famous Whitfield Street, which apparently went across Blackheath near Greenwich Park, where instead was, well, just a heath, but instead of that, and on his uncle's suggestion, he was cycling through the east of the city as the sun was coming up. He knew that soon the roads would get busier, and he was in a hurry, not really paying attention, and using the pavement sometimes as he rode, mainly to cut corners and dip into other areas. He was heading into the Isle of Dogs, just southwest of Canary Wharf; he knew it was a long route, but he was relying on the Thameslink ferry to take him back across to Rotherhithe and Surrey Quays when he was done, and that way he was only a mile or so from home.

Down here was Bartlett Place, or, rather, down here *wasn't* Bartlett Place, a street created between Alpha Grove and Cassilis Road, which had apparently been named on the map after Kieran Bartlett, an employee at Geographers' A-Z Map Company as a "phantom street" to catch anyone stealing their design. Marshall had explained that some cabbies still used "Bartlett Place" as a marker, even if it no longer existed, and was now even blocked off by gates.

Alfie hadn't had problems finding the onetime phantom street; it was a wide walkway with "no access" metal barriers on either side, beside Gainsborough House, a sandstone block of flats. He'd ridden up to them to take a photo and then show it to the others later, but when he arrived, he found it didn't look like the Google Maps image.

For a start, on the west end of the walkway, opposite the no-entry signs of Janet Street, the EMERGENCY ACCESS – NO ENTRY gate was ajar. On the east side, Alfie could see that the other gate was closed, but what immediately drew his eye was the cab.

It was a modern-looking black cab, and it was stationary, about thirty feet down the walkway, parked to the right and against a section of wooden slatted fence. With the gate open, Alfie knew this had to be an illegal parking; the entire blocked-off area was pedestrian only, and through the window, Alfie could see a figure within it, probably a cab driver waiting for an early shift or having a doze after a long night.

*Maybe they parked up, fell asleep and forgot?*

Alfie checked his watch. It was just gone six in the morning, and soon people would go to work. He knew if whoever this was had parked up for a kip, they'd soon be getting a visit from a uniform. He'd rap on the window to wake them up …

But as he got closer, he started to cough.

There was a strong smell of carbon monoxide exhaust fumes, and as he got closer again, he realised that there was a hosepipe sticking out of the side of the cab, the rear driver's side window slightly open to allow the pipe access. Concerned now, Alfie rode up to the driver's door and paused, glancing in.

The car was filled with thick grey smoke, and the driver, barely seen through it, was staring forward.

'Mate,' Alfie said, banging on the window. 'Mate, can you hear me? Are you okay?'

The driver didn't respond because he was quite obviously dead.

'Mate,' Alfie hammered again, his brain not yet registering the fact, but there was still no response from the driver. It was then that Alfie Reynolds realised that the car, although a black cab, was one of the newer electric models, a LEVC TX. He knew this because he'd been eyeing one up for when he passed the Knowledge. It was expensive, but worth it; for a start, you had discounts on various things if you were electric.

But, more importantly, *there was no way this man could have gassed himself to death in an electric car.*

He glanced back and just about visible in the early morning light, through the smoke and fumes emanating inside the car, he could see that the man, although dead, was held up by something around his chest; some kind of strap had kept him on the chair.

Pulling away from the car, Alfie Reynolds realised with horror this wasn't some awful, melancholy suicide. He did the first thing he could think of; he pulled out his phone and, just like he did every other day in his day job, he dialled a number.

'Police,' he said when the call was answered.

'I think I've found a murder.'

# 1

## SMOKE ALARM

WHEN THE CALL CAME THROUGH, DETECTIVE CHIEF INSPECTOR Declan Walsh was driving into work from his house in Hurley, with Detective Inspector Anjli Kapoor by his side.

It was early in the day, late in the week, and unsurprisingly, the M4 motorway had been a nightmare. The original plan, following the events of the last couple of weeks had been to gain some buffer space on their workload, and Declan had hoped to get into the office with time to spare and make a dent in the amount of paperwork they currently had. The unit had been quite busy recently, but many of the cases had been small and quick to solve. However, the problem with a quickly solved case was the amount of paperwork they'd just added to it.

That, and there were a couple of solicitors causing issues with their clients, causing even more paperwork and delays.

It hadn't helped, either, that Detective Superintendent Alex Monroe and Doctor Rosanna Marcos had been away for the last two weeks on a slightly belated honeymoon, leaving, in Monroe's own words, "the sweetie shop in the hands of the

Oompa Loompas", which was both incorrect and mildly offensive at the same time. Still, it'd been a quieter summer than usual, and now, as September was almost starting, Declan was almost looking forward to autumn.

*That and the fact that Jess would be continuing her A Levels, and not hanging around the Temple Inn offices as much.*

It wasn't that he didn't like his daughter being there, it was mainly that in the weeks since Karl Schnitter's death, she'd been more withdrawn than usual and a change in the environment would help her immensely. So much so that Henry Farrow had taken her into Tottenham for a week before she started preparing for sixth form, purely to "show her how real coppers worked", in his own terms.

Declan had wondered how much of this was because of his wife, and Declan's *ex*-wife, Liz wanting more distance between them. Recently, she'd become way colder to Declan, but he couldn't fault that. Being connected to Declan Walsh in any way never seemed to be easy.

It was why he was always so surprised Anjli was still there.

So, claiming the murder scene was technically on their route, and ignoring Billy's protestations that it wasn't anywhere near Temple Inn or the City, Declan had informed Billy that regardless, they'd be picking the case up as soon as they could.

As it was, they only arrived an hour, maybe ninety minutes after the call had come through. It was, however, still enough time for a police cordon to go up, blocking the view of a surprising amount of onlookers for this time of the morning, guarded by PC Esme Cooper. A forensic tent was about fifty feet behind her, over what looked to be a black cab beside some apartment blocks in the middle of the Isle of

Dogs, with suited and masked forensic officers examining the vehicle.

Sergeant Morton De'Geer, their modern-day Viking, seven feet tall and with short blond hair and beard, saw them approach, and walked over to the cordon as PC Cooper led them through.

'Guv,' he said, nodding from Declan to Anjli. 'Other Guv.'

Declan frowned; De'Geer wasn't in the usual forensics one-piece the other forensics officers and SOCOs wore, which was unusual for him.

'No PPE?' he asked, waving his tactical pen at the Sergeant.

'Doctor Marcos arrived before I did, and took the examination on,' De'Geer shrugged. 'Got the impression she needed a distraction, and it's too hot to wear the damn things.'

'I didn't realise they were back from honeymoon.' The statement surprised Anjli. 'I thought it was a three-week trip?'

'I think it was shortened by mutual decision,' De'Geer replied, tapping his nose. 'But nobody's brave enough, or stupid enough, even, to ask.'

Declan understood that statement.

'What have we got?' he asked, pulling on his blue latex gloves. 'Also, why are we here? Surely the Met Police should be on site?'

'I don't think you'll need to do that,' De'Geer said at the reveal of the gloves, nodding back at the car. 'Doctor Marcos had a favour called in. These guys helped us once before, said they were overstretched right now, asked if we could have a look, especially as it looked like a suicide. And D Supt Monroe's remit when he started the unit, has always been that we can take on any and all crimes he likes the look of, so we kind of...'

'Took it over,' Anjli nodded. 'It's a fair point. We've done it before—that Robin Hood convention in Milton Keynes comes to mind.'

'And the Peak District,' De'Geer added. 'Athough that was by Ministerial request, I suppose.'

He looked around the scene.

'There's not much to go on, to be perfectly honest. A young lad came upon it early in the morning. He was riding his bike around here.'

'What time exactly was he riding his bike around here?'

'About six o'clock in the morning.'

Anjli frowned as she pulled out her notebook.

'I didn't think paperboys still existed,' she said. 'Or was he riding to work?'

'He was riding, but not to work,' De'Geer replied. 'More *for* work.'

He motioned across the car park where, against the wall, sitting with his electric bike beside him, was a young man, glumly staring at the scene, his arms folded.

'His name's Alfie Reynolds,' De'Geer explained. 'Twenty-one years old. Training to be a black cab driver.'

'Still not explaining why he's riding a bike early in the bloody morning.'

'He's learning the Knowledge, sir,' De'Geer replied, shrugging. 'I'm assuming he found it better to ride around on a bike in the early hours of the morning than try to do it during rush hour. He works in a call centre during the day. He's training up so that he can become a black cabbie.'

Declan glanced over at Reynolds. He understood the pros and cons of having to work in your off hours when bettering your situation. Many people who took on a side hustle would find themselves working into the early hours of the night. Or, when they were changing jobs and moving into a completely unfamiliar area, hours would be spent learning the new job while working their old one.

Declan had had the same thing happen to him when he left the military police and went to work in Tottenham. He'd spent hours learning the differences between military police rules and Metropolitan Police rules. Surprisingly, he'd eventually passed the tests that allowed him to come in, although he did always wonder whether that was because his father, then the ex-chief of the Tottenham North branch, had pulled some strings.

'Billy was cryptic when he called this in to us,' Declan said as they started towards the black cab. 'He said it was a suicide, but at the same time, not so much.'

'Yes, sir,' De'Geer gave a half-smile. 'Doctor Marcos is all over that at the moment.'

'Victim's name?'

'Ronald Tyler,' De'Geer now read from his notes. 'Black cab driver for twenty-odd years.'

'And he committed suicide?' Anjli asked, noting this down.

'No, Guv,' De'Geer said, pointing over at the black cab, the letters L.E.V.C. on the back above the licence plate and the Hackney carriage plate, which gave the owner the rights to perform the duties of a London black cab driver.

'I was told by Billy he'd been found with carbon monoxide poisoning,' Anjli spoke more cautiously now, aware something was different.

'Yes, ma'am.'

'Stop sir'ing and ma'aming and get to the bloody point,' Declan growled. 'Either he killed himself or he didn't.'

'Well, *sir*, at first sight, it looks like he killed himself,' De'Geer replied, seemingly enjoying the situation. 'You see, he was in his driver's seat. The window's up, but the back window had been dropped an inch, and a hose had been inserted through. It's a standard way for people to commit suicide. They sit in the car, they turn the engine on and let the exhaust fumes enter the car and simply drift off, probably with a load of coughing and vomiting, but the idea romanticised in movies is quite a common one.'

Declan pointed at the back door to the car, where a length of orange hose could be seen poking into the window.

'And that's what happened here?'

'Again, sir, yes and no,' De'Geer shook his head. 'You see, the interior of the car was filled with carbon monoxide and it was definitely what killed Ronald Tyler. However, there are two things that show that this was not suicide.'

'And what are they?' Anjli asked. Looking back at the car, she saw Doctor Rosanna Marcos appear, pulling off her custom-made grey PPE hood, her wild brown hair springing out in all directions.

'First, he'd been ratchet-strapped to the driver's seat,' she explained, walking over and patting De'Geer on the arm. 'Bless Morten, he's so excited that he worked this one out without any help.'

She looked back at Declan.

'Luggage straps, like you have on a roof rack, the ones that you crank, ratchet-wise. One of them had been wrapped around him and ratcheted at the back. It had pinned him to the chair. There was no way he could pull himself out. It was too tight, he probably couldn't even breathe properly.'

'Okay,' Declan said. 'So, somebody ratcheted him to the chair, started the engine, and then left him to die?'

'Well, that's the other problem,' Doctor Marcos looked back at the car, waving a hand out, indicating Declan and Anjli to look at it. 'What do you see?'

Declan examined the car with his eyes, looking for whatever Doctor Marcos was pointing out here.

Almost as one, both Declan and Anjli realised.

'It doesn't have an exhaust,' Declan said.

'It's electric,' Anjli replied.

'There's no way he could have died in the way he did with *this* car,' Doctor Marcos nodded. 'It's an electric black cab. Back in 2018, Transport for London required all new taxis licenced for the first time had to be zero emissions compliant. The L.E.V.C., stands for *London Electric Vehicle Company,* has a range of up to a hundred and fifty miles, and there's about fourteen thousand around London, or so they reckon. They're healthier for the environment, apparently.'

Declan glanced back at the car.

'Wasn't healthy enough for Ronald Tyler,' he said.

'No,' Doctor Marcos replied solemnly. 'But what it means is somebody turned up, strapped Tyler to his seat, stuck a hose in the window, and then used his or her own car to create the carbon monoxide that killed him. Not only was this deliberate, it was definitely a message.'

'Whoever did this wanted people to know that Ronald was murdered,' Declan glanced around. 'Why here, though? It's not exactly a narrow alleyway.'

'No cameras,' Anjli said, looking around. 'I reckon they knew they could park up here, get away with killing Ronald, and then leave. No one would really bother them, two cars parked up. From the looks of things, the hose would have been on the fence side, so any cars going past at the end of the walkway wouldn't even have noticed.'

'But a man, riding down here, learning the Knowledge ...' Declan understood now. 'Why exactly was he cycling around here, anyway?'

'Because of trap streets,' Doctor Marcos shrugged. 'Apparently, his uncle's a cabbie and told him taxi drivers use them as waypoints and locations that help them when they're working through a route. He was learning those today.'

She sighed.

'Although, from the impression I get, I'm not sure if he wants to be a taxi driver anymore.'

Declan looked back to the car.

'Anything else that we should know about?' he asked.

Doctor Marcos shrugged.

'We're about to take the body out,' she said. 'So if we see anything—'

She paused as there was a shout from where the car was. Looking over, Doctor Marcos could see one of the other forensics officers waving their hands and motioning for her to approach.

'Wait here,' she said, her voice now concerned as she pulled on her hood and mask and ran back over.

After a minute of talking to the forensics, she returned to them, a clear plastic bag in her hand, holding it up to show Declan. There was a sheet of torn paper, no more than a strip, in the bag. Declan could read the handwritten words that had been scrawled on one side.

*Crooked Was His Cane*

'Crooked Was His Cane.' Declan frowned. 'What's that supposed to mean? Why are the words all capitalised?'

'Yeah, we didn't get instructions when we found it,' Doctor Marcos replied irritably. Declan wasn't sure if this was because she'd missed it while examining the body the first time. 'It was found in the victim's mouth, placed in the cheek.'

Doctor Marcos was frowning as she stared at the piece of paper.

'We can also change the timeline of death,' she continued.

'How do you work that out?' Anjli asked.

'You strap a man and you place something like this in his mouth, he's going to spit it out,' Doctor Marcos replied, looking back at the body now being removed. 'Now I'm wondering whether the killer put the car fumes into the electric cab, waited until Ronald Tyler was unconscious, returned, shoved the item in his mouth, and then left once more.'

She looked around at the buildings that surrounded the area.

'Do we have any witnesses?' Declan asked, following Doctor Marcos's gaze as he looked up at the apartments surrounding them.

'We have one guy who said he looked out and saw two cars down here around four in the morning before he went off on his shift,' De'Geer now said, reading from his notes. 'But he said all he saw was two cars, each with their bonnets up, facing each other. He assumed one was being jump-started. He wasn't close enough to see that the car was electric and wouldn't have had an engine in the bay.'

'It's a good way of avoiding any interest,' Anjli commented. 'Park up, open up the bonnet, start pumping gas into the other car. As far as anybody thinks as they walk past, they're just trying to get the car working. No one's going to stop, or realise one doesn't have an engine of sorts. Four in the morning, you're going to carry on walking.'

Declan, writing this down, looked back at the car.

'Anything on the vehicle?'

'It's a standard Hackney carriage, electric, has been owned for five years now, since around 2019,' De'Geer read from his notes. 'As I said when you arrived, it's a strange one.'

Declan now found he couldn't take his eyes off the note in the clear bag.

'Crooked Was His Cane.' He repeated. 'Maybe we need to find if there's any connection between that and Tyler ...'

'It's a folk song,' PC Cooper said, walking over, having been relieved at the cordon and hearing the words. 'Crooked Was His Cane. It's a ghost story.'

Declan frowned as he looked back at her.

'Do you know it?'

'A little, sir, my dad's a fan of folk music. I think it's about a ghost who enters someone's cab.'

She shook her head again.

'I'm afraid I don't know it word for word.'

'Luckily, we have someone with an extensive knowledge of Google,' Declan replied. 'Ask Billy to have a look, will you? It probably means nothing, but maybe there's something there.'

He stretched and looked over at Alfie Reynolds, now sipping at a paper cup. The boy looked pale.

'Has somebody spoken to him yet?' he asked.

'Yes, but he doesn't really have a lot to say.'

Declan started over towards Alfie.

'Mister Reynolds?' he asked.

Alfie Reynolds looked up at him; his eyes were haunted.

'I didn't do it,' he said as his first line.

'I know you didn't do it, son.' Declan smiled as he crouched next to him. 'I was told you found this while cycling around learning the Knowledge.'

'Yes, sir.'

'Surely that's driving around central London, not suburbs like this?'

'The Knowledge covers all routes up to six miles from the centre of London,' Alfie replied, almost automatically.

'Ah. Gotcha. And you were looking up trap streets? I don't know much about them, but surely there must have been ones closer to where you live?'

'There's a few,' Alfie admitted. 'I was going to do the one by Greenwich Park, but it's a bit dull. This one's on the route home. Well, it will be when I get the ferry across.'

Declan glanced around.

'So this is a known trap street then, yeah?'

'Well, it's known, but I don't know how well it's known,' Alfie shrugged.

'And you came here because?'

'My uncle suggested it.'

'Your uncle is?'

'Marshall Reynolds. He's a cab driver. Has had the Hackney badge since I was a baby.'

'And your uncle told you to come here today?'

'Yeah, he said to try it,' Alfie replied, looking at the road. 'He knew I travel early when working the streets, said this would be best before rush hour, as it would be empty. And it was mentioned in some BBC show I found on Dailymotion.'

He looked up.

'Looks like someone else had the same idea,' he continued. 'I didn't see who it was. The smoke was thick. I didn't ...'

He trailed off, and Declan patted Alfie on the shoulder.

'We're going to have an officer chat with you, and then we'll get you home.'

He looked over at the electric bike.

'We'll get someone else to ...'

'It's fine,' Alfie interrupted, nervously rising. 'Honestly, I'm literally a mile away. If you can finish up what you need from me, I can go.'

'Are you sure, son? It's been a hectic morning for you.'

Alfie shrugged.

'I think it's best if I just get home, get my head down, and get ready for my next shift at work.'

Declan shrugged, rising.

'Your call,' he replied. 'You know where we are if you need us.'

As Cooper walked over to check over Alfie's statement one last time, Declan walked away, looking back at the tent-covered car to the side.

Someone had brought Ronald Tyler here and killed him. They'd done it in such a way that there was no doubt it was murder, and had left a calling card in his mouth. They'd even waited beside the car as he died.

*But why? And why here?*

Trap street or not, there were gates at either end of the walkway, and one had been deliberately opened. Had Ronald Tyler driven through of his own volition? Or had someone else driven him here and then returned to get their own car?

There was more going on here than the evidence showed.

And what the hell did *Crooked Was His Cane* mean?

# 2

# FOLK SONGS

'ALL RIGHT THEN, KIDDIES,' DETECTIVE SUPERINTENDENT Alexander Monroe said as he stared out at the briefing room. 'We've been cursed by the police gods again, it seems, reminding us never to mention loudly that things are a little dull.'

He stood at the front of the briefing room in a position that usually a DCI would stand, but Declan and Monroe had made an agreement a while back that, even though they'd now promoted themselves out of the positions, there was no way Monroe was going to stop investigating cases, even as a Detective Superintendent. And so Declan, gratefully, as he didn't really want to point-run these cases, had allowed Monroe to stand at the front and talk to everybody. It also gave Declan an element of plausible deniability if things went wrong, which he quite liked.

For the last couple of weeks, Declan had been running point, as Monroe and Doctor Marcos had been on their honeymoon somewhere in the Highlands of Scotland.

Declan wasn't sure how much Monroe had enjoyed the holiday picked by Doctor Marcos, however, as from what he could read from the Facebook posts she'd been putting up, she'd basically been taking him around major murder sites and crime scenes. If ever there was a busman's holiday, it sounded like their honeymoon. If anything, Monroe was probably grateful to be back and doing something else, and Declan had wondered whether this was why they'd cut the holiday short by a week.

'How was the holiday, sir?' PC Cooper asked from the back of the room, sitting next to De'Geer. In front of her, in his usual spot on the computer, was Detective Sergeant Billy Fitzwarren. Declan sat next to Anjli, and the door was ominously empty, usually blocked by Detective Chief Superintendent Bullman, who for some reason hadn't arrived yet, even though today was one of her "work from Temple Inn" days. Doctor Marcos was also missing, currently downstairs, but had promised to come up shortly.

'It was fine, Lassie,' Monroe said, perhaps a little too stiffly. 'And I'll show you all the wee snaps down the line, but can we talk about the murder first, perhaps?'

Cooper reddened and sat back in her chair as Monroe turned and faced the briefing room.

'Ronald Tyler,' he started. 'Fifty-six years old, London cab driver for the last twenty-one of them. No real problems on his record, a couple of speeding fines over the years, but nothing major.'

On the screen behind him, an image of a man in his mid-fifties appeared; it was the Hackney carriage ID of Ronald Tyler.

'Tell me about the driver,' Monroe asked, looking back at the photo. 'Do we have any debts owed? Angry ex-wives?

Lovers who have been spurned or angry boyfriends? He's a cab driver, I know they get around, I've seen the videos.'

'Sir, I think you're looking at the wrong websites if you think that cab drivers get around,' Declan retorted. 'And perhaps you shouldn't be letting your wife know about it either?'

Monroe chuckled.

'So he doesn't have any annoyed ex-girlfriends?'

'He has an ex-wife,' Anjli read from her notes. 'Apparently they broke up four, five years ago. He's got a son who's at university. I think they keep their time equal with him, and for the last four years since the divorce, Ronald Tyler's lived in a small semi-detached house in Haggerston in East London.'

'What about debts? Gambling, perhaps?'

'Doesn't gamble, from what we can find out, supports Arsenal football team, although that's not enough to get him killed,' Declan suggested. 'He does owe on his cab, but it's more of a finance agreement than owing some bloke called Mickey Two-Legs or something like that.'

'Why would he be called Mickey Two-Legs?' De'Geer asked without thinking. 'Surely everybody has two legs; he would just be called Mickey?'

'I was making a point,' Declan glared at the sergeant. 'Do you really want to die on that hill?'

'Not really,' De'Geer held his hand up in a placating gesture.

'Okay, let me get this right,' Monroe grumbled. 'The man doesn't owe any money to at least anybody that we would worry about, doesn't have an ex-wife who hates him, hasn't annoyed anybody recently, yet was found dead and deliberately so. There's more here that we're missing, and we need to know what this is. Does he have any secret money, perhaps, hidden away? Someone needed to steal it from him?'

'If he had the money, surely he would have paid off the loan,' Declan suggested.

'My uncle always told me that cab drivers were always both rich and poor at the same time.' Anjli shrugged. 'You were always owing money for your car and your Hackney badge, but you could simply get into the cab and go make money whenever you wanted.'

'Does your uncle still drive a black cab?' Monroe asked.

Anjli shook her head, laughing.

'God no,' she replied. 'He decided it was too hectic. Also, I think he got annoyed at the fact he was more poor than rich.'

'So much for the term then,' Monroe shrugged, looking back at everybody. 'Okay, so if we're not looking at that, we need to work out why this nice man, who didn't owe money or have gambling debts and hadn't annoyed any mafia from what we can work out, was found dead in a black cab with a note shoved in his mouth.'

'The note's confusing, too,' Declan said.

'Aye, "Crooked Was His Cane",' Monroe nodded. 'Tell me, does anybody know where this comes from?'

'I believe it's a folk song, sir,' Declan looked across the room. 'Billy was going to find out.'

'Billy *has* found out,' Billy interrupted, a smug expression on his face. 'A man named James Harlow wrote the song about fifteen years ago. It's about a ghostly passenger who gets out of a cab and is hit by a car, but is never seen again. I have the lyrics here. Actually, hold on, I can play it to you.'

Billy started tapping around on his keyboard, and on the plasma screen, a YouTube video from about four years ago appeared. It was of a man in his late forties, with an acoustic guitar, long brown hair in a ponytail and a short, well-trimmed beard over a grey woollen cardigan, sitting by a fire in what looked to be a Christmas setting.

'This is a small gig that Harlow did in 2019,' Billy replied. 'From what I can work out, there's about forty people in the audience. The speakers on the laptop aren't loud, but you'll get the gist.'

As the team sat back to listen, the man on the screen, James Harlow, began to sing the song.

*I drove my cab through Wimbledon, now driving through the rain,*
*There was a man, he flagged me down, And Crooked was his Cane.*
*I pulled up by the pavement, his attention I did gain,*
*As he walked up to my window, and he rapped upon the pane.*

*I recall no destination, as the man, he did explain,*
*I recall no explanation, just that Crooked was his Cane.*

*He sat upon the back seat, I continued on again,*
*As he rapped a rhythmic beat out, with his Crooked little Cane.*
*We travelled up towards the Thames, and talking he abstained,*
*As he watched out of the window, while he stroked his Crooked Cane.*

*But as we drove to Hammersmith, he gripped his chest in pain,*
*And asked for me to stop the cab, as he held his Crooked Cane.*
*As we pulled up to the bridge-side, his eyes betrayed his strain,*
*And he tapped upon the back door, with his Crooked little Cane.*

*"I must now leave you, Peter," the man smiled as he explained,*
*And nodded at my meter, he then paid me for my gain.*

*He climbed out of my black cab, and then he smiled at me through rain,*
*I realised, with icy stab, I'd never said my name.*

*He didn't see the bus that struck, as it slid across the lane,*
*The screech of brakes now screamed at me – then the man was gone, again.*
*We never found the body, even though we checked in vain,*
*All we found upon the bridge that night was his Crooked little Cane.*

*And when I checked the fare he gave, I found it was the same,*
*The bank notes he had given me? None did now remain.*
*And so I drive my routes once more, always searching through the rain,*
*For my strange and missing passenger – for I have his Crooked Cane.*

*I recall no destination, as the man, he did explain,*
*I recall no explanation, just that Crooked was his Cane.*

Billy paused the video as it scanned across the applauding audience, the song now over.

'And do we know if this is based on anything truthful?' Declan asked.

'It's a ghost story,' Billy shrugged. 'The best ones are always loosely based on something truthful. It all depends on what else is going on with it. There is one interesting thing, though.'

He started pulling up screen captures from YouTube videos.

'There are four versions of this online that I can find, all by James Harlow. Every one of them has somebody in the comments section at some point talking about 'bindlesticks'.'

'Bindlesticks?' Declan frowned. 'That sounds a bit Rumpelstiltskin, if you ask me.'

'It's actually a term,' Billy replied, pulling up another screenshot – this time, a more traditional image of a young man walking through a medieval setting, a cat in front of him, a stick with a red-spotted bag hanging on the end over his shoulder. 'We all know this traditional image of Dick Whittington, right?'

'Sure,' Declan nodded. 'It's been in pantomimes for a hundred years or so. "Turn again, Dick Whittington, Lord Mayor of London", and all that.'

'Well, it's actually based in part on the true story of Richard Whittington, the Mayor of London, although I don't think he ever had the stick or the cat,' Billy added.

'I'm guessing the stick's important?' Declan asked.

'It is,' Billy smiled. 'You see, the stick that we see here with good old Dick and his cat, that's called a bindle stick. The bindle being the bag on the back. Bindle sticks were traditionally used to hold your items when you travelled, held over your shoulder and is used in the vision of the American hobo riding the trains. You know, before rucksacks became more common in the fifties.'

'So, this is a tramp's stick?' Anjli asked.

At this, however, Billy shook his head.

'No,' he replied. 'There seems to be some kind of confusion between tramps and hobos. Hobos apparently voluntarily want the life of the travelling man or woman; basically a backpacker of the times, whereas a homeless person is someone whose situation is caused by usually external circumstances. Now, you can have homeless people who have chosen to be homeless, and you can have hobos who have been forced into that way of life. However, there seems to be a lot of discussion on whether a hobo is a tramp and a tramp is a hobo. Either way, the hobos had bindle sticks.'

'So, why would this be mentioned on a YouTube video comment?' Declan asked.

'Bindle sticks were often crooked,' Billy added. 'Sure, these pictures of Whittington show a stick that feels like it's a length of bamboo pole, but the bindle at the end of the stick would fall straight off. Crooked sticks were often used.'

'So, a bindle stick was a crooked cane?' Declan shook his head. 'I think we're reaching here. My uncle used to have a walking stick, which was like a twisted branch, so that was crooked. How is that not different?'

'Probably isn't,' Billy replied, shrugging as he read from his laptop screen. 'The first image I have of Dick Whittington is from the cover of *The Famous and Remarkable History of Sir Richard Whittington, Three Times Lord-Mayor of London*, which was printed in 1770. On it, Dick Whittington is walking with his cat, and holds a crooked walking stick. The problem I have is, until I know for sure what's going on with these comments, I'm just having to speculate.'

'And keep speculating, laddie,' Monroe patted Billy on the shoulder, leaning across the table to do so, before looking at the others. 'At the moment, we don't have much to go on. We know a man's been murdered, and we know it was something personal. There's no way you'd do such a thing without it being so. We don't know why it's happened or who did it. And currently, all we have is a story about ghosts, Dick Whittington's pole, and crooked canes. So, get at it.'

He checked his notes.

'Anjli, go speak to the family.'

'Sir?'

'The divorced wife and the kid. See if we can find out anything else. Maybe they'll know something from his past we haven't worked out,' Monroe replied. 'De'Geer, it doesn't look like there's much going on downstairs for you at the moment. So take Cooper and check out his Haggerston house. Maybe he'll have left something we can look into. Declan, you and I will hunt around for some cab drivers. See if we can learn some more stories about the Knowledge and why he might have been here on a trap street.'

'Yes Guv,' Declan seemed surprised at this, but already the room was emptying, with everybody going off to take on their particular task.

As the room emptied, Monroe leant closer to Declan.

'You'll be doing that with me later,' he said. 'First off, I have a request for you. I need you to go down to Westminster and have a chat with your wee friend, the Prime Minister.'

Declan groaned at this.

'I'm sorry, but what's going on now?' he asked.

Monroe folded his arms as he stared at his DCI.

'You think we came home early because we weren't enjoying the honeymoon?' he asked. 'No. Rosanna gained some information that we weren't expecting. A friend of hers passed it on, and it came to me, and we decided we needed to fix this quickly.'

'Sir?'

'Someone's looking to close the Last Chance Saloon, laddie,' Monroe replied. 'The government is claiming they're bringing more police into the city, but they're pressuring units to double up and close areas that aren't needed. Remember how once all the towns had police stations, and now it's phone lines and occasional divisional buildings?

Well, they're looking to do more of that, and we're on the chopping block, laddie.'

'How the hell are we on the chopping block?' Declan was stunned by the comment. 'We've saved the Prime Minister personally several times, we've saved the Queen, we've solved crimes!'

'Aye, and we've also had our share of the consequences of these,' Monroe leant closer, so as not to allow anyone outside to hear. 'We've forced high-ranking chief superintendents and commanders to resign from their positions. We've caused MPs to step down. We've *removed* one Prime Minister too, if you recall.'

'Well, yes, of course, I remember that,' Declan protested. 'But, in the process, we got Charles Baker into the position, so realistically he should be thanking us.'

'I don't think this is all on him,' Monroe shook his head. 'And it didn't help that we recently had a return of a man that we told everybody was dead.'

Declan groaned. The Red Reaper had become quite a popular case again, and considering the fact that a year or two earlier, they'd told everybody that the Red Reaper had run away and was out in the wind, while the government themselves were aware he was in a new CIA identity, the fact he'd returned was a definite egg on the government's face.

'Okay, let me get this right,' Declan sighed, leaning against the doorpost. 'Charles Baker's holding this over us. We do something for him and save our unit, I guess?'

'If it even is Baker who's doing this? Either way, laddie, it's up to you to go to Westminster and find out what's going on, because let's face it, if we close up shop, it's because of you and the Red Reaper.'

Declan sighed.

'He's dead,' he muttered.

'I know, son—'

'He's dead, and he's still destroying our lives.' Declan shook his head as he turned and walked out of the door. 'I am so sick to death of the way this works.'

'Say hi to Baker for us,' Monroe shouted out after him.

## 3

## MEMBERS TERRACE

DECLAN REALLY HATED THE HOUSES OF PARLIAMENT. NOT that he disliked it as a building or location; it was just that every time he went to the Houses of Parliament, bad things usually happened. Either he was blackmailed by the Prime Minister to do something, he was *blackmailing* the Prime Minister to do something; he was saving lives, or he was trying his best to find out answers to cases that Members of Parliament were trying to keep hidden.

Over the last couple of years, Declan and the Last Chance Saloon had been involved way too much with the politics of Westminster, even to where Charles Baker had used Declan as a poster boy when his life was saved during the Queen's State dinner.

He'd also saved *her* life then, although it was short-lived.

Declan had even become known in the media as Charles Baker's "go-to copper", something he wasn't happy about, especially as he hadn't voted for Baker in the first place. The first time Declan had been to the Houses of Parliament, Baker had been a simple MP working in the bowels of Whitehall and accused of murder. Well, he would have been accused of murder if Declan had had his way; as it was, he was purely a suspect. But even back then, Declan knew that Charles Baker played games that nobody else could prove, whether it had been Rattlestone, the removal of his rival Michelle Rose, the Star Chamber he was a part of; all of these areas of power that Charles Baker held within his grasp, all making him a powerful friend, but a more dangerous enemy.

Declan had walked a narrow line where his very career and soul were at risk. And now, it seemed, Baker had one more request.

Declan had done his best to avoid visiting Baker, especially since he had faced him after the Justice case. But as he arrived at the St Stephen's Gate entrance to the Houses of Parliament, he was quite surprised. For a start, the usual lines of paparazzi that would take photos of him seemed disinterested in him today.

Declan was quite happy about this, but at the same time was quite confused.

'What's going on?' he asked one of the guards, who shrugged, pointing back at the paparazzi and crowds watching the main entrance to the Houses of Parliament.

'The new Irish Taoiseach is turning up,' he said. 'He's visiting with the Prime Minister.'

He glanced back at Declan, recognising who he was.

'If you were looking to see your buddy today, you might find it's a problem.'

'He's not my buddy, although I was hoping to have a visit,' Declan replied, nodding a thanks at the guards as he carried on down the ramp that led to the security area and Westminster Great Hall beyond.

He was always impressed with the magnificence of the

building as he walked through it. Governments might come and go, and politicians' careers might rise and fall, but the building itself was a testament to the longevity of British justice and democracy. Nowadays, though, it seemed to be nothing more than a convenient location for politicians to make their own rules up. He tried not to keep this in his thoughts, though, as he made his way up the steps at the end of the Great Hall, firing off a smile as he nodded to the guard who waited at the top, warding curious tourists away. With a return smile, the guard waved him through. If he had kept his face of thunder, he might have been held back and questioned. And the last thing he needed was that.

Declan didn't have a meeting booked. There was no spot in the schedule that had Declan planned into it, but he also knew the moment he'd walked up to the gate and the officer on guard had recognised him, someone somewhere had made a phone call and right now someone connected to Charles Baker would be hurrying to catch Declan before he got too far. After all, in the corridors were cameras, and even if the Irish Taoiseach *was* here, Declan Walsh wandering around could still make a story.

As it was, the face he saw waiting for him surprised Declan.

Jennifer Farnham-Ewing had been Charles Baker's assistant after Will Harrison had been murdered a couple of years earlier, having worked for Harrison in his office before his death. In her early-to-mid-twenties, slim and tall, her long blonde hair pulled into a ponytail and her makeup minimal, she had been ambitious, and often thought she was above all others. But, in the end, her inexperience of youth and her arrogance had cost her downfall. She had once said openly she'd been offered a chance to be an MP, a safe seat in a Conservative stronghold being prepared for her, but had realised that having the ear of the Prime Minister himself gave her more power and had turned it down. Shortly after that, she had found herself in hot water after her meddling with the Prime Minister's Personal Justice bill, creating a CGI video featuring "Lady Justice" which had shown them to have actively hindered a police inquiry.

Jennifer had been removed from Baker's office. Apparently the ruse had been what brought her up from the depths of Whitehall after her previous screw up – barring Declan from the State Dinner he eventually stopped from happening, thus saving everyone's lives from a dangerous poisoner in the catering staff – and the last Declan had heard, she was deep in the basement, working for the Whip's office, her power all but gone.

But here she stood, smiling, her hair pulled into the ponytail she always wore, and an austere navy-blue dress suit over a pink blouse. Declan knew she was in her twenties, but it was almost as if she was making a conscious effort to try to look older. He wondered if this was in some way to convince people she was more grown-up than she'd proven herself to be on other occasions.

'Declan,' she said, with a smile still on her face, even if her eyes didn't match it. 'So good of you to come. Please, walk with me.'

'Jennifer,' Declan replied, a similar humourless smile on his face. 'I thought you were gone from here; removed from politics, as they say.'

'Nobody ever gets removed from politics,' Jennifer said as they started through the hall, turning left down one of the corridors. 'The best always return. How many times have you seen a cabinet minister reduced to the back benches, only to return in triumph years later?'

'True,' Declan replied. 'But rarely with the subordinates. Last I heard, you were in the Whip's office.'

'I no longer work for the Whip,' Jennifer replied smugly. 'I no longer work for any of them.'

It was now that Declan realised they were walking down the corridor towards the Members' Terrace. He turned to ask who they were meeting, but Jennifer had obviously guessed his question, and her smile returned.

'You'll be talking to me today,' she said. 'I am, after all, one of the newest MPs in Parliament.'

She raised her eyebrows as Declan stared in confusion.

'You didn't hear?' she replied. 'Oh, I thought it would have reached your ears by now. Lovely little by-election in Berkshire. Safe Conservative seat. They decided it was a good idea to bring in a fresh face. I'm the "baby of the House" as I'm the youngest current MP, but not the youngest ever elected, as bloody Nadia was six months younger when she got in at twenty-three.'

She leant closer as they walked, conspiratorially linking her arm with Declan's as she spoke softer.

'Of course, it helped that a word from one of their largest donors sealed the deal,' she whispered.

'The largest donor being your father, I suppose?' Declan replied caustically.

Jennifer beamed in response.

'Why, yes,' she said. 'You are absolutely correct.'

They walked out onto the Members' Terrace, where a larger, older woman with greying short hair glared at them from the side.

'That's Nigella Waterstone,' Jennifer waved lazily over at

her. 'She's Charles's lapdog. If I'd stayed where I was, that would have been me.'

She offered a chair as she sat opposite Declan.

'Hungry?'

'No.'

'Good, you won't be here long enough to eat,' Jennifer replied. 'I'll sort you a sandwich out, though. For old time's sake.'

Declan bristled at the memory.

'Look,' he muttered. 'What game is being played here, and how do I get it over and done with?'

'Straight to the point, that's the go-getting detective I remember. Well, my old friend, there's talk of reducing some police units, and through some friendly faces on the select Committee, I might have suggested the Temple Inn unit be placed on the chopping block,' Jennifer replied, perusing the wine menu. 'Is it too early for a Merlot? It's not quite noon.'

'Revenge?' Declan asked, ignoring the comment, as well as the "old friend" line.

Jennifer smiled sweetly and shook her head.

'Oh no,' she replied. 'I have no need for revenge against you. In a way, you've helped me. If I hadn't been forced to leave Charles Baker's side, I would have been strapped to him as he fell downwards, crashing out of power through the leadership contest that's sure to happen this year, stuck to his side like a barnacle on the Titanic. Now, however, I'm the golden child of the Conservative Party, tipped to be an important player in the next Shadow Cabinet.'

'Shadow Cabinet?' Declan raised an eyebrow. 'You don't think you'll be in power?'

Jennifer gave a little knowing wink.

'In a way, even if we do stay in power,' she said, 'I

somehow don't think that Charles Baker will stand there with us. He needs a major win if such a thing is to happen and between you and me, he hasn't done that recently.'

She looked across the Terrace at Nigella.

'Don't worry, Waterstone,' she said. 'If Charles gets fired out of the cannon, you can always come work for me. I have some clout in the lower levels, after all.'

Declan realised at this point that he didn't like the idea of Jennifer Farnham-Ewing having power of any kind. Having met her on multiple occasions, he felt she was possibly the worst person you could have for public service.

'So, what do I need to do to keep us afloat?' he asked. 'I'm guessing you need something from me.'

'Actually, yes,' Jennifer nodded, looking back at him. 'Yes, we do. You remember the Prime Minister's late wife?'

'Donna Baker?' Declan did. It was Donna's apparent suicide, that had led Kendis Taylor into believing that Baker had been involved in a plot, one that cost Kendis her life, and at one point had Declan on the run for terrorism charges. It hadn't been Baker; at the time, he'd just stepped down from being Secretary of State, and it was Malcolm Gladwell, the party's "troubleshooter" who'd been the real instigator.

Of course, when Declan had solved the case, the information he'd passed to Baker himself had also helped with his leadership campaign.

'What about her?' he continued suspiciously.

'Her case was never formally closed,' Jennifer shrugged. 'We would like you to close it, preferably in Mister Baker's favour, as he was never accused or charged of any wrongdoings.'

'I'll see what I can do,' Declan replied, deciding he'd had

enough of the public display, now rising from the table. 'Is there anything else I should know?'

'Yes,' Jennifer rose to match him. 'I'd like you to understand fully that the reason your crime unit is being considered for closure is because of you, Mister Walsh.'

'*Detective Chief Inspector* Walsh, I think you'll find,' Declan was tiring of this conversation. But Jennifer, however, shook her head.

'No, very soon you will be *Mister* Walsh, unless you can explain to an inquiry about certain things we've recently discovered,' she replied. 'The only way to avoid the inquest and to avoid seeing your unit collapse and fade away, like so many others, is to do what we request. Close out the case of Donna's death.'

'How long do I have? We have a murder that we have to solve as well right now.'

'Oh, as long as I can tell the Prime Minister this is definitely being looked at, you can take as long as it needs,' Jennifer smiled warmly. 'We would never try to alter the route of justice after all.'

'Of course not,' Declan laughed. And then paused.

'Why exactly do you say that this is all because of me?'

At the question, Jennifer frowned.

'Well, because of the will,' she said.

'What will?'

As Declan stared in confusion at Jennifer, realisation crossed her face and she laughed.

'Oh my God,' she replied, almost in shock. 'You don't know yet. They haven't told you.'

'Haven't told me what?' Declan was tiring of the game now, and his voice was getting tighter and angrier.

'I'm talking about the will,' Jennifer continued, her voice still laughing. 'Karl Schnitter, the Red Reaper's one.'

'I didn't know he had a will.'

'Few people do yet. We're trying to keep it that way,' Jennifer leant closer, placing a hand on Declan's shoulder in an almost familial way. 'And believe me, Declan, you will probably want to keep it that way as well. Because the Red Reaper, one of the most notorious serial killers in UK history, the man that has been terrifying people for decades, who you gave to the Americans, who then let him return to us, before he killed some more innocent people? He's left you *everything* in his will. All of his money, his items, his properties, the lot.'

She pulled away now, watching Declan as he tried to take in what she was saying.

'So, ask yourself now, *Declan*,' she continued. 'How do you think the press would react when they heard that the DCI who had effectively made his career taking down the Red Reaper was now gaining everything from his estate?'

Declan opened and shut his mouth a couple of times. For a change, he didn't have an answer.

'Anyway, must dash. We've got a little soiree tomorrow I'm helping organise,' Jennifer continued. 'Party to commemorate Queen Elizabeth's memory, and welcome our new Irish Prime Minister friend. I'd say you were barred from arriving, but we did that before, remember?'

'I remember you almost killed everyone with your order.'

'And yet this time you've done it to yourself, haven't you?'

She stared at Declan for a long moment, before looking back at Nigella Waterstone.

'Nigella, be a dear and get DCI Walsh a sandwich to go?' Jennifer breezed away, across the terrace as Declan stared dumbly after her. 'I think he needs to leave now, and *my* aide is doing more important things.'

As Jennifer Farnham-Ewing left Declan alone, Nigella Waterstone stared daggers at Declan.

'I'm not getting a sodding sandwich,' she hissed. 'I was told by the Prime Minister to monitor the conversation.'

'Good, because I don't want one,' Declan replied. 'I'm guessing you're not a fan of our youngest MP?'

Waterstone simply glared silently at him.

'If you can think of any ways I can fulfil this task while also ripping her down a few levels, I'm all ears,' Declan said as he started across the Terrace. 'Say hi to Charles for me.'

She hadn't replied to him, but Declan had seen the smirk cross the face as he mentioned taking Jennifer down a notch.

*The enemy of my enemy is possibly my friend,* he thought to himself. *Even though she works for a different enemy.*

Sighing, he headed back through the Houses of Parliament. He needed to get confirmation of a dead man's will – and fast.

# 4

---

# HOUSE CALLS

RONALD TYLER LIVED IN A SHABBY SEMI-DETACHED HOUSE NEAR the Regents Estate in Haggerston, a small, forgotten suburb between its more affluent neighbours of Dalton and Hoxton.

De'Geer smiled as he looked at the estate. The chances were that even with the weathered appearance, every house here still cost more than his parents' house in Henley; and that was a four-bedroom house with an expansive garden.

They'd been passed a key by one of the forensics officers. Ronald had his items still on him when he died, and De'Geer hadn't been surprised to see they'd not been removed. So, it was with this dead man's key that De'Geer opened the door, Cooper entering behind him.

As houses went, it was well looked after. The walls were a strange brown-yellow mix, giving De'Geer the memory of old, nicotine-stained walls in pubs when he was a child, going along with his parents for Sunday lunches, and he was quite surprised to see horse brasses on one wall. He didn't think anybody under the age of eighty owned horse brasses.

There were various paintings and prints on the wall, but nothing that stood out. And, as De'Geer and Cooper moved through the house, they found nothing of note. No letters or torn notes saying, "I know what you did last summer", or even the words "Crooked Was His Cane" or "Bindlesticks". Eventually, after half an hour of looking around, De'Geer had to admit that there seemed to be nothing that gave any reason why Ronald Tyler would have been targeted in such a way.

Moving away from the admin side, examining the letters, a pack of playing cards and several bills that were placed almost haphazardly onto the dining-room table, they started looking at photo frames on the mantelpiece, searching for connections to people who could then become the next stage of the investigation. The bills were mostly for small amounts, giving the visual image of a man who lived alone, and within his means. There were no excessive tech items, with only a cheap Bluetooth record player in the living room, the type that looked like a suitcase and opened up, connected by a wire to a pair of what looked to be high-end PC speakers, rather than Hi-Fi ones. The photo frames gave little either. Many of them were images of a boy growing up, and De'Geer assumed this must be the son now at university, while a blonde woman, Ronald and the boy were in several others.

*Happier times for Ronald and his family, most likely.*

There were a couple of other photo pictures, including an older photo of a mid-twenties Ronald with three other men, standing beside a black cab. It was the only photo that De'Geer could find that had anybody else in it that wasn't family, so he moved his phone closer and took a photo, sending it to DI Kapoor and Billy, in case it helped somehow.

Maybe Anjli could ask the ex-wife if she knew any of the people in it, for example.

Cooper had found a laptop. There hadn't been a password protecting it, and it had been left on, so she'd quickly searched the desktop, as well as recent browser history; although all Ronald Tyler had apparently searched for in his last few days had been fast food addresses and loan companies.

*Had he reneged on a loan, perhaps?* De'Geer wondered.

The only other website he'd got in his history folder, the previous day in fact, was a two-week old news report from the online page of a Surrey newspaper.

**MAN KILLED IN HIT AND RUN ATTACK.**

De'Geer saw Cooper note the details down, and then she walked away from the laptop as the screensaver turned on.

With the house examined, and with nothing left to discover, Cooper and De'Geer went to leave, but paused in the doorway, as in front of them was a small man, late sixties and Mediterranean in looks, standing on the front step, as if waiting for them to appear.

'He's dead, isn't he?' he asked.

'I'm sorry?'

'Ronald. You wouldn't be walking round his house if something bad hadn't happened.'

'Did you know him?'

'I'm his neighbour.' The man pointed next door. 'My name's Kosta. Kosta Markovic.'

De'Geer took his notebook out and wrote it down.

'How well did you know Mister Tyler?' he asked, the past tense confirming Kosta's concerns.

'Here and there, he's worked shifts, you see. I'd catch him leaving for work, or returning. Nice guy. Never had a problem with him – ahh, it's a damn shame,' Kosta said. 'What was it, mugging? Someone attacked him?'

'Why would you think that?' Cooper asked.

'Well, he's a cabbie, isn't he?' Kosta shrugged. 'He always complained, said it was getting darker, harder to work the routes. Took their lives in their hands, they did when they went out at night, but that was always the more profitable part of the day.'

He shook his head sadly, staring down at the ground.

'I wouldn't have done it, especially with all the harassment stuff.'

'Harassment stuff?' De'Geer looked up from his notepad.

'Oh yeah, cabbies are a tribe and all that, but they still have their fights, you know. He'd changed his route, found a new place, maybe someone wanted to take him down a little.'

'Enough to …' De'Geer didn't finish because Kosta raised his hands to interrupt him in horror.

'Oh God, no,' he stuttered. 'No, no, no. They wouldn't kill each other for that. It's a bloody parking spot, nothing more. I just mean there were, you know, issues.'

'Do you know what kind of issues?'

'No, but I know he said he'd gone to the garage as there'd been problems.'

'Garage?'

'Yeah. Monarch Motors, it's the one the cabbies use around here. Been working for years, they have. They used to fix his car up all the time when it had an engine, but they still did bodywork when needed. I know he took it in recently, someone had smashed his windscreen with a brick or something. He was furious, but what can you do with kids?'

Kosta paused, leaning closer.

'How did he die?' he asked. De'Geer wasn't sure, but he could almost sense a morbid curiosity building up here.

'Shortness of breath,' Cooper interjected, leaning closer. 'And if you know what's good for you, you'll leave it at that, sir.'

Kosta understandably stepped back, once more raising his hands in the air. It seemed to be his default defensive pose.

'I didn't mean anything with that,' he replied.

'It's fine.' De'Geer wanted to return into the house to get away from the neighbour, and noticed Cooper had already beaten him to the punch and had walked back in, obviously not wanting to speak to the shorter man anymore.

Kosta, however, hadn't finished.

'Is this to do with his mate?' he asked. 'The lanky one?'

'What lanky one?' De'Geer couldn't help himself.

'Tall chap, same age, started coming by almost a month ago. Kept banging on the door; we told him if the cab wasn't there then Ronnie wasn't, but he'd still keep banging away. Stopped turning up about a couple of weeks back, so I guess he found him.'

'Perhaps,' De'Geer scratched at his beard. 'Did you get a name?'

'Stuart something,' Kosta nodded. 'Never bothered talking long enough to get the rest. Being honest, it was around the time of the food poisoning, so Ronnie was probably in bed.'

De'Geer reached for his phone, opening up the photo of the four men he'd taken.

'Was he any of these?' he asked.

Kosta took the phone and peered closely at it, squinting, his nose almost touching the screen.

'You can just zoom in,' De'Geer offered.

'I understand how phones work, thanks,' Kosta replied haughtily, tapping at the man on the left, skinnier and taller than the other three. 'Him. Greyer and less hair, but I'd say so.'

'You mentioned food poisoning?'

'Yeah, couple of weeks back, Ron got it bad. Both ends. I only know because he texted me asking for some bog roll. Poor bastard had run out. His ex-wife was supposed to bring some, I think. Turned up one night, and the following morning. Didn't stay over, if you know what I mean. Shows you how bad it gets when you have to call your ex-wife, although she never brought him the bog roll, I still had to do that, which was taking the piss, considering he had deliveries turning up. Bloody doorbell going constantly one evening.'

He scratched his chin.

'I think it was around then some prick took the brick to his windscreen,' he continued. 'Again, cabbies and their fights.'

De'Geer thanked the older man as he took his phone back, but as he was about to ask Kosta another question, he heard a call from Cooper, from inside the house.

'Sarge?'

'Thank you for your time,' De'Geer almost gratefully continued, passing a business card across. 'This is my number. Can you please contact us if anything else comes up?'

'What if you need to speak to me?'

'If we need you, we know where you are.'

Kosta weakly nodded now, almost as if he'd realised he'd overstepped a line. And leaving him at the doorway, De'Geer walked back into the living room.

'I was thinking,' Cooper said as he appeared. 'I had to go and check.'

'What is it?' De'Geer watched as Cooper walked over to the suitcase record player. There were three twelve inch vinyl albums scattered on it; one was *Pink Floyd's Dark Side of the Moon*, another was a *New Order* album he didn't recognise, but the third, which had been under the other two, stood out a little, having been revealed by Cooper. It was a picture of a man with brown hair playing at a small gig. The album, in a typical folk-music style font, announced the name.

*James Harlow – Live at the London Roots Festival, 2019.*

It looked new, barely touched. Ronald Tyler obviously looked after his music.

'What's to reckon that if we took that album and turned it around, we'd see on the playlist "Crooked Was His Cane"?' Cooper asked. After a moment she did so, nodding as her suggestion was confirmed. Opening it up to see the inside of the gatefold, she frowned.

'It's a load of old photos and snippets of songs, but look here, it's signed,' she said. 'In the bottom right-hand corner, under an old photo in the gatefold. "So you never forget."'

'That's not signed,' De'Geer shook his head. 'You need a signature for it to be signed. That's a message.'

'Or a warning.'

De'Geer nodded, texting the name of the garage to Declan and Monroe. *Maybe it was worth visiting.*

'Good work, PC Cooper,' he smiled. 'Finally, it looks like we've got something worth chasing.'

'Why thank you, Sergeant De'Geer,' Cooper beamed back. 'Let's get out of here before you gain an urge to listen to the album, place a lighthouse-keeper's jumper on and go full Folkie on me. After all, you have the beard.'

# 5

## TEARS BEFORE BREAKFAST

LIZZIE TYLER WIPED A TEAR FROM HER EYE AS SHE STARED down at the photo of Ronald that she had picked up after Anjli had informed her of her ex-husband's death.

'It's so unfair,' she said. 'He was a lovely guy, a lovely man.'

'Yet you divorced him,' Anjli continued absently, instantly regretting the comment. 'Sorry, just going through the data.'

At this, Lizzie glared up at Anjli.

'Have you ever been married, Detective Inspector Kapoor?' she asked.

'No,' Anjli admitted. 'Although my partner was divorced.'

'Does he still speak to his wife?'

'Reluctantly.'

'Well, it's not the same for all divorces,' Lizzie walked into the house, waving for Anjli to follow. 'The two of us just grew apart, yeah? One night we were lying in bed and we realised we were more like brother and sister, which might sound bad in that respect, but, I mean ...'

Anjli understood what Lizzie was trying to say, mismatched words or not.

'You didn't love him in the way that a lover should,' she said. 'I've had my share of break-ups. I know how you feel, but I'll be honest, I've never really hung out with them afterwards.'

'Wasn't really an option,' Lizzie shrugged, pointing at a photo on the sideboard of Ronald, her, and a twenty-year-old boy. 'Cavan. He's in his last year at university now. When we broke up, he was starting his A-levels and we couldn't put him through the ringer, so we decided to stay friends.'

'Just like that?' Anjli pulled out a notebook, writing some notes.

'If you want something, you can make it so,' Lizzie nodded. 'It's all about visualisation and compromise, so yeah.'

'Do you know anybody who could have wanted to cause harm to Ronald?'

Anjli wasn't sure, but she was positive that for a split second the mask dropped, as an expression crossed Lizzie's face. It was gone in a second, but Anjli was convinced she saw it.

*Triumph.*

'Ronnie? Nah. Guy was an angel,' Lizzie replied, back to the script now. 'Everybody liked him. You ask around, you'll not hear a bad word said about him.'

Lizzie carried through into the kitchen, where she reached up into a high cabinet and pulled down a bottle of vodka, pouring a glass for herself. She didn't offer Anjli one, and she would have refused, anyway. Lizzie downed the glass in one, re-pouring a fresh shot and holding it up as she considered the question once more.

'I mean, taxi drivers are a bunch of bitchy little bastards but, you know, there's a lot of them out there. They're always fighting for fares and then you've got those guys like Uber and whoever the other names are, all turning up out of nowhere, and then add minicabs in their little offices, usually with no idea what they're doing, relying on sat-navs when they can't even speak English. Not one of them would know Barbican to Mile End, or St Martin's Lane to Fulham Broadway without a bloody app.'

Anjli bristled at the more than racist statement, but she understood the comment. There were people out there who matched this stereotype, but then, every country had that. It was a common trope that the New York taxicab drivers rarely spoke English and came straight off the boat and into the job.

It was often untrue.

*It didn't stop it being believed.*

Racist comments aside, she couldn't help herself as she looked back at Lizzie, who, realising she'd overstepped, held up her hand, pausing Anjli.

'God, I'm sorry. I didn't mean it the way it came out,' she replied. 'It's a frustration at the situation, not at the race or the colour of a driver.'

'I get that,' Anjli nodded. 'I really do. And also, you've had a massive shock. So why don't you tell me about the last time you saw Ronald?'

'I haven't seen him for months,' Lizzie shook her head. 'I mean, we don't visit and hang out. It's mainly when Cavan is home and he's been at university.'

Anjli frowned.

'We're coming to the end of the summer holidays,' she said. 'University's been over for a while now.'

'Yeah, but he has a summer job. He's up in Hull, and it's a lot easier for him to stay up there and get some money over the summer than it is to come down here and hang around. All his friends have moved on, got jobs.'

Anjli noted this down. It sounded that for all the happy-families talk Lizzie was stating, their son preferred to stay elsewhere rather than return to the family unit.

'How long were you married?' she asked, writing the notes.

'Almost sixteen years, until we weren't,' Lizzie said, and there was a slight wistfulness in her voice. 'We got together after ... well, college, I suppose. We just fell into each other, if that makes sense.'

Anjli nodded, writing this down. *Childhood sweethearts, it seemed.*

'We probably would have broken up years back, if it wasn't for Cavan,' Lizzie continued. 'I got pregnant by acci-dent. We'd considered marriage, you know, as a vague sugges-tion, but once Cavan was real and on the horizon, we knew we had to make it legal and all that. I took a back seat, looked after the baby while Ronnie built up his career as a black cab driver.'

'Must have been tough,' Anjli looked back up at the woman facing her. 'I understand the Knowledge seems to be quite intensive. My uncle did it. To have that and an upcoming wedding and a baby on the way ...'

'Oh, he passed the Knowledge before we got together,' Lizzie shook her head. 'He was working long hours though, but our friends kept us both sane.'

'Your friends?'

Lizzie paused, as if realising she'd said too much, and then, with a subtle shift in positioning, she continued.

'Oh, they were more his than mine, from his time learning the Knowledge. I inherited them, you know? There was a group of them who all did the same course. It was one of those London taxi cab schools that does training,' Lizzie explained. 'It meant he didn't have to do it on his own, and I think it helped him a little.'

There was a buzz, and Anjli looked down to see a message arrive from De'Geer. On it was a photo of four young men by a black cab.

'Speak of the devil,' she said, showing the photo to Lizzie. 'Would these be the men he trained with? I'm guessing by the fact that they're beside a cab?'

Lizzie nodded, but her face was no longer one of grief. The eyes had narrowed, the lips thinned. Anjli knew there was an element of distaste here, but she couldn't work out exactly what it was.

'You didn't approve of his friends?'

'I liked his friends fine,' Lizzie said, knocking back the second of the vodka shots.

'Then what is it you don't approve of here?'

'Look, thank you for coming and letting me know, DI Kapoor, but I really can't help with anything else—'

Anjli didn't mean to, but instinctively grabbed the vodka bottle, slamming it down on the table, jerking Lizzie's attention up, her eyes wide as she stared at the woman facing her.

'Which one of them don't you approve of?' Anjli snarled, showing the photo once more. 'The Indian guy? The tall one? Or the posh-looking one?'

After a moment's reluctant silence, Lizzie pointed at the posh-looking one. He, of all of them in the photo, was the only one in what looked to be a suit, although it was possibly trousers and a blazer, with a shirt, the collar unbuttoned, and a loose tie. The others wore jeans and shirts or polo-necks. It was the turn of the millennium and all four were wearing clothing of the era, but the one on the end, the posh-looking one, looked like he was a cut above the others.

'Lance,' Lizzie said, tapping on the suited man. 'Never understood his game.'

'How do you mean?'

'Well, Sandeep, Stuart and Ronald, they needed the job. They had to learn the Knowledge to be cab drivers, but Lance, he came from money,' Lizzie sniffed as she straightened, tapping the side of her head as she continued. 'His dad had threatened to disown him if he didn't prove he could learn something and keep it in there. Rather than helping people or making the world a better place, he decided to become a cab driver. Decided that proving to his dad he could learn the Knowledge was important. He didn't give a damn about the driving. He didn't give a damn about being a cab driver. In fact, after they passed, I don't think he even drove a cab again. He was nothing but a bad influence.'

Anjli wrote this down.

'Do you remember his full name?'

'Lance Curtis,' Lizzie replied. 'But actually, it's Lancelot Curtis-Warner.'

'Curtis-Warner?' Anjli frowned. 'As in *Curtis & Warner,* the toothpaste people?'

'The very same,' Lizzie still shook her head, grabbing the vodka bottle, pouring and downing another shot of vodka before continuing, 'Haven't seen him for years. The last time I saw him, he was on an episode of *Made in Chelsea,* that one about the posh people who live in West London years ago. He turned up as a friend of one of the cast in a scene. I remember seeing him, pointing to Ronald and saying it was Lance, but Ronald wasn't paying attention.'

'Did Ronald still know him at the time of the TV show?'

'Oh, yeah,' Lizzie shook her head. 'It's one of the reasons we actually had fights. I never liked the son of a bitch. Ronald thought the sun shone out of his arse. It was Lance who paid for Ronald's bloody car as well.'

'Car?'

'The electric one he was driving around. They cost a fortune. More than a normal car. Ronald couldn't afford it. Lance stepped in and helped.'

'Why would he do that?'

'Your guess is as good as mine,' Lizzie grumbled. 'That prick never looked out for anybody but himself.'

She sighed, placed her hands on the countertop and stretched, loosening her shoulders.

'But I'm just pissed off, getting drunk and grieving,' she replied. 'Maybe he was fine. Maybe I just didn't like the guy. Either way, though, if there's something going on, you should speak to Curtis-Warner about it.'

Anjli closed her notebook and placed it back inside her jacket.

'Thanks for your time,' she said, already walking back to the main door. 'Oh, one last question, if I may – did Ronald ever talk about a song called "Crooked Was His Cane"?'

It was like Lizzie Tyler was punched, as she stopped in her tracks, gathering her thoughts.

'No,' she replied, after a moment of gaining her composure. 'That is he may have, but we have – I mean we had – different tastes in music.'

'You're sure? You looked a little startled when I mentioned it.'

'Still getting to grips with Ronnie being gone,' Lizzie shook her head now, back in control.

'Well, Ms Tyler, if you—'

'Look,' Lizzie snapped, stopping Anjli. 'Am I under arrest? No? Then come back with a warrant or something if you want to continue. My ex-husband is dead and you're talking gibberish about a bloody folk song! Get out.'

Anjli nodded, turned to the door of the house and left Lizzie Tyler to her own thoughts and memories.

*She was lying.*

Of that, Anjli was sure. She knew the song, and it shook her. Anjli hadn't mentioned it was folk. Perhaps it was a calculated guess, but Anjli doubted it. Whatever "Crooked Was His Cane" was, it was enough to scare Lizzie Tyler to the point she wanted Anjli gone.

But why?

———

# 6

## VIDEO CALLS

In recent years, Billy Fitzwarren hadn't been the biggest fan of going out into the field, preferring instead to sit behind his banks of computer monitors. It wasn't that he was agoraphobic or hated people; it was just that the last times he'd ventured out, *bad* things usually ended up happening. Whether he was walking into scenes involving dead bodies or finding assault rifles aimed at his face, Billy had found that a far safer option was to stay by his computer desk and work the cyber side. However, there were occasions where he needed to speak to people face-to-face.

Luckily for Billy, over the last few years, the videoconferencing industry had become rather popular, and now it was as simple as speaking to somebody through the camera of their phone to gain the face-to-face meetings he needed, while still being able to check expressions for signs of lying.

It wasn't the best, but on occasions like this, Billy was fine with it.

The occasion Billy was referring to was a video call he was about to take with the folk singer James Harlow. He'd managed to find Harlow's number through his management company as, after explaining that he was a police officer working on a case that might have a connection to James, the management company was more than happy to give him Harlow's contact details. So now, at lunchtime, Billy waited for the call to go through.

After a moment, the screen changed, and Billy stared at a man sitting on a sofa, probably using either an iPad or laptop, with the webcam facing him at an upward angle as he peered down at it. The man was in his late forties, maybe fifties, with long brown hair, shaggy around his shoulders, and he wore what people called a lighthouse-keeper jumper – a chunky, cable-designed polo neck in cream. He couldn't look any more like a folk singer if he tried.

'Thank you for agreeing to speak to me,' Billy said. 'I'm Detective Sergeant William Fitzwarren.'

On the other end of the signal, James started speaking, but no sound came out.

'I think you're muted,' Billy said, waving at the screen.

James, confused, carried on speaking.

'No, I can't hear you, I'm afraid. I think you're muted,' Billy groaned inwardly. Although video calls were a blessing at some points, they were also a curse.

Eventually, James pressed the button, and suddenly he could be heard.

'Is that better?' he asked.

'Ah, good. Thank you,' Billy nodded.

'My management said there was some kind of case I could help you with?' James replied. 'I hope I'm not involved in any way.'

'Not necessarily involved,' Billy explained. 'Basically, there's a murder inquiry going on, and it looks like it might have been connected to a song you wrote about fifteen years ago.'

'If anybody's listening to songs I wrote fifteen years ago, they're a superfan, and they probably should be arrested,' James laughed.

Billy didn't laugh.

'The victim had an album of yours,' he replied. 'It was a vinyl double gatefold. A live session of yours, recorded at the 2019 London Roots Festival.'

James nodded.

'I do a dozen such festivals every year. Roots, Cambridge, Moseley, all the big ones. Get good sales from the merch, too. What about it?'

'Well, as I said, the victim had the album, and we think it was connected to the song "Crooked Was His Cane", a song that's on the album.'

'And why would you think that?'

Billy paused.

'I'm afraid I can't really give details of the case,' he said. 'All I can tell you is that we are led to believe that a message was left at a crime scene that was possibly connected to the title.'

'Okay, I get that,' James sat back a little as he replied. 'Song titles have been used many times for messages. Songs like "Imagine" by John Lennon and "Blowin' in the Wind" by Bob Dylan have been used widely as messages of peace and change during protests and movements. Barack Obama referenced titles by Bruce Springsteen and Aretha Franklin in his campaigns, even Black Lives Matter protests used song titles like "Alright" by Kendrick Lamar as subtle rallying cries for justice and resilience.'

Billy, hoping the lecture would end soon, nodded.

'I was hoping you could tell me a little about the song,' he said.

'You've heard it?'

'Yes, and I have the lyrics in front of me.'

James considered the statement, looked around his room, and then gave a mouth shrug, a kind of Robert De Niro impression, although it probably wasn't meant to be such.

'You ever heard of Godley and Creme?' he asked.

Billy frowned, unable to place the name.

'Not off the top of my head.'

'Double act that came out of a band called 10cc back in the seventies,' James nodded. 'Anyway, in eighty-one, they released a song called "Under Your Thumb". Actually reached number three in the charts, highest they ever managed.'

Billy was confused where the conversation was going, but politely held back from asking as James continued.

'Anyway, Under Your Thumb – the song was a ghost story in the kind of style of M. R. James or Charles Dickens,' James explained. 'It was about a man who, sheltering from a thunderstorm, hides in a railway carriage, and while he's there, he finds the spirit of a woman who had jumped from that same train years earlier. He realises the truth when he finds an old newspaper with her name in it. But when she's there, she's screaming that she doesn't want to be under someone's thumb forever, and that's the chorus.'

'Sounds very uplifting and optimistic,' Billy smiled.

James took the joke, laughing.

'It was a ghost story as a song, and it always stuck in my mind when I was a kid,' he continued. 'Anyway, about fifteen years back, I decided to write my own version.'

'Crooked Was His Cane.'

'Yeah. It's not as much of a story as "Under Your Thumb", but I felt it worked. And you think this is involved in a death?'

'Well, one of the reasons I wanted to check into it was that a lot of folk music always have a basis in fact,' Billy added, ignoring the question. 'A story that has travelled around for years might then become a song, and I was wondering how based on facts "Crooked Was His Cane" was.'

'You want to know whether my song of a ghostly man who disappears when hit by a bus, leaving nothing but a cane, is true?' James raised an eyebrow. 'Are you sure you're the police?'

Billy held his hands up, but realised that they probably weren't visible on the screen, so then placed a hand out in front of the camera to show he was backing down slightly.

'I get that,' he replied. 'But inspiration comes from many forms.'

'You need to go back in your police records about twenty years or so,' James said. 'Hammersmith Bridge.'

'What about it?' Billy was already typing the details in.

'Man takes a cab to the middle of the bridge. Furious rainstorm. Says he needs to get out. He's having a panic attack or a heart attack or something, the cab driver wasn't sure. Gets out of the cab. Starts walking across the road. It's late at night. He's had a couple, and he's hit by a bus. Apparently, a double-decker smacked straight into him; simply didn't see him in the night, as it was raining heavily. It didn't veer lanes, the man just basically walked out in front of it.'

Billy typed this down as James continued.

'There was talk he was looking to get out at Hammer-smith Bridge because he was intending to jump, but I've read stories of people who jumped from that bridge, and it's not exactly a guaranteed death if you're looking to commit suicide.'

Billy made an appreciative 'mm' noise, realising the talk was taking a morbid turn.

'Anyway, here's the bit that is the kicker,' James leant closer to the screen as if wanting to make sure his words came through correctly. 'The man walked away from the cab and was hit by a bus, right? The bus carried on, maybe not even realising, the witnesses all ran to make sure the man was still alive, but he wasn't there.'

'What do you mean, he wasn't there?'

'That's literally all the story says. All that was left on the floor was his walking stick, a crooked-looking cane. There was no body, and none of the witnesses saw him leave.'

James didn't answer, instead leaning back on his sofa now.

'Now, nobody came forward and said they'd actually seen it, but there were witnesses who claimed that they'd spoken to *other* witnesses, who in turn claimed *they* had. But no bus driver ever stood forward. It was only the word of a couple of anonymous witnesses who saw it, and stories told to others.'

'There was no body?'

'So the witnesses said,' James replied, shaking his head, eventually answering the question. 'The story isn't the same as I sang, as the witness that contacted the police said she heard the accident, came running up the bridge, saw the cab. There were a couple of men standing around, obviously other passers-by had turned up, and when the witness asked what had happened, they told her what I effectively used in the song.'

'Using what the witnesses said as a basis.'

'Yes,' James replied. 'Anyway, there was no corpse, no

case, and nothing happened. But now that witness, she couldn't get it out of her head. Her next-door neighbour was a police officer, so a couple of days later she told him what she'd seen, thinking it was silly more than anything else. He said he'd raise it with his unit, but as I said, this was twenty-odd years ago. Traffic cameras weren't as prevalent as they are now, and in the middle of a thunderstorm on Hammersmith Bridge, nobody saw anything. The other witnesses were gone, nobody had taken names. They put one of those little yellow boards up, saying, "Were you here? Did you see something?" and no one ever came back. All we have is this woman's opinion of what she was told, and even with that, it's hearsay.'

'So, the story of a man being hit and leaving nothing but a cane resonated with you?' Billy asked.

James nodded once more, but Billy could feel there was something more that hadn't been said.

'Is there anything you'd like to add?' he asked calmly.

James shook his head.

'I'm sure we'll have conversations down the line, officer,' he replied. 'But right now, I'm in the middle of three different things, and I thought I was just having a quick chat. I didn't realise I'd be leaving a statement for a crime that happened twenty years ago, that I used vaguely in a song I wrote.'

He was getting antagonistic, and Billy couldn't quite work out what had done this.

'Well, thank you for your time anyway,' he said, deciding to call the end of the conversation. 'I don't know if it can help, but at least it gives us an idea of something else we can look at. Maybe a cold case from twenty years ago might give us a clue as to why there was an incident that occurred last night.'

'Glad to help,' James said. 'Keep me in the loop if I can help in any other way.'

'One last thing,' Billy held a hand up to stop James from disconnecting the call. 'We've noticed that on several of the videos, many people post comments with just one word. "Bindlesticks." Do you know what this could mean?'

James paled and then shook his head.

'No, sorry, who knows why they post what they post,' he half-whispered. 'It sounds like a joke, detective, and best to leave it at that.'

'Also, the vinyl album, it had a message on it,' Billy added.

'You said one last question, not a dozen.'

'It's important,' Billy insisted. 'It said "so you don't forget". I wondered if you'd ever signed anything like that?'

'Who was it for?'

Billy weighed up his answer, and then decided that as the name would be on the news later that day, he wasn't giving much away by stating it.

'Ronald Tyler. He was a black cab driver.'

'Well, if I did sign it, I don't remember, and if I didn't sign my name, it probably wasn't me, yeah? Maybe it was a gift from someone?'

Before Billy could say anything else, James had disconnected the call, and Billy now stared at a blank screen.

There was something that didn't ring true here, and Billy couldn't quite work out what it was.

He'd have to try to find the witness statement, but a witness claiming that someone had died when the body was not to be found, the actual witnesses to the incident were gone and only a crooked cane had been discovered would likely have been filed and forgotten about. The bus driver hadn't stepped forward, stating he'd hit anybody, because he could have lost his job. The cab driver that had taken the ride wouldn't have passed it on, and if it was a black cab or even a minicab, the chances were it would have been paid by cash back then so there would be no credit card records. The story of the man that climbed out of the car on Hammersmith Bridge, was hit by a bus, and disappeared into nothing, was itself nothing more than an urban legend.

Billy leant back on his gaming chair, muttering to himself. He hated urban legends. There was always a thread of truth in them, but it was never the thread that he wanted to pull on.

*And why had James Harlow paled so when the name "Bindle-sticks" was given?*

Sighing, he returned to the computer system.

There was more here. He just needed to find it.

He knew he just needed to dig a little deeper.

# 7

# HISTORIES

Lance Curtis-Warner hadn't expected visitors that morning. So, when Lizzie Tyler started hammering on the door of his West Chelsea townhouse, it was with an irate glare that he allowed the woman into the room.

'It had better be life or death, Tyler,' he muttered as he walked over to his Nespresso machine and tapped at it idly, trying to coax some kind of espresso from it. Lizzie, stressed but not too stressed to understand how things worked, pushed Lance aside, placed a pod into the top of the machine, and pressed the button. Within a second, the espresso was pouring, and the machine was chugging along as Lizzie turned to face Lance.

'Christ, man,' she said. 'You can't even make a coffee.'

'I have people to do those sorts of things,' Lance groaned as he rubbed the back of his neck. 'Seriously, can we do this some other time? I'm really hungover.'

'Are you? Are you really?' Lizzie leant closer, narrowing her eyes. 'Late night, was it? Or was it more of an early morning?'

'What the bloody hell is that supposed to mean?' Lance replied. 'A late night is always an early morning. Don't you understand how clocks work?'

'Well, if you were around in the early morning, then you might have been with Ronnie,' Lizzie continued. 'Because, let's be honest, someone was with him this morning.'

'Why was someone with him this morning?' Lance asked, bleary eyed and tiring of the game. Lizzie was an attractive woman, and back in the day he knew she'd held a secret crush on him, but any interest he had in her was more the fact she was someone else's, and what other people had was always more interesting to Lance than what he could have himself.

Also, Lance knew without a doubt he could have Lizzie Tyler if he wanted. There'd been enough stolen glances, enough hidden meanings in conversations over the years. It was simply the fact that she'd aged herself out of the running that stopped him from bothering to try.

Walking over to the toaster and this time understanding how to place bread in the top, he waited for an answer, not looking back at the interloper in his kitchen.

'Because someone killed him,' Lizzie eventually snapped back, and her voice sounded broken, like she'd had to gather strength to state the words. 'They strapped him to a seat and pumped carbon monoxide into his cab outside Gainsborough House. You know ... Bartlett bloody Place.'

At this, Lance turned slowly to face her as he held the small espresso cup in his hand.

'You'd better be absolutely bloody lying to me,' he said, his voice emotionless. 'This had better be some kind of really sick and belated April Fools.'

'I wish it was,' Lizzie shook her head. 'The police came to me an hour back. Asked if I knew of any debts he had, of anyone who hated him.'

She straightened, staring directly at Lance.

'She also asked if I knew of "Crooked Was His Cane",' she hissed.

Lance downed the espresso, more as an excuse to gather some thinking time than from the need to drink it; the words spoken would have done a far better job of jolting his system into action. He rubbed his eyes and then walked over to the sink, splashing water onto his face to wake himself up.

'Well, one thing I'll say for you, Lizzie,' he said as he dried his face. 'You're a hell of a hangover cure. Do the others know yet?'

'The others?' Lizzie laughed. 'I came straight here because I know this has something to do with you. Are you telling me the others are involved? Is this because of Stuart? Am I in trouble?'

'We don't know anything yet,' Lance shook his head. 'It could be nothing—'

'Nothing?' Lizzie picked up the discarded espresso cup, throwing it across the kitchen at him, narrowly missing his head as it shattered against the wall. 'My ex-husband is dead because of what you did all those years ago! Probably because of Stuart, too!'

'So what, you're now his fan because he's dead? Don't give me that shit, yeah? We all know you've hated each other for years now.'

Lizzie glared at Lance as he leant against the kitchen counter. In return, Lance raised a finger to stop her from replying to this, but his face was no longer that of a man being calm himself. It was reddening with anger and possibly because of the close call with the coffee cup. There was a very drawn out, uncomfortable moment now in Lance Curtis-Warner's kitchen.

'Thank you for bringing this to my attention,' Lance eventually replied, his voice now cold and emotionless, cutting off any future conversation here. 'I'll look into this and make sure that it's sorted. In the meantime—'

'In the meantime, you can go to hell,' Lizzie turned and stormed back out of the kitchen, heading towards the main door.

As she got to the door, she looked back.

'Oh, and you can keep your car,' she said. 'I won't be taking on the payments for it.'

'Of course not,' Lance had returned to his more amiable self now. 'I would never dream of moving his debt on to you. If poor Ronald has shuffled off this mortal coil, I'll—'

'Shut up,' Lizzie said, turning and slamming the door behind her as she walked out of the house.

There was a long, peaceful moment of solitude in the kitchen.

Lance stared at the door as if expecting Lizzie to appear through it once more.

And then, with a yelp, he jumped as the toast popped out of the toaster.

As he buttered his breakfast then crunched on the crisp toast, he considered the situation. There had only been four of them in the car that night, and none of them wanted to see their lives destroyed if the truth had come out. But they weren't the only ones involved, though. And in a way, Ronald hadn't been involved in Stuart's death a couple of weeks earlier, kept from the shuffle because of his bloody food poisoning.

*Could someone else be cleaning up house now? And why was he at Bartlett Place? What did he know?*

Lance didn't need the answer to that. He knew what Ronald knew. He also knew who'd told him, and what Lance was going to have to do to fix it.

Leaning back against the kitchen counter, he looked up at the ceiling and let out a long, held breath.

'Alexa, play "Crooked Was His Cane",' he whispered.

As the haunting voice of James Harlow now filled the kitchen, Lance stood alone, listening to the song. Like all folk songs, it had a nugget of truth held within.

And, like all folk songs, it wasn't the true story.

*Only Lance, Ronald, Clifford and Stuart knew the true story of that night.*

'Dammit,' he spoke aloud now in the kitchen. 'I'm going to have to speak to him again.'

---

AFTER STUART LAWS HAD BEEN KILLED IN A TERRIBLE HIT-AND-run incident, the case had been pushed upwards, as Surrey Police tried to find anyone who could give information on this.

Detective Sergeant Heather Crawford, a young, ambitious woman in the Addlestone police unit who'd also been given the almost impossible case had reluctantly worked on it, but with no camera footage, no actual witnesses who could give more than "the car hit the man" and no idea of why someone would even do it, outside of incredible rumours and theories including the bloody Yakuza, it quickly fell down the pecking order of her workload, waiting for some revelation to appear, to help solve it – something that was unlikely to happen. It would have stayed in her file drawer, slowly covering with dust, if it hadn't been for the fact Stuart Laws was a known contact of Ronald Tyler, and two weeks after the incident a young police officer named Esme Cooper contacted Surrey Police, having learned of Stuart's death while investigating his details.

It was Detective Sergeant Heather Crawford who gratefully accepted the call, hoping that at best it'd help her solve the case, and at worst give her a way to pass the bloody albatross on to someone else, and keep her fairly spotless closure report. After all, it was coming up to promotion time soon, and the local DI was looking to leave.

'All we have is the coroner's report,' Crawford explained, as Cooper wrote this down on the other end of the phone. 'It was an absolute shitter of a day. Rain was heavy. Visibility was low. Everybody had their heads down or had their hoods up and umbrellas out, which meant they weren't paying attention to the road. They were staring more at their feet, making sure they weren't getting wet. There was a screech of brakes. Stuart Laws went down. The car continued on. By the time people realised what had happened, it was already heading off down the road.'

'Any other details?'

'Nobody got a licence plate. At best, we think it was a 2020 plate, black cab new style, not the less boxy old ones. People ran over to where Stuart lay, crumpled beside a wall. He was still breathing at the time. An ambulance was called, but by the time it arrived, which was only five, ten minutes later, he'd passed away from his injuries.'

'What were the injuries?' Cooper asked.

'Head wound, mainly,' Crawford was reading her notes once more. 'The car hit him straight on and slammed him against the wall. There were obviously injuries to his ribs and legs, and I think his right arm was broken, but it was a slamming of his head against the windscreen and then back against the wall that did it.'

'Do you think it would have broken the windscreen?'

'Impact strong enough to do that much damage? The original report said so,' Crawford replied. 'But to be honest, until somebody actually tries slamming a forehead into a windscreen at speed to replicate it, you can't really tell. It's only theoretical.'

Cooper noted this down. Although there was no guaranteed description of the vehicle, that it was a cab with a potentially smashed windscreen meant there was a chance that some of the local garages around may have had someone come in to have this fixed – which could at least give them a lead.

'It's a shame, really,' Crawford replied.

'The accident?'

'No, that nobody picked up the licence plate,' Crawford's voice was relaxed, and Cooper realised this wasn't that personal to her, just a case she'd been passed that nobody really wanted. 'Basically, in that part of Surrey, you rarely get black cabs unless they're dropping someone off from London, maybe using it as a shortcut to avoid the M25.'

'Do you know which way the cab went?'

'Well, the accident happened on Green Lane, and from what we can work out, it was heading west, towards the junction with the M25,' Crawford clicked her tongue as she considered the question. 'If they were looking to kill him, though, they must have waited a while. He didn't have a regular schedule, being a driver. His jobs were whenever his jobs were, and he parked his car in a driveway down the road.'

'He didn't park outside his house?'

'No,' Crawford's voice was collected and professional as she read her notes. 'Stuart lived in a flat on the High Street. The car he drove was expensive. He wouldn't park it around the back, as he didn't have one of the garages there. So he rented a car parking space outside a new build townhouse about a quarter of a mile down Green Lane. That way, it was in a nicer area, you know? Less likely to get nicked.'

'Was it his own car?'

'Oh, God, no. A man like Stuart Laws couldn't afford a car like that.' Crawford almost laughed, and Cooper was starting to dislike the woman. 'Apparently, he had it on some kind of lease hire agreement.'

'Do you know the company?'

'Not to hand, but I can find it and send it over.'

'That would be appreciated,' Cooper replied, reading out an email that DS Crawford could send all the information to. 'Did anyone forensically examine his home, his emails, phone records, all that?'

There was a long, awkward pause.

'No,' Crawford eventually admitted. 'We were going to, but all signs led to an accident, and we had nothing. I mean, don't get me wrong, we went to look around, and we did flick through the phone records and all that, but nothing out of the ordinary.'

'Could we have that data too?'

'Of course,' Crawford, glad to have got off the hook, replied more jovially now. 'Hey, if you look at it, can you solve a puzzle we have, too?'

'Sure,' Cooper was already writing, waiting for the request.

'One of the last voice messages he had on his phone was a message from an unknown number,' Crawford continued. 'It wasn't a mysterious burner or anything, it was one of those robo-calls that hammer lists of phones. But it was a weird message. Just sang about a crooked cane.'

'Crooked Was His Cane?' Cooper asked, already feeling the air in the room get colder.

'Yeah, that's the one!' Crawford was delighted. 'It was like two lines of a song. I've got it here. "*I recall no destination, as the man, he did explain, I recall no explanation, just that Crooked was his Cane.*" What the hell does it mean?'

'It's a folk song,' Esme replied emotionlessly, her brain already whizzing through the possibilities here.

*Stuart Laws had received the same message that Ronald Tyler had two weeks earlier.*

'Did it come through the same day?' she asked, trying to make her voice sound casual, as if just ticking off a question.

'Yes, but not until the afternoon, after he'd already died,' Crawford replied. 'That's why we never really considered it. Happened about five hours later. Whatever company sent it, they need to update their lists, eh?'

Cooper thanked Crawford for her time and, finishing up the conversation, placed the phone down as she stared at the notes she had taken during the call.

Two weeks ago, Stuart Laws had been murdered by a cab driver. The same day someone had sent him the message "Crooked Was His Cane" by phone.

Last night, Ronald Tyler had been murdered in his cab, but in a way that couldn't have happened legitimately, electric cars not having exhausts. The same phrase had been placed in his mouth.

There were only two other people in the photo that De'Geer had seen: Sandeep Khan and Lancelot Curtis-Warner.

Cooper looked around the office, seeing Anjli, who had returned to her desk.

'Guv?' she said. 'I think I might have something.'

# 8

## NOT NOW KATO

MONROE HAD GONE TO MONARCH AUTOS IN HACKNEY, following the lead given by De'Geer, and Declan had met him there after returning from the Houses of Parliament.

Monroe was waiting outside, and Declan was quite surprised that his boss hadn't entered. As he pulled up, Monroe walked over to him.

'How did it go?' he asked, then stopped as he saw Declan's expression. 'Jesus, laddie, that bad?'

'Jennifer Farnham-Ewing,' Declan replied by explanation, and Monroe visibly shuddered at the name. Whether or not it was done for dramatic intent, Declan couldn't tell.

'I thought she was long gone,' he replied as they started towards Monarch's main entrances.

'Apparently not,' Declan replied with a sigh. 'Apparently she's our youngest member of Parliament now.'

'Someone voted her in?' Monroe shook his head. 'Mary, mother of God, so what do we need to do to keep the unit going?'

'It's a simple request,' Declan replied, pausing, looking at

Monroe. 'But there's something more going on, I can tell. You remember when I was on the run and Kendis was murdered? There was a whole thing about Baker's wife committing suicide?'

'Aye, I remember,' Monroe nodded. After it'd come out during the Victoria Davies case that one victim had actually been an illegitimate son of Baker's, the surrounding press furore had pushed Donna Baker's depression to where she took her own life. However, when Declan had been accused of terrorism by the government, led by Malcolm Gladwell, they'd learnt Gladwell had pressured Donna, a signatory on Rattlestone Securities, and the pressure had been what killed her. Whether it was by Gladstone's own hand, nobody had known, as Baker himself had halted the investigation, claiming that his family just wanted closure.

Nothing more was ever looked into.

'Well, apparently the suicide investigation was never properly closed,' Declan replied. 'The impression I got is Jennifer wants it finished, over and done with. Gave me the impression it's hanging over Charles Baker's head.'

'And you didn't see the man himself?'

'No, his assistant – his new Jennifer, or maybe more Will Harrison, so to speak – named Nigella Waterstone, she stood there glowering at us from across the Members' Terrace, but it was Jennifer who pulled the strings here,' Declan continued. 'I just get the impression that something's going on, something we're missing. It feels more like Baker's getting his ducks in a row, or that Jennifer's doing the same, but possibly not for the same reasons that Baker is.'

'You think she's looking for a hit piece?'

'If we were to look into the suicide, and find it wasn't,'

Declan shrugged his shoulders softly, 'it would cause Baker some serious issues.'

Monroe nodded.

'Okay lad, so what do we do?'

'What they've asked,' Declan replied. 'We find out what happened, we close the case, and if during that time we can work out what the hell game is being played, we stop it. Oh, and we need to check into Karl Schnitter's will.'

'We do? Why?'

'Because apparently he left everything to me,' Declan sighed, ignoring Monroe's shocked expression as he looked up at the garage. 'Is this the place that Anjli mentioned?'

'Aye,' Monroe said. 'It's a local place for cabbies to get their cabs fixed. It's open to the public too, but it does a good trade in black cabs from what I can work out. I thought I'd wait for you.'

'Scared of going in on your own?'

Monroe chuckled.

'Not at all,' he said. 'I know you just want to be where the action is.'

Entering the reception, Declan had turned to speak to Monroe when a voice yelled out.

'Oi oi, Captain Birdseye!'

Declan and Monroe, who hadn't been looking forward as they entered, both turned now to see an embarrassed-looking man standing behind the counter.

'How can I help you, sirs?' he asked.

Irritated by the introduction, Declan held up his warrant card.

'I'm Detective Chief Inspector Walsh,' he said, making sure every word was spoken slowly and with intent. 'And Captain Birdseye here is Detective Superintendent Monroe.'

'Aye,' Monroe added, looking at Declan. 'Although I will point out that *you* might have been the Captain Birdseye he was mentioning.'

Declan glanced back at him.

'I don't have white hair.'

'But you're getting that way, and your beard's getting a bit scraggly.'

The young man at reception looked down beside him and then kicked hard at something out of sight. There was a grunt and another man, older, with grey hair and a black t-shirt, stocky, but more from years of exercise and heavy work than from cake, rose, grinning.

'Sorry guys,' he said, and Declan recognised the accent of the man who had yelled the original statement. 'I was just winding up Richie here. Nothing personal.'

'It's always fun working here,' Richie, the named younger man, grimaced.

'What's the problem? We don't do nicked cars here or chop shop stuff,' the older man said, walking over and holding out a hand. 'I'm Jimmy. I'm the service manager for Monarch.'

'And a budding stand-up comedian too,' Monroe replied, and Declan could tell he was really not warming to this new man. 'We'd like to talk to you about the black cabs that come here for work.'

'What about them?'

'We were hoping there were some drivers here we could chat to, as well as anyone who can help us on a case. We were told you were the go-to garage for Ronald Tyler.'

'Ronnie Tyler? Oh yeah, lovely guy. Came in about a week or two ago.' Jimmy seemed a lot happier to talk. 'He all right?'

'Unfortunately not. Ronald Tyler was found dead this

morning,' Declan shook his head. 'A hose had been piped into his cabin and he died of carbon monoxide poisoning.'

'That's impossible.' Stunned, Jimmy shook his head. 'He's got an electric car.'

'Yes, we know,' Declan replied. 'We also know this was definitely murder, but at the moment we can't find anybody who can tell us why somebody would want Ronald Tyler dead.'

'The problem with black cab drivers,' Monroe added, 'is they don't really have a base like a minicab driver would. They work a lot on their own. We can't find a crew that would have known anything about him. In fact, the only people we know right now who have dealt with Ronald in his work guise ...'

He waved his hand.

'... are in here.'

Jimmy nodded, no longer smiling now.

'I get that,' he replied. 'Yeah, cab drivers are quite solitary. They spend a lot of time on their own. But they do have their tribes.'

Monroe frowned.

'What do you mean by tribes?'

'Look,' Jimmy shrugged. 'They spend all their time on their own but they hang out on cab ranks, they have lunch together, and over the years they get to know each other. The old guys will hang out more together. They'll have their meeting places, a lot of them keep to the same routes, the same locations. If you're parked up for two hours at King's Cross waiting for a fare at rush hour, the chances are you're going to get to know the guy in front and behind you.'

He looked around as he considered his next words.

'But a lot of these relationships go back to the very beginning. We have a lot of cab drivers turn up who still hang out with the same people they walked the routes with.'

'The Knowledge?' Declan asked.

'Yeah, or whatever they call it now. The point is, even though a cab driver drives around on his own, he's never truly alone, if you get what I'm saying.'

Declan did.

'And do you know who Ronald's tribe was?'

'Not really, as I wasn't the one who dealt with him. I just aimed him at whichever mechanic he needed at the time. But I think he—'

He stopped as, from a cupboard to the side, a younger man, about twenty years old, ginger hair, skinny and with freckles leapt out, landing in a karate pose, screaming loudly as he did so.

Declan instinctively went for his extendable baton held up his sleeve of his jacket, something he'd done since his days in the military police. But before he could do anything, Jimmy slapped the younger man on the side of the head.

'Not now, Kato,' he snapped irritably.

The younger man paused, almost as if realising for the first time, as he looked around the garage, that his boss was with two complete strangers.

Jimmy looked back at Monroe.

'Sorry,' he said. 'This job gets boring, you know, so we liven it up.'

'Pink Panther, right?' Monroe smiled. 'I've seen the films. It's where Inspector Clouseau's always attacked by his manservant, Kato.'

'It's become a bit of a game for some of the younger folk,' Jimmy replied, nodding at the redhead, who smiled sheepishly at them both. 'Trying to get one over me. Danny here's been a part of the place since he was a kid. He's taken it enthusiastically, shall we say.'

'Sorry, boss,' Danny said. 'Sorry, guys.'

'They're police,' Jimmy replied, nodding at Declan and Monroe. 'They're here about Ronald Tyler.'

'Ron?' Danny frowned. 'Is he all right?'

'He's dead,' Declan replied.

On hearing this, Danny paled.

'Oh, he was a lovely guy,' he said. 'Always tipped well.'

'He came a lot?'

'He was here now and then,' Danny nodded.

'If he was using an electric car, why was he coming here?' Declan asked. 'Surely there's no reason?'

'We might not be able to fix the engines, so to speak,' Jimmy replied, a sense of professional pride appearing in his voice. 'But we could still do his brakes, his wheels, tyres, his windows, windscreens, wing mirrors—'

'Wing mirrors?' Declan frowned. 'You get a lot of call for that?'

'Yeah, a lot of cabs and cars have their wing mirrors snapped off. It's the same as what used to happen with aerials back in the day. Kids come by, break off the wing mirrors. They think it's funny. It's vandalism and can be fixed, but it's a pain in the arse.'

Danny had wandered off, probably going to do some actual work, or find someone else to annoy who didn't have police officers beside them. Declan turned his attention back to Jimmy.

'So, what did he come in with last time?' he repeated.

Jimmy shrugged.

'Minor vandalism, I think,' he said. 'I mean, it irritated us all, if I'm honest. He came in with a cracked windscreen or something – I'd have to check the notes. It took a day to fix, get a new one in.'

'Smashed by kids?' Declan asked.

Jimmy once more raised his arms in an "I have no idea" shrug.

'Look,' he said. 'All I know is that Ronnie was a nice man, and he was just trying to get ahead at the end of the day. If you need to ask anything else, I suggest—'

He stopped as Monroe, reading a text message, held up a hand to pause him.

'This cracked windscreen you mentioned,' he said, looking up, and Declan noticed his expression had gone deathly cold. Quickly, wondering if he had missed something, he pulled his own phone out and glanced down at the screen. He'd missed a message from Cooper.

> Check the windscreen. Stuart Laws killed in
> hit and run. Head slammed against
> passenger side windscreen of black cab.

'How damaged was it?' Monroe continued.

Jimmy, having not read the text message, frowned.

'Sorry, what do you mean?' he asked.

Monroe looked up from the message, now staring directly at Jimmy.

'What I mean, laddie, is you've told us that Ronald Tyler came in with a damaged windscreen, and I've just had a wee message telling me someone else had a damaged windscreen, and I'd like to see if the two things are related.'

'I'd have to check,' Jimmy stammered, now realising he was a bit out of his depth here. 'Actually, Danny would be the best person to ask.'

He looked back at the ginger-haired mechanic, now across the garage.

'Oi,' he shouted. 'Get back here.'

Reluctantly, Danny wandered back over to them.

'The windscreen that Ronnie Tyler had fixed, did you see it?'

'Sure,' Danny nodded, uncertain in his response, glancing at the two police officers. 'I mean, I did nothing wrong. I didn't overcharge or ...'

'No, no, no, we're not asking that,' Jimmy shook his head. 'What kind of damage was it?'

'Looked like someone had slammed a brick into it,' Danny shrugged.

'And what happened to it?'

'We threw it away, what else would we have done with it?' Danny almost chuckled at this. 'Look, it was just kids, nothing serious. The glass is long gone now, boss. Can I go?'

Jimmy waved Danny away, and as the younger man left, Monroe glanced back at Declan. Cooper had also now sent the records of the conversation she'd had with Crawford as an email, and Declan was reading them as he looked back to his boss.

'Two weeks ago, a man named Stuart Laws was hit by a cab,' he explained to Jimmy. 'His head apparently bounced off the windscreen with such force it cracked it. This was around the same time that Ronald Tyler came in with the broken windscreen.'

'What, you think that Tyler did this?' Jimmy seemed surprised but said nothing more.

Monroe, noticing this, leant closer.

'Aye, that's interesting. You ask what we think, but at no

point have you said, "No, no, he would never do that" or any such protestation.'

He smiled.

'You just stopped, as if you *did* think he could have done it.'

'I didn't know the guy,' Jimmy replied. 'Just saw him when he came in. And as we said, he didn't do engine work anymore. Danny would be the best option.'

He frowned.

'But we wouldn't have thrown the glass *away* away,' he said. 'I mean, it'd be dumped in the skip, but the glass skip only goes once a month – it'd still be here. He should have known that.'

Declan paused, feeling that familiar slide of ice down his spine as he glanced back across the garage. Danny was now marching with purpose across the garage, over to a Rover that was being worked on. The younger man glanced around, his eyes wide in fear, and seeing Declan watching him, he ran to the Rover, opening the driver's door and climbing in, as the surrounding mechanics started shouting at him, telling him to get out and not start the engine.

But Danny wasn't listening.

With the roar of the engine echoing ominously around the garage, he quickly slammed the Rover into reverse, and with the front two wheels careening off the ramp it was currently on, the Rover backed out of the garage and out into the forecourt.

Declan was already running the moment this happened. He didn't know what was going on here, whether Danny was connected to this in some way, or wasn't telling him everything he needed to, but one thing he was sure of was that Danny was scared and trying to escape.

Leaping over a discarded tyre, Declan could hear the mechanics shouting at Danny, and realised that the Rover hadn't been having its engine checked; it had been having its front passenger side tyre replaced. The tyre was still on the car, but the nuts that held the tyre onto it were in a pile by the ramp. The moment Danny spun the car around, the tyre, no longer secured tight by these nuts, simply came off, the axle slamming to the ground as sparks rose, and the now three-wheeled car ground to a halt.

Danny stared in horror as Declan reached the door, baton now in his hand as he rapped on the window.

'I think you need to get out, mate,' he said. 'I think we need to have a chat.'

'I didn't do it,' Danny said, refusing to open the door. 'I saw the blood. I knew something bad had happened. I didn't tell anyone. I can't go to prison for that.'

'Why would you go to prison for seeing blood?' Declan shook his head in disbelief.

'Then why are you so pissed at me?' Danny didn't seem to be the brightest of buttons, and pouted as he spoke.

'What I'm pissed at you about is the fact you tried to run away,' Declan snapped, rapping again on the window. 'Now how about you get out of the car, we see if we can find that windscreen, and you escape spending the night in a jail cell.'

# 9
---

# BRIEFINGS

MONROE RAN A HAND THROUGH HIS HAIR AS HE STARED OUT AT the briefing room in front of him. It was late in the afternoon now, but the room was still quite full. At the back, PC Cooper and Sergeant De'Geer sat together; in front of them, in his usual spot and with laptop in front of him connected to the plasma screen at the front of the room, was Billy, currently typing away, checking emails. On the left, Declan and Anjli sat together, and by the door they had an expected appearance by Detective Chief Superintendent Bullman, who had popped by for the day.

Monroe knew this wasn't because of the case, and was likely more because of the Westminster sub-case they had to sort out, but there was a visible relief in the room that she was there. With only Doctor Marcos not at the briefing, currently in the forensics department downstairs, checking pieces of broken windscreen gained from Monarch Autos, Monroe felt comfortable enough to start.

'Right then, laddies and lassies,' he said, stopping the murmuring in the room as the various conversations paused.

'We've not got one murder anymore, we've now got two. And from the looks of things, one of those bodies might have killed the other. Things are all over the place and we need to have an idea of where we are. So let's start off by trying to work out a chronological timeline of Ronald Tyler and Stuart Laws. Anyone?'

De'Geer stood up, opening his notebook as he started to read from it.

'Ronald Tyler, Stuart Laws, both became cab drivers twenty years ago,' he said. 'Both passed their Knowledge within a month of each other, and both trained at the same Knowledge college.'

Declan held a hand up, looking around.

'Knowledge college,' he said. 'Is that what they call these sorts of places?'

'I don't know if it's the general term,' De'Geer frowned. 'But as it's a college that teaches you the Knowledge, I just assumed it'd be known as that.'

'Sorry, just wondered,' Declan nodded, looking back as he saw Monroe glaring at him.

'It's a school where aspiring taxi drivers go to learn everything they need to know about navigating the streets of a city, particularly London,' De'Geer read from his notes again, and Declan wondered if this had been quickly cribbed from Wikipedia in case Monroe asked. Although Anjli could possibly have helped; he knew her uncle was a cabbie. 'It's not a typical college with classrooms and lectures and that sort of thing; instead, it's more a kind of intensive training situation where students, the potential black cab drivers, memorise thousands of streets, landmarks, and routes. They study maps, learn about traffic regulations, and practise driving to become experts in getting passengers to their destinations efficiently.'

'Are there many of these?' Monroe asked, and Declan again wondered if this was a question to see how deeply De'Geer had researched this.

'A few when I checked,' De'Geer nodded. 'Often they have laminated poster-sized maps of London all over the walls and tables, and the students draw routes across them in whiteboard markers, so they can wipe off. Ronald Tyler and Stuart Laws apparently went to one in Old Street called the College of Knowledge.'

'Sounds like some kind of mental training institute,' Billy chuckled. 'Increase your brain at the College of Knowledge.'

'Actually, yes,' De'Geer grinned. 'By doing the Knowledge, it literally changes the physical structure of the brain. Researchers at UCL have used MRI scans to show that the Hippocampus of people who pass the Knowledge grows by over twenty-five percent, and the neural pathways around it also strengthen. They're physically altering their brains, and retired black cabbies have one of the lowest rates of Alzheimer's on the planet.'

'What, just by learning streets?' Monroe frowned. 'I know streets. But that doesn't mean my brain is superhuman.'

'True, Guv—' De'Geer started, but stopped as Cooper gave a warning nudge. 'What I meant to say is, of course your brain is superhuman, but the Knowledge is about the way you learn. It takes at least two years to pass the Knowledge, because the exams are divided into three categories; a series of exams every two months, which if you pass then goes down to one a month, and then one every three weeks. Each level gets harder, and the time you have left to actually learn more about the city also decreases. If you fail more than two exams on any of the levels you get "red lined", meaning you start the series again from the start. If you've already had to restart once, you go back a series. It's majorly stressful, and you're cramming all the time. Your brain has to literally reconfigure itself.'

'And Stuart Laws and Ronald Tyler were members of this school?' Monroe decided to change subject.

'Same class, or whatever it's called,' De'Geer nodded. 'I spoke to the administration department – well, the man who runs it – an hour ago. They confirmed that in the same course, Stuart Laws, Ronald Tyler, and Lancelot Curtis-Warner, although he was on the books there as Lance Curtis, were definitely working together, along with Sandeep Khan, who's the fourth man in the photo that I took a picture of in Ronald Tyler's house.'

At this, Billy pressed a button, and on the screen, the image of four young men in front of a black cab appeared.

'Okay, so we know they knew each other,' Monroe nodded. 'They all took their Knowledge together, but we also know they went different ways.'

'Yes, sir,' Anjli now took over. 'Ronald Tyler carried on as a cab driver. Stuart Laws, apparently, carried on as a cabbie until about five years ago, when he went into the private sector, upgrading his car to a Mercedes and working for a more elite chauffeur-driven service. Lancelot Curtis-Warner moved into asset finance and bought a variety of other companies. I'd be surprised if he ever drove a cab again.'

'So why did he take the test?' Billy frowned.

'Apparently, according to Lizzie Tyler, he was proving to his dad that he could start something and finish it before he was disowned,' Anjli shrugged as she read from her notes.

'From the sounds of things, he decided that picking the Knowledge was a suitable thing to prove he could learn.'

'Showing off, then?' Declan muttered.

'Pretty much.'

'And Khan?' Monroe looked around the room.

'He's some kind of media influencer who now works in the technology industry,' Billy looked up from the laptop. 'Should have a number in the next hour.'

He pulled a website up onto the plasma screen – it was for a company named *Khan Do Systems.*

'It's a pun on "can do" boss,' he said.

'Aye, I can see that.'

Billy scrolled down, and they could see a variety of options: investment, podcasts, YouTube channels, online courses ... the list went on. And, to the right of these were images of a man, Asian and in good shape for his age, doing a variety of activities: Skydiving, skiing, flying a drone, standing in front of a bookcase with a fanned-out deck of cards in his hands, hosting a podcast and strangely, skiing again.

'Must like skiing,' Declan nodded at the duplicate photo. 'Or he ran out of interesting things.'

'Well, if he did stop being a cabbie, it means he might be alive still, based on his buddies' current situations,' Monroe muttered.

'I recognise the bookcase,' De'Geer spoke up from the back. 'It's the Magic Castle in Los Angeles. You're not allowed to take photos inside, but you can in the lobby, where that is.'

'Magic Castle? As in Disney?' Monroe frowned.

'No, it's a special, members-only club where magicians perform tricks and hang out with people who love magic,' De'Geer replied. 'I've wanted to go for years, but you have to be invited by a member.'

Monroe nodded.

'Okay, well, live in hope, eh, laddie? Have we spoken to Lancelot Curtis-Warner yet?'

'Still trying,' Anjli checked her notes. 'I spoke to his private secretary. It seems that Curtis-Warner won't just take a call from anybody, even if it's in relation to a murder inquiry, unless we're literally banging on the window, looking to arrest him. His words, apparently.'

She smiled.

'We might have an in, though,' she said. 'We'll look into that and see if it can help us in any way.'

Monroe clicked his tongue on the roof of his mouth as he ruminated on all the data given so far.

'So, we have these four men becoming cab drivers. Two stay in the job that we know of for sure of, but over the years the third leaves as well, with only one staying in the role. Nothing seems to happen for twenty-odd years. And then two weeks ago, in terrible weather, Stuart Laws is run down by a black cab.'

He looked over at Cooper.

'You were the one who spoke to Detective Sergeant Crawford in Surrey,' he said. 'What did we get?'

'Crawford had been given the job, but she wasn't sure how she could work it,' Cooper admitted. 'The data she had was incredibly thin on the ground.'

'How so?'

'It was a rainy day. People had their heads down, or they were under umbrellas,' Cooper explained. 'Apparently, Stuart Laws lived on an estate, his car was expensive, he didn't have a garage and he didn't want to have it damaged. So, he'd rented out a parking space on a more expensive driveway, about a ten-minute walk from his house.'

She flipped the page, carrying on.

'He would park up there at night, walk back to his house, and then in the morning, walk back before driving. It was a covered space, so he didn't need to worry about weather damage or anything like that. He was on his way to the car when he was struck. Witnesses said the cab veered off the road, smashed into him, bounced him off the bonnet, his head hitting the windscreen, he slammed against the wall, and then the cab careened back onto the road and carried on. It happened so quickly, nobody picked it up. There were no cameras around, either.'

'Broken windscreen,' Monroe nodded, turning to De'Geer. 'Any news from your boss?'

De'Geer smiled.

'If you mean your wife, Guv,' he said, 'then yes. There's definitely blood on the impact point of the windscreen. It wasn't a brick; or if it was a brick, it was a "bleeding heavily from the face" brick. She's now trying to match it, but obviously it's difficult. The inquest isn't public yet, and the case notes had already moved on, with it being two weeks ago. She said there's a strong possibility this could be Stuart Laws' blood, and it fits the timeline that a day or so afterwards the cab went in.'

He straightened slightly as he looked back at the others.

'However, this doesn't necessarily mean that Ronald Tyler drove the cab,' he said. 'We spoke to a neighbour when we were examining the house, and he said a couple of weeks ago Ronald Tyler had suffered from terrible food poisoning and had been bedridden for a couple of days. He knew this because he'd actually been texted by Ronald asking for help picking up some toilet roll. Apparently, he couldn't leave the house in case he was caught short, and his ex-wife ended up dropping some off, most likely. He also said Tyler had some deliveries too, the doorbell ringing a lot, although it's probably Uber Eats or Deliveroo, if he's house-ridden. It was during this time that the accident happened.'

His eyes widened as he realised he'd forgotten something.

'Mister Markovic also said around the same time Stuart Laws had been knocking on Ronald Tyler's door, but hadn't gained an answer, and didn't come back.'

'Possibly because he was dead,' Monroe muttered. 'But, going from that, there's every possibility here that someone knew that Ronald Tyler was bedridden, borrowed the car, killed Stuart Laws, and then returned it.'

'To do that, though, they would need a lot more information on Ronald Tyler,' Declan scratched at his chin, glancing back at Anjli. 'You said the ex-wife mentioned something about a car leasing agreement?'

'Kind of,' Anjli admitted, nodding. 'His wife said Ronald had gained the loan from Curtis-Warner to cover his new car. I don't know what happened to the last car. Maybe it was given in part exchange, but Curtis-Warner provided the costs.'

Declan mused on this.

'So they must have stayed friends,' he replied. 'Even though Lance wasn't driving a car, he was still close enough to lend the money for a new one, and those cars aren't cheap.'

He glanced over at Billy, who tapped on his computer's keyboard, reading something off the screen.

'Brand new electric car costs around fifty-five grand,' he said. 'If you're a cab driver with an electric car, you're also probably paying out a ton of extras as well. There's no way Ronald Tyler could have afforded that on his own.'

'A reason to speak to Mister Curtis-Warner.'

'Actually, I've got another one,' Billy said, reading the screen once more. 'The DVLA has just come back to me about the Mercedes that Stuart Laws owned. We were right; it was a lease vehicle, owned by LCW Holdings.'

'The LCW standing for Lancelot Curtis-Warner, perhaps?' Bullman said from the door; the first time she'd spoken.

Declan almost jumped. He'd forgotten she was even in the room.

'I'd have to check, but it looks that way, ma'am,' Billy replied.

'So Curtis-Warner paid for the cars of both Stuart Laws and also Ronald Tyler,' Declan shook his head. 'That's either a sign of friendship or a debt owed, and the impression I get is that Curtis-Warner wasn't the kind of guy to owe debts or have friends. We need to find this fourth guy, Sandeep Khan, and find out if there's anything relevant there, too. When Stuart Laws was killed, you said there was a mention of Crooked Canes?'

'Yes, Guv,' Cooper replied. 'It wasn't quite the same, but someone sent some of the song's chorus as a robo-call to Stuart's phone, arriving shortly after he died, left as a voice-mail. Billy's looking into who owned the number.'

'I should have something tomorrow morning,' Billy added.

'Keep on that, and keep on Crawford to send us the infor-mation,' Monroe said. 'Surrey Police might want to dump this on us to get it off their books, so let's get everything we need before the baby lands in our laps.'

He straightened, addressing the room.

'But now let's move on to this Crooked Cane nonsense. What do we have?'

'I spoke to the man who wrote it,' Billy said. 'James Harlow. He explained it was an urban legend he'd heard once that inspired him to write the lyrics. He'd also said to check records from twenty years ago on Hammersmith Bridge for the source of the story, and I spent a lot of the afternoon going through the records until I found what I think he was talking about; an incident that *wasn't* an incident and that nobody can actually prove even happened.'

'Oh, we love those cases,' Declan laughed, and for a moment, the briefing room broke into a more relaxed atmosphere.

'Go on, lad,' Monroe said. 'Tell us why this is a story that isn't a story.'

'A witness said she was walking across Hammersmith Bridge from the south side of the Thames to the north, returning home from a night shift, four o'clock in the morning. She saw a cab parked up and a crowd of witnesses looking confused. They explained the cab driver had been taking a fare to Earls Court when they'd asked to stop on the bridge. The fare, however, instead of getting out on the pavement side, walked out onto the road, and after two steps was hit by a double-decker bus going past at speed.'

'Jesus,' Cooper muttered, reddening at her outburst. 'Sorry.'

'It was raining, it was windy, similar conditions probably to what happened with Stuart Laws, but as other witnesses came running over, the bus didn't stop and had carried on,' Billy continued.

'So how is this a crime that isn't a crime?' Declan frowned.

'Well,' Billy looked back to his screen, reading before turning back to Declan. 'There's no body. In fact, all there was left on the road was a crooked walking cane. That's actually mentioned in the report; the woman said she saw a walking stick that was crooked on the pavement where it'd been moved. She thought at the start that it had been broken, maybe run over by the wheel of the bus, but then she realised it was the design. She described it as one of those quirky walking canes with a twirling curve to the grain and a right angle grip, rather than a hooked one. The cab driver said he was going to call it in and drove off, the witnesses left, and the rain washed away the evidence. Even the stick disappeared.'

He shifted in his seat, scrolling the page.

'When the police looked into it, there were too many discrepancies in the story. For a start, at that time in the morning, there were no buses going across the bridge. Sure, there were night buses travelling through London, but everything went across Putney Bridge, to the East,' he continued. 'Now, granted, there's every opportunity that this was a driver or a mechanic taking a double-decker bus from one depot to another, and maybe possibly didn't even realise he'd hit the man; there was every possibility the bus hit this victim, and he'd got caught underneath the bus, maybe not appearing or coming off until a mile down the road and being written down as another case, but going through it all, I can't find anything like that.'

Declan grimaced; the thought of being trapped under a bus, dying, dragged along the road for a good mile, was his idea of hell.

'But, with no body, no victim, no actual proof apart from a cane that had been left at the side of the road – which then disappeared as well – nothing was ever done about it,' Billy looked at the others and shrugged slightly. 'It fell into one of these legendary "man-that-never-existed" kind of urban myths, and at some point, James Harlow heard it. He liked the basis of the story, realised he could turn it into a song, and that's what he did with "Crooked Was His Cane".'

'So there's nothing personal about it?'

'Not that I can see,' Billy said.

Declan watched his face.

'But you've got something else,' he said. 'You've got that face you sometimes have when you think something more's going on.'

Billy smiled sheepishly.

'It could be nothing,' he replied cautiously. 'So, a lot of responses on the YouTube videos kept putting the word "bindlesticks" up, and I couldn't work out why.'

He spun on his chair to face the rest of the briefing room.

'James Harlow has a brother, about two years younger; I'm not saying the two are connected, but we'd already worked out that a bindlestick is the cane used by a hobo, and James Harlow's brother was known as Bindlesticks.'

'Because he was a hobo?'

'The modern-day equivalent, yes,' Billy said. 'He back-packed around the world from the age of sixteen. I think that James's song is, in a way, a story that both tells an urban legend, but also takes a little from his brother.'

'Do you think his brother could have been the owner of the crooked cane that was struck that night?'

'Possibly, but even if he was, and the body had been found, I don't know how this relates to our case,' Billy sighed, holding a hand up in a resigned expression. 'The four weren't cabbies at this point, so they wouldn't have been taking fares either way. I'm looking into it.'

'Okay,' Monroe replied. 'Let's keep on with finding out why someone might want Ronald Tyler dead, and let's see if Ronald Tyler was the man who could have possibly killed

Stuart Laws – and if not, who could have got his car there and back without forcing entry.'

'The car was electric,' Anjli looked up from her notes. 'Has a range of a hundred and fifty miles. Is this doable?'

'Addlestone's not across the country, lassie,' Monroe gave a slight smile. 'But let's see. Billy?'

'Tyler lived in Haggerston, and the accident was Green Lane in Addlestone,' Billy typed in the addresses. 'M4 and M25, and going through London via the Westway is thirty three miles, so that'd be seventy tops. Even going all the way up the M1 and then back down the M25 would be fifty miles, so a hundred tops. Easily doable.'

Monroe started pacing now; the first time in the briefing he'd done so.

'Okay then. I also think it's time to have a chat with anyone who can get us into the same room with Curtis-Warner,' he suggested. 'We all know what we need to do. Go home, get a good night's sleep. We'll come back to this in the morning.'

As the briefing room rose and shuffled out, Bullman walked in, nodding to Declan.

'Hang around for a moment,' she said as the room emptied, leaving Monroe, Bullman, and Declan alone. 'Talking of people in high places, what do we know?'

Declan shrugged.

'I spoke to Jennifer Farnham-Ewing,' he said. 'She wants the story about Donna Baker's suicide made official. At the moment, apparently, there's a big question mark over its validity, and it could affect some kind of re-election prospects—'

'I don't think it's that.' Bullman shook her head as she broke in. 'When I heard this unit was under observation, I checked into it. They're using the closure as an excuse to force us to sort out a shite job for them. This isn't a case of ending a long-term cold case. It's more something to do with a book.'

'A book?' Declan asked.

Bullman nodded.

'Someone's written a tell-all novel,' she said. 'And in it, it discusses the whole Rattlestone case. It talks about Donna, her connection to Malcolm Gladwell, and I think it's quite damning from what I've heard. Jennifer Farnham-Ewing is either using this to clear her boss, or she's finding a way to make him owe her even more. Either way, Declan, we need to end this story as quickly as we need to solve the other case. Can we do that?'

Declan stared back at his boss's boss and simply shrugged.

'Impossible odds, requirements given to us by Westminster that we can never hope to fulfil?'

He smiled.

'We call that a weekday here.'

# 10

## OLD CRUSHES

In an ideal world, Declan's first call would have been to contact Kendis Taylor. She had been the journalist who'd discovered the entire problem with Rattlestone, Donna Baker, and a whole load of corrupt situations, and had asked for Declan's help to uncover the deep-rooted Westminster corruption. The problem with that, however, was that shortly after she'd asked, Kendis Taylor was dead, having been killed because she'd got too close to Malcolm Gladwell, Will Harrison, and a ton of devious, illegal activities that the then-MP was involved in.

It had ended with Declan solving the case, and avenging Kendis while Gladwell was arrested, and strangely, Charles Baker using his wife's death to boost his own popularity in the press, moved from a vaguely hated ex-front-bench minister to the next possible Prime Minister himself.

Declan chuckled at this.

In effect, Charles Baker *hadn't* been the next Prime Minister. That honour had gone to his leadership rival, Michelle Rose, but she too had been just as corrupt, and had been removed by the Last Chance Saloon after it had been discovered not only had she ordered the murder of Charles Falconer, believing him to be a whistleblower, but also for unknowingly working with a Syrian agent on designing laser weapons forbidden by the Geneva Convention.

Several months later, Charles Baker replaced her.

He owed them for this, but with everything that had happened after the Gladwell case, including the immediate arrival of the Red Reaper, the one thing Declan had never looked into was exactly what Charles Baker had been doing while his wife had died, and whether he had, in fact, been instrumental in it. She had confided in Kendis Taylor before she hanged herself, claiming that she was in fear of her life and Kendis had gained information from her, information on Rattlestone that cost them both their lives. But when all was said and done, nobody had actually checked to see whether Donna Baker, wife of Conservative MP Charles Baker, had taken her life, been *persuaded* to take her life, or had been murdered.

And now there seemed to be a tell-all book, something that was going to cause even more problems down the line, especially with this year likely building towards an upcoming election; Charles Baker was still an unelected Prime Minister after all. Eventually, someone would decide it was time to pay the piper.

The one question Declan didn't have an answer for was who had written the book. Was it a parliamentary undersecretary? An aide? Could it have been someone involved in the act itself? And if so, who would that be?

Declan decided that the easiest thing to do would be to check with Kendis's old editor, Sean Ashby. He'd recently moved from the Guardian, where she'd worked under him in the Features Department, and was now editor-in-chief of *The Individual* newspaper in London. Declan had last spoken to him when Hunt Robinson had been found in the crypt of St. Bride's Church, almost beaten to death, all over a black book of secrets he'd held for decades. After it had all ended, Sean had offered Declan a job; Declan had been about to leave the force, stuck in a situation where, unless he could get himself promoted, he would have to leave the Last Chance Saloon. As it was, he managed to get promoted, but not before Sean had offered him a role as an investigative asset to the paper, more a "private eye for reporters" if he was being honest, and more than double Declan's salary. Declan hadn't taken the job in the end, and instead suggested Theresa "Tessa" Martinez, a former member of the teenage group of crime solvers, *the Magpies.*

But as Kendis's onetime editor, there was every chance that Sean would know more about what was going on here, as well as potentially still holding her notes from the time. So, he had called into *The Individual*, asking to meet. Within half an hour, he'd received an answer saying to meet that evening in a local bar in the city.

Anjli had her own calls to make, so Declan had arranged to meet her back at home. He still couldn't believe that it was only this morning that they had driven in together, stopping to see a murder scene; it felt like days had passed already. And as he made his way to the Trading House pub, off to the side of Guildhall, he found himself having to stretch his spine out, feeling every one of his forty-odd years. Maybe he was getting too old for this. Maybe there was a reason why when you hit DCI, you stopped going out all the time onto cases and spent most of your time at an office.

*It was better on the feet for a start.*

As Declan pushed open the heavy oak door of The Trading House, a gust of cool air and the inaudible murmur of voices welcomed him. The place had been a staple just off Guildhall since the late 1800s, serving as a casual haunt for traders and executives after long hours at the nearby financial hubs in the city. Its walls, lined with old, framed black-and-white photographs of the city's trading history, gave the dimly lit room a sense of importance.

He stepped inside, his eyes taking a moment to adjust to the soft amber lighting that cast shadows over the wooden floor. The bar was straightforward and unpretentious, with a long counter where a few financiers sat quietly, nursing their drinks. Declan noticed the barman, a middle-aged man with a stern face and a quick hand pouring pints, acknowledging regulars with a brief nod. The air was filled with the scent of ale and the faint, underlying hint of decades-old tobacco smoke was ingrained in the furniture. Declan was surprised but not completely sideswiped to see that Sean Ashby hadn't turned up, and instead Tessa Martinez sat at a table, drink in hand, waiting for him.

Tessa Martinez was as beautiful as she'd ever been. Slim, toned, Mediterranean in looks and with short, slightly frizzy black hair framing her stunning brown eyes, she wore a simple blue jacket over a pale blouse, and even with minimal makeup on looked as if she'd just appeared from a photo shoot. She was also a complicated contact for Declan; after all, there weren't many people that Declan still worked with who, when he was a teenage boy, he had a poster of on his wall.

As a teenager, he'd been a fan of *the Magpies,* a group of teenage sleuths whose books entertained everybody to the point they became television celebrities, hosting their own shows and having their own range of merchandise, including a poster of Tessa and Dexter, their dog. A poster that Declan had had on his wall for years, that had helped him decide he wanted to become some kind of detective as he grew up, and had also provided a lifelong crush on the teenage girl, now a stunning woman in her early forties.

It was only when the author of the Magpie books, Reginald Troughton, had been murdered years later and the Magpies had come out of retirement to try to help the Last Chance Saloon find the killer, that Declan learned the truth about the Magpies; how they were a Labour Party plan to brainwash children, how the Magpies were as broken as everything else and how they'd been puppets, told where to go and what to do as other people in the shadows created the mysteries and the accused, in the process often jailing the wrong people.

It was during one of these Magpie cases that Derek Sutton had been arrested and had spent decades in prison for a crime he hadn't committed.

Declan winced as he thought of the name. Derek had been a good man, and he understood why Derek had done what he had when confronted by the Red Reaper, but now Derek was back in Scotland, and there was every chance they would never speak again.

He felt sorry for Monroe, but this was not the time to think of things like that.

Forcing a smile, he walked over, wondering how Anjli would react if she heard that he'd met up for a late-night drink with the woman he'd had a crush on for almost thirty years. Even after being arrested, Tessa had stayed in contact with Declan; she had helped Declan's ex-wife Liz come to terms with the dangers that being connected to Declan had come with, and had brought Declan and his daughter Jess back together after Liz had banned him from seeing her, something he could never repay.

She had been released from prison a few months earlier on appeals and overturned verdicts, a plea deal likely organised through back channels, while people made a point of mentioning her distinguished prior career as a Manchester Detective Inspector, and claiming her crimes were because of a fugue state of pain medication and PTSD, while she was used by people she thought wanted to help her.

Declan sat facing Tessa, noting she'd already bought him a pint of Guinness, waiting on the table.

'I'm guessing you still drink,' she said.

Declan noted the glass of what looked to be a pint of yellow, fizzy water in front of her.

'Soda water and lime,' she said. 'I don't drink anymore.'

'Probably a good idea,' Declan smiled. 'I mean, one problem you had was because of your addiction to drugs.'

'It wasn't quite that bad, but I get what you're saying,' Tessa took the jibe pleasantly.

Declan looked around the bar, checking to see if he was being watched.

'I'm guessing Sean couldn't make it,' he said.

'Less of a case of couldn't, more of a case of didn't want to,' Tessa replied, leaning back in her chair. 'Unfortunately, Declan, you're a little bit toxic right now to be seen with. Especially with the serialisation likely happening in a few weeks if the book goes ahead.'

Declan frowned.

'What do you mean?'

At the question, Tessa straightened up in her chair, confused.

'I assumed that was why you wanted to meet,' she said. 'The book.'

'Yes,' Declan, realising they *were* on the same conversation, nodded eagerly. 'The Charles and Donna Baker tell-all. But we know nothing about this book. We've been told there's—'

'Declan.' The single word cut through Declan's speech, and he paused, realising for the first time that Tessa's face was deathly serious. 'The book isn't about Donna or Charles. The book is about the entire Rattlestone inquiry, and having read the book, or at least an advanced copy, you and the Last Chance Saloon don't come off well.'

Declan felt a shiver of ice slide down his spine.

'Someone's written a book about the unit?'

'Not just someone,' Tessa replied. 'Malcolm Gladwell. He wrote it while he was in prison. Still is in prison, but now he's claiming the book could go towards exonerating him.'

'There's no way he can claim such a thing,' Declan growled menacingly, his hair rising as he realised this wasn't as simple a job as he thought.

*Damn you, Jennifer Farnham-Ewing,* he thought to himself. *You did this deliberately. You wanted your revenge against a unit, and now you got it.*

'It's a hit piece,' Tessa nodded. 'It talks about the relationship Gladwell and Baker had when they worked in the same department many years ago when he was under-secretary and Baker was his under-under-secretary. They talk about the time in the Ministry of Defence, they talk about Baker's connections to the Star Chamber, it's a big, juicy tell-all book, Declan. And in it, he talks about Kendis, her relationship with you during the case, how you were accused of terrorism and ran your own murder enquiry, knowing you were the prime suspect, actively stopping the police from doing what they needed to do.'

Declan groaned; *that* part was true. He hadn't killed Kendis, but Malcolm Gladwell and others had definitely been aiming it at him.

'Let me guess,' Declan said. 'He doesn't mention people like DI Frost or Sutcliffe?'

'Oh, he doesn't talk about anything that goes against his case, he mentions nothing that helps yours,' Tessa chuckled, sipping her drink. 'This is the exoneration of Malcolm Gladwell, how he was a victim of a Conservative plot, how Charles Baker worked with the police to take him down.'

She leant closer.

'Did you find a letter code safe in a mausoleum?'

'Yes,' Declan replied. 'It was a MacNeale & Urban safe, ten-word digit code – Rattlestone—'

'But it wasn't Rattlestone in the end, was it?'

Declan shook his head, realising where this was going.

'I changed it, I thought it'd be funny.'

'Yes,' Tessa leaned back in her chair, watching Declan. 'Yes, it was hilarious changing the code of the safe that held countless secrets within, stuff that people had died for, including Kendis Taylor. It was brilliant to change that code to the words "Declan Walsh".'

'It was a message,' Declan replied defensively. 'A "don't mess with me" message, and Charles Baker got it.'

'Charles Baker got more than that though, didn't he?' Tessa shook her head. 'The files Gladwell had in that safe, apart from the ones that were relevant to the case, you left for Baker to have.'

Declan nodded; he'd made a deal with Baker, the price had been the files.

'Are you telling me that because I left files in a safe and changed the combination to my name as a joke, I'm now some kind of pariah?'

'Malcolm Gladwell is claiming you to be the secret police of Charles Baker,' Tessa snapped back. 'I can't guarantee how much you're going to get attacked by this, for the moment the book comes out, you're going to be nailed to the wall. Baker won't side with you, he'll throw you to the dogs quicker than anything.'

Her anger now dissipating, she relaxed, placing her elbows on the table, her hands under her chin as she rested her head on them.

'Why were we meeting, Declan?' she asked. 'If you weren't aware of this book, then why were you wanting to speak to Sean?'

'I knew there was *a* book, just not it was *this* book. I was here mainly because Jennifer Farnham-Ewing is an MP,' Declan replied, his voice emotionless, stunned at what was going on. 'She used to be Charles Baker's assistant, worked for Will Harrison back in the day, which probably means she knew a lot more than we realised. I thought she was quite ineffective and useless, but it seems she's climbed her way up, and now she's in a position where she's able to put the Last Chance Saloon on the chopping block unless we do something for her.'

'And what would that be?'

'Close Donna Baker's suicide report,' Declan sighed, realising the gravity of the situation. 'It never got sorted. Baker said he didn't want it to continue, grieving family, all that kind of thing, and it just got left. The official record is that she killed herself because of stress connected to all the things that were happening with Malcolm Gladwell, but there's no proof of this.'

'There's every opportunity that she might have still been murdered, and Jennifer Farnham-whatever her name is, wants you to what, close the case?'

'She wants us apparently to solve it,' Declan nodded. 'However, hearing that the book is coming out makes me wonder whether she's trying to cover Baker's back before the book comes out, or use it to leverage her own position.'

'The book is pretty damning about Baker and Donna,' Tessa nodded at this. 'They never really had a loving relationship, and when his illegitimate child came out in the press, the one the mental YouTube evangelist bloke killed, their relationship kind of fell apart. It was well known – even I knew about that and I wasn't even connected.'

Declan ignored the jibe; they hadn't been aware of this, and he was pretty sure Tessa hadn't either, until she spoke to Norman Shipman, her Labour Party backbencher godfather, who happened to also be a member of the bloody Star Chamber with Charles.

'The problem was when she died, it was very convenient for Charles,' Tessa continued. 'He was low in the polls, he was publicly ousted after all the Victoria Davies problems, and having his wife commit suicide because of this made him a victim, gave him a cause to rally behind. Mental health was a big thing, she'd been seeing a therapist over the online attacks, and he was able to use that.'

'Christ,' Declan muttered to himself. 'Please don't tell me we helped him get away with murder?'

Tessa shook her head.

'No, I think Gladwell did it,' she replied. 'Either him or Will Harrison, and if you get down to it, Harrison will be the one who gets blamed in the end, because he's dead and can't defend himself. The problem here, Declan, is that whoever's pulling the strings here has got you aiming at sorting out one thing, when you should be fixing something else.'

'And what's the thing I should be fixing?' Declan asked.

Tessa reached into her bag and pulled out a manuscript. It was bound, but it was obviously an editor's proof.

'This is the book,' she said. 'I shouldn't have it, which means you shouldn't have it, but you need to have a read through this. Because I tell you now, Declan, when this book comes out in a couple of weeks, if it's not stopped or super-injunctioned or whatever, and if you can't prove that Malcolm Gladwell is a lying piece of shit, you will lose everything that you hold dear.'

# 11

## PRIVATE ROOMS

Monroe and Bullman had both tried to get a meeting with Charles Baker to connect to Lancelot Curtis Warner, but all angles, even those with Westminster links seemed to be closed to them. Monroe had muttered that it must be something to do with whatever plan Declan was having to sort out, this Jennifer Farnham-bloody-Ewing issue, but there was still a concern from the refusals. Their access to Westminster was usually quite common, but now they weren't gaining anything.

As it was, it was Anjli that found a way in.

Soho House on Dean Street was a location for creatives and members of the artistic community. Over the years, the membership had grown, and there were a variety of producers, agents, even accountants who were now members; it was incredibly easy to change your LinkedIn profile to make you look like a creative when you were actually some kind of financial advisor, gain your membership and then change it all back. And it was also a home for millionaires, celebrities, and other such types who, with a definite "no photos inside the building" rule across all houses, knew that they could hold their meetings in peace without finding them plastered on the front page. Celebrities had brought their mistresses here over the years, deals and agreements had been made with no one the wiser, and with houses all over the world, to be an "Every House" member of Soho House meant you could go to a multitude of places and do the same.

It was here that Anjli met Eden Storm.

Eden was a billionaire tech magnate who owned musical catalogues and was the son of a long-passed rock star. He was also a man who, almost a couple of years earlier, had expressed his interest in Anjli Kapoor, even dating her on a couple of occasions. After she eventually turned him down, instead choosing Declan, they'd stayed close, and at the start of the year, Anjli and Declan had even attended an event at the Albert Hall with Eden, and had convinced him that his assistant Amanda was possibly the best thing that ever happened to him, and the two of them were quite obviously infatuated with each other. Ever since then, Anjli had been happy to see pictures of Eden and Amanda all over the internet at galas and events. She was still his PA, but it was more of a "partner doing the job" kind of feeling than employee and boss.

That said, Anjli still had a worry every time she met Eden, on whether he was going to try once more to convince her to leave Declan. She was aware this was an arrogance on her part. Why would this gorgeous billionaire man, with a beautiful girlfriend now decide he wanted a frumpy Indian detective inspector as his girlfriend? But more importantly, why was she even considering it?

She chuckled to herself as she arrived at the desk, giving her name and being escorted to a private room at the top of the building. An entire section had been cordoned off for Eden and as she arrived, she saw him seated there, at a large table with what looked to be two advisors, both in suits with no ties (adhering to the Soho House "don't wear ties" creative spaces rule) on one side, and Amanda sitting beside him on the other.

'Soho House has a rule that only three guests can come in at any time with a member,' he smiled as Anjli walked in. 'I told them if they didn't give me four, I would have to buy the building and evict them.'

Anjli chuckled at this; the chances were they knew who Eden was and quite happily allowed him a fourth person, but she allowed the legend to stay.

*Because knowing Eden Storm, he could have done this easily.*

'What can I do for you, Anjli?' Eden now stood, walking over, kissing her hand before sitting back down. The first time she'd seen him, his clothing had been boasting the opulence of his life, he had been wearing a Raf Simons hooded sweater, Ralph Lauren joggers and Nike Vapormax, but now he was in more muted clothing: earthy tones, chinos, a loose woollen jumper, and a baseball cap that Anjli was absolutely sure she'd seen on an episode of *Succession*. This look was known as "quiet luxury" or "old money"; the look was simple but expensive, the labels were non-existent, it was very much a case of if you had to ask, you weren't ready to wear, and Eden Storm looked to have embraced this fully.

Anjli nodded to the others and sat down.

'It's very quick,' she said. 'I understand you have a relationship with Lance Curtis-Warner.'

'I've done some asset finance with him, yes,' Eden nodded. 'Should I be severing all ties?'

'No, not at all,' Anjli shook her head. 'It's just we would

really like to have a word with him, but he's proving hard to find.'

'How come?'

'That he's proving hard to find, or that we want to have a word with him?'

'Let's go with both.' It was Amanda who spoke now.

Anjli straightened in her chair, wondering how to phrase this without making Lancelot, or Lance, look bad.

'Lance is connected to a murder,' she said. 'Not in the actual *murder* way as far as we know, it was somebody he knew back in the day and we believe still kept in contact with. We were hoping to speak to him about the victim, get some more information, but every time we've gone to speak to him about this, we've been blocked.'

'You think he's avoiding you?'

'I genuinely don't know,' Anjli shrugged. 'But the problem we have is we have a group of four friends from twenty years ago, of which two are now dead and as Lance is one of the two survivors, we would really like to have a chat with him.'

Eden laughed.

'I'll make it so,' he waved magnanimously. 'I know he's in London at the moment.'

'How well do you know him?' Anjli couldn't help herself.

'You think I could be a suspect?' Eden rolled his eyes. 'Here we go again.'

Anjli said nothing, she knew this was an act for his friends, and he looked back at her, grinning.

'He's a polo friend,' he continued. 'And I don't mean that we play polo, I mean he's the kind of person you only see at polo matches and events where they know the paps are going to be at. You know the term "star shagger"?'

'I know it under a slightly different term,' Anjli smiled. 'And the second word definitely isn't shagger.'

'I'm being polite in front of my girlfriend,' Eden grinned. 'The idea of a star-whatever you think it is, is somebody who only wants to be famous, hang around with celebrities, and they'll do whatever it takes, including having sex with them. Well, Lance Curtis-Warner is one of those, but instead of wanting to shag stars, he wants to shag newspapers. He wants to be famous. He wants to be known. He wants paparazzi to take photos of him when he walks into a room, does every two-bit interview and podcast he can to "boost his brand", whatever the hell his brand is.'

'Does this happen?' Anjli asked.

'Christ no,' Eden laughed. 'Nobody has a clue who the man is. It's genuinely hilarious.'

He thought about this for a second.

'Which makes me wonder why he's not taking your calls,' he said. 'The Lance Curtis-Warner I know would have instantly taken these. The chance to be seen as part of a double murder, to have that question of "was he the person who did it, did he do it, did he *not* do it", all these questions and answers? That would give him days, weeks of press, and he isn't wanting to see anybody? No, there's something wrong there.'

He nodded to Amanda.

'Could you sort that out for me?' he asked, with a sudden hurried. 'Please, darling?'

Anjli smiled.

'Domesticated life suits you, Eden,' she said, rising from the chair. 'I can't stay long. It's good seeing you again.'

'How are you and Declan?' Eden asked, and it almost

looked like he'd been holding back the question until the last minute, and then finally wasn't able to stop it blurting out.

'We're good,' Anjli grinned.

'You know when you get married, I want an invite to the wedding,' Eden replied. 'I'll even cover the security costs, 'cause you'll need it if I'm there.'

Anjli couldn't help herself. She started laughing loudly.

'I think we've got a long way before we hit that point,' she said. 'But I appreciate it.'

With a nod to the others, Anjli left the building

Once they were alone, Eden turned to the two men.

'Was that okay?' he asked.

The first of the two men, an older man with a grey moustache, nodded.

'I think it's fair that until this book deal is sorted, you should keep your distance from the Last Chance Saloon,' he said. 'I don't think helping them in an inquiry would be very good for your PR if they get hung out to dry.'

Eden stared at the now empty doorway.

'Whatever they need,' he said. 'I'll cover it. If that book comes out, they're gonna have a shit few weeks.'

―――――

GETTING DRUNK WITH THE GIRLS WAS A MISTAKE, AND CORINNE Daniels was already regretting it. Half-past two in the morning and staggering through Islington in the pouring rain, she constantly looked back down the road beside her, searching for a friendly glowing orange light or a taxi that was for hire. She'd tried using the Uber app, but after three or four Uber drivers had claimed to take her request, driven around in circles and then cancelled without any explanation, Corinne started walking. She lived on a new-built estate near the Caledonian Road, and the distance from Islington to King's Cross wasn't that far, especially if you had the magical beer scooter that people who had had a few drinks often used.

The problem was the rain. She'd spent a fortune on her hair, her makeup, and even her dress, which was a one-of-a-kind she'd picked up at a fashion show in Milan. By "picked up", Corinne didn't mean she'd bought it. She worked for a fashion house, and had found it had fallen into her bag when she'd left a fashion show. She'd only worn it a couple of times since, perks of the trade, but she knew the drenching of this downpour, which had only started twenty-five minutes ago, was enough to ruin it forever unless she could find a cab to help her get home quicker and drier.

Of course, at half-past two in the morning on a weekday, when the rain was coming down, *everybody* wanted a cab. Corinne knew the chances of finding anything were slim.

And then, salvation.

As she walked westwards down Theberton Street, now north of Angel Islington, glancing left and right to see if any cabs were coming and, more likely, whether there were any dodgy, shadowy men hanging around – this wasn't the nicest of areas after all – she almost shouted with delight as she glanced north, and saw the yellow lit-up taxi sign of a black cab parked at the side of Gibson Square.

At a run, she started towards the cab, stumbling as her high heels clipped the pavement, almost sending her to the floor so she decided instead to take it carefully, taking a more delicate pace as she ran up to the door, banging on the driver's side.

The driver, however, was staring dead ahead, his eyes wide open, ignoring her as he stared out into the downpour.

'Hey!' she shouted. 'Come on! People are getting wet out here!'

The man said nothing, still staring off into the distance.

'Hey!' Corinne pawed at the driver's side door, irritated, but then froze as the door opened into the rain and she could gain her first clear view of the driver.

He was in his fifties, ginger hair cut short. He was slim, freckled and quite obviously dead. His hair was dry, he hadn't been caught in the rain; however, his face was dripping wet. And his mouth had dribbled water down the front of his shirt, almost as if he had taken a giant mouthful and then let it come out.

Corinne stepped back in horror as she realised the man had been strapped to his seat as well, unable to move and held upright in death. Looking down at his lap, she saw a small piece of blue plastic; she didn't know what it was, but she sure as hell wasn't going to touch it. The man's eyes, however, staring ahead, still made her think for a moment that he might still be alive, that there might still be a chance to save him.

'Hey, are you okay?' she asked, cautiously, pushing at his cheek with her finger.

His mouth opened and more water flooded out of it, along with a piece of paper rolled up, which landed on his lap. Corinne knew she shouldn't have touched it, but she couldn't help it. She reached for the paper, a strange item to be in a mouth, and unrolling it, stared at the words already smudging with the water that were written on it:

# Crooked Was His Cane

Dropping the paper, she stepped back, reaching for her phone. She wasn't going to call for an Uber this time, or any kind of cab. She'd probably get a lift home from the call she was going to make, but she was now aware she'd be spending some time in a police station first.

'Hello, police?' she said. 'I've found a body.'

As Corinne stared, drenched, at the body of the man in front of her, a small part of her mind gave the optimistic hope that at least she'd be dry soon, even if she was sitting in a police interview room.

## 12

## FRESH BODIES

MONROE WAS PACING BACK AND FORTH AT THE FRONT OF THE briefing room as the others took their places. It was a full house today; even Bullman had returned; hovering, as ever, by the door.

'Right then,' he growled. 'Can someone please tell me who in the name of merry Hell Clifford Stone is?'

There was a long moment of quiet as Monroe, watching the briefing room, exploded.

'Come on, people! We're caught off guard here. Can someone tell me what's going on?'

Declan held a hand up, and Monroe turned his anger onto him.

'It's not a bloody school, Declan,' he said.

'I get that, boss,' Declan replied, standing. 'But we were caught on the back foot with this because we were concentrating on the wrong people. Sure, we know there was a group of four people, but that didn't mean that other people weren't going to get killed. We've just been focusing on the wrong area, that's all.'

Monroe mumbled to himself, looking back at the plasma screen where, thanks to Billy, an image of Clifford Stone was now smiling down on everyone.

'I just feel we missed something here,' he mumbled. 'That if we'd worked it out quicker, Mister Stone here wouldn't be dead.'

He was tapping his fingers rhythmically against the desk as he stared at the picture before looking back, seemingly back to normal.

'All right then, lads and lassies,' he said, 'tell me what we have. Rosanna?'

Doctor Marcos, sitting at the back with Sergeant De'Geer, stood up, opening her iPad, reading her notes.

'Body was found at two-thirty this morning on Gibson Square, just off Islington,' she said. 'Corinne Daniels, twenty-four, coming home from some kind of works event, looking for a cab in the rain, saw a black taxi with the orange light on. She thought he was waiting for a fare, wandered over to see if she could book him, and found Clifford Stone dead in the driver's seat.'

'Similar to what happened last time, then?' Anjli asked.

'Yes and no,' Doctor Marcos replied, looking over at her. 'There were parts of the MO that were exactly the same. The victim was ratchet strapped to the seat so he couldn't leave, and a note with the words "Crooked Was His Cane" had been placed in his mouth after death. However, Clifford Stone hadn't been asphyxiated with carbon monoxide.'

She looked around the room.

'Instead, he'd been drowned.'

'So the murderer drowned Clifford Stone, dragged him to the car and then placed him in the driver's position?' Declan asked, confused. 'If that was the case, why would they need to ratchet strap him?'

'Maybe to keep him upright,' Billy suggested from across the room. 'If he was dead, he would just slump forwards, and maybe that's not what the murderer wanted to show.'

'No, I believe he was ratchet strapped to stop him struggling,' Doctor Marcos replied, nodding over at Billy. 'Look in my files. Look for AOI.'

Billy tapped on his computer for a moment, opening up the network profiles. Then, after moving through the file structure, he clicked on an image which appeared on the plasma screen behind Monroe. It was a full-face snorkel mask, the type that people wore on holiday. It wasn't the traditional style of snorkel mask that went over the face and nose, leaving your mouth free to place a snorkel into it, though. This was more of a full-face sheet of plastic that seemed to secure around the entire side of the face. At the top, sticking out at a forty-five-degree angle backwards, was what looked to be the actual snorkel.

'This is a full-face snorkel mask,' Doctor Marcos explained. 'They've been around for a few years now, quite popular at the holiday resorts. You can put it on, put your face in the water, and your vision is pretty much one hundred and eighty degrees. The rubber around the lens creates a suction to the diver's face, sealing out the water, creating a glass or plastic barrier that allows the snorkeller to see underwater, and, because they partition the compartment into a breathing section and a looking section, your hot exhaled breath never connects with the viewport, only around your mouth, so the glass doesn't steam up as much as you would expect.'

'Oh, I've always hated that,' Monroe nodded.

Doctor Marcos raised an eyebrow.

'You're well versed in snorkelling?' she asked, stone faced. Monroe, realising his flippant comment had fallen short, looked back at the plasma screen.

'So how did this kill Clifford Stone?' he asked, changing the subject, deliberately not looking at his wife as she smiled.

Doctor Marcos nodded to Billy to change the photo, and the plasma screen now displayed a broken piece of blue plastic.

'This was found in the driver's seat-well,' she explained. 'I believe it's the top part of a full-face snorkel. The chances are that at some point the murderer came in, placed the mask fully over Clifford Stone's head and removed this piece.'

'Why remove it?' Anjli asked.

'The way snorkels work is that they have a ball-float system,' Doctor Marcos explained. 'In full-face snorkel masks, a ball-float system prevents water from entering the tube when submerged. If water does seep in, it's directed to the chin area of the mask. Here, a special valve allows for easy drainage, keeping the mask dry and breathable. Stops you drowning.'

'But if you remove the ball float, the water can come in freely,' Declan started to understand.

Doctor Marcos waved to Billy to go back to the previous slide. As the image appeared again, she walked over to the plasma screen and pointed at the area around the nose and mouth.

'You would still have the nose and mouth blocked,' she said. 'But if the water's being poured in, there's nowhere for the water to come out. It would dribble out to the sides and probably filled up the inside of the mask eventually, but before that there's nowhere to go, except down the nose and throat. You could take a two-litre bottle of water, pour it into that snorkel, and quite easily drown somebody.'

'That's grim,' Declan said. 'Feels like one of those BBC dramas, you know, the ones where they're in the Bahamas and have to solve murders.'

'Not exactly the kind of thing you expect on a street in Islington,' Monroe mused. 'And I have to say, this feels quite deliberate.'

'How do you mean?' Billy asked, looking up from his laptop.

'Think about it,' Monroe replied. 'The first victim was gassed to death in an electric car. There were easier ways to kill him; possibly this, for example. But they made a point of doing this to give us a message. With this one, Clifford Stone was still driving one of the old-style cabs. There was an exhaust. The murderer could have killed him in exactly the same way that they did Ronald Tyler, and no one would have been any the wiser. But the murderer had to find a new way to kill them. Drowning. How does that relate?'

He shook his head.

'We were lucky the woman found the note as well. The chances are, if we'd have waited until the body was found later, that note would be nothing but mushed paper.'

He stopped tapping the table, lost in thought for a moment, then asked, 'So what do we know about him?'

Billy, as ever the expert on these matters, clicked a button and swiped on the trackpad, bringing up Clifford Stone's driver's licence on the plasma screen.

'Clifford Stone, aged fifty-four,' he read from his page as the others looked up at the screen, 'has been a cab driver for just under twenty-one years, no convictions, a couple of parking fines, lives just outside of London in Surbiton, no family to speak of, has a sister, but we haven't contacted her yet. I don't know if anybody even knows he's dead. His last fare was at one o'clock in the morning, picking somebody up at King's Cross and dropping them at Farringdon.'

'So, sometime between Farringdon and his death, he picked up his murderer,' Monroe stroked at his chin. 'ANPR?'

'We're looking into it,' Billy replied. 'Also, his phone was connected into the sat-nav app Waze, which should have shown some kind of tracking of where he drove, and we're getting that information shortly.'

'The phone was still there?' Declan frowned.

'Forensics suggested that the murderer might have been concerned about being caught,' De'Geer spoke from the back. 'Hence the fact that the broken part of the snorkel wasn't picked up when they left. Our belief at this point is the murderer drowned Clifford Stone, and then, concerned that they might be found quickly, removed the water and the snorkel, placed the piece of paper in the mouth, and then ran.'

'Maybe they were spooked by Corinne Daniels?' Declan suggested.

'No,' Doctor Marcos shook her head. 'His body was damp, but not soaked. If they'd have removed the snorkel mask, it would have been filled with water. It would be the same as pouring a bottle of water all over the front of him. We would have seen that. He had been dead a good hour by the time Corinne found him; we're saying time of death is about one-thirty in the morning.'

'Where did he go to school?' Anjli asked.

'What, secondary?' Billy asked, looking back at her, confused.

'No, to learn the Knowledge,' Anjli replied. 'Was it the

College of Knowledge, by chance? It sounds like he was there around the same time as the four people we've been looking into.'

Billy started flicking through notes.

'Gained his Hackney carriage licence around six, seven months before Ronald Tyler did,' he said. 'There's every chance he could have gone to the College of Knowledge. It doesn't say on the records—'

'But the college itself would know, wouldn't they?' Declan interrupted. 'I think one of us needs to have a chat with them today. Find out exactly what's going on there. This is now a case involving three people, all onetime cab drivers that have died. One was struck by a car. One was gassed and one was drowned.'

'Okay, so we know we need to speak to Curtis-Warner at some point,' Monroe mused. 'Anything more about Sandeep Khan?'

'Apparently he was only a cab driver for about a year, then moved out of the industry,' Cooper, now rising at the back, read from her notes.

'Stopped driving?'

'Yes, sir.'

'So after all that training, he basically walked away from being a cab driver?'

'Not quite.' Cooper shook her head. 'He created a website, and then app, called Oi Taxi.'

'iTaxi?' Declan frowned.

'No, no, no, not *iTaxi*,' Cooper corrected, shaking her head again. '*Oi* Taxi. But the logo did look similar to the Apple logo. It was an app that people could use to hail a London black cab digitally. You didn't have to stand on the street corner with your hand out; you could book it.'

'So, like Uber?' Declan said. 'Or like half a dozen other ways of booking cabs?'

'Yes,' she replied. 'But also not so. There's always been a problem between Uber and black cabs. Black cabs have always claimed that Uber drivers aren't trained, and there have been problems over the years. Uber even lost their licence in London at one point because of threats to safety and the fact there was a lack of vetting process. And then, as recently as a year back, Uber opened up their app to black cab drivers, saying that they could come onto the app as well. So if they were waiting for a fare and nothing was happening, they could take a job with Uber.'

'I bet that went down well,' Monroe replied.

'As well as you would expect, sir,' Cooper smiled. 'I think eighty percent of the cab drivers turned down the deal. It was decided that they would do their own thing. Which, for most of the cab drivers, has been on-the-street bookings, people holding a hand out and waving—'

'Or shouting "Oi, taxi!"' Declan nodded at this.

'Actually, sir, it's illegal to shout and run after a taxi,' Cooper smiled. 'It's the known trope of the taxicab in films, but you're actually supposed to legally stand at the side of the curb and hold out a hand to hail them. No whistles. No screaming out. Nothing.'

'Can we keep on track?' Monroe muttered softly.

Cooper reddened.

'Anyway, Sandeep Khan worked on a website and eventual app which came out a couple of years after he completed his Knowledge, and it seemed to work quite well. The problem was that although it had a monopoly for a while, there were a dozen other ones that appeared once smartphone tech became better; *Taxify*, which is now called *Bolt*,

*Gett, Freenow* and *TaxiApp*, among others. And a lot of people were quite tribal in what app they used.'

'So, if you were a cab driver that was using four different apps, the chances were you weren't getting four times the amount of opportunities, you were just splitting the fees between four different companies ... so what happened?'

'Oi Taxi was one of the brands that came out early, so it gained a solid following, but it started to drop in value,' Cooper continued. 'It was valued at almost twenty million ten years ago, but after it dropped in value, as Uber grabbed a foothold in the market, Khan sold Oi Taxi for eight-point-three million in 2019.'

She smiled.

'Which I would say even if it dropped, it did well, although apparently he still had to take a massive chunk of that and give it to the investment funders who had helped him when he started.'

'He gained investment finance?' Declan looked at the others. 'Am I wrong to think that Lance Curtis-Warner probably pops up in this story as well?'

'Well, they knew each other. Chances are that Sandeep mentioned the idea to Lance and probably gained funding,' Billy suggested.

'What does he do now?' Bullman asked from the door.

'Whatever he damn well wants, Ma'am,' Declan laughed. 'If he's got a few million pounds in his bank account.'

'He runs a company in Shoreditch,' Billy looked from his computer. 'He holds positions on several start-ups. He diversified his money into other areas. He's worth quite a bit now, seems to spend his time doing productivity videos, travelling the world and talking about tech on podcasts he creates.'

He looked over at Anjli.

'I mean, he's not Eden Storm levels of rich, but doing well.'

Anjli bit back a comment at this.

'Actually, on the subject of Eden Storm, he's arranged a meeting with Lance Curtis-Warner,' she said, almost reluctantly, as everybody now looked back at her.

'Eden Storm?' Monroe smiled. 'Ach, lassie. Did you end up having to go speak to your ex-boyfriend about this?'

Anjli cringed, glancing back at Declan. She hadn't mentioned this to him, and his face was one of surprise.

'Sorry,' she muttered. 'I got back late last night, and we didn't really get a chance to talk.'

'I've got no problems with this,' Declan said, but his expression gave off a different impression. 'What did he say?'

'He's worked with Curtis-Warner in asset finance over the years, and he said that he was quite happy to arrange a meeting for us today,' Anjli replied. 'I think, to be honest, if we call Curtis-Warner right now, his people will be prepared.'

'But why would he now risk speaking to us if he wouldn't do it yesterday?' De'Geer was confused by this.

'Because he's now got the risk of losing money from Eden Storm," Declan replied. 'If Eden's turned around and said, "speak to my buddies in the police or I'll kill a contract" Lance is going to speak to his buddies in the police.'

'Or a particular buddy,' Monroe kept smiling. 'A very special buddy.'

'And you can knock that off too, Guv,' Anjli snapped. 'I did it purely so we could get forward in the case, not for anything else. He's a happily taken man now.'

Declan smiled. He trusted Anjli, and he wasn't concerned about the meeting, but it was amusing to see her flustered.

Monroe slammed his hand down on the table as if to end the meeting.

'Right then,' he said. 'We need somebody to go to the College of Knowledge and find out what was going on and see how Clifford Stone was connected to the four we know. We need somebody to speak to Lance Curtis-Warner and find out exactly what the deal was there, and we need somebody to go along and speak to Sandeep Khan and find out if he has any more clue about all this than we do.'

Then it was as if the mood in the briefing room changed, as Monroe straightened and looked around.

'OK then, lads and lassies,' he said, his voice now sombre and done. 'We've talked about the main part, and we know what we need to do about that, but now we think we need to discuss something else.'

## 13

# SECRET BRIEFING

Declan shifted uncomfortably in his seat; he knew this was now the discussion about the fate of the Last Chance Saloon, and as he glanced around the room, he saw everybody had the same expression.

Monroe looked at the back of the room and nodded at De'Geer and Cooper.

'I'm afraid I have to ask you two to leave,' he said.

'Sir?' De'Geer looked confused.

'I need you and PC Cooper to man the phones,' Monroe said, almost conversationally. 'It's nothing personal. It's just we need to discuss something that you shouldn't be involved in.'

'With all due respect, Guv, if this is in relation to the unit being closed,' Cooper added, 'I think we should be involved.'

'Aye, and I get that,' Monroe nodded. 'But what we're about to talk about involves events that happened before both of you turned up, and I'd rather give you a little bit of plausible deniability in the situation.'

He looked around the room.

'Whatever's coming out and aiming for us, well, it's likely to be connected to stuff that happened before these wee guys entered the unit. And if that's the case, then it's unfair on them to be caught in this.'

As the others in the briefing room nodded at this, De'Geer went to complain, and then sighed. Rising from his chair, he motioned for Cooper to do so as well.

'If you don't mind me saying so, sir,' she said, her face reddening. 'This is ...'

Her face paused, scrunching up as she considered the next word.

'... Bush league,' she finished.

Monroe nodded; no smile, but an expression of understanding on his face.

'I know,' he replied. 'It *is* bullshite, and I'm sorry we have to do that.'

Reluctantly, De'Geer and Cooper left the briefing room, and after the door was closed behind them, Bullman entering the room, Monroe turned to Bullman.

'You came in after this, as well,' he added.

'I was Walsh's defence counsel, if you remember,' Bullman placed her hands on her hips. 'I dare you to tell me to bugger off.'

Monroe smiled, nodded, and returned his attention to the others.

'Okay, let's talk about the other elephant in the room,' he said. 'And this bloody favour we're doing to keep the roof above our heads.'

'I spoke to Tessa Martinez,' Declan rose, and then immediately regretted it as the room seemed to stop. Everybody paused in position as if playing a game of statues, and Declan wasn't sure, but he felt that the temperature of the room had dropped a few degrees at the same time.

'You spoke to Tessa Martinez.' It was spoken as a statement, cold and icy as Anjli glared at Declan.

'Yes,' he said. 'I wanted to speak to Sean Ashby but he wouldn't turn up. So he sent Tessa.'

'Convenient.'

'Hold on a second,' Declan straightened. 'I didn't get all pissy when I heard that you were talking to *your* ex-boyfriend.'

'Eden Storm asked me for a few dates and then eventually left me alone when he realised I was seeing you,' Anjli replied coldly. 'You, however, have had a crush on Tessa Martinez for over twenty years and used to have her bloody poster on your wall.'

'And yet I'm still with you,' Declan replied, his tone becoming just as icy. 'It was a business conversation and trust me, at the moment, the impression I get is nobody wants to touch the Last Chance Saloon with a barge pole, so you're bloody stuck with me.'

He looked back at Monroe.

'As you already know, there's a book coming out. It's apparently not good for us. It's *very* not good for Charles Baker, from what I can work out.'

He glanced over at Billy.

'I passed it to our resident cyber-expert to see if he could find some way of using his algorithmic skills to check it through, rather than us all having to sit and read all seven hundred pages written by Malcolm Gladwell.'

Billy nodded as the attention in the room all turned to him now.

'I scanned the pages when DCI Walsh gave it to me,' he

said. 'It took a while, but double-page scanning them, then taking the text and compiling it together gave me a pretty good digital version of the text. I was then able to put it through a couple of algorithms to look up anything that involved the unit, us, and Donna herself.'

'And?' Monroe asked.

'I flicked through the more juicy parts,' Billy replied. 'He really goes to town on the whole "Kendis having some kind of inappropriate relationship with Declan before she died" part of the case.'

Declan raised his eyebrows.

'They said I was her terrorist handler,' he muttered. 'How is that inappropriate?'

'I think he means the part where you helped her break her marital vows,' Anjli nudged him. 'It's okay, I'm fine with that, as it was before you realised I was your one true love. Not Tessa. Me.'

Declan knew Anjli was joking – at least he *hoped* she was joking – and he forced a weak smile at it.

'I should sue.'

'Did you have an inappropriate relationship with Kendis?' Monroe asked softly. 'Leaving her house in the wee hours of the morning, perhaps?'

Declan's face fell.

'Bollocks,' he said. 'I just ... it's just ...'

'You don't want Gladwell making money and gaining his freedom from your loss,' Monroe nodded. 'Aye, we get it. And we need to move it out of our way. Billy, continue.'

Billy straightened and then shrugged.

'It's not great, and even with the jibes at Kendis, which catch DCI Walsh in a kind of friendly fire, it doesn't affect us as bad as it could be. We can pretty much weather a lot of it, but it links us to Charles Baker quite closely. And he comes off badly.'

'Dammed by association, then,' Monroe replied glumly.

'The book is definitely coming out?' Declan asked.

'Well, that's the interesting bit. Possibly not,' Billy replied. 'It's a strange one. There's a publishing deal, but when I chatted to one of their execs this morning, they told me the publishing deal can be stopped at any point by Gladwell. He's only agreed to have a few copies sent out right now, way less than the publisher would usually send, and mainly to people in the press and government who are connected to either Charles Baker or us.'

'Why would he do that?' Declan shook his head at this. 'What's his strategy here?'

'Because he wants to get out of prison,' Monroe muttered. 'That's what he's doing. He wants a pardon; he wants to be released. He's using this as some kind of leverage. If we don't do what he wants, he pulls the trigger, and the book comes out. If we *do* what he wants, the book stays in his vault and he gets to walk free … but the book is still there, in the vault.'

Declan stood back up without realising, his face reddening with anger.

'He killed Kendis Taylor,' he growled. 'It's bad enough he's sullying her name here—'

'Aye, I know, laddie,' Monroe said. 'But at the same time, it's not our place to decide what happens here.'

He chewed on his lip for a moment.

'We need to think about this one carefully,' he continued. 'It could affect the way we continue from now on. The book's out there no matter what. Even if it's not released, there are copies out there that people will see. Billy, I know half of us here don't want to read books and would rather see it on TV, but I think we're going to need copies. We all need to scan this, and fast, and work out exactly what's being aimed at here.'

He looked back at Declan.

'I'd also work out what Jennifer Farnham-Ewing's game is here. Does she want us to free Gladwell, or does she want us to kill this?'

'Kill this?' Anjli frowned.

'Cut off his air supply, send Gladwell back into the void,' Monroe quickly corrected. 'Stop him being a threat once and for all. Remember, this is a man who was part of the super-secret Star Chamber for ages. He's used to ending threats quickly. This here? It sounds like the latest in a long line of them. We know she has ambition, but she also worked for Will Harrison when she started, and he was screwed over by Gladwell, when Laurie Hooper was encouraged to kill him.'

'Before Gladwell then killed Hooper, tasering her repeatedly until she died,' Declan added grimly. 'So, what do we do about this? There's no way he gets to walk from something like that.'

'The only way we can move on Gladwell is to find out more information on what happened with Donna Baker,' Monroe replied. 'Jennifer Farnham-Ewing might be playing the angles, but she's right to do so. With luck her loyalty to both her dead boss and Baker makes her an ally rather than an enemy, but the only one outside of Charles Baker to truly know what happened that night was Kendis Taylor. We need to check Taylor's notes from back then.'

Declan went to reply, to argue this, but stopped. 'We know she was working on a story, and we know she spoke to Donna before she died,' Monroe was pacing now. 'There's every chance Donna confided in her.'

'I remember her saying she took copious digital notes,' Declan suggested. 'So perhaps we might find something in there.'

'It's a start,' Monroe said. 'Do you remember where she put them?'

'That's the problem,' Declan grimaced. 'I thought they were with Sean, but apparently not, so I've got a feeling they're still in the possession of Peter, her widower.'

'The one who hates you, and thought you were having an affair with her?' Billy asked, reddening, before adding. 'Sorry, guv, didn't mean to speak that one aloud.'

'No, you're right,' Declan smiled weakly. 'The last time I saw Peter was after Kendis's funeral. Even though she'd lived with Peter in Putney before her death, she'd grown up in Hurley, like I had, and as such had been buried at St Mary the Virgin Church there. I had kept away from the funeral, but after it ended, I made my way over to pay my respects.'

He winced at the memory.

*'You were just a shag, nothing more than a one-night stand. She loved me, Walsh. Me. Pay your respects to my wife, it's the only time you're allowed to. I know people in this village, and they bloody hate you. They tell me everything, and if I hear you've visited her grave at all after that? I'll kill you.'*

Shaking it off, he took a breath.

'Peter had been waiting. There were words. They weren't good. And it had ended with me being punched hard in the face, Peter having been aware that I had had an affair with his wife. It seemed that although Kendis had told me she and Peter had already come to an agreement about leaving, she had neglected, before we got together, to inform her husband of this.'

He looked away, unable to catch anyone's eyes.

'I felt terrible about this, but immediately after it happened, I'd been placed straight into the Red Reaper's line of sight, and things had been forgotten. If there are any tapes, he'll have them I hope, or at least he'll know where he's placed them.'

He sighed.

'I think I'm going to have to have a chat with an old friend.'

The term was spoken tongue-in-cheek, and there were nods around the room.

'Aye,' Monroe replied. 'You do that, laddie, and you do that fast.'

He leant back against the desk, shaking his head.

'I'd really like the unit to stay open until we could at least solve this case,' he continued. 'So I think we need to look at this as quickly as possible. We'll carry on doing what we can do our end. You guys do what you can do your end, and we'll meet in the middle, aye?'

'Aye, sir,' Declan said, rising, glancing over at Anjli. 'Do you want to come watch me get punched in the face again?'

'As romantic as that sounds,' Anjli replied, 'I think I'll be going to have a chat with a certain college. Try not to get blood on your suit, yeah?'

Declan chuckled.

'Unfortunately for me, I can't promise anything.'

As the others left the briefing room, Declan stared at the plasma screen on the wall, but he wasn't focused on it. His mind was now years earlier, thinking of the last words Kendis Taylor had ever spoken to him.

*'Once I do this, we can go away together. I'll tell Peter. It'll work out. Just watch out for me. I'll be off grid for a few days; then I'll bring the fireworks.'*

The next day she was dead.

He set his jaw, squared his shoulders, and shook himself into the present once more. If Malcolm Gladwell was taking potshots, he'd be aiming at everyone. Declan, the Last Chance Saloon, Baker, even Kendis.

'The hell he will,' he muttered to himself as he walked out of the briefing room.

The last time Peter Taylor saw Declan, he'd punched him in the face, kicked him in the side and spat on him – with good reason, too.

This time, Peter Taylor was going to sit down, bloody well listen, and do exactly what Declan asked him. Or *he'd* be the one on the floor this time.

Declan chuckled at that; he liked the idea of Peter on the floor.

He liked it a *lot*.

---

## 14

---

## COLLEGE OF KNOWLEDGE

ANJLI HAD EXPECTED SOMETHING AKIN TO AN EDUCATIONAL complex when she arrived at the College of Knowledge; maybe *Xavier's School for Gifted Mutants*, or wherever the X-Men in the comics lived. Some kind of stately building, or industrial complex, at the least.

As it turned out, it was what seemed to be an altered *WeWork* building. It was modest in size, and as Anjli stepped into the classroom, she noticed that the air felt heavy with concentration. The walls were covered with big, laminated maps of London, brightly lit by fluorescent lights. Students, varying in age from teens to people in their forties were sitting at their desks, piled with books, notepads, and colourful pens, likely for drawing on the aforementioned laminated maps.

In one corner, two students were quietly discussing a route from Covent Garden to St. Pancras. In the middle of the room, there was a large, old wooden table where a group of students were looking at a complicated section of a map. They were using their fingers to trace routes and calculate distances, looking serious and focused. As she watched, one of them stood up to adjust the map on the wall, pointing out new changes, like a bike lane, or a new building.

The room was mostly quiet, except for the occasional student who would recite a route out loud to themselves as if they were practising for a play. Their voice would be strong and clear, and then they would get some comments or advice from others around them.

Anjli could feel that these students took their studies seriously. They paid for their own education, and like her uncle, they valued the old skill of learning London's streets by heart. Even with modern technology like digital maps, these students preferred to learn by drawing on maps and discussing landmarks. They seemed to connect more with the city this way, learning about places that Anjli wouldn't find just by swiping on a screen.

Cooper stared around the room as well, but Anjli could see that already, the magic within these walls had completely bypassed her.

As she looked back to the classroom, an old, white-haired man grinned as he started walking over to them.

'You must be the ladies who were asking about the Knowledge,' he said.

Anjli nodded with a smile. His grin was infectious, and after everything that had happened so far that day, it was quite nice to see someone actually smile at them.

'DI Kapoor,' she said, holding up her warrant card. 'This is PC Cooper.'

'Oh, a uniformed officer too. Am I in trouble?' His face was still broken into a smile.

'Depends who you are,' Cooper said, her face unsmiling. In fact, Cooper looked quite annoyed, still angry she'd missed the second meeting; and there was an element of feeling that she was being excluded – which, in a way, she was. Anjli had explained on the drive over it was nothing personal, but it was very hard to prove that when you were telling the same person they couldn't be involved in conversations.

The man nodded and spoke as he waved about the classroom.

'I'm Ray Holdsworth, and I run this place for my sins.'

'You teach the Knowledge?'

'I've been doing it for years now.'

Anjli shook his hand.

'Thank you for taking the time to speak to us,' she said. 'I understand you were one of the originals here?'

'Oh Christ, no,' Ray shook his head. 'I've only been here since the nineties. There've been people here teaching the Knowledge for decades. We were one of the first in London, you know.'

'Really?' Anjli nodded, interested.

'But you're not here about the history, are you?' Ray almost mocked as he spoke. 'You want to know about Sandeep, Ronald, Curtis, and Stuart?'

Anjli waggled her hand.

'Yes and no,' she admitted. 'First, I'd like you to tell me about Clifford Stone.'

'Stoney?' Ray frowned. 'What about him?'

'He was found murdered last night,' Anjli replied. 'We're currently working out how he connects to the four other names we gave you.'

Shocked at the news, it was all Ray could do just to nod.

'Well, yes, he was connected to them,' he said eventually. 'There was a group.'

'Not just four?'

'No, the four you called about, they were close. They did everything together, but there were a few others, hangers-on, people who started before them or after them. The main two were Clifford and Beth.'

'Beth?'

'Yes. Dammit, what was her full name?' He gave a weak grin. 'Sorry, it's just, you know, twenty years and all that.'

'Take your time,' Anjli replied patiently. 'We're fine.'

'Beth Stevens, that was it!' Ray grinned. 'Good girl she was, good girl. Sorry, it's just, back then, we only had about three percent of our cab drivers as females, you know? They stood out. And Beth was quite interesting.'

Anjli didn't reply, just waiting for Ray to continue digging his grave.

'I don't mean in that kind of way,' he continued. 'She had a great memory, you know? She could work out the routes without anything to hand, just memorised them. There are three hundred and twenty routes in the Blue Book. She had them all marked out within her first year. She knew every single one.'

Ray pointed at one of the walls where, on one of the giant maps of London, several marked routes could be seen.

'That one there? That's the first route in the Blue Book,' he said. 'It's Manor House Station to Gibson Square. You go south down Green Lanes, right on Brownswood Road, left Blackstock Road, forward Highbury Park—'

Anjli held up a hand to pause him.

'Did you say Gibson Square?'

'Yes.'

'And that's the first route that all the cabbies learn?'

'Yes,' this time, Ray was more cautious in his response. 'Why?'

Anjli glanced at Cooper, deciding whether it was worth telling him.

'Clifford Stone was found at Gibson Square in his cab,' she eventually said. Ray made a cross, but said nothing about this.

'So, you were telling us about Beth Stevens?' Cooper continued, her notebook now in hand.

'Yes, sorry, absolutely. So, Beth had the first one planned within a week, word for word. By the first month, she had the first ten. It takes a lot longer, usually to get into it, but she had it from the start,' there was a hint of pride in Ray's voice. 'Obviously, once the others realised how good she was, they kind of adopted her as quickly as they could, especially the rich prick.'

'Lancelot Curtis-Warner?'

'Yeah, that's the one.' It was obvious from Ray's expression that he wasn't a fan. 'Although he went by the name Lance Curtis, not Lancelot bloody silver-spoon Curtis-Warner.'

Cooper noted down his reaction.

'I mean, the guy was, you know, he came from money, and he wanted to be a cab driver? Bullshit. There was always a plan going on there,' Ray muttered. 'Never worked out what it was, though.'

'His father said he couldn't finish anything,' Cooper replied with a smile, 'Apparently, Curtis-Warner was trying to prove his dad wrong before he was disowned.'

'That was it? He took the sodding Knowledge just to win a bet? Well, that just goes to prove he was a prick,' Ray replied. 'The Knowledge isn't just some kind of Mensa test where you just get brownie points. This is a career, a vocation.'

Anjli had the impression Ray was about to start some kind of evangelical rant about the rights of cab drivers and patted him on the shoulder.

'What happened to Beth?'

'I don't know,' Ray shrugged. 'Once they leave here, they never come back. I mean, we had a couple over the years who came back and helped teach, but once they become cab drivers, they become cab drivers, you know? I believe Sandeep did something with phones, I know the rich prick went off and became even richer. As far as I knew, the rest of them just became cabbies.'

He smiled, looking at the wall covered in London maps.

'But those two, Clifford and Beth, they were definitely part of the team. Well, I mean, in the Knowledge, you come and go, you know? A lot of the people, they would come here when they could, learning the Knowledge in the background while they worked at how to get out of whatever job they had. Sometimes it would be the four of them, sometimes it would be Clifford and a couple of them. Often Beth was around. I mean, they were friends. I don't know if they hung out after passing.'

'Did they all pass at the same time?'

Ray shook his head.

'Clifford was six months before them,' he said, thinking about it. 'Yeah, God, I remember him pissing everybody off.'

'How so?' Anjli asked, noting this down.

'He'd started before everybody else, about a year or so before, but he was slower, so they were slowly catching up with him,' Ray explained. 'He passed the Knowledge, went out and immediately bought himself some second-hand banger of a cab. Didn't bother checking with anybody. Didn't really pay as much attention as he probably should have. But, you know, he needed to get the money in and start earning back the money he'd spent.'

'I'm guessing he didn't spend fifty to sixty thousand on a car,' Cooper said.

'Twenty years back, it wasn't that much. But his was so second hand, it was probably into the double digits,' Ray shook his head. 'The thing was practically an antique, but it still drove, still had an MOT. The problem he had is it didn't pass its conditions of fitness.'

'My uncle's mentioned that before,' Anjli said. 'If you fail, you can't drive it, right?'

Ray nodded.

'Yeah. About eight months after he bought it, he had to scrap it. Start fresh. Simply wouldn't pass. There was a bloody hole in the chassis for a start. If you sat in the back of the cab, you found yourself slowly getting gassed by the exhaust as it came through the boot.'

Anjli wrote this down, noting how similar it sounded to the death of Ronald Tyler.

'I mean, don't get me wrong,' Ray said quickly, realising what he'd said. 'It was just a little bit of smoke, you know, But if you're driving a black cab, that shouldn't be happening. For a start, any luggage in the boot comes out stinking.'

'Anything else?'

'I remember Beth had a boyfriend, and that pissed off a couple of them,' Ray grinned. 'She was a real looker, you know, a real Barbara Windsor type – like the young version from the *Carry On* movies rather than Peggy on *Eastenders*.'

'I've never seen them,' Cooper replied, still writing. 'I understand they're quite misogynistic.'

Ray shrugged.

'They're of their time,' he said, as if this was some kind of explanation. 'Anyway, I can give you the files for them, but all I've got is when they passed, and their administrational records. Would you like them?'

'Please,' Anjli said. 'Anything that we can use.'

She paused.

'Did you teach trap streets?'

'Bloody trap streets. Everybody wants to know about bloody trap streets,' Ray laughed at this. 'There's only half a dozen of them in London, and none of them are relevant. Half the time it's the police plaques they really want to know about.'

Cooper frowned at this.

'Police plaques?'

'We use plaques of fallen police officers as markers. It's part of the system of looking for places of interest that a driver can work via,' Ray nodded. 'Police plaques aren't likely to go anytime soon, and pub names change. One of the runs even passes PC Blakelock's one. We remember you guys.'

'And it's appreciated. Do you know if there was anything else going on?'

'No, not really. The only reason I saw Clifford after he passed was because he was part of the gang and would turn up and see them after he passed, in that bloody banger of a cab. They all went their separate ways. Besides,' he continued, 'I think there was some kind of love triangle thing kicking off at one point and I didn't want to get involved.'

'Love triangle?'

'As I said, Beth was a looker. She attracted a fair share of her interested parties.' Ray shrugged. 'I wasn't one of them.'

Ray paused, squinting his eyes as he thought back.

'Hold on, though.'

He looked across the classroom, calling at another man, in his late forties or early fifties. He was black, with a greying afro over a burgundy sweatshirt and jeans.

'Marshall,' he said, 'can you come over and have a word for a sec?'

Marshall nodded and walked over. Seeing the two women, and noting Cooper in her uniform, he frowned.

'I ain't done anything, have I?' he asked.

'Not yet, mate,' Ray laughed, looking back at Anjli. 'Marshall here's one of our teachers, but he passed his Knowledge around the same time as those guys.'

He looked back at Marshall.

'When you were learning the Knowledge, do you remember Ronnie Tyler and his gang?' he asked. 'Lance Curtis, Clifford Stone, Beth Stevens, Sandeep Khan, Stuart Laws?'

Marshall thought for a moment and then nodded.

'Yeah, they were part of the scene,' he said. 'Didn't hang out with them or anything, but I remember them being around.'

'Do you remember any kind of love triangles there?'

'Love triangles? What, you think Sandeep Khan was having a shag with Stuart Laws or something?' Marshall laughed and then looked back at Anjli and Cooper, staring stonily at him.

'Sorry, of course you want serious answers, don't you?' he said. 'I know Ronnie had a thing for her. And if I'm right, I think Stuart and Clifford both fancied her, too. But nothing ever happened. She wasn't into them. She was into someone else at the time, some other guy. Wasn't a cabbie, I know that for a fact.'

He thought back.

'Only thing I *do* remember is that she was really in love with him. And then they broke up badly.'

'Broke up badly?'

'Yeah, he was a bit of a waster, if I remember correctly,' Marshall was racking his brain, as he thought. 'I just recall someone telling me, possibly Sandeep – I spoke to him the most – that Beth cheated on this guy, and he found out. There was a meeting, and she got battered.'

'Did she press charges?'

'No idea. I heard this all months, maybe even years later.'

'You don't remember his name, do you?'

'What, the name of some ex-boyfriend of somebody I met three times around twenty years ago? You'll be lucky,' Marshall laughed, but it was a nervous one, and Anjli wondered if she was deliberately not being told the full story.

'Yet you can remember over three hundred journeys, road by road?' Anjli raised an eyebrow. 'Surely you're not telling me you couldn't possibly remember such a thing?'

'Now you're just teasing,' Marshall sighed. 'Hold on, let me think.'

There was a moment of silence and in the background, Anjli was distracted by the noise of other students reciting street names as they walked along the maps.

'No, I don't have a name,' he eventually admitted. 'I do remember he had some kind of weird nickname, though.'

'Yeah?'

'Yeah.' Marshall sighed, looking back at Ray. 'It was like a bundle of something.'

'Bundle?' Ray shook his head. 'I think you misheard that, mate.'

'Could it have been Bindle?' Anjli asked, suddenly feeling a sliver of ice slide down her spine. 'As in bindlesticks?'

'Yeah, that's the one,' Marshall laughed. 'Obviously, it's more common than I thought. I'd never heard of the bloody thing before. Does that help?'

'Actually, I believe it does,' Anjli said.

'Well, I wish you luck,' Ray said. 'Give us a second and I'll find the files.'

'You could email them to us if it's easier,' Cooper suggested.

At this, Ray laughed.

'Sweetheart, this place has been going since the sixties,' he said. 'I don't think anything's been put digitally on there. You're going to have to have it on paper, I'm afraid.'

Ray wandered off into the back rooms to find what he needed as Anjli turned to face Cooper.

'Love triangle?' she suggested.

'Maybe, Guv,' Cooper replied. 'But it sounds like it wasn't four in this group, it was six. We need to find this Beth, see if she knows anything, before she too gets added to a list of victims.'

Anjli nodded.

'All right then,' she said as she pulled out her phone, texting Monroe. 'I just hope the others are doing better than us.'

She stopped, looking back at Marshall, now back with a group of students.

'Hold on,' she said. 'Are you Marshall Reynolds?'

Marshall looked back, nodding.

'Yeah, I know where you're going,' he said. 'It was my nephew who found the body.'

'Convenient,' Anjli replied cooly. 'He said you'd aimed

him at trap streets. Any reason why? Ray said you don't really teach them here.'

Marshall went to reply, and his expression was one that looked like he was about to shrug it off, but then he stopped, waved the two officers to join him on the other side of the room and then lowered his voice.

'I saw Ron Tyler a few days back, cab rank in Paddington,' he said. 'I only teach here now and then, I still go out on the routes. Anyway, I wasn't talking to him, but he was chatting with the guy in the cab in front while we waited, yeah? Mentioned he was going to "Bartlett Place" on Wednesday morning. I recognised the name, thought he was taking the piss, but when I saw Alfie, I remembered this, said he should go look it up. I didn't expect him to find Ron's body there.'

'Did you hear him say why he was going there?'

Marshall shrugged.

'It was busy, and I was in the cab, but I think he said he was going to get what was owed to him.'

He sighed.

'I guess he did, in the end. The problem with these sorts of things is it's hard for the children. I was talking to Cavan the other day and he—'

'Hold on,' Anjli frowned. 'Do you mean Cavan Tyler?'

'Yes,' Marshall paused, confused as to why the question was being asked. 'Cavan and Alfie have been friends since they were toddlers. They've grown up together.'

'I understand that,' Anjli said. 'But we were under the assumption that Cavan was in Hull.'

'Oh yeah, he's at university there,' Marshall nodded, his tone brightening as he realised he was still on the same page as Anjli. 'But he's back for the holidays.'

Anjli said nothing to this. She'd been given the impression by Lizzie Tyler that Cavan wasn't home this summer.

'*He has a summer job. He's up in Hull, and it's a lot easier for him to stay up there and get some money over the summer than it is to come down here and hang around. All his friends have moved on, got jobs.*'

This was likely something she was going to have to check into. After all, if Cavan was in London, had Lizzie Tyler been unaware of this ... or lying?

# 15

## UNWELCOME VISITOR

Declan hadn't been to Kendis's house in Putney for almost two years now. In fact, the last time he'd been here had been with Anjli, hoping that the nosy neighbour, Mrs Baldwin wouldn't recognise him, as she stared out at the two police officers arriving to tell Peter Taylor of his wife's death.

The time before that, merely a day earlier, Declan had been sneaking out of there first thing in the morning after a one-night stand, but it turned out to be the last time the two of them were ever intimate. He'd seen her once more in a cemetery; a secret meeting where she was terrified for her life, but then the next time he heard her name, she was dead.

And now he'd returned, staring up at Kendis's house once more.

*No,* he thought to himself, *Kendis hasn't lived here for almost two years now, not since she died. This was Peter Taylor's house now.*

A woman was gardening in the house next door. She looked up, seeing Declan standing at the gate.

'Morning, Mrs Baldwin,' he said, as he straightened his

tie, and with a determined walk, started down the pathway. If the old lady recognised him in any way, she didn't show it, returning to her gardening, not even questioning how this strange, suited man knew her name. Putting her out of his own mind, Declan started steeling himself, preparing for the upcoming confrontation.

If he remembered correctly, Peter often worked shifts, there was every chance he would still be in the house first thing in the morning – or he'd be at work, and Declan's job would become even harder.

He rang the doorbell, waited patiently, and after a couple of moments the door opened, and a familiar face stared out at him.

Peter Taylor.

He stood there, a tall, imposing figure with a rough stubble shading his jaw. He stared, almost in surprise, at Declan on his doorstep, and then his face contorted into an expression of pure anger and hatred.

'You come to my house?' he asked, almost in disbelief. 'You come back here, and knock on my door?'

He was squaring up, and Declan could see he wanted to fight.

'I told you what'd happen if you ever went to her grave – did you honestly think I wanted you to come here? You've got ten seconds to get off my property before I kick the living shit out of you.'

Declan held up his warrant card. It instantly stopped the man in his tracks.

'Peter Taylor, I'm Detective Chief Inspector Declan Walsh of the City of London Police,' he said, tonelessly, stripping every single piece of emotion out of his voice. 'I'm here to speak to you today about the death of Kendis Taylor.'

'You have a nerve,' Peter snapped back.

Declan sighed and stepped closer, moving to the edge of the doorway.

'Listen, Peter,' he said. 'You might not want me here, but I *really* don't want to be facing you, yeah? So the fact that I am here, after all this time, should give you an idea that I need to be here for something very important, and you can either help me, or I'll drag you down to the cells and have your house searched with a fine-tooth comb.'

Peter stared at Declan.

'You wouldn't dare do that,' he said, but now his voice was more uncertain.

'I'll do what I damn well need to,' Declan replied. 'I don't require your time for long, I just need to know if you have a particular item.'

Peter glanced to the side and saw Mrs Baldwin stopping her gardening and watching the two men.

'I suppose you'd better come in then,' he said, motioning reluctantly for Declan to follow him inside, and out of the scrutinised gaze of his neighbour.

The last time Declan had been in the house, he hadn't really paid much attention to it. There had been drinking, and Declan and Kendis hadn't arrived at her empty house to sit in the front room and discuss things. Declan wasn't sure if he'd even reached the front room that night, instead heading straight up the stairs and into the bedroom. The room itself was green, quite an obnoxious shade of green in fact, one that Declan was quite sure Kendis wouldn't have chosen. The walls were simplistic, adorned with a couple of prints, nothing more. And on the bookshelf, there were several ornaments, books and photos in frames. On there, Declan saw a picture of Peter and another woman. He was going to comment on Peter having moved on, and he realised that not only was it around two years or so since Kendis had died, but also that Peter had known one of her last acts alive had been to have an affair.

It probably wasn't the sort of thing that kept you enamoured with someone. That, and that after the funeral Declan had checked into Peter, and learnt he wasn't the angel in the relationship either.

Peter sat down in a chair, and faced Declan, waving for him to sit as well.

'Forgive me if I don't offer you anything,' he said. 'That would take time, and that's something I don't want you to have here.'

'Believe me, the feeling's mutual,' Declan replied, settling into his seat as he pulled out his notebook. 'I'm here in relation to Kendis's last case—'

'The one where you were accused of being some kind of terrorist asset handler?' Peter asked, almost mockingly. 'The one where you ended up getting her killed?'

Declan fought back the urge to argue, to say that he hadn't got Kendis killed, it was Kendis herself who had done that, but he paused, keeping his mouth shut.

'Yeah, you did really well with that, didn't you?' Peter continued. 'Did you ever find the killer?'

Declan knew who the killer was, Malcolm Gladwell, but he also knew that the case had still not come through, and Gladwell, as of yet, had not been accused of this, a governmental gag order placed on it until the trial.

'Listen,' he said, 'I'll get to the point. When Kendis was alive, she was talking to Donna Baker, Charles Baker's wife.'

'Okay, so why should I give a shit about that?'

'Because there's every chance that her legacy is about to be torn apart,' Declan snapped.

'Again with why should I give a shit about that?'

Declan had had enough, and rose, placing his hands on Peter's shoulders, slamming him back into the chair as he leant over, staring down at him.

'The last time we met, you had the jump on me,' he said. 'You took me with a sucker punch and you spat in my face, and I deserved every second for what I did, but do not for one second think that I won't beat the living shite out of you right now, right here, if you do not help me with what I need. I'm here as a police officer, but if you play me, piss me off in any way, I will *not* be, do you understand? You've been told about my past. You know what I'm capable of doing. What I've *done*.'

For the first time, Peter showed concern, fear even, nodding slowly.

'What do you want?' he said.

'Kendis's notes on the Donna Baker case,' Declan replied. 'I know she used to take recordings because she did that while working with my father on a book before she died. I was hoping you'd still have them.'

Peter started to laugh. Declan was about to respond, but Peter held up his hand to pause him, chuckling as he did so.

'You're about six months too late,' he said. 'They're gone. All of her stuff's gone.'

'What do you mean, they're gone?'

'I mean I got rid of all of it,' Peter shrugged. 'Some of it went to her editor, but by then he'd moved papers, so I don't even know if it got there. The rest of it went to a lawyer.'

'Lawyer?'

'Yeah, Malcolm Gladwell's lawyer. He reckoned the tapes

would actually help exonerate his client. Claimed that Malcolm Gladwell hadn't killed her, that it was all a big lie, that you'd been involved in it, and the tapes could answer the questions.'

Declan straightened, staring in horror.

'You absolute cretin,' he growled. 'You utter clown. What you did was destroy her reputation. Malcolm Gladwell didn't want it to clear his name. He wanted it to write a tell-all book, placing himself as the victim.'

'Well, perhaps he is.' Peter rose now to face Declan. 'How do you know he's not?'

'*Because we solved the case!*' Declan shouted. 'He killed Kendis in his family mausoleum in Brompton Cemetery! He tasered her unconscious, then went back to his London apartment, found a letter opener he thought he could frame an aide with and then came back and stabbed her in the chest!'

Peter stared in horror as Declan continued.

'You gave the murderer of your wife everything she ever found out about him, so he could relive the moment for his own sick, selfish reasons.'

'No, no, no.' Peter was shaking his head now, backing away. 'Look, I wasn't happy with her, but I wouldn't have done that.'

'You *did* do that!' Declan screamed. 'You utter—'

Declan reached back into himself to pull himself away from the anger that was building up.

'I should ...' he started, and then paused, shaking his head. 'Did you give him everything?'

'Yes,' Peter replied, then, 'no. I found a box. There were a few tapes in it. They're Dictaphone things that she used to stick in her little voice recorder. She usually used a digital recorder, but she was scared she'd lose data, so sometimes she'd turn it on, keep it on her while she placed the phone on the table. She was always on about backups. She had cloud drives to back up the other cloud drives.'

'Do you have those?' Declan asked. 'Can I see them?'

The fight had drained out of Peter, possibly as he realised he'd possibly helped his dead wife's murderer go free, and he nodded, walking over to the cupboard under the staircase, opening it up and pulling out a cardboard shoebox filled with small tapes.

'Here,' he said, slamming it against Declan's chest. 'There's like ten percent of what she did here. That's all I have.'

Declan took the tapes, turned, and walked to the door.

'If Malcolm Gladwell goes free,' he said, 'and if the book he's written is released, you will have destroyed every single good thing about your wife that you ever had. You were having arguments and fights, I know that. And yes, Kendis and me, we did something stupid I wouldn't have done it if I hadn't believed you weren't already separated. Kendis told me at the time you were, it was only later that she told me you were still in discussions.'

He nodded at the picture of Peter and the new woman.

'Be aware, though. If this does happen to come to pass, and you destroy everything about her, I'll make damn sure that woman there knows everything about you.'

'What do you mean?' Peter frowned.

Declan turned.

'When you punched me and told me never to come back to Hurley, I looked into you,' he replied. 'And I know that during the days you weren't around, when we had our moment—'

'Your "moment"? That's an interesting—'

'I know at the time of *that*, you sure as hell weren't at a conference in Hull, Peter,' Declan ignored the interruption. 'I've never mentioned it because it wasn't relevant then, but it is now. I'll make damn sure the woman in the photo knows, because it *was* her, wasn't it? I'll explain to her that when your wife was murdered by Malcolm Gladwell, you were busy shagging *her* in a hotel in Whitstable.'

Peter opened and shut his mouth twice.

'Oh,' Declan said as he opened the door with one hand, carefully holding the box in the other. 'And I'll visit Kendis's grave when I damn well please, because it looks like you haven't been going for a while. We good on that?'

Peter nodded dumbly and Declan walked out of the door into the front garden, staring at Mrs Baldwin, who had already looked up and was frowning.

'I'm the one who slept with Kendis,' he said, 'and then came back as a police officer. Does that help?'

Mrs Baldwin smiled.

'It does. You said you were his cousin. Thank you so much. Oh,' she noticed the box. 'You're taking some of Kendis's things. That's nice. You should remember her. She was a nice lady.'

'She was indeed,' Declan forced a smile as he walked away down the path. 'The nicest of ladies.'

He paused as his phone rang. Looking down at it, he frowned. It was Bullman.

'Ma'am?' he answered.

'Just a quick one,' Bullman sounded stressed. 'I've just seen Karl Schnitter's will. A day before he died, he arranged for a solicitor to alter his last will and testament. He did indeed leave everything to you.'

'Why?' Declan frowned.

'We're contacting the solicitor right now to ask the same question,' Bullman replied. 'I suggest you leave it with me, and I'll do what I can. You keep on with what you're currently doing and make sure this whole thing doesn't matter.'

Declan sighed, disconnecting the call. So not only did he have a book coming out that character assassinated him, once this will came out, he was screwed anyway.

Sighing, he looked at the tapes.

'You'd better give me a bloody miracle, Kendis,' he muttered. 'Just for old times' sake.'

## 16

## THE RICH PR*CK

From the moment Monroe arrived with De'Geer at LCW Holdings in Farringdon, he knew he didn't like Lance Curtis-Warner.

De'Geer had been sullen for the entire journey, and Monroe understood. It was one thing to be told you couldn't be involved in something because of rank or position, but being unable to help your unit because your unit was keeping you *safe*, was something that De'Geer felt was a little over the top.

Monroe didn't care. He wanted to make sure De'Geer's career in the police was a long and illustrious one. They had almost lost him a few weeks earlier when the Red Reaper had captured him; De'Geer had been badly injured during that time, and there had even been a moment when they'd thought he was dead. As it was, he had escaped shortly before PC Cooper had arrived, and claimed credit for his release – something that still irritated him to this day, even if it was technically correct.

But again, Monroe hadn't cared. De'Geer was family, and

there was no way he was going to have him caught up in any shenanigans that happened before he arrived.

In fact, De'Geer had pointed out that *technically* he should have been involved in the meeting because he *had* been involved with Declan at the time, being one of the Maidenhead Police that had hunted him down in Hurley, and had even been one of the officers that investigated Declan's house when Declan himself was hiding in a secret room. Monroe had chuckled at this, impressed with De'Geer's lateral thinking. But in the end, he'd stuck to his guns, pointing out that if De'Geer was allowed back onto the case, then Cooper would be on her own, and he didn't want to cause problems in *that* particular relationship.

They had arrived at LCW Holdings' offices to find Lance Curtis-Warner still trying to avoid the meeting, but aware that he had to take it, or else lose money. In fact, Curtis-Warner had started the meeting by stating quite clearly that he was only taking the meeting *because* Eden Storm had informed him he would lose money if he didn't. So, sitting in Lance's office, opulently set up as if it was some kind of Victorian gentlemen's club, Monroe faced the desk that Lance sat behind.

'We're here to talk about Ronald Tyler and Stuart Laws,' he said.

'Yes, terrible, terrible news,' Lance nodded sadly. 'I heard about Ronald this morning.'

'You did? Who from?' Monroe leant closer.

'His widow,' Lance replied, but then paused, frowning. 'Is an ex-wife a widow, or is she still an ex-wife? Either way, she contacted me to pass me the terrible news, and of course, I'd heard about Stuart's untimely accident when it happened.'

Monroe watched Lance carefully.

'Untimely accident?' he asked.

'Why yes,' Lance gave no outward sign of concern or fear. 'Do you think it was something worse?'

'Did Elizabeth Tyler tell you how her ex-husband died?'

Lance nodded.

'She did,' he replied. 'And I heard on the cabbie grapevine he was found by Alfie Reynolds, too. That must have been a shock.'

'Cabbie grapevine?'

'I lease cabs to a lot of them, so I'm on a fair few WhatsApp groups.'

'Anything that could help the case?'

'No,' Lance replied almost apologetically. 'But if I hear anything, you'll be the first to know.'

'You said Alfie's name as if you knew him,' De'Geer spoke up now.

'In passing. He's the son of Marshall Reynolds, who I've met here and there. Leased him a cab, once. Long while back, though. Offered the same for Alfie when he passes.'

De'Geer wrote this down as Monroe watched the man in front of them. If Curtis-Warner was hiding anything, he was making a bloody good job of telling them everything.

'So you understand it was murder?'

Again, Lance nodded.

'Are you saying that Stuart Laws' accident was murder too?' he asked.

'Possibly,' Monroe replied. 'We're looking into it. It seems concerning how three of your wee group of Knowledge learners are dead.'

At the number, Lance shook his head.

'I think you're over-exaggerating the numbers there,' he said. 'Ronald and Stuart only make two.'

'Yes, but Clifford Stone makes three,' De'Geer spoke now, still sullen, which added to his seven-foot-tall Viking frame would put the fear of God into anybody.

Lance looked genuinely surprised.

'Clifford Stone is dead?' he shook his head. 'No, that can't be. I only had dinner with him on Monday. It was at the Ivy. My treat, of course. Poor lad could never afford it.'

'We were wondering whether you might have any ideas about who'd be doing this?' Monroe asked.

'You don't think I did it, do you?' Lance looked horrified at the thought.

'Well, as you can understand, sir, we're looking at all options,' De'Geer replied. 'We'd like to *think* you're not the murderer, but still, with the fact that of the six people that we know of currently who knew each other back then, three are dead ...'

'Six people?'

'You, Stuart Laws, Ronald Tyler, Sandeep Khan, Clifford Stone, and we believe a woman named Beth Stevens,' Monroe nodded.

'Beth Stevens?' Lance frowned, but then nodded. 'Oh, of course, yes.'

Monroe noticed this slight change in Lance's tone. It sounded more that he was confused who Beth was, than had forgotten her.

'We're trying to work out why somebody would want three people dead,' he replied. 'And trust me when I say at least two of the deaths were connected.'

'I'm assuming you can't tell me anything more about them?' Lance asked. 'Not because of some kind of ghoulish request. It's just perhaps knowing the way they died would help.'

'One was drowned, one was asphyxiated, and one was struck by a car,' Monroe replied coldly. 'In fact, we believe there's every chance that the car that struck Stuart Laws was the same car that you had leased to Ronald Tyler.'

'Are you thinking I'm connected because of my lease agreements?' Lance laughed at this, more in disbelief than humour. 'My dear man, I helped Ronald Tyler buy a car when his wife left him. He was penniless, driving a knackered old car that wouldn't pass its conditions test. Electric's all the rage at the moment, and I gave him the loan to do so. He part-exchanged his old car in to do it. As for Stuart, he wanted to upgrade his game, work for a new level of client. I helped him gain a car that was worthy of such a chauffeur job.'

He shrugged.

'And it wasn't just the money. I wanted somebody that I knew I could call in if I had a guest, or a work associate that I wanted to have driven somewhere. For the last six months, he's been my personal chauffeur half the time, when I have important meetings to get to. Well, he was. I guess I need to find someone else now.'

Monroe watched Lance as he spoke, ignoring the callous comment.

'Clifford?'

'God knows about bloody Clifford!' Lance snapped. 'As I said, I saw him days ago and nobody was trying to kill him then!'

'Sandeep Khan?'

'I invested in his company, sure, but that was decades ago, we sold up five years back,' Lance was getting flustered now, shaking his head. 'No, this is crazy talk. I'm sorry. This isn't happening. This is a joke, right? Am I on some kind of camera show? Please tell me I'm on some kind of camera show.'

'I'm afraid there's no camera show here,' Monroe replied. 'Is there anything you remember from back then?'

Monroe leant back as Lance Curtis-Warner considered the question.

'We sat in a room full of maps and repeated bloody routes, hour after hour. My dad froze my bank account until almost a year after I passed, so I could prove I stuck to something.'

He smiled and winked.

'Well, he froze one of them, he didn't know about the others.'

Monroe gave it a moment, allowing Lance to calm down before continuing.

'What do you know about the phrase "Crooked Was His Cane"?' he asked.

'I've never heard the bloody song,' Lance snapped back.

At this, however, Monroe looked up from his notebook, his eyebrow raised.

'I don't recall saying it was a song,' he smiled.

'Well, I mean, I know it's the name of a *song*,' Lance replied, flustered. 'No, I meant I've never heard it. That's what I meant.'

'Right,' Monroe replied soothingly. 'Of course, that's exactly what you meant. So how about you tell me where you heard the name from? Because as far as my sergeant and I know, not many people have heard of it, unless they're really into obscure folk musicians.'

'I think Ron Tyler talked about it once,' Lance shrugged. 'It was written by somebody he knew.'

'Oh, aye, Ronald Tyler knew James Harlow, did he?'

If Lance was aware that he was digging himself a larger hole, he didn't show it, shrugging noncommittally as he looked around the room.

'It's just a bloody song title.'

'Aye, but it's a song title that was left at the bodies of both Clifford Stone and Ronald Tyler, and robo-called to Stuart Laws, leaving a recorded message of the bloody chorus,' Monroe answered. 'You can see why it's important, aye?'

'Look,' Lance said defensively. 'I don't know the song, but I know the song exists. I also know that Ron and James Harlow knew each other because of Beth Stevens.'

'You seemed to not remember much about Beth Stevens a minute ago.'

'I remember enough to know that she was going out with Harlow's brother,' Lance replied curtly.

'Do you remember his name?'

Lance folded his arms as he leant back in his chair, glaring at the two officers facing him.

'Look, I wish I could help on that one, but folk music really isn't my thing. Ron was the person you should have spoken to about that, but obviously, he's not going to be answering any questions soon.'

He thought for a moment.

'Logan,' he said, 'Logan Harlow, that was his name.'

'Logan Harlow,' De'Geer wrote this down, speaking the name out loud. 'And he was James Harlow's brother, and was dating Beth Stevens?'

'Well, they were shagging. Whether or not that meant they were seeing each other, I don't know,' Lance seemed reluctant to answer. 'I didn't pay attention that much.'

'Aye,' Monroe's eyes narrowed. 'You've said. Do you know the last time you spoke to Logan Harlow?'

Lance started to laugh.

'Mate, I never really spoke to Logan Harlow,' he replied. 'As I said, I didn't know the Harlows. I didn't realise the song even existed until years later.'

'And what is the connection of the song with Logan Harlow?'

Lance Curtis-Warner sighed, his shoulders slumping.

'Look, all I can say is what I was told second hand, right?' he said, straightening back up as he spoke. 'He was crippled in an accident a few years earlier. Walked with a cane. It was a specially carved one, looked like it was a piece of wood that had been twisted around.'

'A crooked cane?'

'Yeah, maybe.' Lance nodded. 'All I know is that there was a story that came out about a man who disappeared when he was hit by a bus, and James used it as a kind of way of remembering his brother, in a twisted kind of way.'

Monroe placed his pen on top of his notebook, as he looked back at Lance Curtis-Warner.

'Are you telling me that the victim in the song "Crooked Was His Cane" was in fact Logan Harlow, killed when hit by a bus on a bridge?'

'No,' Lance said, and he had such conviction in his tone that it threw Monroe for a second. 'I can tell you without any doubt that was not what happened.'

'And how would you know that, then?'

'Because Logan Harlow drowned himself in Mortlake, in Surrey,' Lance replied. 'He disappeared after a fight with Beth, and hopped up on every pain-killing drug he had, he overdosed, took a swim, and they found his body in the Thames. There's a coroner's report and everything. You can look it up.'

'Aye, we will, laddie,' Monroe nodded. 'Thank you for your time, I'm sorry it took so much to convince you to talk to us.'

'No, I'm the one that's sorry. I tried to kick this can down the street,' Lance replied. 'Soon as I was done there, I was done with that part of my life, if you know what I mean?'

'Yet you kept several of your so-called friends afloat later in life by giving them loans for cars or assisting them in other ways.'

'Yeah, I gave them loans,' Lance nodded. 'I didn't just give them money, it was a business transaction, from my mid-life crisis in my twenties. How many people do *you* hang out with from that time?'

This was aimed at Monroe rather than De'Geer, and Monroe winced. He didn't speak to anyone from that time. Even Derek Sutton was now gone from his life.

'Oh, one other thing,' Lance added. 'Good luck with finding Beth Stevens.'

'How do you mean?' Monroe asked.

'It's not her real name,' Lance shrugged.

'What, her name's not Beth?'

'No, her surname isn't Stevens,' Lance replied, taking a sip from a mug of coffee on his desk, almost as if clearing his throat to continue. 'You see, the college wasn't a place to take the test, it was just a place to learn the routes. They weren't as diligent with gathering information as other places were. You didn't need to show your driving licence – hell, you didn't even need to be a registered driver to learn at the college. All they wanted was people to give them monthly money and learn the routes.'

He waved to a certificate on the wall. Monroe couldn't read it, but he saw Lance's full name on it.

'My full name is Lancelot Curtis-Warner, but I was there as Lance Curtis, if you checked the books. It was something I wanted to ensure that I had anonymity.'

'So, how do you know that Beth Stevens isn't her real name?' De'Geer asked. 'Did you look into her?'

'I didn't – really, I didn't, at the time,' Lance said, his tone a little more defensive than it was a second earlier. 'It's just, when we were there, early on she was friendly to me, you know, quite flirtatious. I was single and nothing happened but it could have; I could see she was attracted to me. Then one day, about two years after I took the Knowledge, way after I'd moved on, a man came to my door. He gave me his name, explained he'd been hired by my father.'

'A private investigator,' Monroe suggested, and Lance nodded.

'It seemed that even though my father had allowed me to do what I needed to do to prove myself to him, he didn't trust me enough to not completely control my life. He'd heard from somebody that Beth and me had been close, she'd had a baby around this time, and so he'd hired this private investigator to look into her, make sure there wasn't a little baby Lance around to cause inheritance issues. The investigator informed me that on doing this, he had learned that back then Stevens wasn't her surname, wasn't even a maiden name, it was completely fictitious. She'd changed her name on the records because she didn't want her family to know she was taking the Knowledge.'

'So, what was her real name?'

Lance shook his head.

'I never asked,' he replied, seriously. 'I didn't care. I never shagged her so the kid wasn't my brat, and as far as I was concerned, it was either Ronald's, Clifford's, Stuart's or

Logan's – before he thought he was a fish. I had no idea who she'd been sleeping with. Also, if she was going to run around with a fake name, I was the last person who could really have a go at her about it, you know? So, I told the private investigator to get out of my house. I didn't want to know, and I was pretty pissed off at Dad as well when I saw him next.'

'Must have been a fun Christmas,' Monroe replied.

Lance chuckled.

'You don't know the half of it,' he said, looking away, deep in thought for a moment.

'I told her once,' he eventually continued, 'at some garden party BBQ bollocks we were all at. By that point, I'd already moved back into finance, and I'd decided this would be my last time seeing everyone. I think Sandeep had also decided it was a loser's game, and was deep into his new life as a tech entrepreneur, and at some point during the afternoon, my curiosity took over and I told Beth that I knew her name wasn't Stevens. I also pointed out I'd never asked what her real name was, and I didn't care why she'd changed it.'

He looked back at Monroe.

'I never brought it up again and shortly after that, she moved on.'

'What do you mean by moved on?'

'I never saw her,' Lance replied.

'And have you seen her since?'

'I'm a millionaire industrialist who does loans for people. She was a woman who wanted to be a cab driver,' Lance's face took on a slightly arrogant, sneering expression. 'If I ever saw her again, it was because she either picked me up in a cab, or she wanted a loan and I don't give loans to people with fake names. Now, if we're done here, I'm very busy.'

Monroe nodded, rising from his chair, passing a card across.

'If you remember anything else, or hear anything on your WhatsApp groups,' he said as he followed De'Geer out of the office.

'If I remember anything else, you'll hear it from my solicitor,' Lance was already scrolling on his tablet, ignoring the two men who'd now left.

———

AS THEY MADE THEIR WAY TO THE ELEVATOR, MONROE LOOKED at De'Geer.

'Curiouser and curiouser,' he muttered, tapping his pen against his chin. 'Three dead bodies, four if you add Harlow's brother, and now we have to find a ghost.'

'So, just a regular day of the week, then, Guv,' De'Geer replied as they entered the carriage. 'And did you see how his demeanour changed? At the start he was all offers to help, but by the end ...'

Monroe smiled.

At least De'Geer wasn't bloody *moping* anymore.

———

# 17

# EAVESDROPPING

'WELL, I MUST ADMIT, DECLAN, YOU'RE NOT EXACTLY THE FIRST person I expected to see right now,' Henry Farrow looked up from his desk, staring at Declan, who was at the door to his office.

'I was passing,' Declan smiled. 'Thought I'd pop in. Need a favour.'

Farrow leant back in his chair, watching Declan carefully. Declan knew that his relationship with Farrow had changed over the last couple of weeks. The last time he'd seen Farrow, he'd been telling him to take Declan's ex-wife – now Farrow's current wife – somewhere safe while the Red Reaper needed to be sorted. He'd also taken Farrow down to the changing rooms of Tottenham North, where, hidden behind a locker had been his backup service revolver.

*The last time Farrow had seen Declan, he'd been loading a Glock 17, possibly to kill a man.*

'Of course you were,' Farrow smiled coldly, disbelieving his line. 'So, what's the favour?'

'I thought it was best to pop in today rather than come

and find you tonight,' Declan said, almost apologetically. 'It's just—'

'I'm glad you came to the office,' Farrow's smile stayed plastered to his lips. It was a nervous one, but there was warmth behind it, nevertheless. 'Bet's not exactly inviting you over at the moment, shall we say?'

'Bet?'

Farrow reddened.

'It's what Liz has asked me to call her now,' he explained. 'She's moving away from the name she used to be known as.'

Declan understood, even if he wasn't happy about this. Elizabeth Walsh had been known as Liz, or Lizzie by Declan for almost twenty years. But in the last few years, Declan had caused her nothing but pain and misery since they'd broken up. First, he'd punched a Catholic priest live on TV, which had her excommunicated from her Catholic reading group. And then over time, she'd repeatedly found herself in the line of danger, simply by being associated with Declan.

Liz Walsh was a constant target. *Bet Farrow,* however, was probably a safer option. Especially with a potential tell-all novel coming out, aimed at sullying the Walsh name.

*Maybe Jess should be strongly urged to take her step-father's surname, too.*

'Well, say hi to her for me,' he said.

Farrow straightened in his chair.

'I hope you don't mind, Declan, but I don't think I'll mention that I've spoken to you,' he said. 'She gets quite angry when she hears your name.'

'I get that.'

'Now, why exactly are you here?'

'I'm looking for an item that I'd left here before leaving,' Declan said.

'Another sodding weapon?'

'No, none of those, I promise. An old Dictaphone that's probably still in a box somewhere, with other stuff I'd forgotten to take.' Declan pulled out one of Kendis's tapes. 'Something that would fit this.'

Farrow frowned as he looked at the tape.

'Should I be asking what this is in connection with?'

'Kendis Taylor, and the last story she worked on.'

'In that case, I *shouldn't* be asking what this is in connection with,' Farrow nodded. 'I've seen a recorder that would fit that. I'll get one of the uniforms to find it.'

'It's okay, I can grab it myself,' Declan said, already aware that he'd overstayed his welcome in the station. 'We're in the middle of a case and I ...'

'Oh, I get it,' Farrow said, and Declan thought he could feel a little irritation in Farrow's voice. 'Always busy, always solving the big case ... no matter what happens.'

'Well, I think that's a bit unfair,' Declan replied.

'Do you?' Farrow asked. 'It's not just Bet who suffered because of their connection to you, is it? I was kidnapped by Luke Snider, attacked, lied to ...'

He took a breath.

'I had to write to the Pope to get permission to marry Bet,' he hissed. 'The bloody *Pope*. And all because of you.'

Declan didn't really have anything to say to this, and simply waited for Farrow to finish. As it was, Farrow stopped himself, shaking his head, and then looked back at Declan, before reaching over to his phone, pressing the intercom.

'Sergeant Byron, are you there?'

'Yes, sir,' a voice spoke down the line.

'Do me a favour. There's a Dictaphone device in lost property.'

'I know the one, sir.'

'Apparently it was ex-DI Walsh's, and he'd like it back. Can you grab it for me?'

'I'll have it at reception for him when he leaves.'

'Thank you.'

Farrow glanced back at Declan.

'Don't take that as a statement that you're not welcome here. You'll always be a part of this unit, even if you decided to leave us for Alexander Monroe,' there was the slightest of smiles at this. 'But I suggest you remember that you're welcome *here*, but not in many other places in Tottenham. And that includes my house.'

He rose to face Declan.

'You will always be a part of Bet's life, as you will always be a part of mine, in a way, purely because of our connection to Jess. But that's it.'

Declan understood and nodded. The recent issues with the Red Reaper had been the last in a long line of problems Declan had found himself with, all landing on DCI Farrow's lap. If the tables had been turned, Declan would have been saying the same thing.

'Thank you for your assistance, Henry,' he said. 'I appreciate it.'

And with the message well and truly given to him, Declan left DCI Farrow's office, possibly for the last time.

---

BYRON WAS AS GOOD AS HIS WORD, AND AS DECLAN ARRIVED AT reception ready to go, the sergeant had the Dictaphone in hand.

'Here you go, sir,' he said, passing it over. 'It's good to see you again.'

Declan smiled but said nothing in response, taking the tape recorder, confirming that it fit Kendis's tape, and then left the unit. He'd find some batteries on the way back; there was a chance the Dictaphone wouldn't be working at the moment. But at least now he could listen to Kendis's tapes. He was going to hear Kendis for the first time in a couple of years; the voice of a dead woman in his ears.

Declan shook his head; Liz changing her name, Kendis returning from the dead, and Tessa Martinez warning him off.

How many other ex-lovers or crushes were going to appear before this case was over?

———

THERE HAD BEEN A PHONE MESSAGE WAITING WHEN DECLAN had arrived back at the office. Fabian Kleid, the solicitor who'd worked for Johnny Lucas since the nineties, and who Declan had run into on several occasions over the last couple of years had called, asking him to call back as soon as he received it.

'Mister Kleid?' Declan said as he returned the call.

'DCI Walsh? Thanks for coming back to me,' Kleid replied down the line. 'As you know, I'm on exclusive retainer to Jonathan Lucas.'

'Has Johnny done something?'

'No, no, Mister Lucas, currently our mutual MP friend, has heard of your situation.'

'How?'

'My dear man, he literally walks through the same Westminster halls,' Kleid replied, almost laughing at this. 'And unable to do anything about either the book or this will you have over your head, he has asked me to help you in any way, on his tab.'

'Really? I ...'

'You don't need to say anything right now,' Kleid continued. 'I have already purloined myself a copy of the manuscript, and when you called, I was already working my way through it. Have you read it?'

'Skimmed.'

'Probably the best way,' Kleid replied. 'It's abysmal. Which is also good, as it shows Mister Gladwell probably wasn't expecting it to get to the release stage, forgoing the editing stage for expedited publishing, in order to get people to help free him.'

'So, what's the next step, then?'

'Well, I think I shall speak to His Majesty's Government, and arrange for an evening chat with Mister Gladwell.'

'You think he'd take that?'

'My dear man, someone turning up for a face-to-face out of the blue is the only thing he's expecting to take,' Kleid laughed. 'I'll call you back when I have times.'

With that, the call was ended, and Declan stared in confusion at the phone. He felt he'd been caught in a tornado and turned around inside, such was the speed of the shift in direction.

However, it also meant he finally felt he could see light at the end of the tunnel.

Of course, they still had the other case to solve, first. And that looked to be a lot harder.

'WELL, BLOODY HELL, WHAT DO YOU KNOW?' RAY HOLDSWORTH laughed as the long-absent figure of Lance Curtis-Warner walked into the classroom. 'The prodigal son returns. Come to start another fight with your dad about the Knowledge? Maybe remember how to drive a cab?'

Lance, who smiled back at Ray weakly, held up a hand.

'Not here to start any fights, Ray,' he said. 'I'm guessing you heard about Ronnie.'

'Yes, and the others,' Ray nodded. 'Terrible thing. Police were by earlier. Anything to do with you?'

'I've barely seen them since we parted,' Lance replied, nodding to a couple of the students who looked up, confused about what was happening. 'Keep going. Route seventy-four's a bastard, but you'll work it out.'

'Lance is a bit of an enigma,' Ray told them as he motioned for Lance to walk past the students and over to his office. 'Took the Knowledge, never drove a cab.'

'I'm not the only one to do it,' Lance added. 'You know that as well as I do.'

He looked around the room.

'Hasn't really changed since I was here,' he observed. 'You've not even got any computers.'

'Don't need them,' Ray replied. 'All I need is A-Zs and a marker.'

Lance bowed slightly, acknowledging the comment.

'So, come on then, why are you really here today?' Ray asked. 'Because let's be serious, you're not here for old times. And I can't see you suddenly wanting to come back here after hearing of the loss of some old friends.'

Lance said nothing, instead staring around the classroom.

'Is Marshall Reynolds around?' he asked.

'Marshall?' Ray seemed surprised by this. 'Yes, I can find him for you.'

He called out to the back office.

'Marshall, the rich prick we were talking about has turned up again.'

If Lance was insulted, he kept quiet. After a second, Marshall Reynolds walked out of the office, looking confused.

'Why do we owe this pleasure? You've not bought the building or something, have you?'

'I was hoping to have a quick word,' Lance said quietly.

Ray frowned, but Marshall shrugged.

'Come on in,' he said. 'I've got nothing to fear from you. You don't own me like you own the others.'

'I don't own anybody,' Lance replied. 'If they've taken lease agreements with me, that's nothing personal, that's purely business.'

'Whatever.' Marshall waved to a door to the side. 'Come on, before I change my mind.'

Lance and Marshall walked through the door and out into an alleyway at the back of the building. It was a fire escape that led to a metal balcony, with steps going down to the ground on the right. Marshall Reynolds turned to face Lance and then gasped as Lance Curtis-Warner grabbed him by the throat, moving quickly forwards, pushing him against the edge of the railings of the balcony.

'You bloody *fool*,' Lance snapped. 'What the hell were you thinking?'

Marshall struggled, pushing Lance aside.

'Don't you dare throw this on me,' he said.

'Bloody Alfie's the one who found the body?' Lance replied. 'What the hell were you doing sending him there?'

'He was looking for trap streets—'

'Don't give me that shit, Marshall! We've never used trap streets!'

'He still needs them for the Knowledge.' Marshall was scared now, shaking his hands, as if to ward Lance off. 'I thought it was a good idea.'

'Who told you about Bartlett Place?' Lance growled softly. 'Why did you send him there Thursday, at six in the morning?'

Marshall frowned at this, narrowing his eyes in suspicion as he stared at Curtis-Warner.

'Wait, what do you *think* was going on?' he asked. 'Look, I was at a cab rank a few days back. Ron Tyler was talking to Cliff Stone. While they were talking, I heard them mention Bartlett Place – you know, the real Broadway Walk. I thought it would be a good trap street for Alfie to go and find. I didn't realise that Ron was going to be found dead there.'

'Bullshit. That would involve you doing something altruistic, and we know you don't do that. What did he see?'

'A bloody dead body, that's what he saw there!' Marshall pushed Lance away now, the anger building as he replied. 'I didn't send him to see that! I wanted to test the lad! It's bad enough I have to teach these buggers during the day, but now I do homework for my nephew. I send him places. Try to make it interesting. I didn't know Ron was gonna be there that time in the morning, just that they mentioned it.'

'Why were they mentioning it?'

'Because they were talking about Bartlett Place!' Marshall shouted. 'Ron was meeting someone there. An investor, I think, because he was talking about getting what was owed to him!'

'In Gainsborough House?'

'What's that?'

'What was once *bloody Bartlett Place!*' Lance almost shouted at Marshall, holding his voice back. 'The only reason it's been bloody mentioned in twenty years!'

Lance went to continue but now paused, as the comment Marshall had made seemed to confuse him.

'Wait,' he said. 'Alfie was genuinely there by accident?'

'Well, yes,' Marshall frowned. 'Ron owed you money, right? Was he looking to buy you out? What's at Bartlett Place?'

Lance looked away, then glanced back.

'So, you weren't anything to do with the call that was made to Stuart Laws, the one that played the music as a voicemail?'

'Why would I have done that?' Marshall responded, his expression a mix of confusion and annoyance.

Lance shook his head.

'Don't tell me you weren't there that night, at the company your nephew works for. I saw the logs.'

Marshall's eyes narrowed at this.

'Wait, how did you see the logs of Alfie's company?' he challenged.

'Because I own the bloody company,' Lance said. 'Remember? I got him the sodding job.'

'I thought it was through a mate of yours?'

'Who runs a company I own, yes,' Lance growled. 'So yeah, I know what you did, but what I don't know is who paid you to do it. I think your nephew and I need to have a chat.'

'My nephew's not connected to any of the shit that you guys did,' Marshall folded his arms. 'Sure, I visited him at work. But I did nothing. And neither did he.'

At this, Lance laughed.

'No,' he said. 'He's probably just the tool that someone used.'

He leant closer once more, pushing Marshall back against the balcony railing again.

'But if I find out that you used *my* company to get a message out to Stuart Laws after he died, we're going to have a problem. You see, to hack the robo-caller needs three things. One, code. And your nephew, bless him, he might be a potential cabbie, but he ain't a coder.'

'And the second?'

'Someone on site to place the code in manually. You and Alfie were both in the office that night, weren't you?'

'I was picking him up from work,' Marshall protested. 'We were going to do a late night run or two.'

He shivered a little as he continued.

'And what's the third?'

Lance smiled; it was a dark, humourless one.

'Third, is you need to have balls of steel, because you're actively going against me,' he said. 'And when you go for the king, you'd better not miss.'

He pulled away.

'Start thinking hard and work out if you remember who paid you to stick that sodding song on a robo-caller, Marshall, because I know it was you, no matter what you say. And try to recall anything else from the conversation you overheard. I want to know who Ronnie believed he was meeting that morning.'

'And then what, tell the police?'

'Christ, no,' Lance snarled. 'Whoever met him likely killed him. And I want to have a chat with them, too.'

# 18

## APP BOY

SANDEEP KHAN WAS SLIM, DARK-HAIRED, GREYING AT THE temples, with a hawkish nose. He wore a fleece sweatshirt with a zip-front piece over jeans, and what looked to be very expensive Nike trainers. He looked wealthy, even though he didn't really show it, and even his watch, a simple-looking smartwatch on his wrist, didn't really scream out that he had money of any kind. He looked like a well-off man, middle-class and entrepreneurial in his business.

He was also walking on a treadmill under a standing desk when Declan arrived in his office.

'I hope you don't mind,' he shouted over the noise of the treadmill. 'I've got to get my steps in.'

'That's fine,' Declan replied. 'I can shout louder as I ask the questions, but others might hear.'

'Oh, don't worry about them,' Sandeep replied, nodding out of the glass window. 'They can't hear much of what happens in here. We're soundproof because we used to do our podcasts over in the corner.'

Declan glanced to the side where, between slatted wood and screens, there were audio dampening foam squares all along the wall.

'Used to?'

'Yeah, we've outgrown the place, so we've upgraded to a new space purely for them,' Sandeep continued, his steps rhythmically hammering as he talked. 'Great deal, too. We do three podcasts every week, there's one about cars and racing, one about wellness and fulfilment, and one about innovations in technology. This way we can film them, start building our YouTube channels.'

'And are you on these podcasts?'

'Christ no,' Sandeep pressed a button, and the treadmill paused for a minute. He turned to Declan and grinned. 'I'm the hand behind the curtain. I'm the Wizard of Oz. They're my flying monkeys.'

Once more, he nodded with his head, gesturing out of the window to his office, before pressing a button and walking again.

'How long have you got left?' Declan asked.

'How do you mean, steps?' Sandeep glanced down at his watch, a Garmin, which seemed to have some kind of running tally on it. 'I'll be finished in an hour, I'm twelve thousand steps short.'

'Twelve thousand steps short?' Declan shook his head. 'I don't think I've walked twelve thousand steps in a day for a long time.'

'I've had to up it,' Sandeep explained. 'I'm in a competition with another entrepreneur. We've said that we can both do twenty-five thousand steps a day for a full month, sharing it on Strava so we can't cheat.'

'And how well are you doing?'

'It's averaged out, but we're in the last days of August and I'm behind. I'll get there in the end. But you're not here to ask me about steps, are you, Detective Chief Inspector? You want to know about the deaths.'

'So you've heard about them, then?'

Sandeep didn't look back, still staring at his screen on his standing desk as he marched to his rhythm of what looked to be three miles an hour.

'I heard about Stuart Laws,' he said over the noise of the treadmill. 'Real shame, that.'

'You knew him well?'

Sandeep nodded.

'As much as one can do with cabbies,' he replied. 'Stuart went alone a while back, more higher-end clients. I used him myself a couple of times.'

'Do you remember the last time you used him?'

Sandeep carried on walking as he spoke.

'About six weeks back, when we closed the deal on the new studio,' he said. 'I needed to get to City Airport after a meeting in London. He took me.'

He chuckled.

'Glad he did, too. I left my messenger bag in the car. He dropped me a message to let me know, I was able to pick it up before I flew. If I'd taken someone less known, or used something like Uber, they probably wouldn't have done that, probably stolen the bloody thing.'

'And Ronald Tyler?'

'He was announced on the news last night.'

Declan wrote this down.

'So you haven't heard about Clifford Stone, then?'

'Clifford?' At the name, Sandeep stumbled on the treadmill as he half turned to look at Declan, half paused while
walking. Gathering his stability once more, he pressed a
button, pausing the treadmill again.

This time, he stepped off it.

'Probably better if I don't do this while we're talking,' he
said. 'I hadn't heard about Clifford. How did he die?'

'He drowned.'

'Shit. Accident?'

'Well, he was strapped to his driving seat when it
happened, so probably not.'

Declan hadn't meant to state the murder. But there was a
feeling, even though Sandeep had asked the question, that he
already knew. There was a common rule that Declan had always
adhered to, where when somebody heard of the death of a friend
or colleague, the first question they would often ask was how the
death happened. It was a morbid curiosity that all humans had.
If somebody asked, they likely and subconsciously wanted to
know because they had this curiosity. But if they *didn't* ask when
hearing a friend had passed, sometimes this could mean that
they already knew, or more importantly, had been involved.

So many people over the years had been convicted purely
because they'd answered the question wrong.

But there was something in Sandeep's eyes showing he
hadn't been that surprised about the manner of Clifford
Stone's passing. Because of this, Declan decided to try something. As Sandeep now walked to a second desk, a chrome
and glass-topped simplistic one with a laptop, a monitor, and
some small desktop items to the side, Declan said, 'You don't
seem that surprised by this.'

He paused, watching Sandeep's reaction.

'I mean, you seemed very concerned when you heard Clifford had passed, but I don't know ...'

He let the sentence trail off, hoping Sandeep would fill in the blanks.

Sandeep did.

'I mean, it sounded very much like what happened to Ronald,' Sandeep replied. 'I don't know, maybe that was why I ...'

He opened and shut his mouth twice, as if his brain had told his voice to shut up. Then he narrowed his eyes, as a thought came to mind.

'Did he have the words in his mouth?' he asked. 'Like Tyler did?'

'"Crooked Was His Cane."' Declan nodded. 'How did you know that? Nobody said that to the press.'

'I asked around the moment I heard the news, and I have very good people who work for me.'

'Does that phrase mean anything to you?'

Sandeep was now sitting at his desk, leaning back in what looked to be some kind of ergonomic gaming chair that even Billy would be jealous of. He slowly nodded.

'Logan Harlow,' he replied. 'You've heard the name?'

Declan shook his head.

'He was the brother of James Harlow, who wrote the song, and the boyfriend of a friend,' Sandeep continued. 'And before he died, he was an investor.'

Declan went to reply, but then frowned as the statement sank in.

'Was this in your Oi Taxi app?'

Sandeep nodded.

'I thought you'd known that,' he frowned. 'We were always

transparent during the funding period. His name is in the records.'

'We're still very early in our investigation,' Declan replied. 'But I was under the assumption that Logan was a glorified backpacker. Just travelled around. Didn't really stay in any jobs.'

'Oh, he was definitely a backpacker. Or whatever you want to call it,' Sandeep laughed. 'But he didn't need to work back then; the guy was minted.'

'Family money?'

'Oh Christ, no, he wasn't like Lance. No, he had an accident. He worked for a toothpaste company in their warehouse; there was an accident, a pallet driver screwed up something and he did his leg in. Walked with a limp from then on, constantly in pain. Used to have a little pharmacy's worth of painkillers in his jacket,' Sandeep explained. 'But there was a payout. Seven figures. Or at least damn close to it. It meant he didn't need to work for a while.'

'The toothpaste company, was it *Curtis & Warner?*' Declan asked. 'The one Lance is the heir to?'

Sandeep grinned.

'You don't sound surprised,' he replied. 'Anyway, before the payout, when he was a teenager, he decided to take a few years off and just travel around. After he gained the payout though, Logan settled down, bought a place, put down roots.'

'So how was he picked to be an investor? Before he died, that is?'

'He offered to place half a million into my app,' Sandeep replied. 'He was one of several investors I had, Lance Curtis-Warner being one of them. I think Beth had suggested it to him. When he ... was found ... well, you know ... the contract was null and void.'

Declan had listened to Sandeep talking as he noted this down. But when he'd stated the words "was found", there had been a momentary pause, before and after. Almost as if he'd meant to say something else, but had changed his mind halfway through.

'But you don't believe Logan Harlow's death was an accident, do you?' Declan said, looking back up. 'It's written all over your face, Mister Khan. How about you tell me what you really believe?'

'I *have* told you.' Sandeep straightened now, and his jawline set. But Declan knew that whatever nervousness he had was now being pushed down by bravado and this new mask.

'Okay,' Declan replied. 'Let's go back to this. You had half a million being placed into your business by Logan Harlow. That's a lot of money. What happened after the money disappeared?'

Sandeep paused for a moment and then shrugged.

'We were in trouble,' he admitted. 'We'd expected to get close to a million in funding and suddenly half of it was gone. We were already in development stages. And the last thing I wanted to do was go back to driving a bloody cab.'

He looked around his office as if searching for something that could inspire him to continue.

'As it was, I needn't have worried,' he continued. 'Lance offered to double his investment. His input went from a quarter of a million to half a million, which only gave us a quarter of a million shortfall, and actually, it was Logan's brother who helped.'

'James Harlow, the folk singer?'

'When Logan passed away, his next of kin was his brother,' Sandeep nodded. 'James was pretty much the only family he had. Much as it was.'

'How do you mean, much as it was?'

Sandeep shifted uncomfortably in his chair.

'I mean, they hated each other,' he explained. 'Logan was always the golden child. The younger brother got away with a lot more, all that self-pitying bullshit. James at this point was mid to late twenties. Logan was twenty-one, maybe twenty-two. Had dropped out after his GCSEs to go backpacking around the world. Never really concentrated on one thing from one day to the next. If he were alive now, he'd probably be diagnosed with ADHD, but back then he was just somebody who could never settle down.'

'Surely James, being a performer, would have accepted that,' Declan frowned. 'Sounds like they had a similar mindset.'

'Yes and no,' Sandeep shook his head, giving the impression it was more no than yes. 'You see, although James was a folk musician, he was a *failed* folk musician. He still had to work in a bar to make ends meet. Half the time the folk songs he wrote were performed in the same pub. He wasn't exactly a success on the circuit back then. And he resented the freedom that Logan had. James had rent that he could just about pay, a job he hated, and a career he wanted but was just out of reach. Logan couldn't give a damn. He was the ultimate free spirit.'

'Is that when he gained the nickname?'

'Bindlesticks? That was after the accident,' Sandeep continued. 'He was working for Curtis & Warner while travelling the States, in one of their warehouses. Wasn't really working that much, but it paid what he needed. Anyway, as I said, he was messing about one day in the loading dock. A pallet toppled, took out his leg. Bad accident.'

'Was he at fault, or was the company?' Declan wrote this down.

'Well, that's where the court case comes in,' Sandeep mouth-shrugged. 'He could walk, but with the aid of a cane, and only after months of physical therapy. His US lawyers claimed he couldn't work anymore because of the injury, when he did what all people seem to do when they're screwed over by multi-national firms.'

'He took them to court,' Declan finished the sentence.

Sandeep grinned.

'He took them to court,' he said. 'Proved the safety levels they had in the US plant were substandard. Expressed outrage at what had happened. Got a few people complaining on his behalf. In the end, he gained a rather nice settlement. Million bucks and costs paid.'

Declan nodded, understanding now.

'Enough to give you a sizeable investment,' he said. 'Especially if you weren't that fussed about money.'

'Yeah, but that wasn't what pissed off James,' Sandeep replied. 'Here was Logan screwing around, doing whatever he wanted to do, while James busts his arse every day. Logan does sod all, messes around at work, and the next thing is he comes home and he's got almost a million pounds in his pocket. James was spitting bullets.'

Sandeep looked as if he was considering not continuing, but seemed to make a quiet decision to ignore that option.

'He didn't care that Logan was permanently in pain, constantly popping painkillers,' he explained, his voice going colder, almost with anger now. 'You know those painkillers you're told if you take too many you can get addicted to? Like in that TV show, "House M.D" with Hugh Laurie, playing a surgeon, that becomes addicted to Vicodin, painkillers, opiates, all that kind of stuff?'

'I know the show,' Declan nodded.

'Well, Logan Harlow made Doctor House look like a rank amateur when it came to knocking back pain pills,' Sandeep shook his head. 'Half the time we saw him, he was spaced out on tramadol and half a dozen others, all mixed together in some mental cocktail. But when he was good, he was good, and when he was bad, he was *bad*. Beth was good for him.'

'Beth Stevens?'

Sandeep nodded.

'She was trying to get him off the pain meds, convincing him that beta blockers were maybe an idea for a while. Seeing if they could find another way to stop the pain, with maybe acupuncture, or other things. He was genuinely cleaning himself up a bit. And then he learnt she shagged his brother one drunken night, had a wobble, took all his meds, and then threw himself off a bridge.'

He sighed.

'Or he jumped off a boat. Nobody knows. All we know is he was found washed up at Mortlake a couple of days after he went missing. Tides at the time suggested that Hammersmith Bridge would have been the option, and of course, we all know in that bloody song when the man was hit by the bus on it, all that was left was his crooked little cane.'

That he'd used the lyrics exactly alerted Declan, and he placed his hands down, now watching the man in front of him.

'Do you think James Harlow wrote about his brother's death?'

'I think James was confused about it,' Sandeep replied.

'You've got to remember he wasn't happy with his brother. They'd had some quite public fights. When Logan had gained his money, James had gone to him, cap in hand, asked him to invest in his next album; thought that with a hundred grand pumped into it, he could get a recording studio, get a good option, maybe get a recording deal. Logan laughed him out of the room, said his music was trite, boring and not what folk music needed to be, and he was putting the money he had into my app. Was he right? I don't know, I find folk music awful, like nails scratching down a chalkboard. James wanted whatever Logan had that he didn't, so if he couldn't have the money, he went for the girlfriend, just to prove he could.'

He leant back in the chair, rocking back and forth for a moment.

'But then, six months after this massive argument, suddenly James is being given eight times what he wanted, through Logan's will. Within months, he'd built a small studio in Stratford, near where the Olympics turned up seven years later.'

Declan listened carefully. The words sounded correct; the reasoning was there, but there was something off in how Sandeep said it, almost as if it was a rehearsed rote for something that didn't actually happen.

*Did Sandeep know something about Logan Harlow's death, something he held over James to gain the investment he required? Had James Harlow done this to spite Lance Curtis, who most likely would have invested the rest of the money if required?*

'Have you spoken to the others recently?'

Sandeep shook his head.

'The last time I spoke to Lance was when I sold the company. Eight-point-three million we went for. He'd paid half the investment amount and had been a joint partner throughout the entire thing, so he made a few fair million.'

'And James Harlow?'

Sandeep grinned.

'Our poor penniless folk singer?' he said, 'The moment we sold back in 2019, he became a multi-millionaire overnight. Never needed to sing again. In fact, he's just built himself a brand new studio with warehouse space, and become a record label.'

———

# 19

# SONS AND FATHERS

BILLY HAD BEEN GRABBING A COFFEE WHEN THE CALL CAME through from the accountancy firm that'd dealt with Logan Harlow's finances all those years ago.

'DS Fitzwarren? Marion Hornby. We spoke on email?'

'Yes, thanks for coming back to me, but I'm not at my desk right now,' Billy replied, phone to his ear as he used his watch to pay for his flat white. 'So if you can email me whatever you have I'd appreciate it.'

'Of course,' the woman's voice came down the line. 'Although there's not much to send if I'm being honest. After Mister Harlow gained his settlement, and you have to understand here I'm reading notes from before my time, he only really made one large withdrawal from the funds.'

'Yeah, we know about that,' Billy replied, quietly annoyed. He'd been hoping for some kind of smoking gun. 'But we'd still appreciate everything, if only for our records, including the investment.'

'Investment?' Marion sounded confused down the line.

'Yes, the one in Oi Taxi, the one he made the withdrawal

for?' Billy paused; his "Spider-sense" was tingling. 'Or do you have something else?'

'I'm sorry, Mister Fitzwarren, but we have nothing named that.' There was the sound of rustling papers, as Marion Hornby searched the records. 'All we have is the property he bought.'

Billy pursed his lips.

'Please, Marion, send me whatever you have,' he said. 'Because I'll be honest, we didn't even know he'd bought any property.'

'We'll do it as soon as we have everything together, but it might take a few hours.'

'Thank you.' Disconnecting the call, Billy considered the options. Declan had heard from Sandeep that James Harlow had gone to his brother, asking for money to record and distribute an album. *Had Logan instead bought him a studio? What else could he have bought?*

He was halfway to the office when he realised he'd left the flat white on a counter in the coffee shop.

———

'SO GLAD OF YOU TO COME AND VISIT, LANCE,' SANDEEP KHAN said as he strode productively on his treadmill. 'I would stop, but, well, I don't really want to, and you won't be here long enough for it to really matter.'

'I know about your bet,' Lance replied lazily, already sitting on the sofa of Sandeep Khan's plush office. 'And that you can't stop walking for five minutes to talk to me face-to-face shows that you've not changed from the spiteful little prick you were back in 2019.'

'I wasn't a spiteful anything back in 2019,' Sandeep

retorted. 'There was no spite in what I did. The company was haemorrhaging money, our valuation had halved in price, and I knew if we didn't sell up then we'd eventually earn nothing.'

At this, Sandeep Khan pressed pause on his treadmill, turning around and stepping off it as the conveyor belt led him off the back.

'Have you noticed how much it's worth at the moment?' he asked. 'If I were to sell it today, I'd only have made just over what we paid for it in the first place. So if I were being spiteful, sure, I'd be spiteful any day of the week if it meant we'd make the money we made.'

'Don't act like you were a messiah,' Lance grumbled back at him. 'All you had to do was wait for Uber to screw up and lose their London licence, for people to return to our app, and for the money to come in. We might have gone down now, but I saw what we were worth at the start of 2020. The valuation you had ten years ago. It was damn near close to what we would have made then, and you know it. You bottled it because you thought someone was going to take it all away in 2019.'

'I have no idea what you mean,' Sandeep replied calmly, wiping his face with a towel. 'So tell me, is this about the money, or about the fact that you seem to be the only person left?'

Lance lazily waved a hand in Sandeep's direction.

'Is it you?' he asked. 'I know you were involved somehow. The coding required for the robo-hack had to be somebody with your set of skills.'

'I'm a multimillionaire,' Sandeep stated. 'Do you think I would turn up personally to do such a thing? I'd hire someone. I'd hire a room of people. Why would I bother spending time on such a minor job when I could outsource just as quickly?'

'Because it's personal,' Lance smiled, but there was no humour behind it. 'Why did you do it?'

'James asked me.'

'And what's Harlow's game?'

'I genuinely don't know,' Sandeep answered. 'He wanted a robo-call to piss you all off. All your numbers were in the list. I'm guessing you don't bother answering your phone that much.'

'Changed the number about six months back,' Lance replied. 'Probably went to the old one. Harlow doesn't have my new number. That would involve me wanting to talk to the prick.'

'Oh, believe me, I think the feeling's mutual,' Sandeep walked over to a small desk fridge, glass-fronted, holding energy drinks inside. 'Mid-afternoon pick-me-up?'

Lance nodded and Sandeep passed over a small tube of aluminium energy. Lance popped the tab and took a long draught before looking back at Sandeep.

'Look me in the eye and tell me you didn't kill Clifford,' he said.

Sandeep frowned, narrowing his eyes as he looked back at Lance.

'Now, interestingly, that was the question I was going to ask you,' he stated, and there was no humour in it. This was a serious comment made by a serious man. 'You're the obvious candidate, after all. He was an angry man, even more so when you made him your bloody chauffeur. Which was a dick move, by the way.'

'Yeah? I didn't see you complaining when you used his

services,' Lance snapped back. 'But then I didn't expect James to make him shit himself over that bloody album.'

'We all got one,' Sandeep replied. 'But only Stuart was stupid enough to kick off.'

'Stuart was an idiot,' Lance replied. 'He was an idiot then, and he was an idiot when he died. And we both know I wasn't the one that killed him, so don't play your games with me.'

'So, why do you think I killed Clifford?' Sandeep asked.

'Clifford came to see me Monday night,' Lance continued between mouthfuls. 'He was worried. Didn't think Stuart dying was enough to stop this from all coming out. Wanted to take down Harlow, convinced it was him.'

Sandeep held up a hand to pause Lance right there.

'Are you convinced too?'

'Hell no,' Lance laughed. 'I think it's you. After all, you've always been a devious bastard. I just can't work out why you'd shit where you eat.'

He rubbed at the bridge of his nose, stressed.

'Did you hear who found the body?'

'Marshall's nephew, wasn't it?'

'Yes, Marshall sent him there.'

'To kill Ronald?'

'No, but I wonder if he was there to find a body. Apparently, Stone was talking.'

'Marshall told you this, or Clifford on your date night?' Sandeep hid a smile.

'Marshall,' Lance confirmed. 'I saw him today, and he told me he overheard Clifford talking to Ronald the same day that I met him later for dinner. Said Ronald was talking about debts being owed and he was going to sort one out Thursday morning at Bartlett Place. Marshall was curious, knew that his nephew would be riding around at that time in the morning, and so told him to have a look. Wondered if he'd get some juicy gossip, perhaps. Or, he was watching Gainsborough House too.'

'I don't know,' Sandeep frowned. 'Marshall was never part of this. Didn't he owe you money?'

'Paid it off a year ago,' Lance laughed. 'I must admit, it surprised the hell out of me. Turned up with twenty-five grand in fifty-pound notes. Told me he was done, that Harlow covered his debt as a "screw you" to me, and he no longer owed me anything. Paid off the cab, then walked out of the room without saying goodbye. The prick didn't even ask for a receipt. Lucky for him I'm quite honourable ...'

He trailed off.

'Anyway,' he said. 'I came to see if it was you.'

Sandeep said nothing, and the moment drew out.

'And Clifford?' Lance continued. 'Was that you cleaning house, sorting out business?'

'No,' Sandeep replied. 'I've never wanted to be part of your business.'

'You aim for the king, you'd better not miss,' Lance replied coldly. 'Logan took money from my family. I wanted to take money from him. James was the same. And let's be honest, he did pretty well from the deal. Still is.'

'Are you going to go and see him?' Sandeep asked.

'Harlow? I don't even know where he is. Sold his studio, apparently. Needs a bigger dick-measuring location.'

'He's got a gig tonight at Archspace, under the arches at Haggerston,' Sandeep shrugged. 'You should pop by, say hello. Maybe he'll tell you who did the things you think I did. Maybe *he'll* tell you who killed Ronald Tyler, Stuart Laws, and Clifford Stone.'

'Go on, walk your bloody steps,' Lance rose angrily, leaving the office as Sandeep returned to his treadmill with a smile.

He didn't start it immediately, though. His mind was elsewhere.

Stuart Laws, and a messenger bag.

'You bloody idiot,' he muttered to himself as he started his next wave of steps.

———

LANCE SAID NOTHING MORE AS HE WALKED THROUGH THE reception, and it was only once he'd stormed over to the elevator, that he pulled out his phone and dialled a number.

It answered on the third try.

'Cavan,' he said. 'It's Lance Curtis-Warner. We need to speak. It's about you, your real father, and a shit-ton of cash.'

———

# 20

# HOME AUDIO

By the time Declan got back to the office, it was early afternoon. He sequestered himself into one of the interview rooms, headphones on, as he listened to the recordings. It was strange hearing Kendis's voice for the first time in nearly two years. The tapes were exactly as he remembered, straight and to the point. The recorder was turned on at some point before the conversations would start, ignored as Kendis and whoever she was interviewing spoke, likely closer to the iPhone or other digital recorder that she was using at the time. Declan had several hours' worth of recordings to listen to and was hoping he wouldn't need to go through them all, but Kendis had a haphazard style of organisation, made worse because she had likely passed away before organising these properly.

So, Declan decided to work backwards, chronologically, finding the most recent ones and moving his way towards the earlier dates. Nothing he had were from the days leading up to her death; they would have been too new, too recent to have been placed in the storage she used here. In fact, the most recent recording was one with Will Harrison, where Will had informed Kendis that there had been no misadventure with the death the previous day of Donna Baker.

Declan had leant back at this; he hadn't considered the fact that she would have spoken to Baker's aides so soon after that, but still reached for an earlier tape to see if something else would happen.

He was onto the third tape, and the second hour when Anjli walked into the room, seeing him listening.

'Anything?' she asked.

Declan shook his head as Anjli came and sat opposite him. He could tell there was something wrong, but couldn't quite work out what it was.

'Are you okay?' she eventually asked, nodding at the tapes.

Declan gave a smile.

'It's weird,' he replied, 'hearing her talk, knowing she's gone. It's been two years; I hadn't really remembered what her voice sounded like.'

'Was Peter okay with this?'

'I don't think he was that happy,' Declan shrugged. 'But then, what could he do? There wasn't really much of an opportunity he had to get out of giving these to me once I'd started demanding them.'

He leant back in the chair.

'He gave the digital copies to Malcolm Gladwell,' he said. 'Whether it was because he genuinely didn't believe Gladwell killed her, or because he wanted to sully her memory, I don't know.'

He shook his head.

'I should have done more, Anjli. I know this isn't the kind

of thing you want to hear, me saying that the woman I loved back as a teenager—'

Anjli placed a hand on Declan's own.

'I'm aware how much you loved her, Declan,' she said. 'And I know you'd just started getting back together with her, and I can't be jealous of that. This was before we got together. I mean, she was back in your life when you first came to the unit.'

Declan shrugged, remembering the surprise he'd felt when he saw she'd been working with his father while cleaning out his office.

'Still isn't great,' he said.

The tape had been playing in the background, and he paused, one ear still to the headphone, and rewound a section.

'Are you okay?'

Declan pulled the headphones out, glancing back down at the recorder to make sure the volume was up.

'This is the day of Donna's death, as much as I can work out,' he said. 'Kendis has been interviewing her, talking about Rattlestone and her connection. She's been denying it, but Kendis is quite insistent.'

He looked back at Anjli.

'Malcolm Gladwell's just arrived, told Donna he needs to speak to her. Listen.'

The recorder started to play. Malcolm Gladwell's voice echoed through the interview room.

*'If you don't mind, Miss Taylor, I need to speak to Donna Baker alone. Take your digital recorder with you.'*

Kendis's voice then came through.

*'That's fine,'* she said. *'I'll be right outside. I'll see you in a bit.'*

This was obviously said to Donna and there was the

sound of Kendis pushing a chair back and leaving the room. Declan wondered if she had accidentally forgotten to turn the analogue recorder off, or whether this was deliberate; some way of catching more information in the process.

Declan leant closer to the recorder, listening as the voices continued.

'*You shouldn't be talking to her,*' Gladwell repeated. '*She's bad news.*'

'*She's the only one who listens,*' Donna replied, angry. '*I should never have listened to you.*'

'*Now wait a moment, Mrs Baker,*' Gladwell sounded indignant now. '*I never told you to sign your name onto all those companies. I never told you to take the money that your husband was making.*'

'*No, but you made it damn hard for me not to, didn't you?*' Donna snapped back. '*Don't for one second think that I don't know what you did, Malcolm.*'

'*And so what? Talking to the journalist is your confession?*'

There was movement. It sounded like Gladwell was moving closer and his lowered voice confirmed this.

'*I suggest you keep that for a priest,*' he hissed. '*I can give you a few details of some very friendly priests who don't tell the press what they hear.*'

There was a pause. Declan glanced at Anjli.

'He's a real piece of work,' she said. 'We're calling it a night in a minute. Nothing's coming through from forensics before morning, and we need new eyes on this.'

'I'll be there in a minute,' Declan nodded, and Anjli left the interview room as Declan returned to the tape.

On it, Gladwell continued.

'*You don't want something bad to happen. After all, confessions are one thing. Having the priest read your last rites is another.*'

*'Are you threatening me?'* Donna sounded nervous.

*'I don't need to threaten you,'* Gladwell chuckled. *'I've got enough information on you and what you've done to destroy you and your husband. Everything that you've built up, I'll remove in a second.'*

'Whatever Harrison or his little blonde bitch told you is a lie,' a defiant Donna said.

*'Well, you can tell that to the police. I'm sure they'd be very interested to hear about your business actions.'*

There was a pause. And then Gladwell spoke again.

*'Of course, even if the police did believe what you said and didn't press charges, your husband's career would be gone. Over. As quickly as it would take me to say the words "insider dealing".'*

*'What do you want me to do?'*

*'I think you need to make your decision on how important your husband's career is to you.'* There was pacing. Gladwell's voice fading and then returning, as if he was walking around the room. *'For a start, you need to tell that journalist to piss off to where she came from.'*

*'And if I don't?'* a very defiant Donna asked.

*'Don't test me, Mrs Baker.'*

*'If I go down, you go down too, Malcolm,'* Donna replied angrily. *'I know about your safe and I've got a pretty good idea of what the code is. Even if I didn't know, I'm sure the police could find a way of getting in.'*

'If you did that, you would destroy your husband's career.'

'What choice do I have? You're telling me if I don't comply, you'll destroy his career. And if I find a way to stop you, I'll destroy it as well. We've got enough money. He's made millions on the lecture circuit—'

'Your husband wants to be Prime Minister.'

'My husband wants to stay out of prison,' Donna seemed

calmer now, more assured and in control. *'This whole Devington issue brought up a can of worms that's been hanging over his head for years. That can of worms is now gone, however. He survived it quite easily.'*

There was the sound of smashing, and Declan, not expecting this, jumped back. Through the speakers, the sound of an angry pacing Malcolm Gladwell could be heard.

*'Don't talk back to me, you little bitch!'* he snapped, growling at the woman who was in the room with him. *'I made your husband, when he was a shitty little backbencher, in the middle of goddamn nowhere. I kept him next to me when everybody else said he should have gone. I made him the man he is.'*

There was a pause, and his voice lowered, but as he was still beside the microphone, the voice didn't drop, as the tone became more venomous, more vicious.

*'I even knew about the son,'* Gladwell said. *'Did you know about that?'*

*'Even Charles didn't know.'*

*'Oh, don't be so sure.'* Gladwell's voice was mocking. *'If I could find out, he could. If he didn't, it was simply because he couldn't be bothered, it wasn't worth his time, didn't fit in with his plans. Do you still fit in with his plans, Donna? Because the last I heard, you've been losing your rag a lot over his pre-marital relationships.'*

*'What happened before we were married was none of my concern,'* Donna replied, forcing herself to stay calm.

*'You speak the lie so well,'* Gladwell said coldly. *'But we both know it's just a lie. That before you got married, you and your husband were literally strangers, brought together for political reasons.'*

*'It's not true. No—'*

*'Be serious, Donna. You can play the innocent bitch as much as*

*you want, but we all know that you quite happily shut your eyes as much as he did. As long as you got your fancy parties and your Centre Court Wimbledon tickets, you couldn't give a damn what he did.'*

'Shut up. Just shut up.' Donna's voice was rising now, becoming more hysterical.

*'What's the matter, Donna?'* Gladwell was mocking now. *'You're not going to do something bad, are you? Please don't hurt yourself. I don't know what I'd do if you passed away horribly due to some self-inflicted suicide attempt.'*

*'You're sick. You're twisted.'*

*'No, Donna,'* Gladwell laughed. *'I'm not sick or twisted at all. I'm exactly as I always was. Just like I was when you wanted more of me.'*

*'That was a mistake—'*

*'Was it?'* Gladwell's voice lowered again, and Declan found it harder to hear as Gladwell continued through the speaker. *'Because if I remember correctly, you wanted sick and twisted when you threw your clothes off and begged me to take you.'*

*'Shut up.'*

*'Oh, I know. You were drunk. It was a mistake ... but was it? You wanted me. Look at me. Look at your husband. You know he only runs now because I do. He couldn't hold a torch to me, and you know it. Do you lie awake at night thinking about me?'*

Declan could hear sobbing now. Donna Baker was crying.

*'You know the worst thing,'* Gladwell said, suddenly emotionless, his voice serious. *'You claim it was a mistake and you cry about what you did, but for me, it was a half an hour shag that released some stress, nothing more. I don't think of it. I don't think of you. In fact, the emotional existence I have in relation to*

*that night we had is probably the same amount that your husband has every night.'*

He paused.

*'I wonder if he sees her face when he screws you?'*

*'Shut up.'*

*'I wonder if Sarah Hinksman appears in his dreams while you get down on your knees and—'*

*'Shut up!'* There was a second smashing sound. The door then slammed open on the audio, and Kendis Taylor's voice re-entered the conversation.

*'Are you okay, Donna?'*

*'Get the hell out of here,'* Gladwell snapped. *'You have no right—'*

*'And neither do you,'* Kendis replied. *'You really want to do this, Malcolm? Because we can have this conversation right now. On the record.'*

Declan smiled. Kendis wasn't backing down. And interestingly, it sounded like Malcolm Gladwell did, because the next thing he said was calmer, softer.

*'You're right, Kendis. I apologise. I was just stressed, there are things going on that you don't know about, and I apologise. And to you as well, Donna.'*

*'That's fine, Malcolm,'* Donna replied. It almost sounded like she believed him. Declan wondered what Malcolm's game was and then remembered what had happened shortly afterwards. He'd convinced Kendis Taylor he was a whistleblower, and he was probably already planning his future plans at this point, and realised halfway through his tirade that he had to keep this woman on his side.

*'Kendis, I think we should carry on in the other room,'* Donna said quickly. *'Come with me.'*

There was no sound for a while, apart from the crash of a

door as it slammed shut, and then the sound of a phone being used, the tones of numbers being pressed as Malcolm Gladwell made a phone call.

'Frost, it's me,' he said, and Declan had a shiver go down his spine. He couldn't hear the other side of the conversation, but he knew without a doubt that the man that Gladwell was talking to now was Detective Inspector Frost, otherwise known as the man with the rimless glasses. 'We need to remove Baker's wife before she does something stupid.'

There was a pause, probably while he listened to Frost's suggestion.

'I don't care what your excuses are,' he snapped. 'I want her removed. No, an accident, I think.'

And then Gladwell must have had an idea because his voice suddenly became a lot lighter, a lot more relaxed as he continued.

'Actually forget that, I think I know what to do.'

There was a pause, another silent moment where Declan assumed he had finished one call and begun a second, because a moment later, Declan heard Gladwell speak again.

'Doctor Trudeau, it's Gladwell.'

There was a pause as someone on the other end of the phone spoke. It was minimal, barely audible, but it sounded like a woman's voice coming through the smartphone speaker.

'Donna Baker's about to book another meeting with you,' he continued. 'If you haven't heard from her by this afternoon, I suggest you give her a call to prod her. I want her in your office by the end of the day.'

Another break, and then Declan's skin crawled as he heard the last words.

'I want you to do your thing,' Gladwell finished. 'I don't care *what you need to do, what mumbo-jumbo hypnosis it takes, or meditational thinking you use, but by the end of tonight, I want Donna Baker putting a noose around her neck and ending it. Tell her it'll be better if she's gone. Tell her the pain will stop, and her husband would be safer with Donna out of the way. I don't care what you do.'*

He stopped, and Declan could hear the faint voice on the other end getting louder and more agitated.

*'You think I care about your oaths?'* Gladwell laughed. *'If I release what I have on you, you'll be in prison for life. All you're doing here is risking the possibility of losing your licence. I suggest you do what I say, or it'll be bad for you. Almost as bad as it will be for Mister Baker.'*

There were no other sounds. Gladwell obviously finished his phone call, and then left the room, the door shutting behind him.

Declan fast-forwarded through the tape. It was three minutes later when the door opened once again. Someone walked over to the tape recorder, and the recording was stopped. Kendis, grabbing the evidence before she left, most likely.

Declan whistled to himself as he leant back in his chair, staring at the tape recorder. Kendis had gone into the other room with her voice recorder, and so this tape would not have arrived on Malcolm Gladwell's prison desk when Peter sent everything else over. He didn't even know it existed. More importantly, the chances were that Kendis had never had a chance to listen to this, as within a matter of days she was gone. If she had, she wouldn't have trusted Gladwell as much as she did, at the end.

*Damn you, Kendis,* Declan thought to himself. *If you'd only listened to your tape, you might not have gone to the mausoleum that night. You might not have trusted Gladwell, and you might not have died.*

But the fact of the matter was that Gladwell had been involved in Donna Baker's suicide. Although he hadn't been the one that placed the noose around her neck, he was just as active. All Declan had to do now was work out what the hell Doctor Trudeau's role in this was.

Also, who the hell Doctor Trudeau was.

---

BILLY HAD BEEN LOOKING FOR SOMETHING, ANYTHING THAT could help in the case, but the one thing he kept going back to was the video of James Harlow singing his song on YouTube. He'd watched it a dozen times now, each time knowing something was shining out at him, but he couldn't work out what it was.

The song was on again, on silent, as Billy didn't want to piss off the others in the office. De'Geer was talking quietly to Anjli as he worked, and so Billy silently watched the video from 2019 once more, where James was performing in front of a Christmas fire, a small crowd gathered, no more than thirty or forty people—

Billy paused the video as it scanned the audience.

*There.*

He'd known something was up, but now he'd finally seen it. There, sitting in jumper and Christmas cracker crown with the other members of the audience was Ronald Tyler, two teenage boys beside him. But he wasn't smiling. In fact, he looked as if he was about to leap across the room and strangle Harlow. The camera moved quickly from him, and wasn't seen again.

Billy reversed the footage, returning to the audience, freezing the image as he watched it, frame by frame.

'Anjli,' Billy said as he looked around. 'I think you should see this.'

Anjli walked over, leaning past Billy as she stared at the image.

On it, Ronald sat in the audience, a face of thunder.

'That's Tyler, isn't it?' Billy asked. 'I'm not going mad, right?'

'No, you're not,' Anjli said as she tapped the screen. 'And the kid beside him? I saw him yesterday in a photo. That's Cavan Tyler, Ronald's son.'

'What about the other kid?'

Anjli peered closer at the image, and her eyes widened.

'You know, I think that's a young Alfie Reynolds,' she replied. 'The lad who found Ronald Tyler's body.'

She leant back.

'I think we need to chat to both of them,' she said. 'Something doesn't look right, and it's not the chunky jumpers.'

## 21

## PARTY FROCK

Bᴜʟʟᴍᴀɴ ʜᴀᴅ ɴᴇᴠᴇʀ ʙᴇᴇɴ ᴀ ꜰᴀɴ ᴏꜰ ʙʟᴀᴄᴋ-ᴛɪᴇ ᴅɪɴɴᴇʀs, preferring far simpler pub fare than the course after course that the Houses of Parliament provided. It was made even more awkward for her, knowing that she was running a unit that had found out once that the caterers of these events wanted to kill the people that were there; something that concerned her every time she took a bite of the salmon fillet she had on the plate in front of her. However, whether people knew it or not, she was seeing David Bradbury, who was currently the Commander of the City of London Police, one of the highest jobs you could get, and unfortunately a role that required him to appear at such events, in his full City of London Police finery.

*At least I don't have to wear my uniform*, she thought to herself. *I can get away with a pretty dress paid for by the taxpayer.*

Growing up as a working-class copper, Bullman wasn't happy with that part of the deal, but if the taxpayer paid for the pretty dress she was wearing, it meant she didn't have to, and there was a part of her that was quite happy with that.

*God forbid if I ever did become rich, I think I very much would become a let-them-eat-cake kind of person.*

There was a long break between the dessert and the final coffees and petit fours; this was usually when the speeches started.

Charles Baker had stood up and waxed lyrical about the late Queen Elizabeth, talking about the many times that he had met her, and acting almost like they were best friends before she passed. It was short, and mercifully sweet however, and Bullman noted Baker looked uncomfortable, distracted even.

*Understandable, really.*

And then it was the turn of the Irish Taoiseach, Patrick Reilly, to stand up and give a few words. Bullman didn't envy the man, but Reilly was politically tactful and spoke for several minutes without actively giving a compliment while at the same time being incredibly complimentary.

Bullman was impressed. She'd even taken down a few choice phrases to use herself the next time she had to speak about somebody that she didn't like. She was sure that the Taoiseach had liked the Queen, it was simply bad timing he'd turned up to meet the Prime Minister on the day they were having a bit of a memorial bash.

After the speeches, people started to stand and wander around, the "networking" part of the evening, and an opportunity for surreptitious meetings to be started. Bullman had nodded to Bradbury (who knew the reasons why she'd turned up that night), rose from her chair and had walked across the dining room, heading towards Jennifer Farnham-Ewing, who, seeing Bullman approach, had risen from the chair herself, placing her napkin to the side and walking out to intercept the Detective Chief Superintendent.

*Clever girl. Probably doesn't want people to know that she's talking to me.*

'How does it feel to be safely eating a dinner in here?' Jennifer smiled, waving around. 'It's the same room that your police turned into a circus.'

'If I recall correctly, Miss Farnham-Ewing, this is the same room that you barred the police from attending, almost killing our Majesty herself, a Prime Minister, several Ministers, and, well, quite a lot of people, really.'

Jennifer Farnham-Ewing gave a sickly smile back.

'Now we've given the traditional veiled insults,' she said, 'can we speak like grown-ups?'

'Always,' Bullman replied. 'Let's start by you telling me what exactly you're playing at.'

'I'm trying to save a career.'

'That's admirable,' Bullman nodded. 'And whose career are you trying to save exactly?'

'I've already told Detective Chief Inspector Walsh that the Prime Minister—'

'Please, don't give me that crap,' Bullman snapped back, interrupting. 'Can I tell you what I already know?'

Jennifer didn't reply, simply nodding an acceptance, probably smarting from the interruption.

'I've been thinking about your job,' Bullman said. 'Not the job you have. I'm on about the job that you *used* to have. You know, when you used to work for Will Harrison.'

She smiled, allowing their moment to stretch out.

'You remember Will Harrison, right?'

Jennifer replied coldly, 'Of course I remember him.'

'Well, here's the thing that *we* remember.' Bullman took Jennifer lightly by the arm and led her towards one of the side doors, making sure that the conversation was more private. 'We know Will Harrison was working with Malcolm Gladwell. We also know Will Harrison was a sneaky little shit who deserved everything he got. Maybe not being murdered, that was quite harsh, but we both know that it was Malcolm Gladwell who had done it. But here's the thing, when all this was going on, you worked for Will Harrison, didn't you? I recall seeing you hovering in the background when we cornered Laurie Hooper in her Ford Focus.'

Bullman patted Jennifer on the shoulder.

'You would have been the person putting to life all this sneaky shit that he was doing. You would have been the person typing up the memos, making sure the meetings were sorted out, keeping an eye on the phone-call log, while he was working on Laurie Hooper, and taking his shot at Gladwell, all while Gladwell was playing games behind everyone else's backs,' she hissed. 'Everything that happened, there you were, loyally working for him. But when he died, you moved quickly, getting out of the way of any bodies falling, shall we say?'

She leaned closer now they were in a corridor, more alone than they were before.

'Now you've decided to take a shot at siding with us, because you think we can help you, and I'll be honest, we will, because we have to. But know this, if you'd have come to us hands open asking for our assistance—'

'You wouldn't have given it to me,' Jennifer snapped back. 'You guys hate me.'

'You've not exactly endeared yourself to us, that's true,'

Bullman smiled. 'But you forget, the people on the front line, the police, they solve crimes, they don't play the politics game. You have to go higher to do that. Charles Baker is an albatross around our neck, but when he wins, we look good. So it's in our interest to make him win. But there's only a finite amount of times that Baker will win, as well you know. So, when he does inevitably fall, we will need somebody else who would champion us.'

Bullman gave a wide, beatific smile.

'That could be you, Miss Farnham-Ewing, "Baby" of the House. Now, I would really like you to tell me if there's anything else we're missing here, so we can save both our jobs, and yours.'

---

'THANK YOU VERY MUCH. YOU'VE BEEN A WONDERFUL AUDIENCE. Please stay safe on the way home.'

James Harlow held a hand up, waving out from the Archspace stage at his audience of fans. There weren't many in the audience. It was a Friday night, but it was also a folk club evening, and they never really had that many people. If there'd been more than a couple of hundred in the venue, he'd have been impressed. Ticket sales had been down. And he was probably performing at a loss yet again.

Walking through the backstage area, he carried on down a small corridor, jumping four steps down to a slightly lower part of it, and ducked into a small room on the right-hand side where, hastily taped on a piece of A4 paper, was the name:

James Harlow
Performer.

*That's all I am today,* he thought to himself as he walked into the room. *Performer.*

There was no rider, no food waiting for him, no staff, no catering, just a small table with a mirror on it to prepare himself, a stand to hold his guitar, and his bag. There wasn't even a sofa if he brought some friends in, which had annoyed him, strangely. The thought about the lack of seating had come to mind because, as he walked into the room, he saw the man standing at the side, arms folded, waiting.

'Did you see the show?' he asked, not looking at Lance Curtis-Warner, placing his guitar down on the stand and grabbing a bottle of water from the table.

'No, sorry,' Lance replied, amiably, a curved walking stick in his hand as he leaned against the wall. 'I think your music's shit, so I didn't really want to be seen listening to it. I paid someone a small amount of money to let me come to your room. It's amazing how little they accepted. I suppose not being famous or "good at music" in any way helps. Or is it simply the fact that folk music is so undeniably hated by the masses that anyone can get anywhere?'

James ignored the insults. He'd been expecting Lance to appear, just not at the end of a long and tiring performance, and not holding a replica of his brother's cane.

'You like that?' he asked. 'It was waiting for me when I arrived. Box office have no idea who sent it. Had a little note on it, saying "so you don't forget", which I thought was a nice touch. Did you send it?'

Lance shook his head, placing the cane back down.

'No,' he replied. 'And if it wasn't me, I think we both know who likely did. I'm just here so you can tell me what's going on. I know it was you that paid Marshall Reynolds to play your stupid song on robo-calls, and I know you spoke with Sandeep Khan about working out the coding to get it through there.'

James frowned.

'I have no idea what you're talking about, but I'm sure you'll explain whatever tinfoil-hat conspiracy theory you're peddling,' he sneered.

'Don't lie to me, James. I'd like to know why you were sending that song to Stuart the day he died.'

James held a hand up.

'Wait a second,' he replied, shaking his head. 'You don't seriously think that I did this deliberately?'

'This is a joke to you,' Lance growled. 'You genuinely don't care that people are dead.'

'Did you care when you killed my brother?'

'Oh, no. Don't for one second claim to be some kind of virtuous angel on this!' Furious, Lance picked up a mug next to him and hurled it across the dressing room at Harlow, the cup smashing against the wall. 'You hated him! It was your idea in the first place to get him to lose his money!'

'There were a lot of things happening at the time. I was distracted,' James replied, ignoring the smashed mug. 'But I wasn't the one who screwed someone out of property.'

'You didn't complain though, did you?' Lance snapped back. 'Do you know why Stuart Laws was so nervous? Why he was trying to contact Ronald Tyler?'

James shook his head.

'I'm sure you're going to tell me.'

'He'd had a dose of realism,' Lance replied. 'When you

played your stupid games and sent him that album, you gave him a new focus on life. That sodding message made him think you knew everything and were gunning for him.'

'Nice idea, but it's bollocks,' James snapped back. 'Because Stuart told me everything himself. Why would I gun for the man who gave me the information?'

'When?' Lance frowned.

'Shortly after you bought him a shiny car for his silence,' Lance smiled. 'He'd decided he wanted a fresh start, knew you'd stop him. So he brokered a deal through Marshall, scared I'd kick off, I suppose. He turned up, offering information for money.'

'What kind of information and what kind of money?'

'Well, that's the kicker, isn't it?' James replied. 'It was a lot of money, and it was a lot of information. But Stuart, poor stupid Stuart, he'd forgotten how to play the game, forgotten how when you offer information for money, you get the money *before* you give the information. I gave it to Marshall instead, a kind of "finder's fee", as I also realised it'd get him out from under your boot, too.'

'What did Stuart tell you?'

'The truth about what happened that night,' James placed the water bottle down, now turning to face Lance. 'I know exactly what happened to my brother. Did he deserve it? Yes. I've got no love lost there. But he also told me some other things. Did you know that Ronnie Tyler's son *wasn't* Ronnie Tyler's son? That Beth Stevens had confided in Stuart, of all people, the news she was pregnant with Logan's child? He would have been the heir to Logan's estate. Not me. He had a right to contact the courts. Demand a substantial payout, including the property in Gainsborough House. Which would have opened up the inquiry again. Maybe looked at dates, and the impossibility of them.'

James laughed.

'The problem was, I already knew. Poor Stuart, thinking he had the truth about Logan's real son, and there I was, having realised it five years earlier, when I saw the lad and realised he was the spit of my brother at that age.'

He reached across and strummed the neck of his acoustic guitar gently, the discordant notes echoing around the small dressing room.

'I didn't do anything, I knew he was just trying to save his skin. That's why he got an album, just like you did. And Ronald, and Beth, and Sandeep, and Clifford. Every sodding one of you involved in Logan's death. I might have hated him, but he was blood. I'd do everything for blood.'

'But yet you never sent the robo-call?'

'I honestly have no clue what you're talking about.'

Lance watched James.

'You'd do anything for blood,' he repeated. 'That include Cavan?'

'He's Logan's blood, not my blood,' James shrugged. 'He can piss right off.'

'That's where you're wrong,' Lance smiled. 'He is your blood. From that one-night-stand you had purely to piss your brother off. Should have used a condom, buddy.'

'Bullshit.'

Lance pulled out a sheet of paper, tossing it over.

'My dad did a paternity test on Cavan when he was born,' he explained. 'I was told by a private investigator that I wasn't the dad, but neither was Ronald. I assumed it was Logan, but imagine my surprise when I saw it was you.'

James read the sheet, horrified.

'Cavan's my son?' he whispered. He went to speak, but then stopped as he saw Lance had pulled a phone from within his jacket, holding it out.

'You see, this is the problem we have,' Lance walked over to James. 'Your actual son, and what we do about it.'

James stared at the video on Lance's phone. It was Cavan, unconscious, tied to a chair.

'He put up a good fight,' Lance said. 'But in the end, I made him an offer he couldn't refuse. Your life for his. I mean, you never acted like family, so why should he care?'

'You're here to kill me?' James asked nervously, all arrogance now gone.

'God no,' Lance smiled. 'We can't let the old ghosts return, so you're going to help me explain away the more recent murders, because let's face it, it was you, wasn't it? The albums kind of telegraphed it.'

'And how did I do that?'

'Ronald, well, you gassed him. And Clifford, well, he drowned. That was everything that happened to your brother, after all. You were just gaining retribution.'

'And Stuart? Did I hit him with a cab, like he did Logan?'

Lance shook his head.

'No, someone else killed Stuart,' he replied. 'Unfortunately, I'm involved in that, too, so we'll be adding that to your tally though, tie everything off with a neat little bow.'

Lance looked back at the video, now paused on his phone.

'Anyway, let's crack on with this, shall we?' he suggested, picking up the walking stick. 'This really does look like the real thing. Might even be, I suppose. Did you know it was also connected to the attack on your brother, all those years ago?'

'How?' James replied angrily, but didn't continue as, with one swift motion, Lance Curtis-Warner swung the cane viciously at his head, knocking him to the ground.

'Because we did that to him before we stuffed his arse in the boot of a cab,' Lance finished, staring down at the unconscious folk singer.

## 22

---

# A NEW DAY

DECLAN AND ANJLI HAD RIDDEN IN TOGETHER AGAIN THE
following day, and arrived half an hour earlier than usual,
even though it was a Saturday. Nevertheless, they were still
the last two to enter the building, and Monroe had a scowl on
his face, pacing back and forth at the front of the briefing
room as they walked in.

'About bloody time too,' he snapped, nodding for them to
sit in their usual chairs, next to Bullman, who looked more
than a little hungover, and who was leaning back on hers,
watching Declan with some amusement.

'Late for class,' she said. 'The teacher's going to be angry.'

Declan glanced around the briefing room and saw it was
a packed house. Apart from Bullman and Monroe, Doctor
Marcos and De'Geer were sitting at the back, Cooper next to
them, and Billy was at his desk, connecting the laptop to the
screen.

'Did you all have to wait for us?' he asked.

'No, my husband's just being a miserable git,' Doctor

Marcos smiled. 'Well, now everybody's here, darling, why don't you start?'

Monroe paused, glared down at his wife, and then, almost as if a button had been switched, his anger dissipated and he simply seemed to deflate.

'I'm annoyed,' he said. 'I spent ages getting this unit up to speed. They even came in and fixed the walls and gave us more feet on the ground, and ...'

He sighed.

'Anyway,' he shook his head. 'We'll come to that in a minute. What do we have that's different from what we had yesterday?'

'Logan Harlow,' Declan said, looking around the room. 'Apparently, he's not the travelling hobo we thought he was.'

'Aye,' Monroe nodded. 'De'Geer and I discovered the same thing.'

He nodded at the Viking at the back.

'Would you care to inform us what you found out?'

'Yes, sir,' De'Geer stood now. 'It seems Logan disappeared almost twenty years ago, but then was found a couple of days later, washed up at the Thames at Mortlake. Witnesses claimed he'd last been seen in North London, near Islington, and he'd been depressed and in pain at the time, because of a leg injury that was constantly painful.'

'I don't know about you, but I see foul play, even if the coroner at the time said it was likely to be an accident or suicide,' Monroe muttered.

'There was definitely something going on,' Doctor Marcos said, standing up. 'I checked the coroner's reports, and also examined the notes from the autopsy that was done on Logan Harlow. He definitely overdosed on pain meds and drowned. The Thames' water was in his lungs. But what was interesting is there was also a large amount of carbon monoxide poisoning. Now, last I saw, the Thames wasn't filled with carbon monoxide, which meant that he was either fed a packet of tramadol, almost murdered in the same way that Ron Tyler was and *then* drowned, or something else was going on.'

'What could it mean?'

Doctor Marcos shrugged.

'Honestly, the chances are he was in a smoky environment immediately before he overdosed and drowned,' she said. 'Carbon monoxide is quite specific. Maybe he was in a garage or somewhere else, we don't know yet, and we possibly never will, because as of this point, it's a twenty-year cold case with a half-arsed autopsy.'

'So we don't think it was suicide then,' Declan nodded. 'What happened to the money after he passed?'

'It would have gone to his next of kin,' Billy said, looking back from his laptop. 'He didn't have a wife or children. It would have, therefore, probably gone to his brother. I'm waiting for paperwork from the accountants who dealt with him, but they're a little slow, mainly as it's all paper rather than digital files.'

He shuddered, likely at the thought of a non-digital workplace.

'So, James Harlow would have made enough to record his song,' Declan said. 'That's convenient, but is it a reason for murder?'

'You said Sandeep Khan mentioned him sleeping with Beth Stevens,' Anjli replied. 'And we all know stupider things have happened for love. Do you think they were having an affair, or was this more of a one-sided relationship?'

'Sandeep gave the impression it was a drunken mistake,'

Declan said. 'We should ask Beth Stevens when we finally meet her. Billy?'

'Still no luck finding anyone of that name,' Billy grumbled.

'Okay. Next?' Monroe moved things on as Billy tapped on his laptop.

'We have CCTV from King's Cross, the night Clifford Stone died,' he explained as he pulled up a grainy black and white video. 'It's quite zoomed in, and I won't be taking questions on why I can't just upscale it like they do in the movies. But ANPR shows this is Clifford Stone's cab, and he's been flagged down on the Caledonian Road.'

They watched as on the screen a hooded figure ran over and spoke through the driver's window for a moment.

'The rain hasn't started yet, but he's keeping the hood up,' Doctor Marcos muttered as she watched. 'I say "he" as the skeletal structure looks like a match for a male, but I'd need better imagery. Can you upscale it, Billy?'

Billy ignored Doctor Monroe's jibe as Anjli leant closer.

'He's wearing a rucksack,' she commented. 'One large enough for ratchets and a snorkel mask.'

'Aye, and probably enough for a two litre bottle of water in it, too,' Monroe muttered. 'See if you can find this man on any other cameras, Billy, preferably with a face to show. And is that—'

'Yeah,' Billy nodded as he paused another image, this time showing something slim and dark in the passenger's hand. 'He has a walking cane with him. I can't get a better view, but it feels off, considering the whole hoodie and rucksack look.'

There was a groan to Declan's side, and he saw Bullman holding her head.

'Anyone got any painkillers?' she asked, looking around the room. 'I think I had too many shandies at last night's event to commemorate Queen Elizabeth the Second.'

She looked at Declan with a smile.

'I think you were missed off the list due to what happened the last time you turned up to a state banquet with her there.'

'Jennifer mentioned it when we met,' Declan nodded. 'Even made a comment on how this time she didn't even need to bar me, as I'd done it to myself with the book and Schnitter's will.'

'That and the fact everyone hates us right now,' Monroe muttered.

Declan went to add to this, but then paused.

'Lilibet,' he said.

'Lilibet?' Monroe frowned. 'Are you having a stroke?'

'Lilibet was the nickname that Queen Elizabeth's family gave her,' Declan said. 'Elizabeth. Lilibet. It was Lily and Bet, together.'

'I don't really know where you're going with this,' Monroe said. 'Should we all wait while you work it out, or shall we just come back later?'

Declan had risen, however, and was already pacing.

'I saw Henry Farrow yesterday,' he said. 'When I picked up the tape recorder. He said Bet didn't want to see me anymore.'

'Bet being?' Monroe looked around the room. 'Am I missing something here?'

'Bet is Lizzie,' Declan replied. 'Apparently both "Liz" and "Lizzie" are what I used to call her, and since we're no longer talking at the moment, she wanted to not be reminded of it. She had a chat with her new husband, and now he calls her Bet.'

'Because Elizabeth has Lizzie and Beth in it,' Anjli said,

now understanding where Declan was going. 'Are you thinking that Lizzie Tyler is actually *Beth* Tyler?'

'Billy's literally just said we've not been able to find Beth Stevens,' Declan said. 'And Lance did say to you it wasn't her real name. Do we have Lizzie Tyler's maiden name?'

'Hang on, I'll have it here,' Billy started typing. After a second, he sat back, staring at the screen, then tapped a button to push it onto the plasma screen behind Monroe.

'Elizabeth Stefanos,' Declan said, reading the screen. 'Lizzie, for short.'

'Beth Stevens, to people she doesn't want to know her true name,' Monroe added. 'Bloody hell, the sixth member of the cabbie club was Ronald Tyler's sodding wife.'

'And the woman who was dating Logan Harlow before he died,' Declan said.

Anjli slammed her fist against the desk in impotent fury.

'It was right there, all the bloody time,' she said, reading from her notebook. 'She even said "Not one of them would know Barbican to Mile End, or St Martin's Lane to Fulham Broadway without a bloody app" when we saw her.'

She looked at Billy, who, in some psychic way knew what she wanted, and typed on the laptop keyboard.

'Barbican to Mile End is run twelve,' he replied. 'And St Martin's Lane to Fulham Broadway is run a hundred and eighty-six.'

As Anjli glowered at everyone in the room, there was a buzz outside the briefing room as one phone in the office rang, halting her flow. Cooper rose quickly, walking outside and answering. The momentary pause was enough for Monroe to pace back and forth a few times, muttering to himself.

'We need to bring her in,' he said. 'Find out why she's bloody playing with us—'

He stopped as Cooper walked back to the doorway.

'That was front desk,' she said. 'Marshall Reynolds is downstairs.'

'The uncle of the kid who found the body?' Monroe frowned. 'Why's he turning up this time in the morning?'

'No idea, guv,' Cooper replied. 'Shall I put him in Interview Room One?'

'Make it Two,' Declan said. 'I still have a box of tapes in one.'

He looked at Anjli, also frowning.

'Did he give you any indication he'd be turning up when you spoke?'

Anjli shook her head.

'I didn't even know he'd be there when I went to the college,' she said. 'You want me in the room?'

'No,' Monroe shook his head. 'We still have more to discuss. Hang around the building, once we're done, we'll be continuing. Until then, I want fresh faces in there, see if that shakes him. Declan?'

Declan nodded.

'Let's see what Marshall Reynolds has to say,' he said.

# 23

---

# CONFESSION

M<small>ARSHALL</small> R<small>EYNOLDS SAT IN THE INTERVIEW ROOM</small>, <small>HEAD IN</small> his hands, as Declan entered, Monroe beside him.

'Mister Reynolds,' he said. 'I understand you'd like to talk to us.'

Marshall looked up, and his eyes looked haunted.

'My nephew,' he said. 'Alfie, he's nothing to do with this, okay? I'm here today because I don't want him losing his future for a stupid thing that I did.'

'Okay,' Declan nodded. 'Why don't you tell me about the stupid thing?'

Marshall nodded.

'Alfie works for a company, right?' he said. 'Telemarketing. Robo-calls.'

'We know,' Monroe said. 'We gained that from him during his statement, when he was explaining why he wanted to leave and become a cab driver.'

'Yeah, well, what he didn't explain to you is that they also do a lot of marketing stuff,' Marshall replied. 'So you can pay his company and they'll phone people up, and when the phone's answered, they'll play a recorded message to you. "You've won a contest" or "Congratulations" or "Have you thought about life insurance?" All those kinds of things.'

'Okay, and this is important how?'

'Because, well, I might have put one in the company's system one night,' Marshall added, uncomfortably. 'I was paid five grand to do it, and I shared it with Alfie.'

'Who paid you to do this?'

'James Harlow.'

At this, Monroe's eyes narrowed.

'Are you telling me that folk singer James Harlow paid you to send the chorus of his song to Stuart Laws' phone?'

'Yes and no,' Marshall replied. 'Look, I'm not proud of it, okay? But I was told he wanted to do some kind of advertising, yeah? Thought it'd be clever to have it so that when people answered the phone, they'd hear his song. He was streaming on Spotify or something, he was probably hoping it'd remind them to listen to it, maybe buy the album, and maybe he'd make some money. Gave me five grand and a list of about a thousand phone numbers he'd been given by a marketing company. Just said to get them entered into the system and dial them up.'

'And you didn't check the numbers?'

'No,' Marshall replied. 'There were a thousand of them. How the hell was I gonna do that? It was five grand. Easy money. I split half with Alfie. He hated the job anyway, didn't care what was going on, and he knew how the system worked. We went over one night and put the data in, set it up and let it go.'

He frowned as he looked away.

'The problem was the code had an issue, and it took almost forty-eight hours to go through the system,' he said. 'James wanted it to go through on a Monday and it didn't go through till the Wednesday, a couple of weeks back.'

Declan understood what Marshall was saying. The message that Stuart Laws *should* have got would have arrived before he died, rather than after.

*A warning, perhaps, rather than an epitaph.*

'Why are you telling us this?'

'Because the company Alfie works for is owned by Lance Curtis-Warner,' Marshall replied. 'He came to me yesterday and kicked off, saying he'd been going through the logs. He knew I was there that night.'

He gave a visible sigh as the ramifications of what had happened that night sunk in.

'He told me Stuart had received the message after he died, and I realised this would put Alfie in the crosshairs if it came out. I mean, come on, the guy who finds the body also sent a message to another? I couldn't do that to him, as this was my screw up.'

Declan stared at the man in front of him.

'Look, I don't care what happens to me,' Marshall continued. 'But Alfie, he's got his whole life ahead of him, you know? All I did was play some music to some people. I didn't realise it was part of any message. I didn't realise ...'

He trailed off.

'When you were at the school, did you ever hear of Beth and Logan being together?' Declan asked.

'Of course.'

'And did you ever hear of her sleeping with his brother? And this time, tell us the truth. Don't make out you don't have a clue what's going on, yeah?'

Marshall eyed Declan cautiously.

'There were rumours bouncing around the Knowledge school,' he nodded. 'Whether they were true or not, I don't know, but the scuttlebutt was that James, who was now kind of part of the scene because of his brother, had met Beth – and they'd ended up getting drunk and sleeping with each other. Logan found out and had really gone to town on Beth. It was the same night Stuart Laws had passed his Knowledge, I think; everyone was out getting drunk. We were in a pub. I was there at the time, so was Sandeep Khan, but he didn't drink. Stuart also wasn't drinking that night.'

'He didn't drink?'

'I think it was because he'd just passed the Knowledge, wanted to stay clear-headed, I don't know. Anyway, the news came in that Beth, who'd gone to have a heart-to-heart with Logan, had been beaten badly, and the lads went out to find him.'

'The lads?' Monroe asked.

'Clifford, Ronnie, Stuart, Lance,' Marshall confirmed. 'They took Clifford's cab, but Clifford was too drunk, so Stuart, being the only sober one, drove.'

Marshall shook his head.

'Sandeep didn't want to get involved, said it wasn't his problem. The guy was always quite cold. I also heard that at the time that Logan was investing heavily in a website thing Sandeep wanted to create, and I think Sandeep was worried that facing off with Logan about this would screw the deal. So Sandeep decided not to do anything.'

'Why didn't you go?'

'Wasn't my crowd,' Marshall replied. 'They want to go and play chivalric knights, literally in Lancelot's case, that's fine. Wasn't my argument. Besides, I was tired, and I was calling it a night, I had an early run in the morning. I passed my Knowledge a while earlier, so I was an actual cabbie at this point.'

'What happened?'

'No one knows. The following day, all of them are claiming they couldn't find him, but Logan's never seen again. Two days later, he's found dead in Bull's Alley dock in Mortlake. Everyone assumes that either distraught by what he did, or because of his own depression and pain, he overdosed on his painkillers, jumped off a bridge and killed himself.'

He leant closer now.

'But I know he didn't. I know *they* bloody did it. And James knows as well. That song of his, "Crooked Was His Cane", I listened to it when we did the robo-call. I'd never heard it before; it wasn't really my thing. But it was a message, wasn't it? Crooked cane guy gets hit by a bus, body's never found? Pretty bloody obvious,' he muttered. 'Anyway, turned out fine for everybody, didn't it? Everybody else became cab drivers. Sandeep got his company going, made millions. Lance continued being a rich wanker. Life goes on, as they say.'

Monroe nodded at this.

'We'll take this as a witness statement,' he said. 'But you still haven't explained how you knew where Ronald Tyler was when you sent Alfie there.'

Marshall sighed, slumping into the chair.

'As I said to your colleague,' he replied. 'I was at a cab rank on Monday. I was behind Ron Tyler, and he was talking to Clifford Stone.'

'You speak to either of them much?'

Marshall shook his head.

'I'm not usually on the same runs. I think I've spoken to both of them at cab stops here and there, but nothing more. I couldn't hear much of what they were saying, but they were talking about Bartlett Place, which is a known trap street. It's a running joke; whenever you want to do something dodgy, go "off clock" you go to Bartlett Place.'

He shifted in his seat.

'It pricked my ears when I heard them say it. But this sounded like he actually wanted to go there. He said he'd had enough, and he wanted his payday, wanted what was owed to him.'

He shrugged.

'He said he was going to be there first thing Thursday morning. It was about three days from when he said it.'

'Thursday. The day he was found dead,' Monroe mused. 'And you thought if you sent Alfie there, he'd be able to see who Ronald was meeting with, maybe even hear the information? This wasn't testing the Knowledge. This was using your nephew as a spy.'

Marshall Reynolds said nothing, staring directly at Monroe now.

'I'm not proud, but I'm not apologetic. Alfie was riding his bike around London around then, so there was a chance he'd see something.'

'Why didn't you go?'

Marshall waved a hand at his afro.

'I'm known,' he said. 'Kid on a bike? Less so.'

Monroe shifted in his seat.

'Do you know why Ronald Tyler might have been killed?'

'Only person I know who hated him was his wife,' Marshall shook his head.

'Lizzie Tyler? She didn't give us that impression earlier.'

'Maybe death changed her thoughts on him,' Marshall shrugged. 'I know, however, she hadn't spoken to him for a good year or so; seems she'd had a massive row with Ronnie in late 2019, and things better left unsaid had come out.'

'Like what?'

'I wasn't there, I wouldn't know,' Marshall's attitude altered now, as if he was tiring of being helpful. 'You know, Cavan Tyler's a bastard, right? He's not Ronnie's biological kid.'

Declan stared at the cabbie.

'If he's not Tyler's kid,' he asked, 'then who the bloody hell is he?'

'No idea, never asked, but the smart money's on him being Logan, considering the birth timeline.'

Declan looked down at his notes. *From the looks of things, James Harlow had a lot to answer for.*

He leant back, watching Marshall.

'Lizzie Tyler,' he said. 'Is Beth Stevens, right?'

Marshall paled, and then nodded.

'And you never said this before because…?'

'You never asked,' Marshall replied. 'But honestly? I never considered it. I didn't really spend time with them after the marriage. And she took his surname.'

Declan cursed his stupidity. *They could have learnt this way earlier, if someone had just connected the names for them.*

'Hold on,' he read his notes again. 'You said "but I was told he wanted to do some kind of advertising" when you spoke about James. So you didn't deal with James Harlow direct?'

'Well, no,' Marshall said, before leaning back in the chair and folding his arms. 'It was through Sandeep Khan.'

Declan walked out into the corridor with Monroe, as PC Cooper entered to take the official statement of Marshall Reynolds.

'So Logan was a wanker, and possibly an unknowing father. And it looks like they killed him one night in retaliation,' he said. 'Now what?'

'Now, laddie, we work out which of these buggers we have to arrest,' Monroe replied. 'Ronald Tyler and his wife having a barney is interesting, though. I wonder if she discovered the truth of that night?'

'Makes her sickbed visit the neighbour mentioned a little more suspicious, too,' Declan mused. 'Why visit the man you apparently hate when he's ill?'

'Maybe to gloat, laddie?' Monroe smiled. 'Of course, we then have the question of why she lied about seeing him to Anjli, too.'

He took a moment to stretch out his spine, grunting as a loud and concerning click sound was heard.

'Right, it'll take Esme a few minutes to make it official,' he eventually said. 'I think we need to see what else is going on.'

Declan went to reply but then noticed his phone had lit up.

'Sorry, Guv, but Johnny Lucas's solicitor just texted,' he said. 'There's a meeting planned in a couple of hours with Gladwell. He's asked if I can go along. I can tell him—'

'You'll tell him you can make it,' Monroe insisted. 'Look, laddie. If we don't fix the Gladwell problem, then it doesn't matter if we solve this case or not, we'll still be closed. We'll work on the now, while you sort out our bloody future.'

Declan nodded and started off down the corridor.

'And don't do anything I'd be ashamed of!' Monroe called after him.

Declan grinned.

*That didn't leave much.*

## 24

VISITING HOURS

LIZZIE TYLER WAS IN HER CAR WHEN ANJLI AND COOPER arrived, Cooper pulling up the squad car in front of the driveway, effectively blocking Lizzie from leaving.

As Anjli climbed out of the passenger side, Lizzie seemed to want to stay inside her vehicle, but then eventually turned off the engine and emerged from the driver's side.

'I do hope we're not interrupting you, Mrs Tyler,' Anjli said, noticing the suitcase resting on the back seat. 'Going on a trip?'

Lizzie glanced back at the suitcase and paled.

'Yes,' she admitted. 'Just a day or two. Me and Cavan are going to get away from the press. They're contacting us constantly asking for information about his father.'

'So Cavan's come home then?' Anjli asked.

'Well, no,' Lizzie replied cautiously. 'He'll be arriving today. He couldn't make it yesterday. Apparently the press found him at his Hull house. He spent the day hiding from them, missed the train, so he was catching the first one this morning.'

'That's interesting,' Anjli said, 'that he was still in Hull until this morning.'

If Lizzie agreed with the curious note, she didn't reply with anything.

'Look, I really do need to go,' she said, nodding at Cooper, who was now standing beside the driver's side of the car. 'If you could move your squad car?'

'We only have a couple of quick questions, Mrs Tyler,' Anjli continued, ignoring the statement, 'and then we'll go. Don't worry, we won't be here long.'

'Can it be done here?' Lizzie Tyler asked. 'It's just I've locked up, and I'd rather not have to go through the security again.'

'That's fine,' Anjli replied, glancing back at the house. 'It's more of a clearing up some concerns. You see, some of the things you told us a couple of days ago aren't matching with what we've now been told.'

'Like what?'

Anjli pulled out her notebook.

'When we saw you the day of your ex-husband's murder, you told us that when you broke up, it was because you felt like you were brother and sister, that you were still close, and for your son's sake, you'd made a point of staying together over the years, making sure he had the most normal life he could possibly have.'

Lizzie didn't reply. It was almost as if she knew what was coming next.

'Yet when we've spoken to other people,' Anjli continued, 'we found that you and your husband had actually split back in 2019 because of a large fight. A fight that seemed to be connected to James Harlow, and a song that you claimed not to know.'

Lizzie still didn't respond.

'The people we spoke to told us you and Ronald were actually antagonistic with each other. You hated him. There was no love lost at all,' Cooper now spoke. 'Yet just over two weeks ago, on the day that Stuart Laws was hit by a London taxi – a London taxi we believe matched the one that your husband drove – you visited him twice while he was ill with food poisoning, even though you told DI Kapoor here you'd not seen him for months.'

Lizzie straightened her jaw set as she turned her gaze from Anjli to Cooper.

'Yeah, I hated him,' she admitted. 'We'd always had our problems, but something came out, he lost his rag and, honestly, I'd had enough of his shit. So when he started bitching, I just told him to piss off. We spoke little over the years, but that didn't mean that I wouldn't care. So when I heard he'd been taken down with what he reckoned was the norovirus, I went over to visit.'

Anjli nodded, writing this down in the notebook. Lizzie glanced to the side, and following her gaze, Anjli saw the slightest rustle of a net curtain behind one of the windows.

*Looks like the neighbours are taking an interest,* she thought to herself, as Lizzie Tyler sighed and looked back at Anjli.

'Any more questions?'

'Oh, we have a few,' Anjli replied. 'Why you lied to us about your past as Beth Stevens, your relationship with Logan Harlow ...'

'The true parentage of your son,' Cooper added for good measure. 'And some others, you know how it goes.'

Lizzie glanced nervously back at the window and eventually deflated slightly, as she waved back at the door.

'I suppose you'd better come in then,' she said.

'Yes, that would be for the best,' Anjli smiled. 'After you.'

———————

MALCOLM GLADWELL HAD NEVER FELT SO POPULAR.

He'd been waiting for his trial for almost two years now, and in that time he had had his fair share of solicitors and reporters wanting to ask his side of the story, but since the manuscript had been released to a select few people, mainly politicians and movers and shakers in the political industry, he had found himself overwhelmed with meeting requests.

On remand during that time, he was only given a set amount of availability when he could have these meetings, but as his defence counsel claimed this was a valid part of any appeal he would be making against these crimes being levelled against him, he was given a little more sway in the amount of people he could speak to.

He'd had a new name appear on the list today, however, one he hadn't expected, or been informed in advance about.

*Fabian Kleid.*

He was sure he had recognised the name from some-where. Fabian wasn't exactly the most commonplace of names, but he couldn't quite figure out where he knew the man from. He'd asked around, but this had been quite a short-notice meeting, booked the same morning. That they couldn't wait until the weekend was over was incred-ibly promising. And so Gladwell had accepted it, guessing this was somebody wanting to make some kind of offer, but using a contact that didn't have sway. It was a common gambit in Westminster; when you wanted to take a punt at someone, or convince them to help you take a shot at someone else, you never went direct. You would often use a middleman, usually somebody completely out of the game, giving them, and you, plausible deniability.

What he hadn't expected as he walked into the room though, was that there was a *second* person sitting beside Kleid.

Fabian Kleid was middle-aged, stick thin and with dyed, jet-black hair cut into a wedge style. He wore an expensive suit, and had a smile on his face as he sat at the desk; beside him, with an equally knowing smile, was Detective Chief Inspector Declan Walsh.

The last time Gladwell had seen Walsh had been in Charles Baker's office when he'd been arrested and removed, ignominiously, from his role in Westminster. He'd dreamt of the time he would next see Declan. He had hoped it would be on the outside, however, as Declan himself was dragged away in handcuffs.

'I'm not talking to that man,' he said, stopping at the door and nodding at Declan.

'That's fine,' Fabian replied. 'You're here to see me. Mister Walsh is purely here to give confirmation on context for some of the information we're sharing.'

Gladwell sighed, walking reluctantly over and sitting in the chair facing them.

'I'm here anyway,' he said. 'We might as well get on with it. Have you come to beg my forgiveness? Tell me what you're going to do to get me out?'

'You're not getting out of here—' Declan said, and then stopped as Fabian raised a hand.

'Please, Detective Chief Inspector Walsh,' he said, a rather pained expression on his face. 'As we said earlier on, you're not here to talk, you're here as a witness.'

Declan held his hand up, and Fabian turned to look back at Gladwell.

'*Now* I know where I know you from,' Gladwell growled. 'You're the East End scumbag Johnny Lucas's solicitor, aren't you?'

'I am,' Fabian replied, unconcerned as to any statement made, opening up his notebook and reading from the papers held within. 'You believe that by releasing this manuscript, you were effectively holding several people for ransom. Detective Chief Inspector Walsh, his colleagues at the City of London police unit, and several members of Parliament, including the Prime Minister.'

He looked up from his notes.

'Have I missed anyone?'

'No, you seem perfectly clear about what you're saying,' Gladwell replied, unconcerned.

'Good,' Fabian returned to his notes. 'You seem to believe that this manuscript will exonerate you somehow, show that you were a victim in a targeted campaign by both Kendis Taylor and her then-secret lover, Declan Walsh.'

'He had an agenda against me,' Gladwell nodded. 'And when my colleague, Will Harrison, went off the rails—'

'Don't you dare,' Declan started, but stopped as Fabian held a hand up.

'Please,' he said. 'Continue.'

'When your friend next to you decided to come for me for Will Harrison's crimes, he destroyed my life,' Gladwell muttered. 'I was an innocent man who had his career removed by a public servant who should have known better.'

'You believed that releasing a book was a wise idea?'

'Sure, I know it was risky,' Gladwell smiled. 'When you have everything to lose, you don't rattle the cage. Secrets could spill out of it, and you've done it to yourself. Everything you've built up over the years is gone in a flash, and you have nothing. But sometimes you need to roll that dice.'

Fabian considered the statement and wrote something down in the book.

'It was a very bold move,' he smiled as he carried on, giving the impression of someone on the same side. 'But, as you're probably aware, Detective Chief Inspector Walsh is not here in connection with the death of Kendis Taylor. He's here in connection with the death of Donna Baker, the Prime Minister's late wife.'

Gladwell hadn't seemed to expect this, and his eyebrows furrowed together.

'What about Donna?' he asked.

'She was weak. She was mentally incapable,' Fabian answered the line. 'Yes, she would be, wouldn't she? With all the problems that were happening, being blamed for being the signatory of a dozen different less-than-authentic companies, hearing about the son that her husband never knew he had, and of course all the problems with him trying to run for Parliament and then Prime Minister himself, I can see how these would mount up.'

He looked up from a notebook, staring at Gladwell.

'You are aware, by the way, that the information you were given by Peter Taylor, the audio files of her meetings with Donna Baker, weren't complete, aren't you?'

Gladwell watched Fabian for a long moment before turning his attention to Declan.

'What did you do?' he asked.

'Would you like me to speak?' Declan replied calmly.

'What did you *do*?' Gladwell repeated.

Declan, with a nod from Fabian, shifted position.

'Kendis also took analogue audio recordings on tape,' he said. 'The last few hadn't been placed in her filing system before you killed her, and therefore you didn't get them.'

Gladwell glowered at Declan.

'And what exactly are we talking about here?'

'Do you remember when you told Donna not to speak to Kendis?' Declan smiled. 'On the day that she died, you came in and you told Kendis to move. In fact …'

He looked down at his notebook.

'On the day in question, I believe you said, "*If you don't mind, Miss Taylor, I need to speak to Donna Baker alone*" or something along those lines.'

Gladwell nodded.

'Yes,' he said. 'Kendis Taylor left, and I was on my own. I suggested to Donna that she shouldn't speak to this woman anymore and then we went our separate ways.'

'No,' Declan replied calmly. 'You didn't. What you actually did was threaten Donna, send her away, and make two phone calls. One to Detective Inspector Frost, or whatever his real name was, followed by another to Donna's therapist.'

'I don't recall that,' Gladwell shook his head. 'I think what you're doing here is listening to the assumed ravings of a madwoman who can't be contested and whose word can't be proven.'

'Oh no,' Declan replied, pulling out a tape recorder. 'We have the tapes.'

He pressed a button and Gladwell's voice could be heard.

*'You speak the lie so well, but we both know it's just a lie. That before you got married, you and your husband were literally strangers, brought together for political reasons.'*

*'It's not true. No—'*

*'Be serious, Donna. You can play the innocent bitch as much as*

*you want, but we all know that you quite happily shut your eyes as much as he did. As long as you got your fancy parties and your Centre Court Wimbledon tickets, you couldn't give a damn what he did.'*

Declan looked back at Gladwell.

'Whoops,' he smiled. 'You sent her out of the room, but you left the tape recorder in there. This never got mentioned because, well, Kendis was dead later that day.'

*'Shut up. Just shut up.'*

*'What's the matter, Donna? You're not going to do something bad, are you? Please don't hurt yourself. I don't know what I'd do if you passed away horribly due to some self-inflicted suicide—'*

Declan paused the tape, looking back at Gladwell.

'This isn't the first time we've got you on tape. If you recall, we recorded everything Detective Inspector Frost did on his final day alive. We had you found repeatedly tasering Laurie Hooper in Will Harrison's flat, or as you liked to say in that message, "taking care of business".'

Gladwell looked around the room as if expecting someone else to appear from nowhere.

'There's one other thing I don't think you realise,' Declan said. 'When I went into that mausoleum that night, opened up your family safe using the name *Rattlestone* and then changed it stupidly, I admit, to my own name, I removed every file inside it and took photos.'

He pulled out his phone, opening it up and scrolling through a series of sheets of paper on the screen.

'I have everything here about the Balkans debacle in 2015,' he replied. 'If I release it, it would destroy Charles Baker's re-election chances, but it would also kill any chance you have of continuing to breathe.'

He looked at Fabian as he placed his phone away.

'You see, this prison has a lot of military types in it,' he explained. 'A lot of the prison guards are ex-military and sadly, so are a lot of the prisoners. How do you think they'll respond when they hear how many soldiers died because of you? How safe do you think you'll be walking through this prison every day, knowing that every other man here wants you dead and has been trained by your own government to do it really well?'

'I'd rather talk to you,' Gladwell stated, turning back to face Fabian, but Declan hadn't finished and was now leaning across the table.

'Whatever you're doing, it ends,' he said coldly. 'You thought you had something on us? Well, you don't. You want to kill my career? I'm fine with that. You want to try to destroy a good journalist's career? I'm *less* happy about that. I know you killed Kendis Taylor. I know you tasered her unconscious, went home, found a blade, and then stabbed her, trying to force the blame onto Will Harrison. And you might get away with that when you eventually go to trial, but I'll make damn sure you don't walk free on any kind of technicality first.'

He straightened now, towering over the now terrified Gladwell, forward winding the tape to a set number on the side. This done, he played it.

*I don't care what you need to do, what mumbo-jumbo hypnosis it takes, or meditational thinking you use, but by the end of tonight, I want Donna Baker putting a noose around her neck and ending it. Tell her it'll be better if she's gone. Tell her the pain will stop, and her husband would be safer with Donna out of the way. I don't care what you do. You think I care about your oaths? If I release what I have on you, you'll be in prison for life. All you're doing here is risking the possibility of losing your licence. I suggest you do what I say, or it'll be bad for you. Almost as bad as it will be for Mister Baker.'*

Once more, Declan turned off the recorder.

'I have you on tape telling Doctor Trudeau to convince Donna Baker to kill herself,' Declan stepped away from the table as he spoke. 'Mister Kleid here spoke to Doctor Trudeau last night. She's been offered immunity if she speaks against you in the trial. She claims that you convinced her to press a mentally disturbed woman to commit suicide. It's enough to give you manslaughter. That, and everything else we have on you, will destroy everything you think you can do to us.'

He looked back at Fabian.

'We understand there's a get-out clause on this contract,' Fabian took on the conversation now. 'That, if you decided so, the book would not be printed. We assume this was because you wanted people to release you, and if released, the black-mail you'd have given them through this book would not be needed. I now encourage you to consider not releasing that book after all, because if you *were* to release that book, my client here would release every single sheet he took from your mausoleum, as well as releasing the recordings that he has – and these are not the *only* ones. You would be deemed a joke within an hour of the book's release. You would probably be dead within a day.'

Fabian smiled.

'Please, let the legal system judge your case. Maybe it will be profitable for you.'

Gladwell said nothing as Declan nodded to Fabian, and the two of them rose from their chairs and walked towards the main door.

'You have until midnight tomorrow,' Declan said, turning

back one last time. 'If you haven't cancelled the book deal by then, I'll go live Monday morning before you release it.'

Gladwell sat back in his chair as Declan and Fabian left, then he started slamming his head against the desk repeatedly at force, screaming loudly until the guards dragged him from it.

'I need to speak to my agent,' he shouted, blood streaming down his forehead as they pulled him away and back to the infirmary. 'I need to speak with her now!'

**25**

---

## THE OTHER SHOE

BILLY WAS AT HIS DESK GOING THROUGH CCTV IMAGES, WHEN De'Geer arrived with a twelve-inch vinyl album in the largest Ziplock baggy Billy had ever seen.

'I understand you are asking about this,' he said, placing it down on the desk.

'Yes, thanks,' Billy replied, looking up. 'Can I ...'

He left the sentence hanging, and De'Geer, smiling, opened up the baggy.

'You can touch it,' he nodded. 'We've checked it for finger-prints, and, to be honest, I think it was nothing more than just an album.'

'I think we might be wrong about that,' Billy said, as he gently eased the vinyl album out of the baggy, placing it on his desk, and then opening it up.

Inside the gatefold sleeve was the signed comment.

*So you don't forget.*

'This is what you found in Ronald Tyler's house,' Billy said. 'But I think there's more to it. Look at this.'

The inside of the gatefold had been designed in a particular way, to show old photographs from James Harlow's life. Pictures of James as a child, an adult, playing gigs; it was an anthology-style gatefold imagery, used in hundreds of albums over the years.

There were, however, a couple of other photos; ones of James with his brother and what looked to be a young James with his family, but it was the picture beside the signed text that Billy tapped at.

'This,' he said. 'Look where it's written.'

De'Geer squinted as he looked down.

'It's beside the photo of Logan Harlow,' he replied, finally realising where Billy was going with this.

'What if this is a message?' Billy picked his phone up and took a photo of the signature. 'What if this is James Harlow saying he knows something about Logan Harlow, something he's passed on here as a message to Ronald Tyler? This wasn't just a simple "So you don't forget" type message. This was an actual image of his brother with the text written underneath, and to me, this sounds like James telling Ronald that he knows.'

'Knows what, though? That Ronald killed Logan?'

Billy shrugged as his eyes scrolled down the imagery, stopping at the tiny text at the bottom of the gatefold sleeve.

'Look at this,' he tapped the album as he continued. 'The album's a live show from 2019, but the vinyl wasn't printed until this year. In fact, it was released a month ago.'

'A month?' De'Geer frowned, stroking at his Viking beard. 'That would be a week or two before Stuart Laws started hammering on Ronald Tyler's door.'

'When everything went wrong,' Billy nodded as he looked back at the album. 'I wonder how many other people received this in the post?'

He picked up his phone and started texting Anjli.

'Let's find out.'

---

LIZZIE HADN'T BEEN LYING WHEN SHE'D MENTIONED THE security; there was a four-digit alarm and several locks that had to be released before they could re-enter the house.

Anjli noted as they did so that Cavan Tyler was nowhere to be seen, which gave her the question now on whether Lizzie Tyler actually *was* aware that her son wasn't up north right now.

'It's true,' Lizzie said as she walked into the kitchen, once more reaching for the cabinet, although this time, rather than grabbing a bottle of vodka, she pulled down a pack of instant coffee, turning on the kettle. 'Cavan wasn't Ronnie's.'

'Did Ronald know?'

'Not at the start,' Lizzie shook her head. 'We'd got together soon after Logan's death. It was a physical thing at first.'

'You mean you were shagging each other?' Cooper replied bluntly and then reddened. 'Sorry, I didn't mean it to come out like it did.'

'No, but you are right,' Lizzie nodded. 'I found out about Logan's death, and Ronald was there for me. It was almost like he was psychic, knew something was wrong. We got drunk and we ended up sleeping together. We were together here and there for the space of about a week. It was purely sexual, no emotions.'

She shrugged.

'I needed somebody there.'

'We don't need to know the full details of your sex life,' Anjli replied. 'But we still need to know the timeline. Did you have an affair with James Harlow?'

'Not after the death,' Lizzie shook her head. 'And before that, it was a single night of idiocy. I wasn't proud of this time in my life.'

She placed a spoonful of coffee into a mug.

'James hung around after Logan died, though; nothing naughty, and he disappeared within a couple of days. It was almost as if he wanted to confirm I wasn't going to cause any problems with the will, and once he was sure, he buggered off.'

'What about the will?'

'Logan had apparently promised to place everything in my name. Said he loved me, wanted to get married. Said he had a massive surprise for me,' Lizzie leaned against the counter. 'But then there were two sides to Logan. If he wasn't proclaiming his love, he was hitting me. He was Jekyll and Hyde, and it wasn't working.'

'So you broke up?'

'The night we had our final fight, I'd had enough, walked away from it all,' Lizzie nodded, her voice soft, melancholy as she spoke. 'Well, more *limped*. After Logan died, James was worried that Logan, as some kind of apology, had made some big gesture before he topped himself, and I'd end up getting all the money that was now owed effectively, to James, but nothing ever turned up. I didn't contest it, I didn't want it. And Ronald, well, he was there for me, you know, so I didn't need anything from the Harlows.'

'What about Clifford Stone?'

'Clifford was a loser,' Lizzie shook her head. 'Clifford,

Stuart, Ronald, they all bloody loved me. Well, claimed they did. Of course, I was the only woman in the room. Out of all of them, I think Ronald was the only one who actually cared.'

Anjli wrote this down.

'When did you know Cavan wasn't Ronald's son?'

'Not for years,' Lizzie replied. 'We were happy, and I'd moved on. And then, in 2019, something happened, and Ronald suddenly had his suspicions. He confronted me. We argued, but by that point I too had noticed certain things. Characteristics that Cavan had as a teenage kid, that reminded me very much of Logan. I went through the dates and realised that there was every chance that, in a two-week period, I'd slept with Logan, Ronald and James. Although ...'

She stopped, as if checking herself.

'No, no, it was just technically Logan and Ronald. It was a coin toss. We always knew I'd become pregnant early in our relationship, but we never contested it, we never questioned it.'

'So, what happened in 2019?' Cooper asked.

'James Harlow gained a lot of money,' Lizzie replied. 'He'd invested in Sandeep Khan's Oi Taxi project, taking on some of the investment that Logan had promised. The app was sold in early 2019, and he'd made a chunk of money. He celebrated with a tour.'

Anjli wrote this down.

'October 2019,' she said. 'Some of the songs are on YouTube. Ronald went to the gig, didn't he?'

Lizzie nodded.

'He was always keeping an eye on James,' she replied. 'They weren't close or anything like that. He wasn't even a fan of the music, to an extent. Then he got an invite, which said to bring Cavan and me, and he was given three tickets. I didn't want to go. By that point, I'd worked out that Cavan was Logan's son. I mean, I must have even somehow known when I named him.'

'Why?' Cooper asked.

'Logan? It's a Gaelic word; "lagan" or "lag" which means "little hollow", and Cavan, in Irish is "cabhán," which means "grassy hill" or "hollow",' Lizzie shook her head. 'Even subconsciously, I knew. We should have discussed it years earlier, but we'd never done anything. I'd never spoken to Cavan about it. Until a biological test was done, there was nothing to learn and, well, we weren't letting that happen anytime soon.'

She sighed.

'Anyway, I didn't want to go to the gig. I didn't want to see James, I didn't want to be reminded of what happened with Logan, so I gave the ticket away.'

'You gave it to Alfie Reynolds?'

Lizzie nodded.

'Alfie and Cavan had grown up together, you know? The sons of the cabbies kind of hung out as kids. But anyway, they went to the gig, and James had videos playing on TVs on either side of him; old family photos, because a lot of his tour then was about his past and his childhood, and there were childhood photos of both him and Logan as he sang his songs.'

'Let me guess, at some point during the gig, a teenage photo of Logan appeared, and he was a spitting image of your son.'

'So I was told,' Lizzie nodded. 'Ronald was furious. For the first time, he realised he'd been cuckolded. It wasn't deliberate. I'd always hoped that he was the father, but I'd known for years he wasn't. That night, afterwards, he had a fight with James. *How dare he do this?* James didn't care. He was pressing at a wound, seeing what happened, and during that time, he pointed out that he'd worked out Cavan was Logan's son a lot earlier, seeing photos over the years. He was staking his claim, pointing out that he had a nephew, and he wanted access. Although we learnt later he didn't give a shit about it, and it was all about screwing over Ronnie.'

She looked away.

'Anyway, Ronnie came back home. We had a fight. During it, I'd mentioned that I'd always suspected, and he felt betrayed, walked out. There were other reasons we broke up. It wasn't just purely because of Cavan's parentage, but by that point, Cavan was starting his A-levels. He was head down. We didn't tell him why we'd broken up, and James, to our knowledge, didn't press the matter. We asked him to wait until Cavan had finished university before telling him.'

She shrugged as, behind her, the kettle boiled.

'And then what?' Anjli asked.

Lizzie looked up, her eyes red with tears.

'James screwed us,' she said. 'He met up with Cavan a couple of years ago, told him the truth. By this point, Ronald had been distant, barely talking to him. Cavan didn't understand why, and now suddenly he had a reason. He was angry. Cut off all ties with us. He'd spent more time in Hull than down here. It was a new life for him, and when he did come down here, he used the house like a bed-and-breakfast, spending most of his time with Alfie in Bermondsey. Probably down right now, as much as I know.'

'When you came to see your husband, when he was sick,' Anjli changed the subject, 'did you take his car keys? Did you take Ronald Tyler's car and drive it down to Surrey?'

'Wait, you think I did it?' Lizzie held the mug in front of her like a shield. 'I loved Ronald. Why would I--'

'You might have loved him, but that doesn't mean you liked him,' Anjli interrupted coldly. 'Also, do you know why Stuart Laws was banging on Ronald Tyler's door a month ago?'

'Because I sent him there,' Lizzie backed against the counter, giving the look of a woman trying to gain distance from Cooper and Anjli. 'He turned up at the door – terrified me, he did. Like a man possessed. Hadn't realised we'd split, came looking for Ronnie. I gave him the new address and told him to piss off.'

'Okay then, so why was he looking for him in the first place?'

Lizzie went to reply, and Anjli could see from her expression she was about to blow this off, try to change the subject, but then she stopped herself, sighing, looking to the floor. Then she walked off, out of the kitchen without another word. Anjli was about to suggest to Cooper to follow her when Lizzie came back with a vinyl album in her hand.

A familiar looking one.

'Here,' Lizzie said, opening it up, showing the middle gatefold. 'I'm guessing you've seen the same one at Ronnie's. It wasn't just me and Ronnie who got these a few weeks ago. This was why Stuart turned up. He was in pieces. I had to bring him in, sit him down ... you've seen the vodka bottle already, yeah? He downed half of it in five minutes.'

Anjli watched Lizzie carefully.

'And why do you think he was so stressed?' she asked. 'Surely the message is about Logan being Cavan's father, based on the positioning of the message?'

'Oh, sure, yeah—' Lizzie started, but Anjli shook her head.

'Come on, Lizzie, or Beth, or whatever you want to be called,' she said. 'You don't need to try to play us for fools. We're pretty much convinced Stuart was involved in the death of Logan all those years ago.'

At the comment, Lizzie Tyler's expression changed or, rather, it lessened. It was as if all emotion drained out, leaving a cold, blank expression.

'You're damned right he was,' she said. 'He drove the car that hit Logan.'

She threw the vinyl album onto the table as she paced now.

'He sent all of us a copy of the album,' she said. 'Lance got one too, but he tossed it, I believe. James probably did other stuff, too, to screw with people.'

'He did,' Anjli nodded. 'He had a robo-call company phone all of them, playing part of "Crooked Was His Cane" but whether any of them heard it, we don't know.'

She reopened the notebook.

'So, Stuart turns up, he's panicking ... he then leaves here and goes to Ronald. Why?'

'Because he thought James was sending a message. I mean, he was, but Stuart thought it was a more *final* one, if you get what I'm saying,' Lizzie walked to the rear door, staring out of it as she continued. 'Stuart was saying he was going to go to the police, tell them what had happened. But he was mumbling, kept talking about the "messenger," whoever that was.'

'And what *had* happened?' Cooper asked.

Lizzie shrugged, knowing everything was over now.

'That night, twenty years ago ... they hit Logan with a car,' she said. 'Stuart veered off the road, struck him as he went to run for Gibson Square. They got out, smacked him in the head with his own cane to knock him out, overdosed him with his own meds to try to fix him, and dumped him in the cab's boot. I don't think they'd thought through what they did next. And they'd gone off script.'

'Script?'

Lizzie didn't answer, lost in her memories.

'Anyway, when he turned up, I told Stuart to speak to Ronnie first, but he was out driving. I knew Stuart was losing it, and the next step would be to give up everything.'

'But why did you care?' Anjli frowned, deciding to return to the previous comment. 'You'd been beaten by Logan, but you weren't in the car with them.'

Lizzie turned to face Anjli, tears running down her face.

'Because I paid Stuart to do it,' she said. 'I borrowed five grand and gave it to him, told him to break Logan's bloody legs. Even called Logan, telling him to meet me back at Gibson Square, said I had something important to say, so he'd be there.'

She took a deep breath, looking up at the ceiling.

'It's my fault he's dead,' she said. 'Though I never said to kill him. But I couldn't let Stuart tell anyone, so I went to Ronald and told him everything.'

'And Ronald went to Surrey and struck him with a cab?' Cooper asked gently.

'Yes,' Lizzie nodded now. 'He did it. That's the God's own truth.'

'Except it isn't, is it?' Anjli played a hunch. 'Ronald's neighbour saw you the day of the accident, as well as a visit the night before. Ronald was bedridden, and you were visiting him, weren't you? Or were you placing back the cab keys you'd borrowed, when you realised you had to do the job yourself; killing Stuart Laws?'

Lizzie Tyler, aka Beth Stevens, aka Beth Stephanos bit back a sob—

And then ran for the back door, yanking it open as she went to escape through it.

Cooper had been ready, though, and tackled her to the floor, knocking the discarded coffee mug aside as she landed on Lizzie's back, pinning her arms to her sides.

'I think we need to have a chat about this at the station,' Anjli pulled out her handcuffs, looking at the spilt coffee. 'Oh, that's a shame. You've ruined that nice vinyl album.'

————

## 26

## HOUSING LADDER

DECLAN HADN'T EXPECTED BUNTING AND INDOOR FIREWORKS when he returned to the Temple Inn offices, but at the very least, he had expected a couple of high-fives and a "well done". After all, it seemed, to all intents and purposes as if Malcolm Gladwell was no longer a threat to the unit.

What he found instead was an office in a state of agitation, with Anjli running from her desk over to Billy and back.

'What's going on?' he asked, looking around.

'Lizzie Tyler's upstairs,' Anjli replied, looking back at him, pausing mid-stride. 'We've almost confirmed she was the one who drove Ron Tyler's cab that morning and killed Stuart Laws.'

'She was?' Declan placed his bag on the desk and turned back to face the others. 'Do we know why?'

'Apparently, she paid five thousand pounds to Stuart Laws to run Logan Harlow over, twenty years ago,' Billy said, looking back from his monitors. 'Stuart had started stressing when the vinyl albums had arrived a month back.'

'They all got one,' Anjli added before Billy continued.

'Each album had the same message from James Harlow written on them. Stuart had taken it as a message that Harlow knew about the murder of Logan.'

Declan whistled.

'I literally went out for half an hour,' he said.

'It was longer than that, laddie,' Monroe said, walking out of Declan's office. 'I hope you don't mind, I requisitioned yours because Bullman's in mine.'

'That's fine, Guv,' Declan replied. 'What else do we have?'

'We now know that Cavan Tyler's aware that Ronald Tyler wasn't his father, and that Logan Harlow was, in fact, his real biological dad.'

'Confirmed?'

'Seems so,' Billy replied. 'If the others were all drunk, but Stuart hadn't been drinking that night, and that's *why* he was driving, I wonder whether this had already been decided in advance, and he knew that Clifford getting drunk would give him the option to drive the car?'

'It's a question we can't ask him,' Declan replied.

'No, but we can bloody ask Sandeep Khan and Lance Curtis-Warner,' Monroe muttered. 'Do we have anything on them yet?'

'Sandeep's not answering his phone, so I'm trying to track him another way,' Billy looked back over. 'The walking contest he's got going? He mentioned it on his podcast, and his rival's Jeff Morrison, a crypto king influencer. We've reached out to Jeff's people and they've promised us his Strava details.'

'And how does that work?' Declan frowned.

'They promised to keep things transparent to stop cheating,' Billy explained. 'All month they've logged every step on Strava and used the Beacon service. It's a feature that lets you share your live location with up to three people who can track your progress in real time.'

'And Sandeep shared this with Jeff?'

'And vice versa, and only with them, as it's not public knowledge. However, with Jeff sharing it with us, we're allowed to examine it,' Billy nodded. 'Which means the moment we get access, we can check where he is, using Jeff's login. However, we have a slight problem with Lance.'

'Now what would that be?' Monroe turned to face Billy. 'Let me guess, he's missing?'

'Actually, yes, sir,' Billy replied. 'He went out yesterday evening, told his PA he wouldn't be around for a while, and didn't turn up this morning. It's not like him, apparently. They've checked his house, they've called him repeatedly, they've tracked his phone, but everything's in his car.'

'And where's his car?' Declan asked.

'Haggerston,' Billy replied. 'About a hundred yards away from a folk club where James Harlow was performing last night.'

'So, you think Lance went to see James Harlow?'

'Possibly,' Billy returned to his keyboard, typing. 'I'm checking CCTV at the event venue to see if I can pick him up, but as of yet, I've not seen anything. But one thing I can say is, if his PA's correct, Lance Curtis-Warner went to see James Harlow last night and didn't come back. Also, they had someone check the dressing room, and they found a smashed ceramic mug with a stain on the wall from where it'd been thrown, and blood on the carpet. There was definitely a fight.'

'Considering the fact that he's the fourth of four that potentially killed James's brother,' Declan added, 'that's not a good thing.'

'We also have an idea of how Logan Harlow died,' Billy

continued as he turned back to his monitors. 'De'Geer's checking it at the moment, but it's based on the various murders matched with what Doctor Marcos could grab from the original coroner's report from twenty-odd years ago.'

'Go on,' Declan said.

'Logan Harlow was found in Mortlake, having drowned in the Thames,' Anjli replied. 'However, he also had an incredible amount of painkillers in his blood, carbon monoxide poisoning and injuries that would suggest being hit by a car.'

'There was one other wound which we can't quite work out. It was small and narrow and to the head, but that could have been from the edge of the bridge when he jumped or even something he hit when he landed, we don't know,' Billy admitted. 'However Lizzie Tyler mentioned they struck him with his own walking stick, and that could match.'

'The hypothetical situation at the moment, though,' Monroe added, walking over to Anjli's desk, 'is that Stuart Laws saw Logan Harlow in Gibson Square and hit him with a car. They – this being Stuart, Ronald, Lance and Clifford – then took him, knocked him out with his own crooked cane, and dumped him in the boot of the aforementioned cab. But this is where the wheels came off the car – although not literally – because Stuart had been told to hurt Logan, not kill him. The others were drunk and couldn't decide about what to do now they had Logan. This was about ten-thirty, eleven o'clock at night.'

'Makes sense,' Declan nodded. 'They're still a few hours ahead of the witness statement here, so if this was the case, they'd probably stick him in the cab's boot and drive around for several hours trying to work out what to do. Maybe even feed him painkillers to kill whatever extra discomfort they added. Eventually, around three in the morning, they decide to stop and pull Logan out, to see if being hit by a car and kidnapped might actually have scared him into being a potentially decent human being ...'

Declan then groaned.

'Clifford Jones's car failed the conditions, didn't it?'

Anjli nodded.

'Ray Holdsworth said to us that when Clifford bought the car, it had a hole in the chassis,' she replied. 'The boot would fill with carbon monoxide, making luggage stink. If Logan went into the boot and was driven around for hours, he would have breathed that in. When they opened it up, they'd have realised from the amount of smoke coming out, and probably the smell in the cab itself, that they'd effectively gassed him to death.'

'By this point, they were near Hammersmith Bridge, so they probably decided to drive up and throw him over the edge,' Monroe took the hypothetical story on now. 'This time in the morning, twenty-odd years ago, cameras weren't as prolific as they are now. They probably thought they could pull up, wait for a quiet moment, dump him over the side and people would assume that the suicidal, painkiller-addicted man had killed himself.'

'And that's what people saw that night,' Declan nodded now, understanding. 'A witness walked onto the bridge, found four men standing around. They claimed it had been an accident. They hadn't yet thrown the cane over the side, and they came up with this story of a man being hit, and other witnesses all seeing it. It was raining, it was cold, and no one really cared.'

He frowned.

'But the autopsy report said he drowned, he wasn't gassed.'

'Exactly!' Monroe slapped the desk hard. 'That's the point. Logan Harlow was unconscious, but not dead. Not one of those idiot bampots checked him for a pulse. They threw him over the side and the Thames did the rest! They murdered him, laddie, in three different ways. They thought they'd killed him with the car, they thought they'd gassed him in the boot, and then they threw him in the water and let him drown.'

'The murder of Stuart Laws seems to be coincidence,' Anjli was stretching now, rubbing the back of her neck. 'Lizzie Tyler was worried it would come out that she tried to have Logan murdered, possibly affecting her son and his future. She knee-jerk reacted, went to speak to Ronald about it, found he was sick, and we think she took his car and hit Stuart, killing him, smashing his head against the bonnet. She hasn't confessed yet, though.'

'Ronald then takes the car into the garage to get it fixed, thinking it's kids,' Monroe nodded.

Declan desperately needed a coffee.

'Hold on,' he said. 'Around the same time, James Harlow used his song "Crooked Was His Cane" as a robo-call. Was that connected?'

'We found it on Stuart's phone because, well, he was dead and wasn't answering them,' Monroe shrugged. 'But the others, maybe they got them, maybe they didn't. One thing's for sure, whether or not James did this deliberately, we don't know yet.'

Billy's phone rang. Checking the number, he said, 'I need to take this, I'm sorry,' rose quickly and walked out of the room.

With Billy now missing, Declan considered what had been said.

'Okay then. Stuart Laws hit by a car, Ronald Tyler gassed, Clifford Stone drowned,' he looked around the room. 'What's left for Lance Curtis-Warner, if he's indeed been taken?'

'Aye, laddie, that's the problem,' Monroe muttered. 'If he's got taken by someone, either Cavan or James or whatever, we have no bloody idea what's in store for him.'

'I think I need to go and have a chat with Mister Harlow,' Declan said. 'As soon as I find him, that is.'

'Aye, and once we find Mister Khan, we'll have a chat with him, too. Anjli and De'Geer? When Khan's located, go grab him. Rosanna can go through the forensics again.'

'And what about you and Bullman?' Declan asked.

'She's sorting out our ... other issue,' Monroe replied. 'It seems after you and Mister Kleid visited our other friend today, he wants to talk.'

His words were cut short as Billy re-entered the room, a smile on his face.

'Who was it?' Declan asked.

'An estate agent that Logan Harlow's accountants had put me in touch with,' Billy replied.

'Oh, aye?' Monroe raised an eyebrow. 'Laddie, if you're going to buy another mansion, can you do it in your own time?'

Billy smiled, sitting back in the chair.

'It's actually in relation to trap streets,' he said. 'I'd left my notebook by my computer, so I had to run out and get it.'

'When you say trap street, do you mean Bartlett Place?' Declan asked.

Billy nodded, pulling up an image on the screen. It was one they'd seen before, the Google Maps imagery of what was believed to be the onetime Bartlett Place.

'So there's a TV show, right?' he said. 'Alfie Reynolds

mentioned his dad had suggested he watch it, and I found it on Dailymotion. It's twenty years old, and probably recorded straight from BBC Two, but back in 2005 there was a show called *Map Man*, where Nicholas Crane would travel around and look at various maps.'

'Sounds fascinating,' Monroe rolled his eyes.

'Well, it was fascinating enough for two seasons,' Billy smiled politely. 'In one of them, they talk about the creation of the A to Z, how it was built up from one lady, Phyllis Pearsall, walking around London over years, collecting every street, but it also talks about trap streets, or as they call them, "phantom streets". In the episode, Crane goes to find a street which doesn't exist yet on the map. He calls in the A to Z people, who turn up and map a new-build estate in Canary Wharf, in E14—'

'Where Bartlett Place is.'

'Well, that's the thing,' Billy said. 'In the episode, we learn Bartlett Place is a phantom street created by the A to Z to stop people ripping off their maps. In fact, it's named after Kieran Bartlett, who in the episode is actually the person fixing the maps, so it was obviously a more recent addition than something from decades earlier.'

'So, I'm guessing that your conversation about television shows is connected to why Ronald Tyler was found there?' Declan asked.

'I think so,' Billy nodded. 'You see, in the episode, one reason Crane can't find the street is because it's a new-build estate, and checking into the records, I saw it was built around 2004 as a large selection of apartments and flats.'

Billy started going through records on his laptop.

'The average price for one of these was somewhere

between one hundred and fifty to two hundred and fifty thousand pounds, back then.'

'Jesus,' Monroe muttered. 'And that's twenty years ago. I wonder what they're worth now.'

'About three times the price,' Billy said. 'Estimations at the moment show an apartment that was, say, two hundred thousand pounds in 2004 is now six, sometimes maybe seven hundred thousand pounds. And here's the interesting thing ... Logan Harlow owned one of the apartments.'

'Harlow did?' Declan frowned. 'I'm guessing this was after the payout?'

'Yes,' Billy replied. 'He bought the apartment the moment it hit the market, about six, seven months before he died, and around the time he met Beth Stevens. However, from the looks of the details here, he paid cash, two hundred grand, for a massive discount off the asking price.'

'Quite a substantial chunk of his money.'

'True, but it meant no mortgage, and the value would only go up,' Anjli replied. 'It's a wise investment.'

'Aye, and something for him and Beth to move into if they carried on their relationship. It seems the Bindlesticks back-packer wanted to settle down.'

Billy nodded at Monroe's comment.

'But that's not all. You see, after Logan died, everything went to his brother James, which would have included the apartment and probably a large amount of death taxes. But shortly before Logan died, he put the apartment into some kind of trust, making Sandeep Khan the executor.'

'Which bypasses death taxes, I assume,' Declan replied.

'Exactly. So, I was looking into Lance Curtis-Warner,' Billy continued. 'I knew he'd been broke when he'd invested in Sandeep Khan's software, having been cut off from his funds.

From what I can work out, he'd drained his other accounts to cover that investment. However, he still had some kind of off-the-books income, because he continued living the life he had up to that point, until about six months after Logan passed away, when Lance Curtis-Warner takes a hundred-grand loan to invest in another company.'

'There's nothing surprising about that, surely,' Declan replied. 'He's the heir to billions—'

'He's the heir to billions who's effectively been cut off from the sweetie jar,' Monroe added. 'Banks would still want something as collateral, so what did he give them?'

'The document I found shows that, six months after the death of Logan Harlow, Lance Curtis-Warner owned a third of the apartment off Bartlett Place and used that.'

'Who owned the other two-thirds?' Declan asked.

'According to the records, James Harlow and Sandeep Khan.'

Billy tapped on the screen, and more documents appeared, overlaying each other.

'The day before Logan Harlow was found dead, and through his executor—'

'Sandeep Khan.'

'Yes, he arranged to sell his apartment in Gainsborough House to Lance, James, and Sandeep for the price of £1 each.'

'That's a fairly significant loss,' Monroe raised an eyebrow.

'Even if it was, he couldn't have,' Declan shook his head at this. 'When they found his body, they said he'd been in the water for two days.'

'Nobody paid attention, as it had already gone through at that point,' Billy shrugged. 'They'd had the paperwork ready for a while, and somehow, after he drowned, but before he was found, Logan Harlow raised himself from the dead, split his apartment between three people for three quid, and then went back to the Thames.'

'And James Harlow inherited the rest of his money and invested it with Sandeep,' Anjli muttered to herself. 'Maybe gaining part of this apartment could have been a bribe.'

'Selling it at the time would have made them just under a hundred grand each,' Billy replied. 'Death taxes on a full sale would have knocked it almost down by half, unless passed down the family line.'

He looked back at the room.

'But they never sold the apartment. They still own it, and for the last twenty years, that apartment has been rented out by a management company on their behalf. It brings in around two and a half grand a month in rent. My estimations are, that over the twenty years, it's probably made them double what the apartment originally cost in profits.'

'Did anyone know about this?'

'I don't think so,' Billy replied. 'But think about it; Logan's got a kid. If it comes up now that Logan had an heir, this apartment ... well, that could technically be something a legal team would use to reopen Logan's case. People would finally work out that the timing doesn't match.'

'It would open a can of worms they weren't expecting,' Declan nodded. 'Plus open them up to blackmail by Ronald Tyler.'

'What makes you think that?'

'Because he went there at six in the morning,' Declan said. 'He told Clifford Stone he was going to get what was owed to him or something along those lines. What if Ronald Tyler realised almost three-quarters of a million pounds worth of apartment was money gained by criminal means? If he could prove they took this apartment from Logan while he was dead but not found, it'd end them. That's worth a large bag of hush money.'

He paused, frowning.

'And what's the matter with you?' Monroe asked. 'You look like you saw a bloody ghost!'

Declan looked around the room, frowning, before continuing.

'Something Gladwell said, it's still resonating with me,' he said. 'I'll come back to you on it.'

Nodding, Monroe clapped his hands, looking back to the room.

'Okay then. We have a motive, finally!' he cried out. 'Let's find some people to arrest!'

27
_____

# STEP COUNT

After leaving the briefing room, Billy had been working through Lance Curtis-Warner's phone GPS records. LCW Holdings had given him access to them, in hopes he could learn anything where Lance was right now, following the discovery of broken crockery and blood. As it was, he couldn't; the phone had been left in the car he'd parked up near the venue, but one thing it meant was that Billy could check the whereabouts of Lance over the last few weeks.

Unsurprisingly, the phone hadn't been in Gibson Square recently, nor had it been anywhere near any old trap streets, but there was one address it visited a few weeks earlier that raised alarm bells.

He would have continued, but the Strava passcode and web URL for Sandeep Khan's Garmin had finally arrived from Jeff Morrison's PA, and Billy, now alone at his monitor station, logged into the system. Everything Declan had told him about Sandeep Khan's step contest seemed to be true. The Strava that was connected had begun counting steps at the start of the month, and Billy could see that there was an average of twenty to twenty-five thousand steps every day. Sandeep Khan still hadn't reached his target, and Billy could see from the data that Jeff was only a mile away from reaching his. However, it wasn't the step count that interested Billy, it was the Strava real-time data. Billy had read up about the Strava Beacon app, and had learned it was a push update every fifteen-seconds, which meant that four times a minute, the location of the person using the Strava app would appear.

Currently, Sandeep Khan's Garmin watch, connected to Strava, was somewhere in Stratford, not far from the Olympic Park.

Billy leant back, frowning. That wasn't anywhere near Khan's Shoreditch office or podcast studios, and, to his knowledge, Sandeep Khan didn't live anywhere near there. It was, however, very close to James Harlow's old recording studio.

*Was Sandeep with James? If so, was Lance with them?*

Billy was about to pass the information on when he paused, looking back at the app.

*It showed Sandeep's Strava footage for the entire month.*

The data within could give Billy an in-depth tracking map of everywhere Sandeep Khan had been since the start of August, a time that covered the deaths of Ron Tyler, Clifford Stone, and Stuart Laws.

Billy looked around the office. He knew that what he was thinking was technically *not* legal, rather than *il*legal. But there was a good argument to state that Sandeep Khan not answering his phone could mean he was in mortal danger and, therefore, checking into his history could give Billy what he needed.

*And Jeff Morrison had said to do whatever they wanted with the data.*

'Hey, Guv,' he said. 'Is it okay if I check this data? Maybe see if Sandeep Khan was anywhere suspicious?'

It was spoken softly, but not loud enough to even reach Bullman in her office.

'You're not angry if I do this?' Billy continued at the same level and, receiving no answer, he smiled.

'All right then,' he said, moving into the database data. 'I performed due diligence and was not told to back off. Let's have a quick peek.'

He scrolled back through the data, starting chronologically, going back to the day Stuart Laws had been murdered. However, as expected, Sandeep Khan hadn't been in Surrey around that time. There was, however, an address that popped up that surprised Billy, from the evening *before* Stuart Laws died. And as he progressed through the month, Billy leant back in his chair, whistling to himself, staring at the data in front of him.

He turned back to the other window, and reopening Lance Curtis-Warner's records, another lengthy database of code and numbers, Billy looked through that as well. Chronologically, the last known location of the phone was the car outside the club where James Harlow had played the previous night. But once he checked the other dates, cross-referencing them with Sandeep's, Bullman, emerging from her office and seeing his expression, walked over.

'What do you have?' she asked as Billy looked back at her.

'Is D Supt Monroe upstairs talking to Lizzie Tyler still?' he asked.

Bullman stared at the ceiling.

'Using my psychic powers, I would assume he's talking to her or Marshall,' she replied. 'What have you found?'

Billy looked back at the screen.

'The night before Stuart Laws died,' he started, 'the neighbour claimed that Ronald Tyler was bedridden with food poisoning, and that his wife had visited him once during the night and then again on the day after. He said there were also lots of deliveries, people knocking on the door. I don't think they were deliveries, ma'am.'

'Go on,' Bullman went closer, checking the data he could see. 'Who are we looking at here?'

'The one on the left is Lance Curtis-Warner,' Billy explained. 'His people sent me his phone's GPS codes, hoping we could find him.'

'Did we?'

'No, because the phone's in his car outside the gig venue, but it *has* shown me something else – that he was at Ronald Tyler's house that night.'

'And the other?'

'It's the monthly Strava location information for Sandeep Khan,' Billy replied. 'He was there, too. And I reckon if you checked the Waze records on his phone, you'll see Clifford Stone turned up at Tyler's as well.'

Bullman tapped her lip.

'And you gained this how?'

'The rival in Sandeep's step challenge sent me the details,' Billy said, ignoring the fluffed legalities here.

'So Sandeep Khan, Lance Curtis-Warner, Lizzie and Ronald Tyler and possibly Clifford Stone were all at Ronald Tyler's house the night before Stuart Laws' death,' Bullman made a "hmm" noise before continuing. 'That's a star chamber. That's people deciding what to do about Stuart, a "who would rid me of this turbulent priest" moment. But no James Harlow?'

Billy shook his head.

'Harlow was most likely arranging the robo-call with Sandeep Khan at this point,' he said. 'Sandeep would have done it after the meeting, I'm guessing.'

'Sounds like Sandeep Khan is more involved in this than we thought. Do we get anything else from Curtis-Warner?'

Billy paused a line of data, noting it down.

'Not much,' he admitted. 'He visited Sandeep Khan yesterday afternoon, and also Monarch Autos after the Guvs visited, but that's not uncommon, as he has cars leased that get checked up there. But I've only just received this, so I need some more time to go through it.'

'What else do you have? You have that expression Declan's pointed out before.'

Billy opened up the CCTV taken from King's Cross of the hooded man standing beside Clifford Stone's car, walking stick just about visible in his hand.

'It's time-stamped here, see,' he said, sitting down. 'King's Cross Station. It's actually heading south on Pancras Road. You come out and you queue up—'

'I know the cab stop,' Bullman nodded. 'And we've seen this before, unless you have facial recognition software that can look through hoods.'

'I think I might have better, ma'am,' Billy replied. 'Sandeep Khan's Strava information has him in the same location at the exact same time. If it isn't him standing there watching the car, he's inside it.'

He showed the line of data that he'd seen this on.

'Added to that, ma'am, the next time he gains any step count – which basically means the next time he's walking – well, it's in Gibson Square, half an hour later.'

He paused as a thought came to mind.

'Sorry, I just need to ...' he trailed off, already typing and pulling up his browser windows. In one of the browser windows, the page of Sandeep Khan's podcast appeared. They'd seen it before; Billy had shown it in one of the earlier briefings.

But now, Billy stared at it.

'There was something that threw me about this,' he said. 'Besides all the services the website boasts on offer, there are pictures of Sandeep doing exciting activities: hiking, swimming, skiing, magic, all that kind of stuff. But there are two photos here that are the same image.'

'And?' Bullman frowned.

'And if you're designing a website, you don't put the same image twice,' Billy replied. 'It's a placeholder photo until something new goes in.'

'Okay, so maybe they need a new photo?'

'Yes, ma'am, but the question is why?'

He started typing in the browser tab again, opening up a website called the *Wayback Machine.*

'This website takes snapshots of everything on the internet,' he says. 'You can go back years and discover how a website has progressed throughout time. As you can see here, the podcast page was snapped by the machine two months ago and seven months ago, so if we look at the more recent one—'

He paused as the Wayback Machine's browser slowly loaded the same web page.

'It looks exactly the same,' Bullman replied.

'No, look,' Billy said. 'That duplicate photo isn't there.'

Bullman watched as Billy scrolled down, revealing the now-changed photo of Sandeep Khan. In the older, now-removed image, he was standing on what looked to be a Caribbean beach.

And in his right hand was a *full-face blue snorkel mask.*

'Sandeep Khan removed this some time in the last four weeks,' Billy replied. 'There's nothing else in this photo that would cause it to be removed. No other person, no branding ...'

He faded off. He didn't need to continue. Bullman understood.

'Sandeep Khan removed this photo because he didn't want us knowing he'd used a full-face mask,' she said. 'Also, the top of *that* mask looks very similar to the one we found in Clifford Stone's car.'

She straightened, looking down at the screen.

'Sandeep Khan knows how the snorkel works. He owns one of those snorkels, or at least has used one. He's also near Clifford Stone on the night in question. Why wouldn't he have hidden his steps?'

'Probably didn't think about it,' Billy replied. 'I mean, the only reason I found it was because he's missing and we were worried. If he hadn't been a suspect, we wouldn't have been checking into this. It's just pure luck. And as we're near the end of the month, he's probably become more lax.'

'Where is he now?' Bullman snarled.

Billy checked.

'Right here,' he said, pointing at a spot on a Google map that appeared. 'Near the London Stadium, in Stratford.'

Bullman leant closer.

'And what the bloody hell is that place?' she asked.

---

'IT'S A RECORDING STUDIO OWNED BY JAMES HARLOW,' Marshall Reynolds said, leaning back on his chair, all attempts at pretence now stopped. 'That is, it used to be. He built a new building when he had made some more money from the sale of the taxi app.'

'Who uses it now?' Monroe asked, looking at Declan beside him for any suggestions. Until they could work out where James Harlow was, there was no point in leaving the building, and so Declan had decided to help Monroe.

'I don't know,' Marshall admitted. 'I think he sold it, as someone else was moving in or something.'

'You seem to be very knowledgeable about James Harlow,' Monroe muttered. 'Maybe you're closer than we thought.'

Marshall sighed, shaking his head slightly, more as an effort of resignation than of denial.

'I had debts,' he said, 'about a year back, at the time my car had broken down and I needed money. Curtis-Warner was upping his percentage, claiming I had to give him more each month for the lease of the car.'

'And so you went to see James Harlow?'

'Christ no,' Marshall shrugged his head. 'First, I went to see Sandeep.'

'Did Sandeep help you?'

'In a way. You see, *he* was the one who put me in touch with James Harlow,' Marshall shrugged, looking away. 'I might hate the family, but he's got deep pockets, you know?'

Monroe leant closer.

'So what happened to Sandeep and Lance, in your opinion? And remember, laddie, that brevity is the source of all hope for you. We have possibly two people missing.'

Marshall shook his head.

'They're not missing,' he said. 'They decided to go off-grid.'

'What makes you think that?'

'Because I know them both,' he said. 'There is absolutely no reason why Lance would have been taken by James. It's Sandeep who hates his bloody guts.'

'But Sandeep would work with James, right?' Monroe replied. 'You said he helped with the coding for the robo-call.'

'He also gave us the money,' Marshall admitted. 'Said it was from James. I had no reason to disbelieve him. It's the Harlows. They have form for this sort of petty shit.'

---

'YEAH, THEY WERE IN THE ROOM,' LIZZIE TYLER WIPED HER eyes with the tissue passed to her by Cooper, as Anjli noted this down. 'Me, Ronnie, Clifford, Sandeep and Lance.'

'And why was Sandeep there?' Anjli looked up. 'He wasn't there when Logan was hit?'

'Neither was I,' Lizzie protested.

'Yes, but you paid for the thing,' Anjli replied calmly. 'You were as much a part of this as they were. Sandeep, though ...'

'He was part of it. He loaned me the money back then.'

'He did? Why?'

'I don't know why. Maybe he felt sorry for me. I paid him back in a couple of weeks, and it was swept under the rug,' Lizzie shrugged. 'To be honest, I don't know why he was there. But it was good he was, as we couldn't decide what to do.'

'He made the decision?'

Lizzie shook her head.

'We all knew Stuart had to go,' she said. 'He knew too much, and he was talking about going to the police, going on about "messengers". But there needed to be a plan. Ronald had food poisoning from a dodgy drive-thru meal the previous night, so he was let off the deal.'

'Deal?'

Lizzie nodded.

'Ronnie had a pack of cards. Sandeep shuffled them, and then we all took one from him. The lowest card did the deed, so to speak. Most honest way to do it. Sandeep even took one himself, to show he was part of this.'

'Did he now?' Anjli asked, realising what had truly happened here. Sandeep was a fan of card magic; that was shown by the photo on the webpage. It stood to reason he knew some of the tricks. Forcing a card wasn't that hard; he'd known exactly who to give it to.

'You drew the lowest, didn't you?' she continued.

Lizzie nodded.

'Five of diamonds,' she admitted. 'But I need to explain; we weren't looking to kill Stuart. The plan was to scare him. Rough him up.'

'But it was wet and slippery that morning, wasn't it? What happened, you lost control?'

'I hadn't driven an electric cab before. I didn't realise how quickly it accelerated,' Lizzie looked away. 'I came at him too fast. I knew he was dead the moment he bounced off the windscreen.'

There was a long, silent moment in the interview room.

'He killed Logan, though,' she muttered. 'He was only supposed to hit him.'

'Like *you* were only supposed to,' Anjli replied.

Lizzie Tyler didn't respond. She knew he was right.

DOCTOR MARCOS WASN'T SURE WHY SHE HAD CHECKED THE black cab for emissions. Clifford Stone's vehicle was impounded because it was associated with a victim's death, rather than being a murder weapon itself. But while she had waited for some responses, she had been staring at the car in the impound lot. There was something not quite right – something she had missed. There was every chance that Clifford Stone had been part of something many years ago, something for which he'd been killed, but was she over-thinking the situation?

She turned to one of the forensic officers.

'Long shot, but do you have a gas chromatography-mass spectrometer around?'

'I don't think we have one in the kit,' they said, looking confused. Doctor Marcos grimaced. They weren't her usual crew; she was borrowing from another department.

She stared at the car.

'Have you got the keys?' she asked.

'Yes.'

'This is going to sound strange, but I want you to start the car and keep it going until I say stop.'

'And what are you going to do?' the officer asked, frowning.

'I'm going to stand behind it with an evidence baggie and fill it up with exhaust fumes,' Doctor Marcos smiled. The forensics officer stared at her as if she was mad, but walked over to the car, leaning in and turning it on. It spluttered to life. It was old, ten years old, and the exhaust was shaking; possibly one of the brackets holding it to the chassis had gone, but it did the job. Doctor Marcos pulled out a baggie, placing it over the exhaust for a couple of seconds, then she pulled it off quickly before the plastic melted on the hot exhaust.

Coughing, she zipped it up.

'You do know that'll escape?' the forensics officer asked.

Doctor Marcos nodded.

'I just need trace elements,' she said with a smile. 'You can turn it off now. It's done its job.'

———

# 28

# MIXING DESKS

MONROE WAS WALKING DOWN FROM THE INTERVIEW ROOM when he received the call from Doctor Marcos to come to the ground floor. Muttering to himself and hoping this wasn't anything to do with the week he'd cut short on the honeymoon, Monroe strolled down the steps to the forensic labs and morgue to find Doctor Marcos sitting there with a baggie in front of her and a smile on her face.

'I've just solved one of your crimes,' she said with a grin.

'And how have you done that?' Monroe asked.

Doctor Marcos tapped at the baggie.

'This was filled with the exhaust from Clifford Stone's car,' she explained. 'We didn't have the right equipment, so I had to improvise. Once I got to a lab I could use, I tested it.'

'Aye, and how did you do that, lassie, or am I going to regret asking?'

Doctor Marcos grinned, rubbing her hands together in anticipation of the lecture.

'First, I gathered exhaust samples directly from Clifford Stone's cab. Did it all under strict lab conditions to avoid any contamination; I was really meticulous about capturing the samples accurately to ensure we're comparing apples to apples, so to speak.'

'And how did you create this lab condition?'

'I took an evidence baggie and stuck it on the exhaust,' Doctor Marcos smiled. 'It did the job, Alex. I brought it to Lambeth as they have the big toys, and used two principal methods for the analysis. For organic compounds—'

'Organic compounds?'

'Key compounds from engine oil, like hydrocarbons, phthalates, and specific markers from additives,' Doctor Marcos explained. 'What engine oil do you use in your car?'

Monroe considered this.

'Castrol Magnatec—'

'Right, so if we were looking at your exhaust, we'd find traces that match that. These traces, for example, wouldn't match their GTX range. And, as Stone had a small container with some oil in, probably for emergencies in the boot of his cab, we know what we're looking for here.'

Monroe nodded, understanding this.

'So, knowing that, we went with gas chromatography-mass spectrometry, and for any metals – those tiny traces that come from engine wear or oil additives – we used inductively coupled plasma mass spectrometry.'

'These are all made up *Star Trek* words, aren't they?'

'You wish, nerd-boy. Anyway, it's detailed work, looking for specific markers and all that,' Doctor Marcos continued. 'We already had the lab reports from the exhaust fumes in Ronald Tyler's car. With the car being electric, there were no contrasting exhaust fumes to dilute this, and comparing the two, I can see it's a match.'

She pumped the air with a fist.

'Doctor Marcos solves the crime,' she said. 'Go me.'

'Are you telling me that Clifford Stone's car was the one that killed Ron Tyler?'

'It's not conclusive, but definitely compelling. Environmental factors and sample degradation are always wild cards in forensic science, but the profiles matched more closely than I expected,' Doctor Marcos replied. 'The chemical signatures and metal concentrations of both samples were consistent with what we'd predict from a car that had been at both scenes. What I can't prove is whether Clifford Stone was the driver at the time, but I'm sure you can work that one out, checking his Waze or Google Maps data.'

Monroe nodded.

'Billy can match that,' he said, already walking to the door to pass this along. 'This is great work, thank you.'

He turned back to look at her.

'Marshall Reynolds said Clifford Stone was talking to Ron Tyler,' he said. 'I wonder if this was why he did this.'

Doctor Marcos smiled.

'You look so sexy when you think you're being a detective,' she said. 'Give me half an hour and I'll solve the rest for you.'

---

AFTER THE INTERVIEW, AND AS MONROE WENT TO VISIT Doctor Marcos, Declan was checking for updates on James Harlow's location using his old desk – as Monroe had requisitioned his office again – when Sergeant Mastakin, usually found at the front desk, popped his head through the door.

'DCI Walsh?' he asked. 'Sorry to interrupt you, but your car alarm keeps going off.'

Declan frowned. His police-issue Audi wasn't exactly the newest of cars on the block, and in the Temple Inn car park, there were a multitude of newer, more expensive-looking cars.

After all, Temple Inn was also home to a lot of barristers when they weren't at court.

For someone to keep targeting his car seemed a bit odd.

*Maybe it was an easier one to break into,* he thought to himself as he grabbed his jacket and walked down the stairs, following Sergeant Mastakin back to the front desk.

Walking out into the open, Declan crossed King's Bench Walk, hurrying over to where his car was parked. It wasn't flashing, and there was no alarm going, but Declan knew the alarm would sound for thirty seconds and then stop, repeating shortly after.

*Best to check it, anyway.*

As he approached the car, however, he saw a figure peel away from the tree to the left.

He was an old man, late sixties, wearing a long, three-quarter length navy overcoat-style jacket. He had short cropped gunmetal-grey hair, and his face was pockmarked along the left-hand side, as if someone had once used it as a brake against gravel, or he'd had something acidic thrown against him. Some kind of injury, definitely.

The way he held himself gave Declan the impression that this man was ex-police, or something similar.

Army, maybe. Security services? Most likely.

*Oh God*, he thought to himself, *tell me Charles Baker isn't sending people to see me again.*

'Are you Walsh?' the man asked, walking over.

'Depends who's asking,' Declan replied. 'Are you the joker that's been playing with my car?'

'Needed to get you out of the station without raising suspicion,' the man said. 'The name's Strange.'

'Your name is strange, or—'

'Bernard Strange. I didn't ask for the surname, and I don't appreciate any jokes.'

Declan held a hand up, forcing back the three quick one-liners he'd already considered.

'Can you follow me, please?' The new arrival continued, waving at the car park. 'I have a slightly delicate request for you.'

'Ask me it here.'

'I would, but it's not from me.'

Declan sighed, and followed the strange, pockmarked man – although he couldn't really call him strange if his surname was Strange – over to a Range Rover with black tinted windows, parked at the far end of the car parking area. He opened the door, and Declan looked in, and was surprised to see a man in his eighties sitting there waiting for him.

He was slim, his hair almost gone, white and wispy remnants on the sides. He was tanned, with a small collection of liver spots over his pate. He wore an expensive pinstripe, double-breasted suit with a pink tie. And from the Rolex Declan could see on his wrist, this man was incredibly rich.

'My name is Timothy Curtis-Warner,' he said, as Declan stood at the doorway to the Range Rover. 'I believe you've been trying to find my son.'

He waved a hand dismissively, as if to invite Declan into the car, but not caring too much if Declan did or not.

Declan glanced at Mister Strange, who had already walked around to the passenger's side. Shrugging, he clambered into the car, closing the door behind him.

'You could have come into the building,' he said. 'We have comfortable rooms and—'

'I can't be seen going into a police station,' Timothy explained. 'It's bad enough my son is bringing my family's name into disrepute; for me to be seen going into a police station would just start the paparazzi up.'

'I don't know if you've noticed,' Declan said, looking out of the window. 'We have little paparazzi around here.'

'Believe me, Detective Chief Inspector, within ten minutes of me entering your unit, you'd have a dozen paparazzi at the front watching. The ancient old recluse having an awayday here? It'd be news, I'm sure. And don't tell me it's not the first time you've had it. I know who you are, I've read up.'

Declan nodded, accepting the statement.

'Are you here to tell me where your son is? Are you here to help us find him?'

Timothy shook his head.

'I was hoping you could give me information,' he replied. 'His PA contacted my office in a state, claiming he'd gone off grid, his phone left in a car. Bernard here went and had a look.'

'It's only showing that it's in his car, because it turned off while beside his car,' Bernard replied. 'I checked, it's not in there. He could still have it on him, he's just chosen not to turn it on to make calls or receive or send messages. I looked in the venue, there's broken crockery and blood, but not enough to fear vital organs being spilled.'

Declan nodded.

'Okay,' he replied. 'Again with the "this could have been a phone call".'

'I understand he attended a concert by a folk musician named James Harlow,' Timothy asked.

'That's believed to be correct,' Declan replied, wondering where the conversation was now going.

Timothy looked across to the passenger seat where Bernard turned to face them.

'About twenty years ago,' he said, 'maybe a little less, I was hired by Mister Curtis-Warner here to check into his son's past.'

'Private Investigator?'

'I was, now I'm on retainer as Mister Curtis-Warner's counsel.'

'So work-for-hire Private Investigator,' Declan smiled as Bernard gave a short nod. 'This investigation was when Lance was training to be a cab driver, I assume?'

Timothy slumped back in his seat.

'Lance was a bit of a disappointment to the family,' he explained. 'Always partying, never really paying attention. I'd threatened to disown him at one point for his drug-taking and, well, let's just say his dalliances had got out of hand. I gave him an ultimatum, shall we say. He had to prove he could make money, prove he could take a project and carry it on until the end.'

He shook his head but displayed the slightest smile, almost of pride, as he continued.

'So yes, he took the Knowledge, something I'd never even considered, and during that time he found financing opportunities in the market he could move into and, to his credit, he did this. But he was still ...'

He looked away, staring out of the window.

'*Whoring*,' he muttered.

There was a long, uncomfortable moment of silence in the car. Declan didn't want to continue in case it diverted

Timothy from whatever he was going to say, but at the same time, he wasn't sure where the conversation was going.

'There was a woman,' Timothy continued.

'Beth Stevens?'

'Yes, but that wasn't her real name.'

'We know,' Declan replied. 'Elizabeth Stephanos.'

The revelation seemed to surprise Timothy, as if he hadn't considered that the police would even work this one out.

'Why, yes,' he said. 'Have you spoken to her?'

'She's a person of interest,' Declan nodded. 'She's the widow of one of the murder victims.'

'Yes, Ronald Tyler,' Timothy nodded. 'He was one of Lance's friends and took many loans from him over the years. But that's not the reason we've come to talk to you. It's James Harlow we want to talk to you about.'

Declan leant closer.

'If you have something that can tell me what James Harlow is playing at, we'd greatly appreciate it.'

'What James Harlow is playing at?' Timothy shook his head, confused. 'What do you know that I don't?'

'Mister Curtis-Warner, we are led to believe that your son was involved in the murder of Logan Harlow twenty years ago,' Declan explained. 'We also believe that twenty years later, James Harlow, learning about this, has started some kind of campaign against the four men involved, which caused them to turn against each other. We already know that Stuart Laws, one of the four, was murdered after they met up one night to discuss him. And since then, two other people from the original four are dead. Lance is the last one. So, your son is either the last of this line of victims—'

'Or he's the one doing it,' Bernard saw where Declan was going with this.

'At the moment, we have no knowledge of why James Harlow would have started this campaign,' Declan nodded. 'He worked with Sandeep Khan and your son for many years as an investor in Khan's company, and from what we can work out, he owns an equal share in an E14 apartment, again with Khan and your son. Gained a lot of money five years ago, and the only thing that we can work out is that he discovered in the last few years that Cavan Tyler, Lizzie Tyler's son, is actually Logan Harlow's biological son.'

'That's another reason why we've come to speak to you,' Bernard pulled out a sheet of paper, passing it across. 'As Mister Curtis-Warner said, twenty years ago he was worried about Lance's lifestyle, shall we say, and brought me in to check into it. We were concerned he'd done something stupid because we'd heard that the girl, Elizabeth, although she called herself Beth, was pregnant. We worried this was some kind of scam to try to gain money from Lance, claiming that on a drunken binge he got her pregnant and "oh no, now he must give her money every month for the rest of his life". It's more common than you would expect.'

Declan nodded as he looked down the lines.

'This is a DNA test,' he said. 'Paternity?'

'Yes,' Bernard replied. 'When the baby was born we managed to do a paternity test against Lance, and found that he wasn't the father, which is what we expected, but to be sure we'd also cross-compared it to both Ronald Tyler and Logan.'

'You're making it sound like neither of them were the father?'

'No,' Bernard replied, passing a second piece of paper across. 'So, curious, we got creative. My department, that is, not the company. We looked into a rumour that on the night Logan disappeared, he'd had a fight with Miss Stephanos about an affair she'd had with James, and so we managed to gain DNA evidence. And surprise, surprise, it was a match. James Harlow is Cavan Tyler's father.'

'Did Lance ever know this?' Declan shook his head – nothing in this case had surprised him, but this had got close.

Bernard laughed.

'DCI Walsh, Lance Curtis-Warner has *always* known this,' he said. 'This was part of the review that we gave him, when we told him about what we'd found a year after the baby was born. He was unhappy his father had got into his life in such detail, but ...'

He turned away, looking out of the window.

'Perhaps we should have kept it from him,' he said. 'But over the last twenty years, Lance Curtis-Warner has been the only person who I know of outside of this car that knows that James Harlow is Cavan Tyler's true father. Even the mother didn't know, convinced it was his brother.'

'Jesus,' Declan said. 'Can I keep this?'

'We have many copies,' Timothy said. 'But please, if you find Lance is involved in something terrible, can you do your best to keep it from the press? We would be grateful.'

'I'll do what I can,' Declan said. 'But if we find he's involved criminally, there's not a lot I can really do.'

He paused, looking back at Bernard.

'Actually, how grateful?' he asked.

'What do you need?' Bernard smiled. 'I'm guessing it's something off the books?'

'If I give you a name, can you look into them?' Declan asked. 'Just to check? If you were this good twenty years ago you must be pretty bloody brilliant right now. And unfortunately, anything we do off-books, especially with this one, is likely to be scrutinised.'

'Give me the name. I'll have a look and you'll have something by the end of today.'

Declan folded up the paper, placing it into his inside pocket.

'Jennifer Farnham-Ewing,' he said. 'She's an MP. I'm particularly curious about her movements when she worked for Will Harrison a few years back.'

'Consider it done,' Bernard replied, noting it down. 'If, somehow, we can keep Mister Curtis-Warner's son out of the press.'

'I can't promise that,' Declan said. 'If I find he's in any way connected to the murders, he will have to face justice.'

'And that's perfectly fine,' Timothy said. 'But the moment that happens, *if* it does, please understand the finest solicitors known to man or beast will appear on your doorstep. Because murderer or not, he's my child. And a father will do everything for his child.'

Declan shook Timothy Curtis-Warner's hand.

'Yes, they will,' he replied. 'I'd do whatever it took to keep my daughter safe.'

Walking from the car, Declan froze in the car park; the memory of Gladwell came to his mind again, a particular line he'd spoken while talking to Declan and Fabian Kleid.

*'When you have everything to lose, you don't rattle the cage. Secrets could spill out of it, and you've done it to yourself. Everything you've built up over the years is gone in a flash, and you have nothing.'*

Declan finally now knew what it was about the words that had tweaked at his thoughts.

And suddenly, he had an idea about what was really going on.

———

## 29

***

# WAKEY WAKEY

'Do you think we have this the wrong way around?' Declan asked as he stood in the main office, having recently returned from his downstairs meeting. 'I mean, if Lance's dad's correct, then for twenty years, Lance Curtis-Warner has known that Cavan Tyler is actually James Harlow's son and has never once told them.'

The office was full: Billy at his monitor, Anjli at her desk, Monroe beside her and De'Geer standing beside Bullman. Only Cooper, called downstairs to reception moments earlier, and Doctor Marcos, still examining carbon monoxide in her office, weren't there.

'Maybe he feels it wasn't his place to say?' Monroe suggested.

'But surely he would have corrected them when they started saying it was Logan's son?' Declan added. 'It would have been a matter of just simply replying and saying, "Actually, I think you'll find ..." as the damage had already been done, and at least that way James would know.'

He shook his head.

'What if he's *not* the victim of a kidnapping here? What if he's been playing a game as long as James has? What does he lose? Or, rather, what does he gain from the deaths of the others?'

Monroe considered the question.

'Maybe his father would disown him again,' he suggested. 'The Curtis & Warner money is quite significant. You're talking billions when his father dies, and he's not exactly getting any younger. Also, if the news gets out about Lance knowing James was Cavan's father, it could bring to light the dodgy real estate dealings he was involved in, twenty years ago.'

'Boss,' Billy said from across the room, breaking the moment.

'What have you found, laddie?' Monroe glanced over at him.

'That apartment that we found in E14,' Billy tapped his screen. 'The one we worked out was owned by Lance, Sandeep, and James?'

'Okay, laddie, spit it out.'

'It's not anymore.'

'I thought you said they had never sold it,' Declan frowned.

'They haven't,' Billy replied. 'But the deeds were re-filed a month and a half ago.'

'Remortgaging, perhaps?' Anjli suggested.

Billy shook his head as he turned to her.

'More of an estate swap,' he said. 'James Harlow sold his recording studio. His old one, that is.'

Billy tapped on his keyboard, swiping on his trackpad, working through some of the digital files he'd been sent, with a speed which made Declan wonder whether Billy was actually reading them, or using some kind of psychic mind control. Eventually, Billy stopped and turned back with a smile.

'Six weeks ago,' he said triumphantly. 'James Harlow sold his third of the apartment to Sandeep Khan for one pound, the same price they did the original deal.'

'You would have thought they would have added at least some inflation,' Declan smiled. 'So, why would he do that, then? Surely that's just losing money.'

'Well, it wasn't just a pound,' Billy read from the screen. 'It was a pound and the deeds to his recording studio.'

Declan thought back to when he met Sandeep.

'He needed a new recording studio for his podcasts,' he said. 'Stratford's not too far from Haggerston, it makes a little sense.'

'But there's a dozen different places he could have gone to where he works,' Billy replied. 'You throw a stone in Shoreditch and you'll find a mixing desk.'

'Aye,' Monroe replied. 'But this mixing desk came with an advantage.'

He looked back at the others.

'Think about it. This isn't about James Harlow gaining more of his brother's apartment. This is Sandeep Khan removing evidence. By purchasing the recording studio, he's saving himself time and stress by not having to find a different one, but he's also selling off part of a property that could bite him on the arse any time soon.'

'The building's probably worth about the same as the apartment is now,' Declan replied. 'By doing this, they save a lot of legal and solicitor fees. It's a straight swap, in a way.'

He paused.

'Sandeep told me he hadn't started the podcast yet, but

you just said it was six weeks ago, so technically that place is empty.'

'Probably would be,' Billy nodded as he carried on working through the notes. 'I mean, it *was* an actual recording studio first. They probably had to do it up, add some comfy chairs, a table or two.'

'Why do you need all that for a radio show?' Monroe frowned.

'It's a podcast,' Billy replied, 'not a radio show. A lot of them now are filmed, so you can actually see them on YouTube and watch them as they happen. It's like a television interview rather than a radio. You need a set so doing that in a musical recording studio probably wouldn't look as good. Also, the acoustics there would have been made for instruments, and they probably want it to be more something for sound.'

'Have you got an address?'

'Yes Guv.' Billy held a finger up, as if testing the wind as he stared at the screen. 'Hold on. There's a clause. Sandeep buys for a pound and his share of the apartment, but as James has no next of kin, if he dies before Sandeep does, Sandeep gains both his and James's shares back.'

'Clever,' Bullman nodded. 'That would become a new deed. Sandeep would be seen as gaining two-thirds of a property, rather than gaining a third and re-gaining another.'

'And if Lance dies, then Sandeep has a case for the whole thing,' Declan added. 'Because I bet he's got that planned somehow.'

'If Sandeep owns that building, then that explains why he's there,' Monroe said. 'I think we need to see what's going on.'

He paused.

'You've got his Strava details for the last month, right?'

'Yes, sir,' Billy replied. 'But I hadn't really gone into it because of legalities.'

'To hell with legalities,' Monroe snapped. 'Can you check quickly if Sandeep Khan has been there any time in the last month?'

Billy worked on his computer for a moment.

'Since acquiring the location, he's only been there once, after the deal was settled,' he said. 'Apart from that, no.'

'So, why would he be there right now, on a Saturday afternoon?' Monroe nodded to himself. 'Declan, I think it's time to go bring Sandeep in for the murder of Clifford Stone, among others.'

'Hold on,' Declan was shaking his head. 'Stuart Laws' phone. We have records, right?'

Billy nodded, pulling up the details.

'What are you thinking?'

'Messages sent from Stuart Laws to Sandeep, six weeks ago,' Declan said. 'The day he made the deal.'

Billy check the phone records, and then sent one to the plasma screen.

TO: SANDEEP KHAN

I have your messenger bag still – you left it in the car.

I had to open it to confirm it was yours.
Sorry.

'Sandeep told me he sorted the deal for his new studio right before flying from City Airport,' Declan mused. 'He was taken there by Stuart, who sent that message when he realised Sandeep left his messenger bag in the car.'

'And if he'd just been and sorted the deal, then the paperwork would have been in it,' Anjli replied, her eyes widening in realisation. 'He would have seen the dates, the names … the original sale date would have been on it. He could have realised the truth. Lizzie Tyler said that when Stuart was banging on her door a month back, he mentioned the "messenger". What if he meant the bag, not a person?'

'It also gives another reason Sandeep would want Stuart Laws silenced,' Declan had already walked over to his desk, grabbing his jacket. 'We need to speak with Sandeep right now.'

'Take a few people with you,' Monroe added. 'I have a feeling this isn't going to be as simple as we thought it would be.'

⸻

THE FIRST THING JAMES HARLOW TASTED AS HE REGAINED consciousness was the metallic tang of blood in his mouth. Frowning, he groaned to himself as his temple throbbed, reaching up and grabbing at it, his eyes still closed, and almost too scared to open.

*What had he done last night?*

He remembered playing a gig under the arches, going back to his dressing room … the rest was fuzzy—

*'Remember how I said this was for you? Well, in a way it is, because it's also connected to the attack on your brother, all those years ago—'*

James jerked awake, throwing his hands up to deflect the imaginary cane that swung at him, sliding off the wooden chair he'd been dumped on as he did so.

*He remembered.*

He also recognised his current cell; a recording studio

play room, devoid of all instruments, only one light and a wide-open window to an almost pitch-black sound desk area in his view. The walls were soundproofed, the wooden door to the outside likely locked. There would be nobody here, as he'd locked the doors and padlocked them himself, when he moved to his new studios a few months back – and as far as he knew, the new owner, Sandeep Khan, was still refurbishing.

Rising, he looked around the room; it wasn't large, but it was fair-sized, enough space for three or four people to sit and play music, as was originally planned. However, the equipment for such a thing was now gone, but moved to his newer recording studios, and all that seemed to be left were two large microphone stands, the type that could move around like monitor arms, both hanging from the ceiling, each of which connected into separate microphones, one aimed in each direction, primarily at two chairs. These looked comfy, with a cool, grey, leather upholstery that faced each other across a mahogany coffee table. On each chair's arms were over-ear headphones, and it looked, to James's first impressions, like some kind of interview room. It definitely wasn't how James had left it, several months earlier, when he'd moved.

He looked at the soundproofing on the walls. Some of this had also been changed. He'd had twenty-year-old proofing when he'd started the studio. Good for the time, but nowhere near the levels that people had now. But, over the years, pieces of soundproofing had fallen off, petrified, crumbled away into nothing. This had now been fixed, adding newer technology, as well as some neon lights along the side, for uplighting and aesthetic value.

A momentary humour passed through James. *Maybe he*

*was the next guest on the podcast.* But before he could even chuckle at such a thing, the gravity of his situation came back to mind.

Lance Curtis-Warner had smashed him in the face with a crooked handle of what looked to be his brother's cane. It had hurt like buggery, drawing blood on his temple, but the tip of the handle had clipped the gum, explaining the blood inside his mouth.

It was now he remembered the video, followed by the additional news that Cavan Tyler, his nephew, was actually his *son.*

*That* was something he hadn't expected.

He didn't know if he could trust Lance; he'd need to speak to Beth, find out if she knew any of this, maybe even find out if Ronald had known. There was a whole list of things he'd have to do, including checking the Curtis-Warner private investigator's records to see what had happened all those years ago.

Though, of course, all of this would also involve James Harlow making it out of here alive.

'Hello,' he shouted. 'Is there anybody there?'

There was no answer.

'Come on, you prick!' James shouted. 'You've brought me here. What do you want?'

There was a noise behind him, and he turned around, facing the darkened control room.

'I'm not going to let you go,' the voice of Lance Curtis-Warner spoke through the speakers. 'But I could have been harsher. I could have chained you to a speaker stand, or something.'

'Is this your idea of a joke?' James shouted back, suddenly aware that the soundproofed walls meant no matter how loud he was, nobody would hear him. 'What the hell were you thinking?'

'I was thinking how you did all these terrible things,' Lance said as he now walked up to the window, only just clear through the glass. 'And how your son is going to suffer because of it.'

James walked over to one of the comfortable chairs and sat down in it.

'You want to do this, then you come in here and do it, you arrogant little shit,' he muttered. 'How dare you, of all people, try to throw this on me?'

'No concern over your son and his wellbeing? I can't say I'm that surprised,' Lance mocked.

'Of course I'm concerned,' James half rose from the chair. 'But for my nephew! I can't take your word and a piece of paper! I'll need to confirm it myself.'

'Why bother?' Lance replied calmly. 'After all, it's not like you'll let him into your life or anything.'

At this, James sighed, looking up at the ceiling.

'I have no heirs,' he said. 'No little James's running around. If he is my legal son, then he'll be my next of kin.'

He looked back at the window.

'But even as my biological *nephew* he's still my bloody next of kin, so quit with this bullshit and show me Cavan before I add you to the growing list of other dead onetime wannabe cabbies!'

Lance tutted as he shook his head sadly in response.

'See?' he said, looking to the side. 'Always with the plans, the lies. Always looking how to get on, threatening, killing …'

'No, wait,' James held his hands up. 'I didn't mean it like that. I didn't—'

He stopped as the lights in the mixing studio control

room lit up, and James saw for the first time Lance, watching him ... with Cavan Tyler beside him.

Cavan Tyler, who didn't seem to be bound or restrained.

'Did you send the albums?' Cavan asked, his voice picked up by the microphone, and passing through the speakers.

'Albums?' James was still groggy and confused, but then, on realising, nodded, continuing sarcastically. 'Oh, I might have sent some albums a few weeks back. A gift for all my friends.'

'What about robo-calls?' Lance now asked.

James shook his head.

'That wasn't me,' he said. 'I swear. Whoever sent messages to your phones, reminding you of what you did, I applaud them, don't get me wrong, but I never arranged any of it.'

'So you didn't pay Alfie and his dad five grand to do it?' Cavan frowned.

'The question isn't "did I" but "who did", James risked touching his temple again, wincing as it hurt. 'As in if I didn't do it, then someone had to pay them. And whoever gave them the money, it wasn't me.'

'Alfie said Sandeep Khan did that.'

'Well, there you go,' James shrugged. 'It was Sandeep who'd decided to screw with them.'

'"Them" being?' Cavan folded his arms.

'Your step-father, Ronald Tyler, Stuart Laws, Clifford Stone and that prick beside you.'

James looked back up at the ceiling, considering his next words carefully.

'I've made a lot of money over my life, and it's not been because of my actual talent,' he said. 'Just the fact that I was lucky enough to invest in something that did well, like Lance there did. But the people I invested with weren't the best of people, Cavan. They had secrets, as you're well aware of.'

'Everybody has secrets,' Cavan replied. 'Why should yours be any different?'

'I think you sent that message deliberately to spook us,' Lance now spoke. 'I think you were just looking to prod us, get us worrying. Buggering around, playing with the people you believed killed your poor, mentally ill brother, all those years ago. You sent a vinyl album with that bloody song on to us. You wrote a single message into each one, reminding us to remember what we did, whatever that was. You then sent a robo-call playing that song's chorus. You were harassing us, James, mentally attacking poor, broken souls like Stuart Laws.'

'*I didn't send the robo-calls!*' James screamed out.

'See?' Unperturbed by the outburst, Lance looked back at Cavan. 'He didn't deny the harassment.'

'I know that Stuart Laws came to see you,' Cavan spoke now through the window. 'He was scared, wasn't he? And then you killed him, because you were scared of him telling everybody what you planned to do. I know you sent out threats, how you killed my stepdad, how you were the one who truly killed your brother, knowing, as his only heir, you'd gain the money. Money that meant my mum didn't get a penny, even though he'd promised her. Money you never even offered her.'

James shook his head.

'This is not true,' he responded. 'You've got to listen to me.'

'I don't have to listen to you at all,' Cavan looked back at Lance now. 'I've been told the truth, and you—'

'You've been told a pack of lies,' a new voice spoke now, as

Sandeep Khan walked into the recording studio control room. 'Hello, Cavan. Hello, Lance. Fancy seeing you here.'

'Thank God,' James whispered. 'Finally, a grown-up appears.'

'Mister Khan?' Cavan frowned. 'What are you doing here?'

'I came to make sure that this prick isn't lying to you,' Sandeep smiled, nodding over at Lance. 'You see, this wonderful studio is mine, and the moment you walked in, I got an alarm on my phone. The cameras showed it was you, so I thought I'd pop by.'

'We came into the building three hours ago,' Lance frowned. 'Why didn't you come in then?'

'Because I needed to wait for the right moment,' Sandeep grinned. 'So, what are we doing here? Screwing around with poor little Cavan? Or is Harlow there laying down tracks for his apology tour?'

He looked at Cavan.

'You know he's your dad, right?' he asked innocently. 'Oh, shit, did I give it away and spoil the surprise for ...'

He nodded theatrically at James, as if worried he'd given out a terrible secret.

'Sandeep, I know this is your building and everything, but I'm fixing things,' Lance said.

'What, by having Cavan and James kill each other in my recording studio?' Sandeep shook his head. 'It's a solid idea, but nah, not happening.'

'What does he mean "kill each other"—' Cavan started, but the question died in his mouth as Lance picked up the walking cane and backhanded him, sending him to the ground.

Lance spun back, facing Sandeep, brandishing the cane as a weapon.

'You weren't supposed to be here,' he snarled. 'You said your podcasts started next month, so I thought I had a few days. And the place is insured, anyway.'

'You were going to burn it down!' Sandeep was delighted. 'Let me guess. Cavan learns he's the son of James, blames him for Ronald's murder, they fight in his old studio, and then whoosh! The whole place goes up! I mean, there's a ton of flammable old tapes and crappy old sound proofing. And you get to walk away from the murders, free as a bird.'

He shook his head.

'There's only one problem with that,' he said, reaching into his pocket and pulling out a gun. It was a black semiautomatic with a dark-brown grip.

'This was my father's when he was a police officer in Mumbai,' Sandeep explained. 'He managed to get it over with him when they emigrated, and I inherited it when he died.'

He looked down at it, turning it in his hand.

'It's a Pistol Auto 9mm 1A, also known as an Indian Ordinance Factories 9mm pistol,' he explained. 'Basically, it's a licenced copy of the Browning Hi-Power. Thirteen rounds in the chamber, easily enough for you.'

Lance stared in horror at Sandeep.

'You mean to shoot me?' he was stunned by what he felt was a betrayal.

'No,' Sandeep waved his hand at the door to the studio, a key in the lock. 'I want the two of you in there with James, and then I'll just burn you all to ash. Far better story now you're there too, Lance. I'll even tearfully explain how you'd gone to save Cavan, but died in the process, a hero. Or maybe I'll say James did that and you're the killer. I mean, you even placed your fingerprints all over Logan's old cane for me.

Even I wasn't stupid enough to not use gloves when I left it in the dressing room. I was hoping he'd pick it up, but this works so much better ...'

He smiled.

'With you and James dead, I'll own the Bartlett Place apartment outright. And with Cavan dead, I won't have to give the money to someone else when I sell it, throwing you both under the bus for the murders.'

He paused.

'No, wait,' he corrected himself. 'People going under buses are the realm of James's songs, aren't they?'

Cavan, now rising, gingerly grabbing at his jaw, glared at Sandeep.

'Bartlett Place,' he muttered. 'Ronald knew, didn't he?'

'Oh, don't call him by his name, call him "Dad,"' Sandeep smiled. 'After all, looking at your real one, he's the best option you ever had.'

He waved the gun menacingly.

'Now, get into the bloody studio booth before I shoot you in the face,' he said. 'I've fixed the soundproofing, but I really don't want to test it.'

———

# 30

# STUDIO TOUR

Declan stood outside the Stratford office building where James Harlow's onetime recording studio had been, Anjli and De'Geer beside him.

There was no boarding, no sign to state this was a recording studio; it looked nothing more than a business village of varying-sized offices, just like a dozen others in the area.

*Although that might have been what James Harlow had been going for*, Declan thought to himself as he looked around the car park.

Currently, his Audi was the only vehicle there; the squad cars were hidden around the corner, in case it gave Sandeep advanced warning, and he escaped.

'I could have been a music producer,' Declan muttered.

At this strange statement, Anjli looked at him.

'And since when have you been a music-producing expert?' she asked.

'Since the *Alternator* case,' Declan replied, shrugging. 'I started watching videos about how to use mixing desks. It's quite simplistic, actually, until you get really detailed.'

'Yeah, and those pesky details are always the thing that let people down, Guv,' De'Geer replied, and Declan was sure he saw a wink pass between De'Geer and Anjli. 'Anybody can be anything. That doesn't necessarily mean anybody can be *good* at anything.'

'Just saying,' Declan was sulking now. 'I know my way around a basic mixing desk.'

'He's watched five videos on it and he thinks he's Mark Ronson,' Anjli shook her head. 'So, how do you want to play this?'

'Carefully,' Declan checked his sleeve, making sure his extendable police baton was secured up there. 'We don't know how far Sandeep's gone, let alone how far he'll go, here. The man didn't strike me as someone who would act without a plan, so whatever he's doing, it's not improvised.'

'You think anyone's with him?' De'Geer was checking a window, to no avail.

'If James and Lance are here, it solves a lot of questions,' Declan shrugged. 'So, my plan is—'

'To go in alone, get them talking, show off your amazing deductive powers and basically get them to confess while we sneak in to arrest them?' Anjli interrupted with a smile.

'I wasn't going to say that exactly,' Declan muttered. 'How did you come up with that?'

'Because it's what you always do,' Anjli waved at the building. 'Go on then, DCI Walsh. Go do your stuff, save the day and solve the case. We'll have your back when you inevitably stick your arse into the fire.'

'And why would you think I'd do that?' Declan started to the main door, pulling out his lock pick kit.

Anjli laughed.

'Because it's what you always do,' she finished.

———

RELUCTANTLY, AND BLEEDING FROM THE EYEBROW, LANCE HAD followed Cavan into the studio, while Sandeep had trained his gun on them, following them to the doorway between mixing room and studio.

'You won't get away with this,' Lance muttered, wiping at his wound and grimacing as he saw the blood.

'Of course I will,' Sandeep smiled. 'Didn't you hear? All the deaths? It was James there, gaining vengeance.'

'Including Stuart?'

'Sure,' Sandeep waved for Lance to move deeper into the room. 'With you dead, only Beth remains. And as she was the one that killed him, she won't be confessing soon. She'll back up whatever statement I make.'

He looked at the walls sadly.

'I'm annoyed I have to burn this lovely place down after all we did, but with the insurance money, I'll make a better one.'

James glowered at Sandeep.

'Karma will get you for this.'

'Will it? Oh no, please no. I'm quaking in my boots,' Sandeep deadpanned. 'Shut up and sit down. This is your greatest performance. You're about to become a household name. All you ever dreamed of.'

There was the sound of a door closing outside the studio mixing room, and Sandeep, hiding the gun for a moment, looked back as the door into the mixing room opened slowly.

'You don't mind me interrupting anything, do you?'

Declan smiled as he walked into the room. 'I just so love recording studios.'

He took a long look around the room.

'I haven't been in one since a year or two ago,' he continued. 'Ram Studios in Hayes. Lots of problems there. Murders, complaints about money, people lying to each other ...'

He shrugged, noting the weapon in Sandeep's hand, now brought up.

'Just like now,' he finished, unconcerned.

Sandeep stared back at him, his eyes glaring daggers in his direction.

'Nice gun,' Declan added with a smile. 'Hope you've got a permit for it.'

'I'm sorry you're here, Detective Chief Inspector,' Sandeep said. 'I really wish you hadn't. But, unfortunately, the fact you've turned up means that you now must become part of this story.'

'And what story would that be?' Declan said, peering through the glass at Lance, James, and Cavan. 'I mean, it's quite an interesting one, from the looks of things. Maybe I could work it out. I'm quite intelligent. We could maybe do it as a podcast.'

He started flicking switches on the mixing board.

'Would you please stop buggering around with my expensive equipment?' Sandeep muttered.

'Why do you care?' Lance shouted out. 'You were going to burn the place down a minute ago.'

'Well, now it's a little bit more complicated, isn't it?' Sandeep replied, gun still trained on Declan, who stepped back, holding his hand up from the mixing desk.

'It all started twenty-odd years ago, didn't it?' Declan asked. 'All of you learning the Knowledge, wanting to become cab drivers, or in Lance's case, get his money owed to him by his dad who, by this point, was convinced he was completely useless.'

He gave Lance a smile.

'Don't get me wrong, I'm impressed at what you did. Doesn't stop you being a dick, though, does it?'

Lance gave an uncaring shrug as Declan turned back to Sandeep.

'So, there we are, twenty years ago, all of you doing the Knowledge, and you pull in Beth Stevens into your little group. She's really good at it, but when Beth turns up, you also gain her boyfriend, Logan Harlow, and in a way, Logan's brother James.'

He nodded over to James now, who had walked back to the chair and sat down on it, casually.

'You met Sandeep first, didn't you?' Declan asked.

'Yeah,' James nodded. 'Logan invited me to something, I didn't want to go, but it was after he had made his money.'

'At this point, Logan had gained his settlement from a crippling accident—not really "making money" though, is it?' Declan asked, looking through the window, back at Lance. 'But he'd kept it quiet, hadn't he? Didn't want people to know he was rich. Maybe even Beth didn't know. But at some point you learned who he was, didn't you?'

Lance nodded.

'Wasn't that difficult,' he said. 'Not many people screw over my family and survive.'

He looked over at James.

'Although I suppose he didn't either.'

'So, Logan meets the team, then James meets the team, Lance realises who Logan is, and starts to cultivate an attitude of hatred towards him,' Declan continued. 'He knows Ronald,

Clifford, and Stuart are all besotted with Beth, so it's easy to turn them all against him. He even sits down with James one night over a beer, and convinces him to help take away Logan's money, before he spends it all on frivolous things like apartments on Bartlett Place.'

At this, Sandeep shook his head.

'That wasn't frivolous,' he growled.

'Oh, I know,' Declan replied. 'To be honest, this seems to be the only clever investment that Logan Harlow made. So, how did you become his executor exactly?'

'You've got to understand that Logan wasn't exactly a financial whiz kid,' Sandeep shrugged. 'He'd left school with barely any GCSEs, he'd travelled the world working menial jobs, he wasn't a brain surgeon or anything like that. We'd met a couple of times and we got on. It helped that the only other person with money was Lance, and he'd proven himself to be an absolute tosser.'

'Hey!' Lance protested, but a wave from the gun silenced him back up as Sandeep continued.

'So, a few times when Logan was asking questions, I was able to give him help. I wasn't rich myself,' he shrugged. 'But I obviously had a face he could trust.'

'And trust he did,' Declan replied. 'Because he made you a signatory.'

'It wasn't quite the same as that,' Sandeep said. 'I didn't have access to his money. It was when he invested in my company that happened. I'd given him all the bells and whistles, shown him how much the app could make. He'd been watching the other cabbies and seen how much money a good cab driver could make in a week, and he saw the value of getting them to pay *him* to make money. Funny enough, he decided he wanted to put in most of the money he'd gained from the settlement into it.'

'And why would he do that?' Declan asked, frowning. 'I mean, he's in constant pain and he's literally throwing it all away?'

Sandeep straightened angrily, the gun barrel swinging back to aim at Declan.

'He threw nothing away,' he snapped. 'He was guaranteed over ten per cent profit in the first year. You show me a bank account that could give him that. He'd gain that back after twelve months as well. It wasn't stuck in there for perpetuity. I just needed seed money to start everything.'

The gun lowered slightly though, as Sandeep sighed.

'But he'd just spent a ton of cash on the apartment, and was spending money like there was no tomorrow. My bank was concerned, and so he offered the place for collateral. Said if he reneged on the deal, I could have it, sell it off and use that. He wasn't exactly well-versed in the forms of finance, and I wasn't going to say no. I needed the money.'

'And how did Lance get involved?'

'I saw a deal,' Lance replied arrogantly, still unable to show humility now his life was in danger.

'When Lance had heard that Logan was involved, he put his money in immediately, and it was almost like some kind of pissing game between the two,' Sandeep laughed at this. 'Lance matched Logan, so Logan had to add a bit more. Lance then threw another twenty grand in, so Logan went up a bit higher.'

He looked back at Lance.

'I only found out years later that this was his intention, to make Logan Harlow spend every spare penny he had.'

He shrugged.

'But he wouldn't have been broke, even if he lost everything,' he said. 'He paid for the apartment in cash. He could have sold that at any point for a cool quarter of a million. But Logan Harlow didn't care about money.'

His voice had trailed off, almost sad.

'You genuinely liked Logan, didn't you?' Declan asked, idly flicking a couple more switches, but stopping as Sandeep glared at him and, gun now once again aimed at his head and with Sandeep motioning for him to walk, he left the mixing room and entered the studio area through the door.

'At the start, sure,' Sandeep nodded as Declan passed by. 'He was a free spirit. He understood why I wanted to create a business. But then the painkillers started to *not* become enough for him. He upped his medicine, he took more than he should have, and he became a Jekyll and Hyde character. Sometimes he was lovely and fun to be near, and other times he was ...'

He glanced over at Lance.

'More like him,' he explained. 'An absolute egotistical prick. Didn't help that he wasn't talking to his brother, and had created some kind of strong rift there. Beth was trying to clean him up, but he took that as control, something he'd travelled the world to get away from. Things weren't going great.'

Now with everyone in the same room, he walked over to a comfy chair, resting back on the arm as he kept his weapon trained on the others.

'We genuinely thought Beth and Logan would break up. I was concerned because my fear was if Logan left the group, he might not want to keep his money with me—'

'And so you started to plan for phase two,' Declan said.

'There was no conscious plan,' Sandeep replied. 'But I was considering my options ... and then Logan got violent.'

He looked over at Cavan.

'You see, Logan was jealous. Insanely so. He didn't like the fact that Beth was adored by her friends. Had already told her that when she passed the Knowledge, he wanted her to drop all ties with them. And to be honest, Beth probably would have. She loved him. But then there was an argument. She got drunk, and James took his moment to shoot his shot, as they say. Slept with her, but it wasn't because he wanted her.'

James sighed.

'It was revenge, nothing more. When Logan turned me down, he killed my dream. He took something important from me. I decided to take something from him.'

'The problem was, as soon as he'd slept with her, he made sure everybody knew,' Sandeep carried on. 'Off the record, of course. "Don't tell anyone, but ..." and all that. Of course, it came back to Logan. He was furious.'

'And he attacked Beth,' Declan took over now. 'She came to find you all. This was the night Stuart Laws passed his Knowledge. You'd all had a few drinks – apart from you, Sandeep.'

'Didn't feel like it.'

'So, Beth turns up, battered, and in tears. And you provided her the help she needed, didn't you?'

'By that point, I'd already realised that Logan was a loose cannon,' Sandeep nodded. 'I had to find another way.'

'And another way was to give her the funds to pay Stuart to kill Logan.'

'He was only supposed to scare him off,' Lance muttered.

'No, he wanted Logan dead,' James said, nodding at

Sandeep. 'He talked to me later, and with hindsight, I can see it now.'

'You wanted that too!' Sandeep snapped back, looking over at Declan. 'You see, I'd already worked out that James was Logan's only heir. So I asked if Logan did pass away, what would James do with the money? James promised to invest in my company, with a few caveats.'

'Was one of the caveats that he owned part of the apartment?'

Sandeep shook his head.

'That was my suggestion,' he replied. 'I'd realised at this point Logan was falling apart, and I knew the paperwork I had. Well, I could adjust it, put it into my name, perhaps sell it off and gain money that way for the app. But James came up with a different idea.'

'James, when he inherited the money, would take over Logan's investments, and you would all share the property,' Declan said.

'You make it sound so simple,' Lance replied. 'I think you'll find there were a lot more legalities involved.'

He paused.

'No, actually it *was* that simple, when you think about it.'

'But here was the problem,' Declan said. 'At some point, you found out she was pregnant, didn't you?'

Sandeep nodded.

'Logan called me the same night. Utterly broken. Convinced he'd screwed everything up, begging me to help him find a way to get Beth back. He would do anything for her. Put the apartment in her name, even, so that if they did break up, she had something. I could see that the investment was going to disappear quickly.'

'So, when Beth turned up, crying her eyes out, you, the

only sober person there apart from Stuart Laws, decided to create your own endgame,' Declan said. 'You convinced Beth to end her relationship with Logan. Permanently.'

He shrugged as he looked around the room.

'Perhaps you convinced others to join in? Ronnie, Stuart, Clifford, they were over the moon that somebody was telling Beth to walk away from Logan. Gave them a chance for themselves. They didn't yet know she was pregnant. But you kept quiet. Simply gave her the money.'

Sandeep shook his head.

'He was the only other sober person there, and he hated Logan more than anything. He was also broke, so I offered him five grand to break his legs.'

'And that was the plan, wasn't it?' Declan said. 'Find Logan, smack him with the car, hurt him. But meanwhile ... you had a darker idea, didn't you?'

Sandeep said nothing, so Declan moved closer.

'You'd already decided he needed to die so you could survive. Just like twenty years later, you decided others needed to die. Only this time, your plans were much bigger.'

# 31

# LARGER PLANS

SANDEEP GLARED BALEFULLY AT DECLAN, BUT IT WAS LANCE who spoke.

'He didn't have the balls for it,' he said. 'But I did. I told Stuart that if he could finish the job I'd help him finance his first car.'

He shrugged.

'We were drunk, it was bravado. I didn't know what I was doing. I was idiotic, and I regret it. But what can you do, I'm a passionate man.'

Declan stared coldly at Lance.

'But then it didn't go to plan, did it?' he said. 'Stuart found him in Gibson Square after Beth told him to meet her. He would have done anything for her at this point. Logan was broken and desperate, and then when you arrived, he probably ran, scared. How far did you hunt him before you took him down?'

'A matter of yards, nothing more,' Lance replied. 'He couldn't run fast, you see. On account of his leg.'

'So,' Declan replied, 'you hit him. The problem was, he

was hit, but not dead. You forced the painkillers down his throat, telling everybody that the painkillers would help with whatever happened, but meanwhile you were trying to overdose him.'

'You can't prove that,' Lance replied.

'What I *can* prove is that you then struck him with his own walking stick, tossing him and the stick into the boot of Clifford's non-condition-passing cab,' Declan continued. 'But now you're all flapping; what do you do? You can't let him go, he might call the police. This has gone from the bravado-filled attack to attempted murder.'

He looked back at Sandeep.

'Apart from you, of course,' he said. 'Because you hadn't gone. You hadn't wanted anything to do with this.'

Sandeep shrugged.

'Wasn't my fight.'

'Nah,' Declan said. 'It was your fight. But it was a *different* fight for the others.'

He paced the room, keeping Lance in his line of vision.

'So, now you drive around for a while, trying to work it out, and suddenly one of you smells the exhaust fumes leaking through, and Clifford realises in horror what's going on,' he continued, his voice lowering as anger took over. 'You stop at the side of a bridge and open up the boot, and, well, Logan's dead. Gassed. You don't know what to do. And then one of you, maybe Lance, we'll never know ... he suggests just heaving the body over the side. "He's had a load of painkillers. No-one will know. He'll float up the next day, another suicide." And so you do that. Three in the morning, you toss him over the side, one more dead body for the Thames. But he wasn't dead, was he? You see, the painkillers you'd given him had knocked him unconscious, so deep that he wouldn't revive, and when he fell in the water, it also stopped him being able to swim.'

He stopped, glaring directly at Lance now.

'That was the moment you killed Logan Harlow,' he said. 'Turning up two days later at Mortlake, the autopsy just assumed that he'd killed himself, the bruises from being hit by boats, or the bridge itself. There were no other witnesses, apart from one woman who had turned up and seen you standing around the side. But you'd given her this fantastical story, cobbled from scratch, about how this man in a cab had asked to stop ... and then been hit by a bus, before disappearing. And then everything went along quite tickety-boo for the next fifteen years.'

'You make it sound so simple,' Lance muttered.

'Murder is simple,' Declan said back. 'It's the aftermath that isn't. Logan was dead, legally, nothing seemed to land on your shoulders. You gained a secret apartment and the passive income from rent made you lots of money. Ronald and Lizzie got together. Life moved on. Even Lance was welcomed back into his family's bosom and James, hearing the rumour while looking into his brother's death, wrote a song about it. But then things changed about five years ago, didn't they?'

'And why would that be?' Lance, bored with this now, played with his nails as he waited for a response.

Declan looked back at him,

'Because in 2019, you sold Oi Taxi,' he said. 'Or rather Sandeep did at James's insistence. James was broke, spending money left, right, and centre for a career that wasn't working, and realised that he had a chunk of money just waiting, if you'd only sell the company. Lance wasn't happy about this, but two out of three made the decision. Maybe James pressured you, reminded you that you had an apartment that technically was given by a dead man. I don't know what it was, but the money came in, and James went on tour. Was it around then you learned about Cavan?'

The last part was aimed at James, who shook his head.

'I'd realised it a few years earlier,' he replied. 'There was something about Cavan's mannerisms that reminded me of Logan. But I soon realised that Ronald didn't know. I wasn't even sure if Lizzie knew. So I invited them to a gig, put loads of pictures up of young Logan. I really wanted both of them to see that even though they'd killed him, he was still around.'

'You know, this is a lot of work for somebody you didn't like,' Declan said, 'and for somebody you gained money from.'

'He's blood,' James said.

'Yeah, we've already had that conversation,' Sandeep sighed audibly. 'James doesn't think much about blood, though, although he's reassessing that, now he knows Cavan's his son.'

'Yeah, so now we get to Cavan,' Declan said, turning to face the younger man. 'Fifteen years old, used as a pawn. Ronald's worked out you're not his and that he's been lied to, takes it out on you, doesn't go down well. I get that. And then a couple of years ago, James comes and finds you, tells you that you're Logan's kid?'

Cavan didn't reply, just nodded.

'So Cavan is James's project for a while, but then he gets bored again,' Declan said. 'But by now, things have gone wrong. Stuart doesn't want to be a cab driver anymore, but needs money to get a new car. Starts to pressure Sandeep and Lance, reminding them of what happened back when they were all starting off. Leverages a nice vehicle from Lance. Hush money, even if he has to work for it.'

'He never complained about the work.'

'He never complained to *you* about the work,' Sandeep muttered. 'All of us, we heard it.'

'Ronald Tyler is doing the same, gaining loan upon loan from Lance, who probably feels guilty, especially once Ronald learns Cavan isn't his kid, something that Lance knew from the moment his father gave him the paternity test,' Declan replied. 'Or maybe not. I don't know if you feel guilt.'

Lance said nothing, glowering at Declan as he continued.

'Life went on until James released the album,' Declan looked around the room. 'I know you recorded it live at a festival, but is this where you mixed it? Is this where the magic happened?'

He shook his head sadly.

'Couldn't help yourself, could you?' he said. 'You had everything in front of you, no one was even considering you to be a murderer, and you still had to press buttons. Made a nice album, and then sent copies to everybody, with little cryptic notes telling them to remember. But you were just playing games, weren't you?'

James shrugged, looking away, refusing to reply.

'The message? It was ambiguous. Meant different things. To Ron and Lizzie, it was remembering the father of their child. To the others, it was remembering what had happened to Logan. But Stuart saw it differently. Stuart thought you were coming for him after what he'd told you, and that spurred him into action. Especially as he knew a little more than the rest.'

'What's that supposed to mean?' Lance frowned.

'It means Stuart Laws knew about Bartlett Place,' Declan

explained. 'He picked Sandeep up after he made the deal for this place, and when Sandeep accidentally left his messenger bag in Stuart's car, he looked inside it to find the identity of the bag's owner.'

He winked theatrically at Sandeep.

'Of course, we all know he likely did it to see what you were up to,' he added. 'Imagine his surprise when he saw the apartment deeds, including the one where Logan signed it over to you the day *after* Stuart helped kill him.'

He looked back at Lance.

'That's why Sandeep was with you at Ronald's house, the night before Stuart's accident.'

'Bullshit!' Sandeep snapped. 'There's no way you can prove—'

'Nice watch,' Declan said, cutting Sandeep off. 'How's your Strava step count going?'

Sandeep looked down at his watch, realising, then, even knowing it was pointless now, he pulled it off and tossed it to the floor.

'Clever,' he muttered.

'Not as clever as your sleight of hand magic,' Declan replied. 'Our Sergeant recognised the Magic Castle in your photos. You might not be good enough to fool Penn and Teller, but you're good enough to force a card on someone. Low card loses, and you made damn sure that was Lizzie Tyler.'

Lance genuinely looked impressed as he stared at Sandeep.

'Stuart threatened me,' Sandeep muttered. 'Said he knew about the apartment, he'd seen the papers. The album spooked him, and he wanted enough money to start a new life. I said I'd think about it. But I knew he was a liability. So I leant into the album story, said to everyone how Stuart, spooked by memories of Logan's death was going to grass us all to the police. We all met to discuss it and decided Stuart needed to go.'

'*You* decided, more like,' Lance growled. 'All that "I'm here impartially" bollocks.'

Declan waited a moment.

'To add to this, you'd already set Marshall and Alfie up to robo-call everyone with a line of the chorus of "Crooked Was His Cane" the same day,' he said. 'Timing it so it'd arrive after the death, and throw more blame on James, while using Lance's company as your blunt weapon.'

Sandeep looked to argue, but then stopped.

'So, if this is true, why did I kill the others?' he asked. 'I had no fight with Ronald.'

'True, until he found out about your apartment,' Declan replied. 'Even though you'd sold it on, it could still land on you, and Stuart had told him what he saw. Ronald was furious, wasn't he? Felt he should be cut in, perhaps? Decided to shake you down, find out about the place and then come back to you with everything. He had the address, so he intended to stake it out. But he made the mistake of telling Clifford at a cab rank. And then, the same night, Clifford passed this on to Lance at dinner, not realising he was signing Ronald's death certificate.'

'Excuse me,' Cavan held a nervous hand up. 'How?'

'Because Lance realised where Clifford was going with this and distanced himself,' Declan replied. 'Clifford then left to his own devices, not told during the dinner to kill Ronald, but not actively told *not* to kill him. Maybe try to warn him off instead.'

He looked at Sandeep.

'Did he call you?'

'Only after he did it,' Sandeep admitted. 'And yes, he admitted it to me. They'd had a fight, he tried to shake Ronald off, reminding him of his involvement with Logan and Stuart's deaths, but Ronald argued, said he was ill, hadn't been involved with Stuart's death. It got heated, and Clifford ended up choking Ronald out. He realised he was screwed, so faked a suicide. Strapped Ronald in, then called me for advice, about five in the sodding morning. I told him to find a hose and gas Ronald to push the suicide angle, and also to place the note in his mouth.'

'Because that would lead to James again.'

Sandeep nodded.

'I didn't know Alfie was turning up, that was Marshall playing silly bastards,' he admitted. Clifford came back to me later, said he'd done it, killed Ronald. It was only later I learnt he'd used his own cab, as Ronald didn't have an exhaust. Dopey bastard never even mentioned that to me, and then ran before taking the bloody strap off. I realised he'd screwed up, he'd be found out, so I told him to meet with me the next day.'

'King's Cross Station,' Declan replied. 'You brought that stick, too.'

Sandeep went to argue, but then simply smiled and nodded.

'Well done,' he said. 'I arranged to meet him at King's Cross, and I said to take me to Gibson Square. He should have known when I gave the address, but as we've heard already, he was a dopey bastard.'

'He was your friend,' Lance snapped.

'Was he?' Sandeep turned back to Lance now. 'In the

same way he was yours? Of course not. He was just some cabbie who owed you money.'

'So you placed the snorkel over his face, drowned him, and then stuck another note in the mouth,' Declan said, bringing the attention back over to him now. 'We know you had experience with the full-face snorkel, because you tried to hide a photo of you with one.'

'I was panicking,' Sandeep muttered. 'I sucker punched him, and while he shook that off, I got the strap around him. Once this was on, he was stuck. But I was flapping by then, lost the top of the snorkel, and it was too dark to find it. I didn't want to scrabble around, so I just ran for it.'

Declan sighed, looking around the studio.

'And so we come to this,' he said. 'Your last chance to clean everything up. You lead Lance down a road that paints him as the next victim by James, even sending the cane so he sees it. You know he'll strike first, and you wait to see what he does. But he doesn't do what you hoped.'

Sandeep shook his head, looking over at Lance now.

'I'd hoped he'd turn up, kick a fight off, hammer James to death with the cane,' he said. 'Or James hammered him. I didn't care, really. I would have fixed whatever happened next, anyway.'

'And me?' Cavan straightened angrily. 'What was I in this to you?'

'You?' Sandeep sniffed dismissively. 'Cavan, you were nothing. I didn't even know you were James's son. Trust me, if I had, I'd have removed you way earlier.'

'Because your new deal here says if James dies, you get his two-thirds of the apartment, but if he has a direct heir, that changes,' Declan said. 'You'd have needed to kill him anyway, right?'

Sandeep shrugged.

'Logan's brat or James's one, he'd have had a say in his father's affairs,' he replied. 'The apartment would have come up.'

Declan looked at each of the men in turn.

'Well, it goes without saying, Sandeep, you're under arrest,' he said. 'Lots of murders kinda do that. Lance, you're under arrest too; accessory to Stuart Laws' death, and also Logan Harlow's. Probably other stuff, too.'

He looked over at James now.

'You? Well, you were just a prick,' he said. 'Unfortunately, we can't arrest you for that, but we can arrest you for being complicit in the theft of the Gainsborough House apartment, signed off the day after Logan died.'

'I was under the belief it was legal,' James smiled coldly. 'You can't prove I didn't know – even if I did.'

Declan smiled back at James.

'Well, I guess this means the podcast is over,' he said. 'I'll be taking you all in now—'

'I think you forget who has the gun,' Sandeep waved the pistol in his hand for emphasis. 'You're going nowhere. You don't have any proof of half your accusations, and you won't be leaving here alive.'

'I don't need proof,' Declan frowned, looking around. 'You just gave a confession.'

'But when the witness is dead ...' Sandeep raised the gun, before pausing. 'No, screw it. You can burn with the others.'

'You didn't think I was the witness, did you?' Declan waggled his hand in a "tut tut" gesture as he looked back at the mixing desk through the window. 'Did you get all that?'

'We did, Guv,' De'Geer said as he came into view, Anjli beside him. 'The audio is perfect. Well equalised.'

'You see, when you said I was "buggering around" with your mixing desk, I was starting the system up,' Declan explained. 'Everything since then has been recorded through the microphones, just like the podcasts you were planning to make here. So, yeah. I pretty much have the confession. And a shit-ton of evidence, too.'

Sandeep's eyes narrowed, and Declan knew he was about to fire the gun, but before he could, screaming, Cavan grabbed the walking cane and swung it at Sandeep, hitting him hard in the head, the gun firing wildly as Sandeep went down. Cavan went to strike again, but stopped as James, rising, grabbed him from behind, pinning his arms.

'No, son,' he said. 'That bastard needs to pay.'

He looked at Lance, standing in utter shock now.

'They both need to pay.'

Declan kicked the gun from the fallen Sandeep, stepping back as the door opened, and Anjli and De'Geer came in, handcuffs at the ready.

'And they will,' Declan replied calmly. 'Believe me, on that.'

# EPILOGUE

IT DIDN'T TAKE LONG FOR THE HOUSE OF CARDS TO COLLAPSE. With the entire plan on tape, with Lance now pushing for a plea deal, thanks to the expensive solicitors paid for by his father, and with Lizzie Tyler now finding ways to screw everyone in return, the case was starting to become incredibly messy, and more of an administrational nightmare than anyone had expected.

One positive thing that came out of it, however, was James and Cavan's new relationship. Although cold at the start, the moment he'd thought he was about to lose Cavan, something had woken inside James, and even if it was a little reluctant, he had promised to do good by his new son. The case against James would likely fall apart anyway, and Logan's items would still go to him, but he'd promised to build a relationship with his new son who, with a mother about to go to jail and a "father" who was dead, was now alone.

Alfie and Marshall Reynolds were also let go; all they'd been were pawns, and the only thing either could be done for was the robo-call, but not in relation to any murders. Alfie lost his job, though.

He didn't seem too crushed by it.

As for Sandeep, he knew he was screwed, and from the moment he arrived at the interview room, his narrative was already changing as he tried to wheedle out of yet another problem.

But that didn't matter for the team at the Last Chance Saloon, as they'd already moved on from this case, and were onto the next problem.

———

Declan didn't wait long before Bernard Strange came back to him with information on his recent assignment, contacting him the following week to arrange a meeting.

Declan had picked up the dossier Bernard had created in a printed format, rather than digital, probably because Bernard didn't want any footprint leading back to him, and returned to the unit where they went over everything inside it, planning their next step.

Bernard hadn't found much that they didn't already know, but one thing he had found was whom Jennifer Farnham-Ewing was spending her time with, now she was an MP.

There were a lot of familiar names; right-wing, conservative MPs that had connections at points in the past to both Rattlestone and Pierce Associates, and who had been earning small amounts of consultancy money with Phoenix Industries, the company that had replaced both Pierce Associates and Rattlestone, until it too folded recently.

With the information Bernard had found, Declan now knew exactly how to fix this.

So, after making a couple of phone calls, he put on his best suit and went to Westminster for a light lunch.

———

WHEN JENNIFER FARNHAM-EWING HAD RECEIVED THE invitation to lunch on the Members' Terrace, she had expressed interest. It was a right-wing oriented group that had requested her attendance, one she had been courting for a while now, and more importantly, one that Malcolm Gladwell, up to a couple of years earlier, had been heavily involved in. They were a more extreme form of the 1922 committee, in the sense that they could make or break a party leader, depending on whether or not they liked them.

Jennifer Farnham-Ewing had many years ahead of her; she was aware of this. She could make her enemies now and still come out on top at the end, but she was also ambitious and impatient. There was no need to wait until the end of her career to make a name for herself, especially with a variety of issues over her head.

*She wanted it now. And this meeting could help with that.*

She had hoped that Declan Walsh and his cohort of idiot coppers had managed to fulfil what she required him to do; getting Charles Baker off the hook, while allowing Malcolm Gladwell to release his book. This way, she was seen as the loyal Conservative Party MP doing her best for party and country, while not letting personal connections get the better.

She had read the book. She knew she came off well in it. Gladwell had never really dealt with her, mainly spending his time speaking to Will Harrison before his death. Even so, there was that concern that somewhere was a deep, dark secret waiting to come out.

Jennifer Farnham-Ewing hated deep, dark secrets.

She wondered whether this invitation was connected to Gladwell; maybe he'd heard of her rise in Parliament and had suggested they speak to her. She was well aware that several MPs had still been keeping in touch with him through unofficial routes, not stupid enough to let themselves be seen publicly with a known murderer, after all.

Jennifer chuckled to herself as she walked through the central lobby, passing the journalists talking to camera.

*The amount of MPs in this building who conversed with murderers on a daily basis was alarmingly high.*

Walking onto the Members' Terrace, she straightened and smiled, remembering the old adage she had always been taught of "tits and teeth out", before stumbling to a halt as she realised the meeting she was attending was not the one she *thought* she was attending.

The Members' Terrace was closed for a private function. The private function seemed to be for Jennifer Farnham-Ewing, because on a table at the far end, Jennifer could see Charles Baker and DCI Declan Walsh. She turned to walk away as if realising she had mistakenly picked the wrong time, but found her exit blocked by Nigella Waterstone.

'You're right on time,' Waterstone smiled, irritatingly smug and arrogant. 'This way.'

Numb and confused at what was actually happening, Jennifer meekly followed Waterstone over to the table where, waiting for her, were the two people she *really* didn't want to speak to right now.

'Jennifer,' Charles smiled, standing up and holding a hand out to shake hers, ever the outward impression of a friendly party member. 'I understand you have been trying to save my career.'

'Yes, Prime Minister,' Jennifer nodded, deciding to see where this went. 'I read the book, and I realised it needed to be fixed.'

'I misjudged you,' Charles continued to smile. 'I thought you were an enemy, once you were back in Parliament ... but you're the same as you were when you worked for Will Harrison, aren't you? Loyal to the party and your Prime Minister.'

Jennifer was not sure what was going on, but smiled weakly, hoping that non-answering, but expressing some kind of positive emotion, could gain her some breathing space.

Charles, who had been eating a Caesar salad before rising to shake her hand, returned to it, attacking the lettuce with his fork.

'You will be happy to know that whatever you did has worked,' he said. 'Mister Walsh here has once more pulled my fat out of the fire.'

'Really?' Jennifer asked, looking confused at Declan. 'The book isn't coming out?'

'Mister Gladwell has decided it is best for him to let justice rule,' Declan explained. 'He feels the book he wrote would be an unjust biasing of his case, and would rather he was freed on his own merit than in a court of public opinion.'

Declan was eating a sandwich, what looked to be a BLT, and he ate a mouthful with a grin, chewing on it, savouring the moment, waiting before continuing.

'These are good sandwiches,' he smiled. 'I don't know why I've never tried one before.'

Jennifer kept her composure; she knew he was testing her.

Declan dabbed at his mouth with his napkin, sat back in his chair and stared at her.

'I didn't know what your game was, to start with,' he said. 'I mean, Charles Baker screwed you over with the whole "Justice" thing and dumped you down to the whip in the middle of nowhere, but you didn't exactly help yourself with your various cock-ups.'

Jennifer kept quiet, glaring at Declan across the table as he continued,

'But then here you were, literally threatening the life of my unit to get him off the hook,' he shook his head. 'Truly masterfully done, making yourself look both loyal and eager to help, while preparing the knives for his back.'

Jennifer wasn't sure if she was being mocked or not, but erred on the side of caution and simply nodded.

Declan took another mouthful, chewing, his expression pondering, thinking about what he was about to say next.

'But it didn't matter, did it really?' he said. 'You thought you'd win either way. If Charles Baker was taken down by Gladwell, well, someone else would come in. Maybe Tamara Banks, or Joanna Karolides. She is quite popular these days. Maybe even Robertson, the new defence secretary. I understand he's a nice right-wing friend to have. Even used to speak to Will Harrison back in the Rattlestone days, I understand.'

Jennifer frowned as Declan continued.

'And then, if he didn't get taken down, he'd see you as an ally, as he does right now – until the book would be leaked, somehow, most likely by Gladwell. The press would get it, and it'd start all over again. What would they say, when they realised that, on knowing the book was coming out, the Prime Minister's office had asked their pet copper to close his wife's murder?'

'But Charles didn't ask,' Jennifer replied carefully.

'You can play that card with me if you want,' Charles replied. 'But we've checked your logs. It seems when you left, you kept your admin credentials. Several things have been moved around, and your request to Declan, off the books, seemingly came from your replacement.'

At this bombshell statement, Nigella Waterstone stepped up beside her.

'You don't like me, and I don't like you,' she said. 'That's fine, that's how it works here, but I don't appreciate being put in front of a firing squad for you and your ambitions.'

Jennifer's mind was racing as she tried to work out how she could salvage something from whatever this was.

'I'm glad my plan helped,' she forced a smile, 'to assist you in staying in power.'

'But that wasn't what you wanted to do, was it?' Declan asked. 'You see, we had someone look into you – off the books, but very good at what he does – and he found you've been taking meetings with a lot of Malcolm Gladwell's old friends.'

'The same ones you thought you were meeting for lunch,' Baker continued. 'You see, you don't really feel the same way they do, but you're also aware they're powerful, and with Gladwell gone, it's good to be seen as a possible ally of his rather than an enemy, especially with me likely to be challenged in the next few months for the leadership.'

He glanced briefly at Waterstone before taking one more mouthful of salad.

'You tried to play the game close to your chest, but it failed, Jennifer,' he said. 'We know it was you that leaked the book out in the first place, sent a copy by Malcolm. We know you spoke to him frequently through intermediaries. We also know that you were the one who put him in touch with Peter

Taylor, Kendis Taylor's widower, to gain the tapes to help him.'

Declan leant forward now.

'But he didn't get all the tapes, you see,' he added. 'And what he missed was enough to damn any chance he had of releasing that book and staying alive. The book's gone, Jennifer. It won't be turning up, and if any leaked copies come out, they'll be destroyed. There's a super injunction already coming out from Malcolm himself. He's realised he has to look like a good little soldier as well, if he wants to survive.'

Declan now reached down to his side and placed a cardboard folder onto the table.

'But here's a very interesting thing,' he said. 'When I arrested Malcolm Gladwell, back when he killed Kendis Taylor; and believe me, he *killed* Kendis Taylor, we also know he convinced Donna Baker to see a therapist, one who'd been blackmailed and cajoled by Malcolm to convince Donna to take her own life, knowing she was fragile and suggestible. And, well, that's where it lands on you.'

'I had no idea about this,' Jennifer shook her head vehemently, looking back at Charles. 'I was trying to help. I didn't know she was still seeing Doctor Trudeau.'

'But that's the problem,' Declan replied. 'You did. In fact, you were the one who brought Trudeau into the situation, and convinced Donna she needed to be looked at by her. We know this, because when I opened that safe of Malcolm Gladwell's and took out the files, the ones that kept Charles here in power, I took photos of every one of them. And having a look at them last night, imagine my surprise when I realised your name turns up, doing Will's bidding, of course, but in the process of booking the appointments between Donna Baker and Doctor Trudeau.'

'Hold on,' Jennifer stuttered, looking around, now realising this was more than just a chat, more than just a threat even; she was fighting for her own career. 'I was just doing my job. I was his assistant. I worked in his department.'

'Oh, I'm aware of that,' Declan said. 'And I don't think that you were involved in anything that happened back then. You aren't that intelligent.'

He smiled darkly.

'But what I do have, Jennifer, are records of you booking meetings for Donna Baker with the very therapist that, paid for and blackmailed by Malcolm Gladwell, convinced her to take her own life. How do you think that will look when your Prime Minister, the man who lost his wife, goes public? How do you think that'll help you when the party takes the whip from you and dumps you in the back benches where the independents sit until the by-election that removes you? My boss told you that we always need friends in Westminster. The question really is, though, how long you'll be here?'

Slowly, Jennifer turned and stared at Charles Baker, who equally slowly nodded his head.

'I'm glad to have you in my party,' he said. 'And I expect you to be one of my most loyal MPs while I'm in power. In fact, I would expect you to dive in front of any bullets fired at me across that floor, or in the back rooms you've become so fond of frequenting.'

He rose, placing his fork onto his half-eaten plate, and nodding to Waterstone to follow him.

'Because the moment you step out of line, you conniving little cow, I will make sure that everybody knows just how involved you were in all of this. How you made your play and failed on your first go.'

He shrugged.

'Maybe Karolides *will* become Prime Minister after me,' he smiled. 'She's quite basic, really. You would probably do better against her. As for me, I'll see you at Prime Minister's Questions. Nice and early.'

This said, he turned and left, Waterstone following – although not before turning back and briefly smiling evilly at Jennifer.

'Jesus, that was harsh,' Declan replied, still munching on his sandwich. 'I wouldn't take that. I'd find somewhere and hide. That burn you just got. That can be seen from space.'

Jennifer stood, numb, unsure of what was happening.

Declan pointed at the sandwich.

'I'm just going to finish this and then I'll go,' he said. 'You don't need to wait. I'm sure you've got a lot of phone calls to make right now; promises you might have made, you now have to renege on. But hey, that's politics. For you, it's probably a weekday.'

---

DECLAN FELT QUITE SMUG AS HE RETURNED TO THE LAST Chance Saloon's Temple Inn that afternoon. With Jennifer Farnham-Ewing now back in her box, and Malcolm Gladwell reluctantly agreeing to return to his own, things seemed calmer. Declan wasn't an idiot, though; he knew that down the line, Gladwell would return. He knew that Jennifer Farnham-Ewing would likely do the same, after all, she was still an MP, with a bright future ahead of her, whether or not he liked it. He wondered if he could somehow use Johnny Lucas while he was an MP, although the thoughts he'd been having of late were more along the lines of Johnny Lucas sorting her out in his old line of work.

*Possibly not the best thing to be thinking.*

But when all was said and done, they'd solved a case, stopped a book coming out that could affect their unit, and managed to score one for the winning team against ambitious, two-faced politicians.

He hadn't expected such a sombre response when he arrived.

'Ah, Declan, I need to speak to you,' Monroe said, seeing him enter. 'My office, please.'

Declan noticed Anjli and Billy standing beside his computer. Anjli went to walk towards Declan, but a cough from Monroe stopped her.

'Lassie, this is my conversation to have,' he said.

'What's going on?' Declan asked.

'I thought it'd be better if we—'

'I don't care what you think is better, Guv,' Declan said, looking around. 'You're all looking at me like I've died. Let's not have this theatrical bollocks, just tell me what's happened.'

He paused.

'*Has* someone died? Oh God, it's not one of us, is it?'

Monroe paused at the entrance to his office and took a deep breath, letting it out loud and with resignation, before nodding to Billy.

'Show him, laddie.'

Billy didn't speak as he opened up the browser window. In fact, he opened four browser windows, all news pages, all showing variations of the same story. But it was the top news piece that Declan got to see in its full glory.

**SERIAL KILLER GIVES COP HUNTING HIM EVERYTHING IN WILL**

Under it was a picture of Karl Schnitter and Declan. They were separate photos, from different times, but obviously, the message was clear. The threat that Jennifer Farnham-Ewing had mentioned about the will of Karl Schnitter coming out had come true.

'They're all quite harsh,' Monroe said. 'And they all follow the same beats, which to me says they've been given some kind of carefully crafted leak. Probably Farnham-Ewing's middle finger gesture once she realised it was the only play she could make.'

Declan was reading the screen.

'It says here I deliberately let him go, gave him to the Americans, who gave him a new life. And then when he returned, as a thank you, he promised to keep giving me everything when he died. That's not what happened.'

He paused, looking up.

'Well, it's *mostly* not happened. I mean, yeah, sure, I let him go, but that's because I wanted him in a black site cell where the CIA couldn't find him. And I didn't know about the will when he came back ...'

He trailed off, realising he was babbling.

'They go deeper, laddie,' Monroe said. 'They've got pictures of you and your father with him.'

'What do you mean?' Declan frowned.

'Do you remember how we first found out that Karl was a killer?'

'Yeah, it was a photo of him in the *Maidenhead Advertiser,* a *Comic Relief* event in 2013.'

'Aye,' Monroe replied. 'There are pictures of Patrick and him at the same event.'

'They were friends back then,' Declan said. 'My dad didn't know ... nobody knew at the time he was a murderer!'

'It doesn't matter what you think and what I think, laddie. The press has photos of you and your father with a known serial killer. Years later, instead of arresting him, you let him free and you've gained everything from his will.'

Declan glared around the room.

'If anyone here believes—'

'Don't be an idiot, laddie,' Monroe snapped. 'None of us believe you're anything more than the man you are. Christ, if we did, then Anjli would have already beaten the shite out of us, let alone you. But the press loves stories. And this is going to be here for a while. We need to get ahead of it and fast. We need to find a way of killing this now.'

He looked around.

'We just had one of the biggest wins of our career,' he raised his voice so everyone heard. 'Saved ourselves, stopped the government from being embarrassed, and we *still* have this appear. Winning a large case isn't helping us this time.'

'What will then?' Declan asked.

Monroe walked over to him, placed a fatherly hand on his shoulder, and shook his head.

'Laddie, this time I don't think there's anything that can be done to help you,' he said.

'This time, I think you and all of us are right and truly screwed.'

DCI Walsh and the team of the *Last Chance Saloon* will return in their next thriller

# A POCKET FULL OF POSIES

Order Now at Amazon:

www.mybook.to/apocketfullofposies

# ACKNOWLEDGEMENTS

When you write a series of books, you find that there are a ton of people out there who help you, sometimes without even realising, and so I wanted to say thanks.

There are people I need to thank, and they know who they are, including my brother Chris Lee, Jacqueline Beard MBE, who has copyedited all my books since the very beginning, and editor Sian Phillips, all of whom have made my books way better than they have every right to be.

Also, I couldn't have done this without my growing army of ARC and beta readers, who not only show me where I falter, but also raise awareness of me in the social media world, ensuring that other people learn of my books.

But mainly, I tip my hat and thank you. *The reader.* Who once took a chance on an unknown author in a pile of Kindle books, and thought you'd give them a go, and who has carried on this far with them, as well as the spin off books I now release.

I write Declan Walsh for you. He (and his team) solves crimes for you. And with luck, he'll keep on solving them for a very long time.

*Jack Gatland / Tony Lee,*
   *London, June 2024*

# ABOUT THE AUTHOR

**Jack Gatland** is the pen name of *#1 New York Times Bestselling Author* Tony Lee, who has been writing in all media for thirty-five years, including comics, graphic novels, middle grade books, audio drama, TV and film for *DC Comics, Marvel, BBC, ITV, Random House, Penguin USA, Hachette* and a ton of other publishers and broadcasters.

These have included licences such as *Doctor Who, Spider Man, X-Men, Star Trek, Battlestar Galactica, MacGyver,* BBC's *Doctors, Wallace and Gromit* and *Shrek*, as well as work created with musicians such as *Ozzy Osbourne, Joe Satriani, Beartooth, Pantera, Megadeth, Iron Maiden* and *Bruce Dickinson.*

As Tony, he's toured the world talking to reluctant readers with his 'Change The Channel' school tours, and lectures on screenwriting, story craft and comic scripting for festivals and conferences such as *Raindance* in London and both *Author Nation* and *20Books* globally.

An introvert West Londoner by heart, he lives with his wife Tracy and dog Fosco, just outside London.

**Locations In The Book**

The locations and items I use in my books are real, if altered slightly for dramatic intent.

**Bartlett Place** did once exist, and was used in the TV episode we spoke of in the novel, *Map Man*, a BBC show where Nicholas Crane would travel around and look at various maps. It's long gone now, though, as are many others. But there are "Trap Streets" all over the world. I can't give any links, but if you were to search for the show and "Dailymotion," I'm sure you'd find it...

**The Houses of Parliament** are real (obviously) and everything that I say about it is real as well. I've even attended the *Sherlock Holmes Society of London* dinners there.

**The Trading House** exists; historically part of medieval guildhalls, the trading house served as a central hub for merchants and artisans to conduct business and exchange goods. Located within the guildhall, it facilitated local and international trade, fostering economic growth and cultural exchange. Over time, its functions evolved to meet the needs of emerging markets.

Today, the Trading House bar, located on Gresham Street in London, is housed in a Victorian building that was once the Bank of New Zealand. This establishment, part of The New World Trading Company, opened its doors in 2014 and has quickly become a notable spot in the City's dining and drinking scene. The bar draws inspiration from the East India Trading Company and features a unique blend of historical ambiance and modern hospitality.

The interior of The Trading House is decorated with quirky Victorian-era details, including a stuffed albino peacock, mounted animal heads, and old maps, creating a distinctively eclectic atmosphere reminiscent of a Victorian library. The venue also boasts impressive architectural features like a hand-carved ceiling and spiral staircases, adding to its historical charm.

I also have personal knowledge of the place, as it's where I held a small gathering after gaining my *Freedom of the City of London*, next door in the Guildhall, back in 2023!

**The Boxing Club** near Meath Gardens doesn't exist - but the location used is the current **Globe Town Social Club**, within **Green Lens Studios**, a community centre formerly known as Eastbourne House, that I would pass occasionally in my 20s.

**Hurley-Upon-Thames** is a real village, and one that I visited many times from the age of 8 until 16, as my parents and I would spend our spring and summer weekends at the local campsite. It's a location that means a lot to me, my second home throughout my childhood, and so I've decided that this should be the 'home base' for Declan. And by the time book four came out, I'd completely destroyed its reputation!

If you're interested in seeing what the *real* locations look like, I post 'behind the scenes' location images on my Instagram feed. This will continue through all the books, after leaving a suitable amount of time to avoid spoilers, and I suggest you follow it.

In fact, feel free to follow me on all my social media by clicking on the links below. Over time these can be places where we can engage, discuss Declan and put the world to rights.

www.jackgatland.com
www.hoodemanmedia.com

Visit Jack's Reader's Group Page
(Mainly for fans to discuss his books):
https://www.facebook.com/groups/jackgatland

Subscribe to Jack's Readers List:
https://bit.ly/jackgatlandVIP

www.facebook.com/jackgatlandbooks
www.twitter.com/jackgatlandbook
ww.instagram.com/jackgatland

**Want more books by Jack Gatland? Turn the page...**

THE THEFT OF A **PRICELESS** PAINTING...
A GANGSTER WITH A **CRIPPLING DEBT**...
A **BODY COUNT** RISING BY THE HOUR...

**AND ELLIE RECKLESS IS CAUGHT IN THE MIDDLE.**

# JACK GATLAND

# PAINT
# — THE —
# DEAD

**A 'COP FOR CRIMINALS' ELLIE RECKLESS NOVEL**

A NEW PROCEDURAL CRIME SERIES WITH
A TWIST - FROM THE CREATOR OF THE
BESTSELLING 'DI DECLAN WALSH' SERIES

**AVAILABLE ON AMAZON / KINDLE UNLIMITED**

THEY TRIED TO KILL HIM...
NOW HE'S OUT FOR **REVENGE.**

NEW YORK TIMES #1 BESTSELLER **TONY LEE** WRITING AS

# JACK GATLAND

THE MURDER OF AN **MI5 AGENT**...
A BURNED SPY **ON THE RUN** FROM HIS OWN PEOPLE...
AN ENEMY OUT TO **STOP HIM** AT ANY COST...
AND A **PRESIDENT** ABOUT TO BE **ASSASSINATED**...

# SLEEPING SOLDIERS

A **TOM MARLOWE** THRILLER

BOOK 1 IN A NEW SERIES OF THRILLERS IN THE STYLE OF
**JASON BOURNE, JOHN MILTON** OR **BURN NOTICE,** AND
SPINNING OUT OF THE **DECLAN WALSH** SERIES OF BOOKS

AVAILABLE ON AMAZON / KINDLE UNLIMITED

Printed in Great Britain
by Amazon